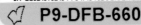
Praise for Kurt Vonnegut's
BAGOMBO SNUFF BOX

"A good showing." — *People*

"These tales are worth reading; with the other early stories in *Welcome to the Monkey House*, they provide fans with the complete test-tube Vonnegut." — *Entertainment Weekly*

"The stories . . . are snappy and often humorous, gentle even when sad. Some have trick endings — the early Vonnegut, he tells us, was an admirer of O. Henry. Most have morals. And the characters know what the morals are; the willingness of even the pretentious and deluded among them to learn from their comeuppances reflects a kind of optimism we don't expect from the author of *Slaughterhouse-Five* and *Cat's Cradle*." — *Los Angeles Times*

"It is fascinating to read the author as he was developing his distinctive style and voice that would subsequently fashion novels such as *Cat's Cradle* and *Slaughterhouse-Five* . . . The stories in this collection still resonate in the new millenium . . . There are many gems . . . The stories, full of fast-moving dialogue and zany characters, rarely miss their mark." — *The Florida Times-Union*

"A pleasant sampler of the comic science fiction and anecdotal-style humor that later matured into the black comedy of his best novels . . : Here's proof that Vonnegut was always drop-dead funny, that he had a knack for knowing that every good joke must be attached to an idea." — *Milwaukee Journal Sentinel*

"Vonnegut fans can rejoice at publication of *Bagombo Snuff Box* . . . This pleasing assortment of wicked techno-satire and cautionary wisdom, mostly written and published in the '50s, represents the balance of Mr. Vonnegut's unpublished short work." — *The Dallas Morning News*

"An on-target, satisfying collection of quirky plot lines and rapidly developed characters who usually manage to rise above their ordinary stations and predicaments." — *Chicago Tribune*

continued . . .

Books by Kurt Vonnegut

PLAYER PIANO

THE SIRENS OF TITAN

MOTHER NIGHT

CAT'S CRADLE

GOD BLESS YOU, MR. ROSEWATER

WELCOME TO THE MONKEY HOUSE

SLAUGHTERHOUSE-FIVE

HAPPY BIRTHDAY, WANDA JUNE

BREAKFAST OF CHAMPIONS

WAMPETERS, FOMA & GRANFALLOONS

SLAPSTICK

JAILBIRD

PALM SUNDAY

DEADEYE DICK

GALÁPAGOS

BLUEBEARD

HOCUS POCUS

FATES WORSE THAN DEATH

TIMEQUAKE

BAGOMBO SNUFF BOX

Bagombo Snuff Box

UNCOLLECTED SHORT FICTION

Kurt Vonnegut

Ⓑ

BERKLEY BOOKS, NEW YORK

BAGOMBO SNUFF BOX

A Berkley Book / published by arrangement with
the author

PRINTING HISTORY
G. P. Putnam's Sons hardcover edition / August 1999
Berkley trade paperback edition / August 2000

The Penguin Putnam Inc. World Wide Web site address is
http://www.penguinputnam.com

ISBN: 0-425-17446-8

BERKLEY®
Berkley Books are published by The Berkley Publishing Group,
a division of Penguin Putnam Inc.,
BERKLEY and the "B" design are trademarks
belonging to Penguin Putnam Inc.

PRINTED IN THE UNITED STATES OF AMERICA

20 19 18 17 16

As in my other works of fiction:

All persons living and dead are purely coincidental, and should not be construed. No names have been changed in order to protect the innocent. Angels protect the innocent as a matter of Heavenly routine.

In memory of my first agents,
Kenneth Littauer
and Max Wilkinson,
who taught me how to write

Contents

Bagombo Snuff Box

Preface

Kurt Vonnegut has achieved wide recognition as one of the best American novelists of the second half of the twentieth century, on the strength of such works as *Slaughterhouse-Five*, *Cat's Cradle*, *Breakfast of Champions*, and *Bluebeard*. His skills as a short story writer have attracted less attention. In the first decade and more of his career, Vonnegut's short fiction enjoyed a wide readership in the leading magazines of the day. Throughout the fifties and early sixties, he wrote many stories, which were published in *Collier's*, *The Saturday Evening Post*, *Cosmopolitan*, *Argosy*, *Redbook*, and other magazines. Twenty-three stories were collected in *Welcome to the Monkey House*; now, with this volume, the others can be found in a single collection, too.

Vonnegut's short fiction commanded a ready market, appearing in the best of the glossy wide-circulation magazines, and remained in demand while those publications thrived. It was ingenious, varied, and well written. Collected in *Welcome to the Monkey House*, or as anthologized, it has continued to find a readership. As popular fiction, these stories are accomplished in their energy, humor, and insight. It is important that the twenty-odd known stories not collected in *Monkey House* be preserved in book form, for they have their place in the Vonnegut canon as surely as his acclaimed novels. It is in these stories where he honed his skills that we see evolve the range of Vonnegut's talents, and the topics and techniques further developed in his later work.

Vonnegut began writing short stories in the late 1940s, while employed in public relations at General Electric in Schenectady, New York. Earlier, he had cut his teeth on journalism: while attending Shortridge High School in Indianapolis (1936–1940), he had been a regular contributor to and managing editor of its daily newspaper, *The Shortridge Echo*, and in college he worked on *The Cornell Daily Sun*. In his columns he creates characters, and one begins to see the humor and witty social iconoclasm evident in the mature work. The war intervened, with the dramatic circumstances that would be the stuff of his masterpiece, *Slaughterhouse-Five*, yet Vonnegut's course to becoming a writer had already been set.

After the war, popular magazines featuring short stories flourished in the United States. The late forties and early fifties were still a largely television-free era, with a steady demand for entertaining reading material. In 1949, Vonnegut sent "Report on the Barnhouse Effect" to *Collier's*. Knox Burger, who was fiction editor there, recognized the author's name from Cornell, where Burger had been editor of the campus humor magazine, *The Widow,* and gave the story his attention. After some revisions, "Barnhouse" became Vonnegut's first story to be accepted for publication. Burger was helpful also in introducing Vonnegut to Kenneth Littauer and Max Wilkinson, two agents with long experience in guiding aspiring writers. Their advice on the writing of a well-made story was invaluable (and even finds its way into the eight rules Vonnegut sets forth in his introduction to this collection). Having soon placed more stories, and with the apparent assurance of a market for his fiction, Vonnegut quit General Electric, moved to Cape Cod, and devoted himself full-time to writing.

This collection includes stories that draw on Vonnegut's World War Two experiences. The events on which *Slaughterhouse-Five* was based are by now widely known: how Vonnegut was captured by the Germans at the Battle of the Bulge, was held as a prisoner of war in Dresden, was sheltered in an underground meat storage room when that city was incinerated in massive air raids, and after the Nazi defeat wandered briefly in a Germany awash in refugees before he was reunited with American forces. "*Der Arme Dolmetscher,*" "Souvenir," and "The Cruise of *The Jolly Roger*" treat the aftermath of war with a varying mix of humor and poignancy.

Many of the stories offer fascinating insights into attitudes and preoccupations of Americans in the fifties. At General Electric the motto was "Progress is our most important product," a slogan that sums up the decade's optimism and the extension of the wartime can-do spirit. There was widespread belief in the ability of science and technology to go on improving everyday life. The assumption of a stable society that could offer the average family a happy home, financial advancement, and living conditions made easier and more glamorous by ever better gadgetry provides the context for these stories. Vonnegut questions this rosy vision, however, by showing that such ostensible progress may come at human cost. Thus do the home owners in "The Package" discover the inadequacy of the glitz embodied in their new gadget-laden house in a high-income suburb and decide they prefer the solidity of their old lives, and thus does the community of "Poor Little Rich Town" come to choose old ways over new and modest means over the affluence promised by developers. The theme is repeated in Vonnegut's first novel, the contemporary *Player Piano* (1952), and in much of his later fiction.

Pretense does not fare well in these stories. People who put on airs are usually exposed, often by children. Youngsters expose the egotistical gangster in "A Present for Big Saint Nick," and a nine-year-old trips up the show-off salesman in "Bagombo Snuff Box." At times pretense becomes a way of getting through life, as it does for the star performer's husband in "Unpaid Consultant," who invents an imaginary role for himself in order to retain a sense of importance. Kitty Cahoun, of "Custom-Made Bride," rebels against the pretense of the "Falloleen" role into which her designer husband would mold her. And young Kiah of "The Powder-Blue Dragon" finds only disillusionment in his attempt to pretend his way into a more sophisticated world by way of an exotic sports car. Such stories prefigure the warning sounded in *Mother Night*: "We are what we pretend to be, so we must be careful about what we pretend to be."

As in the novels, occupation often determines identity—at least in the case of men. Father-son relationships, which recur also in the novels, may help define the identities of both parent and child—see "This Son of Mine." The relationship is seldom comfortable, partly because of its propensity to impose an identity on the son, and partly because the father fears how he may be viewed by the son.

If there is one aspect of the stories that, more than any other, may make them seem dated, it is the roles of the women. After all, large numbers of married women in this era did not work outside the home, and they often took their standard for how they should dress, cook, decorate, entertain, or parent from some of the very magazines in which these stories appeared. While one would hardly expect stories written in the fifties to exhibit the kind of sensitivity to women's concerns so powerfully expressed in the novels *Galápagos* and *Bluebeard*, they already point that way. Even the romantic tales "A Night for Love" and "Find Me a Dream" demonstrate the burdensome expectations that can be placed on women in a man's world. "Lovers Anonymous," published in 1963, treats humorously the social awkwardness occasioned by the newly emergent "women's liberation."

The short story requires quick character definition, and these stories reveal how adept Vonnegut was at establishing a recognizable personality in a few paragraphs. That facility carries over into the novels, where character often seems subservient to message. Indeed, the more psychologically complex personalities, *Mother Night*'s Howard Campbell or *Bluebeard*'s Rabo Karabekian, for instance, are developed with a minimum of physical description. Some of the characterizations in these stories—the high school band director George M. Helmholtz, who is featured in three, comes to mind—might be prototypes for those in the novels.

Several stories rely on a convenient narrator, someone like a storm window salesman or a financial advisor, with access to many different social settings. Such a person can enter the homes of rich celebrities, as happens in "Custom-Made Bride" and "Unpaid Consultant," and deliver matter-of-fact observations. These narrators lend the immediacy of an intimate voice, a presence who, by virtue of being there, authenticates the account. Often theirs is the perspective of sound common sense that keeps the bizarre grounded in the everyday, and their wry commentary or ironic tone is a source of humor.

Vonnegut's humorous stories fit that American tradition of the tall tale epitomized by Mark Twain. "Tom Edison's Shaggy Dog," which appears in *Welcome to the Monkey House*, is the classic example of the form. Both "Mnemonics" and "Any Reasonable Offer" in this collection rise to an abrupt joke ending. Untraditional is Vonnegut's use of humor in science fiction stories. He characteristically seizes on the comic possibilities of the otherworldly settings and bizarre events typical of science fiction. "Thanasphere" belongs in the category of comic science fiction, the story combining space travel (then only an exciting prospect) and conventional notions of the spirits of the dead being "up there." If the story's humor is tinged with poignancy, that, too, is characteristic of Vonnegut. *Player Piano* and *The Sirens of Titan*, novels cast in the science fiction mode, abound in plot developments that are at once comic and painful, as does the classic short story "Epicac," which appears in *Welcome to the Monkey House*.

Television contributed to the end of Vonnegut's career as a

short story writer. The magazines that had been eager buyers of stories suffered from losses of readership and advertising revenues. And the audience for magazine stories turned increasingly to television for entertainment, while the advertisers who were the magazines' lifeblood found the new medium irresistible. Some magazines folded, some changed format, some shrank. Vonnegut switched to writing novels—first paperback originals, *The Sirens of Titan* (1959) and *Mother Night* (1961), and then, beginning with *Cat's Cradle* (1963), hardcover. All of his novels, now fourteen in number, remain in print.

As mentioned earlier, *Welcome to the Monkey House* (1968) included twenty-three stories. Of these, eleven had appeared in an earlier collection, now out of print and a rare find, *Canary in a Cat House* (1961). "Hal Irwin's Magic Lamp," included in that collection but not in *Monkey House*, is included also here, though in a different version from the original. The rest remained uncollected. Preparing a study (*The Short Fiction of Kurt Vonnegut*, Greenwood Press, 1997) took me into musty archives, retrieving Vonnegut contributions from bound volumes of *The Saturday Evening Post*, *Collier's*, and other magazines. It seemed obvious that these scattered tales deserved a proper home of their own, just as those in print in *Welcome to the Monkey House* have. Naturally I was delighted that Kurt Vonnegut shared my enthusiasm for the idea.

One curiosity for those interested in literary details. "*Der Arme Dolmetscher*" (The Poor Interpreter) is referred to on the copyright page of *Welcome to the Monkey House* and was included in the manuscript of that collection, but does not appear in the published work. The citation says that it appeared in *The Atlantic Monthly* with the title "Das Ganz Arm Dolmetscher," although in fact *Atlantic* used the shorter, grammatically correct title. Another curiosity: Although it did not appear until July 1955, it may have been accepted much earlier; the headnote describes Vonnegut as working at General Electric, when he had left the company by 1950.

Peter Reed

Introduction

My longtime friend and critic Professor Peter Reed, of the English Department at the University of Minnesota, made it his business to find these stories from my distant past. Otherwise, they might never have seen the light of day again. I myself hadn't saved one scrap of paper from that part of my life. I didn't think I would amount to a hill of beans. All I wanted to do was support a family.

Peter's quest was that of a scholar. I nevertheless asked him to go an extra mile for me, by providing an informal preface to what is in fact his rather than my collection.

God bless you, Dr. Reed, I think.

. . . . .

These stories, and twenty-three of similar quality in my previous hardcover collection, *Welcome to the Monkey House*, were written at the very end of a golden age of magazine fiction in this country. For about fifty years, until 1953, say, stories like these were a mild but popular form of entertainment in millions of homes, my own included.

This old man's hope has to be that some of his earliest tales, for all their mildness and innocence and clumsiness, may, in these coarse times, still entertain.

They would not be reprinted now, if novels I had written around the same time had not, better late than never, received critical attention. My children were adults by then, and I was middle-aged. These stories, printed in magazines fat with fiction and advertising, magazines now in most cases defunct, were expected to be among the living about as long as individual lightning bugs.

That anything I have written is in print today is due to the efforts of one publisher, Seymour "Sam" Lawrence (1927–1994). When I was broke in 1965, and teaching at the Writers' Workshop at the University of Iowa all alone, completely out of print, having separated myself from my family on Cape Cod in order to support them, Sam bought rights to my books, for peanuts, from publishers, both hardcover and softcover, who had given up on me. Sam thrust my books back into the myopic public eye again.

CPR! Cardiopulmonary resuscitation of this author who was all but dead!

Thus encouraged, this Lazarus wrote *Slaughterhouse-Five* for Sam. That made my reputation. I am a Humanist, and so am not entitled to expect an afterlife for myself or anyone. But at Seymour Lawrence's memorial service at New York City's Harvard Club five years ago, I said this with all my heart: "Sam is up in Heaven now."

I returned to Dresden, incidentally, the setting for *Slaughterhouse-Five*, on October 7th, 1998. I was taken down into the cellar where I and about a hundred other American POWs survived a firestorm that suffocated or incinerated 135,000 or so other human beings. It reduced the "Florence of the Elbe" to a jagged moonscape.

While I was down in that cellar again, this thought came to me: "Because I have lived so long, I am one of the few persons on Earth who saw an Atlantis before it disappeared forever beneath the waves."

Short stories can have greatness, short as they have to be. Several knocked my socks off when I was still in high school. Ernest Hemingway's "The Short Happy Life of Francis Macomber" and Saki's "The Open Window" and O. Henry's "The Gift of the Magi" and Ambrose Bierce's "An Occurrence at Owl Creek Bridge" spring to mind. But there is no greatness in this or my other collection, nor was there meant to be.

My own stories may be interesting, nonetheless, as relics from a time, before there was television, when an author might support a family by writing stories that satisfied uncritical readers of magazines, and earning thereby enough free time in which to write serious novels. When I became a full-time freelance in 1950, I expected to be doing that for the rest of my life.

I was in such good company with a prospectus like that. Hemingway had written for *Esquire*, F. Scott Fitzgerald for *The*

Saturday Evening Post, William Faulkner for *Collier's*, John Steinbeck for *The Woman's Home Companion*!

Say what you want about me, I never wrote for a magazine called *The Woman's Home Companion*, but there was a time when I would have been most happy to. And I add this thought: Just because a woman is stuck alone at home, with her husband at work and her kids at school, that doesn't mean she is an imbecile.

Publication of this book makes me want to talk about the peculiar and beneficial effect a short story can have on us, which makes it different from a novel or movie or play or TV show.

If I am to make my point, though, you must first imagine with me a scene in the home of my childhood and youth in Indianapolis, in the middle of the previous Great Depression. The previous Great Depression lasted from the stock market crash on October 24th, 1929, until the Japanese did us the favor, for the sheer hell of it, of bombing our comatose fleet of warships in Pearl Harbor, on December 7th, 1941. The little yellow bastards, as we used to call them, were bored to tears with the Great Depression. So were we.

Imagine that it is 1938 again. I am sixteen again. I come home again from yet another lousy day at Shortridge High School. Mother, who does not work outside the home, says there is a new *Saturday Evening Post* on the coffee table. It is raining outside, and I am unpopular. But I can't turn on a magazine like a TV set. I have to pick it up, or it will go on lying there, dead as a doornail. An unassisted magazine has no get-up-and-go.

After I pick it up, I have to make all one hundred sixty pounds of male adolescent meat and bones comfortable in an easy chair. Then I have to leaf through the magazine with my fingertips, so my eyes can shop for a story with a stimulating title and illustration.

Illustrators during the golden age of American magazine fiction used to get as much money as the authors whose stories they illustrated. They were often as famous as, or even more famous than, the authors. Norman Rockwell was their Michelangelo.

While I shop for a story, my eyes also see ads for automobiles and cigarettes and hand lotions and so on. It is advertisers, not readers, who pay the true costs of such a voluptuous publication. And God bless them for doing that. But consider the incredible thing I myself have to do in turn. I turn my brains on!

That isn't the half of it. With my brains all fired up, I do the nearly impossible thing that you are doing now, dear reader. I make sense of idiosyncratic arrangements, in horizontal lines, of nothing but twenty-six phonetic symbols, ten Arabic numerals, and perhaps eight punctuation marks, on a sheet of bleached and flattened wood pulp!

But get this: While I am reading, my pulse and breathing slow down. My high school troubles drop away. I am in a pleasant state somewhere between sleep and restfulness.

OK?

And then, after however long it takes to read a short story, ten minutes, say, I spring out of the chair. I put *The Saturday Evening Post* back on the coffee table for somebody else.

OK?

So then my architect dad comes home from work, or more likely from no work, since the little yellow bastards haven't bombed Pearl Harbor yet. I tell him I have read a story he might enjoy. I tell him to sit in the easy chair whose cushion is still dented and warmed by my teenage butt.

Dad sits. I pick up the magazine and open it to the story. Dad is tired and blue. Dad starts to read. His pulse and breathing slow down. His troubles drop away, and so on.

Yes! And our little domestic playlet, true to life in the 1930s, dear reader, proves exactly what? It proves that a short story, because of its physiological and psychological effects on a human being, is more closely related to Buddhist styles of meditation than it is to any other form of narrative entertainment.

What you have in this volume, then, and in every other collection of short stories, is a bunch of Buddhist catnaps.

Reading a novel, *War and Peace*, for example, is no catnap. Because a novel is so long, reading one is like being married forever to somebody nobody else knows or cares about. Definitely not refreshing!

Oh sure, we had radios before we had TV. But radios can't hold our attention, can't take control of our emotions, except in times of war. Radios can't make us sit still. Unlike print and plays and movies and boob tubes, radios don't give us anything for our restless eyes to do.

Listen: After I came home from World War Two, a brevet corporal twenty-two years old, I didn't want to be a fiction writer. I married my childhood sweetheart Jane Marie Cox, also from Indianapolis, up in Heaven now, and enrolled as a graduate student in the Anthropology Department of the University of Chicago. But I didn't want to be an anthropologist, either. I only hoped to find out more about human beings. I was going to be a journalist!

To that end, I also took a job as a police reporter for the Chicago City News Bureau. The News Bureau was supported by all four Chicago dailies back then, as a sensor for breaking news, prowling the city night and day, and as a training ground. The only way to get a job on one of those papers, short of nepotism, was to go through the News Bureau's hazing first.

But it became obvious that no newspaper positions were going to open up in Chicago or anywhere else for several years. Reporters had come home from the war to reclaim their jobs, and the women who had replaced them would not quit. The women were terrific. They should not have quit.

And then the Department of Anthropology rejected my M.A. thesis, which proved that similarities between the Cubist painters in Paris in 1907 and the leaders of Native American, or Injun, uprisings late in the nineteenth century could not be ignored. The Department said it was unprofessional.

Slowly but surely, Fate, which had spared my life in Dresden, now began to shape me into a fiction writer and a failure until I was a bleeding forty-seven years of age! But first I had to be a publicity hack for General Electric in Schenectady, New York.

While writing publicity releases at GE, I had a boss named George. George taped to the outside of his office door cartoons he felt had some bearing on the company or the kind of work we did. One cartoon was of two guys in the office of a buggy whip factory. A chart on the wall showed their business had dropped to zero. One guy was saying to the other, "It can't be our product's quality. We make the finest buggy whips in the world." George posted that cartoon to celebrate how GE, with its wonderful new products, was making a lot of other companies feel as though they were trying to sell buggy whips.

A broken-down movie actor named Ronald Reagan was working for the company. He was on the road all the time, lecturing to chambers of commerce and power companies and so on about the evils of socialism. We never met, so I remain a socialist.

While my future two-term president was burbling out on the rubber-chicken circuit in 1950, I started writing short stories at nights and on weekends. Jane and I had two kids by then. I needed more money than GE would pay me. I also wanted, if possible, more self-respect.

There was a crazy seller's market for short stories in 1950. There were four weekly magazines that published three or more of the things in every issue. Six monthlies did the same.

I got me an agent. If I sent him a story that didn't quite work, wouldn't quite satisfy a reader, he would tell me how to fix it. Agents and editors back then could tell a writer how to fine-tune a story as though they were pit mechanics and the story were a race car. With help like that, I sold one, and then two, and then three stories, and banked more money than a year's salary at GE.

I quit GE and started my first novel, *Player Piano*. It is a lampoon on GE. I bit the hand that used to feed me. The book predicted what has indeed come to pass, a day when machines, because they are so dependable and efficient and tireless, and getting cheaper all the time, are taking the halfway decent jobs from human beings.

I moved our family of four to Cape Cod, first to Province-town. I met Norman Mailer there. He was my age. He had been a college-educated infantry private like me, and he was already a world figure, because of his great war novel *The Naked and the Dead*. I admired him then, and do today. He is majestic. He is royalty. So was Jacqueline Onassis. So was Joe DiMaggio. So is Muhammad Ali. So is Arthur Miller.

We moved from Provincetown to Osterville, still on the Cape. But only three years after I left Schenectady, advertisers started withdrawing their money from magazines. The Buddhist catnaps coming out of my typewriter were becoming as obsolete as buggy whips.

One monthly that had bought several of my stories, *Cosmopolitan*, now survives as a harrowingly explicit sex manual.

That same year, 1953, Ray Bradbury published *Fahrenheit 451*. The title refers to the kindling point of paper. That is how hot you have to get a book or a magazine before it bursts into flame. The leading male character makes his living burning printed matter. Nobody reads anymore. Many ordinary, rinky-dink homes like Ray's and mine have a room with floor-to-ceiling TV screens on all four walls, with one chair in the middle.

The actors and actresses on all four walls of TV are scripted to acknowledge whoever is sitting in the chair in the middle, even if nobody is sitting in the chair in the middle, as a friend or relative in the midst of things. The wife of the guy who burns up paper is unhappy. He can afford only three screens. His wife can't stand not knowing what's happening on the missing fourth screen, because the TV actors and actresses are the only people she loves, the only ones anywhere she gives a damn about.

Fahrenheit 451 was published before we and most of our neighbors in Osterville even owned TVs. Ray Bradbury himself may not have owned one. He still may not own one. To this day, Ray can't drive a car and hates to ride in airplanes.

In any case, Ray was sure as heck prescient. Just as people with dysfunctional kidneys are getting perfect ones from hospitals nowadays, Americans with dysfunctional social lives, like the woman in Ray's book, are getting perfect friends and relatives from their TV sets. And around the clock!

Ray missed the boat about how many screens would be required for a successful people-transplant. One lousy little Sony can do the job, night and day. All it takes besides that is actors and actresses, telling the news, selling stuff, in soap operas or whatever, who treat whoever is watching, even if nobody is watching, like family.

"Hell is other people," said Jean-Paul Sartre. "Hell is other real people," is what he should have said.

You can't fight progress. The best you can do is ignore it, until it finally takes your livelihood and self-respect away. General Electric itself was made to feel like a buggy whip factory for a time, as Bell Labs and others cornered patents on transistors and their uses, while GE was still shunting electrons this way and that with vacuum tubes.

Too big to fail, though, as I was not, GE recovered sufficiently to lay off thousands and poison the Hudson River with PCBs.

. . . . .

By 1953, Jane and I had three kids. So I taught English in a boarding school there on the Cape. Then I wrote ads for an industrial agency in Boston. I wrote a couple of paperback originals, *The Sirens of Titan* and *Mother Night*. They were never reviewed. I got for each of them what I used to get for a short story.

I tried to sell some of the first Saab automobiles to come into this country. The doors opened into the wind. There was a roller-blind behind the front grille, which you could operate with a chain under the dashboard. That was to keep your engine warm in the wintertime. You had to mix oil with your gasoline every time you filled the tank of those early Saabs. If you ever forgot to do that, the engine would revert to the ore state. One engine I chipped away from a Saab chassis with a cold chisel and a sledge looked like a meteor!

If you left a Saab parked for more than a day, the oil settled like maple syrup to the bottom of the gas tank. When you started it up, the exhaust would black out a whole neighborhood. One time I blacked out Woods Hole that way. I was coughing like everybody else, I couldn't imagine where all that smoke had come from.

Then I took to teaching creative writing, first at Iowa, then at Harvard, and then at City College in New York. Joseph Heller, author of *Catch-22*, was teaching at City College also. He said to me that if it hadn't been for the war, he would have been in the dry-cleaning business. I said to him that if it hadn't

55555

5555555

been for the war, I would have been garden editor of *The Indianapolis Star*.

. . . .

Now lend me your ears. Here is Creative Writing 101:

1. Use the time of a total stranger in such a way that he or she will not feel the time was wasted.
2. Give the reader at least one character he or she can root for.
3. Every character should want something, even if it is only a glass of water.
4. Every sentence must do one of two things—reveal character or advance the action.
5. Start as close to the end as possible.
6. Be a sadist. No matter how sweet and innocent your leading characters, make awful things happen to them—in order that the reader may see what they are made of.
7. Write to please just one person. If you open a window and make love to the world, so to speak, your story will get pneumonia.
8. Give your readers as much information as possible as soon as possible. To heck with suspense. Readers should have such complete understanding of what is going on, where and why, that they could finish the story themselves, should cockroaches eat the last few pages.

The greatest American short story writer of my generation was Flannery O'Connor (1925–1964). She broke practically every one of my rules but the first. Great writers tend to do that.

. . . .

Ms. O'Connor may or may not have broken my seventh rule, "Write to please just one person." There is no way for us to find out for sure, unless, of course, there is a Heaven after all, and she's there, and the rest of us are going there, and we can ask her.

I'm almost sure she didn't break rule seven. The late American psychiatrist Dr. Edmund Bergler, who claimed to have treated more professional writers than any other shrink, said in his book *The Writer and Psychoanalysis* that most writers in his experience wrote to please one person they knew well, even if they didn't realize they were doing that. It wasn't a trick of the fiction trade. It was simply a natural human thing to do, whether or not it could make a story better.

Dr. Bergler said it commonly required psychoanalysis before his patients could know for whom they had been writing. But as soon as I finished his book, and then thought for only a couple of minutes, I knew it was my sister Allie I had been writing for. She is the person the stories in this book were written for. Anything I knew Allie wouldn't like I crossed out. Everything I knew she would get a kick out of I left in.

Allie is up in Heaven now, with my first wife Jane and Sam Lawrence and Flannery O'Connor and Dr. Bergler, but I still write to please her. Allie was funny in real life. That gives me permission to be funny, too. Allie and I were very close.

In my opinion, a story written for one person pleases a reader, dear reader, because it makes him or her a part of the action. It makes the reader feel, even though he or she doesn't know it, as though he or she is eavesdropping on a fascinating conversation between two people at the next table, say, in a restaurant.

That's my educated guess.

Here is another: A reader likes a story written for just one person because the reader can sense, again without knowing it, that the story has boundaries like a playing field. The story can't go simply anywhere. This, I feel, invites readers to come off the sidelines, to get into the game with the author. Where is the story going next? Where should it go? No fair! Hopeless situation! Touchdown!

Remember my rule number eight? "Give your readers as much information as possible as soon as possible"? That's so they can play along. Where, outside the Groves of Academe, does anybody like a story where so much information is withheld or arcane that there is no way for readers to play along?

The boundaries to the playing fields of my short stories, and my novels, too, were once the boundaries of the soul of my only sister. She lives on that way.

Amen.

Kurt Vonnegut

Thanasphere

At noon, Wednesday, July 26th, windowpanes in the small mountain towns of Sevier County, Tennessee, were rattled by the shock and faint thunder of a distant explosion rolling down the northwest slopes of the Great Smokies. The explosion came from the general direction of the closely guarded Air Force experimental station in the forest ten miles northwest of Elkmont.

Said the Air Force Office of Public Information, "No comment."

That evening, amateur astronomers in Omaha, Nebraska, and Glenwood, Iowa, reported independently that a speck had crossed the face of the full moon at 9:57 p.m. There was a flurry of excitement on the news wires. Astronomers at the major North American observatories denied that they had seen it.

They lied.

In Boston, on the morning of Thursday, July 27th, an enterprising newsman sought out Dr. Bernard Groszinger, youthful rocket consultant for the Air Force. "Is it possible that what crossed the moon was a spaceship?" the newsman asked.

Dr. Groszinger laughed at the question. "My own opinion is that we're beginning another cycle of flying-saucer scares," he said. "This time everyone's seeing spaceships between us and the moon. You can tell your readers this, my friend: No rocket ship will leave the earth for at least another twenty years."

He lied.

He knew a great deal more than he was saying, but somewhat less than he himself thought. He did not believe in ghosts, for instance—and had yet to learn of the Thanasphere.

Dr. Groszinger rested his long legs on his cluttered desktop, and watched his secretary conduct the disappointed newsman through the locked door, past the armed guards. He lit a cigarette and tried to relax before going back into the stale air and tension of the radio room. IS YOUR SAFE LOCKED? asked a sign on the wall, tacked there by a diligent security officer. The sign annoyed him. Security officers, security regulations only served to slow his work, to make him think about things he had no time to think about.

The secret papers in the safe weren't secrets. They said what had been known for centuries: Given fundamental physics, it follows that a projectile fired into space in direction x, at y miles per hour, will travel in the arc z. Dr. Groszinger modified the equation: Given fundamental physics and one billion dollars.

Impending war had offered him the opportunity to try the experiment. The threat of war was an incident, the military men about him an irritating condition of work—*the experiment* was the heart of the matter.

There were no unknowns, he reflected, finding contentment in the dependability of the physical world. Young Dr. Groszinger smiled, thinking of Christopher Columbus and his crew, who hadn't known what lay ahead of them, who had been scared stiff by sea monsters that didn't exist. Maybe the average person of today felt the same way about space. The Age of Superstition still had a few years to run.

But the man in the spaceship two thousand miles from earth had no unknowns to fear. The sullen Major Allen Rice would have nothing surprising to report in his radio messages. He could only confirm what reason had already revealed about outer space.

The major American observatories, working closely with the project, reported that the ship was now moving around the earth in the predicted orbit at the predicted velocity. Soon, anytime now, the first message in history from outer space would be received in the radio room. The broadcast could be on an ultra-high-frequency band where no one had ever sent or received messages before.

The first message was overdue, but nothing had gone wrong—nothing *could* go wrong, Dr. Groszinger assured himself again. Machines, not men, were guiding the flight. The man was a mere observer, piloted to his lonely vantage point by infallible electronic brains, swifter than his own. He had controls in his ship, but only for gliding down through the atmosphere, when and if they brought him back from space. He was equipped to stay for several years.

Even the man was as much like a machine as possible, Dr. Groszinger thought with satisfaction. He was quick, strong, unemotional. Psychiatrists had picked Major Rice from a hundred volunteers, and predicted that he would function as perfectly as the rocket motors, the metal hull, and the electronic controls. His specifications: Husky, twenty-nine years of age, fifty-five missions over Europe during the Second World War without a sign of fatigue, a childless widower, melancholy and solitary, a career soldier, a demon for work.

The Major's mission? Simple: To report weather conditions over enemy territory, and to observe the accuracy of guided atomic missiles in the event of war.

Major Rice was fixed in the solar system, two thousand miles above the earth now—close by, really—the distance from New York to Salt Lake City, not far enough away to see much of the polar icecaps, even. With a telescope, Rice could pick out small towns and the wakes of ships without much trouble. It would be breathtaking to watch the enormous blue-and-green ball, to see night creeping around it, and clouds and storms growing and swirling over its face.

Dr. Groszinger tamped out his cigarette, absently lit another almost at once, and strode down the corridor to the small laboratory where the radio equipment had been set up.

Lieutenant General Franklin Dane, head of Project Cyclops, sat next to the radio operator, his uniform rumpled, his collar open. The General stared expectantly at the loudspeaker before him. The floor was littered with sandwich wrappings and cigarette butts. Coffee-filled paper cups stood before the General and the radio operator, and beside the canvas chair where Groszinger had spent the night waiting.

General Dane nodded to Groszinger and motioned with his hand for silence.

"Able Baker Fox, this is Dog Easy Charley. Able Baker Fox,

this is Dog Easy Charley . . ." droned the radio operator wearily, using the code names. "Can you hear me, Able Baker Fox? Can you—"

The loudspeaker crackled, then, tuned to its peak volume, boomed: "This is Able Baker Fox. Come in, Dog Easy Charley. Over."

General Dane jumped to his feet and embraced Groszinger. They laughed idiotically and pounded each other on the back. The General snatched the microphone from the radio operator. "You made it. Able Baker Fox! Right on course! What's it like, boy? What's it feel like? Over." Groszinger, his arm draped around the General's shoulders, leaned forward eagerly, his ear a few inches from the speaker. The radio operator turned the volume down, so that they could hear something of the quality of Major Rice's voice.

The voice came through again, soft, hesitant. The tone disturbed Groszinger—he had wanted it to be crisp, sharp, efficient.

"This side of the earth's dark, very dark just now. And I feel like I'm falling—the way you said I would. Over."

"Is anything the matter?" asked the General anxiously. "You sound as though something—"

The Major cut in before he could finish: "There! Did you hear that?"

"Able Baker Fox, we can't hear anything," said the General, looking perplexed at Groszinger. "What is it—some kind of noise in your receiver? Over."

"A child," said the Major. "I hear a child crying. Don't you hear it? And now—listen!—now an old man is trying to comfort it." His voice seemed farther away, as though he were no longer speaking directly into his microphone.

"That's impossible, ridiculous!" said Groszinger. "Check your set, Able Baker Fox, check your set. Over."

"They're getting louder now. The voices are louder. I can't hear you very well above them. It's like standing in the middle of a crowd, with everybody trying to get my attention at once. It's like . . ." The message trailed off. They could hear a shushing sound in the speaker. The Major's transmitter was still on.

"Can you hear me, Able Baker Fox? Answer! Can you hear me?" called General Dane.

The shushing noise stopped. The General and Groszinger stared blankly at the speaker.

"Able Baker Fox, this is Dog Easy Charley," chanted the radio operator. "Able Baker Fox, this is Dog Easy Charley. . . ."

Groszinger, his eyes shielded from the glaring ceiling light of the radio room by a newspaper, lay fully dressed on the cot that had been brought in for him. Every few minutes he ran his long, slender fingers through his tangled hair and swore. His machine had worked perfectly, *was* working perfectly. The one thing he had not designed, the damn man in it, had failed, had destroyed the whole experiment.

They had been trying for six hours to reestablish contact with the lunatic who peered down at earth from his tiny steel moon and heard voices.

"He's coming in again, sir," said the radio operator. "This is Dog Easy Charley. Come in, Able Baker Fox. Over."

"This is Able Baker Fox. Clear weather over Zones Seven, Eleven, Nineteen, and Twenty-three. Zones One, Two, Three, Four, Five, and Six overcast. Storm seems to be shaping up over

Zones Eight and Nine, moving south by southwest at about eighteen miles an hour. Over."

"He's OK now," said the General, relieved.

Groszinger remained supine, his head still covered with the newspaper. "Ask him about the voices," he said.

"You don't hear the voices anymore, *do* you, Able Baker Fox?"

"What do you mean, I don't hear them? I can hear them better than I can hear you. Over."

"He's out of his head," said Groszinger, sitting up.

"I heard that," said Major Rice. "Maybe I am. It shouldn't be too hard to check. All you have to do is find out if an Andrew Tobin died in Evansville, Indiana, on February 17, 1927. Over."

"I don't follow you, Able Baker Fox," said the General. "Who was Andrew Tobin? Over."

"He's one of the voices." There was an uncomfortable pause. Major Rice cleared his throat. "Claims his brother murdered him. Over."

The radio operator had risen slowly from his stool, his face chalk-white. Groszinger pushed him back down and took the microphone from the General's now limp hand.

"Either you've lost your mind, or this is the most sophomoric practical joke in history, Able Baker Fox," said Groszinger. "This is *Groszinger* you're talking to, and you're dumber than I think you are if you think you can kid me." He nodded. "Over."

"I can't hear you very well anymore, Dog Easy Charley. Sorry, but the voices are getting louder."

"Rice! Straighten out!" said Groszinger.

"There—I caught that: Mrs. Pamela Ritter wants her husband to marry again, for the sake of the children. He lives at—"

"Stop it!"

"He lives at 1577 Damon Place, in Scotia, New York. Over and out."

General Dane shook Groszinger's shoulder gently. "You've been asleep five hours," he said. "It's midnight." He handed him a cup of coffee. "We've got some more messages. Interested?"

Groszinger sipped the coffee. "Is he still raving?"

"He still hears the voices, if that's what you mean." The General dropped two unopened telegrams in Groszinger's lap. "Thought you might like to be the one to open these."

Groszinger laughed. "Went ahead and checked Scotia and Evansville, did you? God help this army, if all the generals are as superstitious as you, my friend."

"OK, OK, you're the scientist, you're the brain-box. That's why I want *you* to open the telegrams. I want you to tell me what in hell's going on."

Groszinger opened one of the telegrams.

HARVEY RITTER LISTED FOR 1577 DAMON PLACE, SCOTIA. GE ENGINEER. WIDOWER, TWO CHILDREN. DECEASED WIFE NAMED PAMELA. DO YOU NEED MORE INFORMATION? R. B. FAILEY, CHIEF, SCOTIA POLICE

He shrugged and handed the message to General Dane, then opened the other telegram:

RECORDS SHOW ANDREW TOBIN DIED IN HUNTING ACCIDENT FEBRUARY 17, 1927. BROTHER PAUL LEADING BUSINESSMAN.

OWNS COAL BUSINESS STARTED BY ANDREW. CAN FURNISH FUR-
THER DETAILS IF NEEDED. F. B. JOHNSON, CHIEF, EVANSVILLE P.D.

"I'm not surprised," said Groszinger. "I expected something like this. I suppose you're firmly convinced now that our friend Major Rice has found outer space populated by ghosts?"

"Well, I'd say he's sure as hell found it populated by some-thing," said the General.

Groszinger wadded the second telegram in his fist and threw it across the room, missing the wastebasket by a foot. He folded his hands and affected the patient, priestlike pose he used in lecturing freshman physics classes. "At first, my friend, we had two possible conclusions: Either Major Rice was insane, or he was pulling off a spectacular hoax." He twiddled his thumbs, waiting for the General to digest this intelligence. "Now that we know his spirit messages deal with real people, we've got to conclude that he has planned and is now carrying out some sort of hoax. He got his names and addresses before he took off. God knows what he hopes to accomplish by it. God knows what we can do to make him stop it. That's your problem, I'd say."

The General's eyes narrowed. "So he's trying to jimmy the project, is he? We'll see, by God, we'll see." The radio operator was dozing. The General slapped him on the back. "On the ball, Sergeant, on the ball. Keep calling Rice till you get him, understand?"

The radio operator had to call only once.

"This is Able Baker Fox. Come in, Dog Easy Charley." Major Rice's voice was tired.

"This is Dog Easy Charley," said General Dane. "We've had enough of your voices, Able Baker Fox—do you understand? We don't want to hear any more about them. We're onto your little game. I don't know what your angle is, but I do know I'll bring you back down and slap you on a rock pile in Leavenworth so fast you'll leave your teeth up there. Do we understand each other?" The General bit the tip from a fresh cigar fiercely. "Over."

"Did you check those names and addresses? Over."

The General looked at Groszinger, who frowned and shook his head. "Sure we did. That doesn't prove anything. So you've got a list of names and addresses up there. So what does that prove? Over."

"You say those names checked? Over."

"I'm telling you to quit it, Rice. Right now. Forget the voices, do you hear? Give me a weather report. Over."

"Clear patches over Zones Eleven, Fifteen, and Sixteen. Looks like a solid overcast in One, Two, and Three. All clear in the rest. Over."

"That's more like it, Able Baker Fox," said the General. "We'll forget about the voices, eh? Over."

"There's an old woman calling out something in a German accent. Is Dr. Groszinger there? I think she's calling his name. She's asking him not to get too wound up in his work—not to—"

Groszinger leaned over the radio operator's shoulder and snapped off the switch on the receiver. "Of all the cheap, sickening stunts," he said.

"Let's hear what he has to say," said the General. "Thought you were a scientist."

Groszinger glared at him defiantly, snapped on the receiver, and stood back, his hands on his hips.

"—saying something in German," continued the voice of Major Rice. "Can't understand it. Maybe you can. I'll give it to you the way it sounds: '*Alles geben die Götter, die unendlichen, ihren Lieblingen, ganz. Alle—*'"

Groszinger turned down the volume. "'*Alle Freuden, die unendlichen, alle Schmerzen, die unendlichen, ganz,*'" he said faintly. "That's how it ends." He sat down on the cot. "It's my mother's favorite quotation—something from Goethe."

"I can threaten him again," said the General.

"What for?" Groszinger shrugged and smiled. "Outer space *is* full of voices." He laughed nervously. "*There's* something to pep up a physics textbook."

"An omen, sir—it's an omen," blurted the radio operator.

"What the hell do you mean, an omen?" said the General. "So outer space is filled with ghosts. That doesn't surprise me."

"Nothing would, then," said Groszinger.

"That's exactly right. I'd be a hell of a general if anything would. For all I know, the moon is made of green cheese. So what. All I want is a man out there to tell me that I'm hitting what I'm shooting at. I don't give a damn what's going on in outer space."

"Don't you see, sir?" said the radio operator. "Don't you see? It's an omen. When people find out about all the spirits out there they'll forget about war. They won't want to think about anything but the spirits."

"Relax, Sergeant," said the General. "Nobody's going to find out about them, understand?"

"You can't suppress a discovery like this," said Groszinger.

"You're nuts if you think I can't," said General Dane. "How're you going to tell anybody about this business without telling them we've got a rocket ship out there?"

"They've got a right to know," said the radio operator.

"If the world finds out we have that ship out there, that's

the start of World War Three," said the General. "Now tell me you want that. The enemy won't have any choice but to try and blow the hell out of us before we can put Major Rice to any use. And there'd be nothing for us to do but try and blow the hell out of them first. Is that what you want?"

"No, sir," said the radio operator. "I guess not, sir."

"Well, we can experiment, anyway," said Groszinger. "We can find out as much as possible about what the spirits are like. We can send Rice into a wider orbit to find out how far out he can hear the voices, and whether—"

"Not on Air Force funds, you can't," said General Dane. "That isn't what Rice is out there for. We can't afford to piddle around. We need him right there."

"All right, all right," said Groszinger. "Then let's hear what he has to say."

"Tune him in, Sergeant," said the General.

"Yes, sir." The radio operator fiddled with the dials. "He doesn't seem to be transmitting now, sir." The shushing noise of a transmitter cut into the hum of the loudspeaker. "I guess he's coming in again. Able Baker Fox, this is Dog Easy Charley—"

"King Two X-ray William Love, this is William Five Zebra Zebra King in Dallas," said the loudspeaker. The voice had a soft drawl and was pitched higher than Major Rice's.

A bass voice answered: "This is King Two X-ray William Love in Albany. Come in W5ZZK, I hear you well. How do you hear me? Over."

"You're clear as a bell, K2XWL—twenty-five thousand megacycles on the button. I'm trying to cut down on my drift with a—"

The voice of Major Rice interrupted. "I can't hear you

clearly, Dog Easy Charley. The voices are a steady roar now. I can catch bits of what they're saying. Grantland Whitman, the Hollywood actor, is yelling that his will was tampered with by his nephew Carl. He says—"

"Say again, K2XWL," said the drawling voice. "I must have misunderstood you. Over."

"I didn't say anything, W5ZZK. What was that about Grantland Whitman? Over."

"The crowd's quieting down," said Major Rice. "Now there's just one voice—a young woman, I think. It's so soft I can't make out what she's saying."

"What's going on, K2XWL? Can you hear me, K2XWL?"

"She's calling my name. Do you hear it? She's calling my name," said Major Rice.

"Jam the frequency, dammit!" cried the General. "Yell, whistle—do something!"

Early-morning traffic past the university came to a honking, bad-tempered stop, as Groszinger absently crossed the street against the light, on his way back to his office and the radio room. He looked up in surprise, mumbled an apology, and hurried to the curb. He had had a solitary breakfast in an all-night diner a block and a half from the laboratory building, and then he'd taken a long walk. He had hoped that getting away for a couple of hours would clear his head—but the feeling of confusion and helplessness was still with him. Did the world have a right to know, or didn't it?

There had been no more messages from Major Rice. At the General's orders, the frequency had been jammed. Now the unexpected eavesdroppers could hear nothing but a steady whine at 25,000 megacycles. General Dane had reported the dilemma to Washington shortly after midnight. Perhaps orders as to what to do with Major Rice had come through by now.

Groszinger paused in a patch of sunlight on the laboratory building's steps, and read again the front-page news story, which ran fancifully for a column, beneath the headline "Mystery Radio Message Reveals Possible Will Fraud." The story told of two radio amateurs, experimenting illegally on the supposedly unused ultra-high-frequency band, who had been amazed to hear a man chattering about voices and a will. The amateurs had broken the law, operating on an unassigned frequency, but they hadn't kept their mouths shut about their discovery. Now hams all over the world would be building sets so they could listen in, too.

"Morning, sir. Nice morning, isn't it?" said a guard coming off duty. He was a cheerful Irishman.

"Fine morning, all right," agreed Groszinger. "Clouding up a little in the west, maybe." He wondered what the guard would say if he told him what he knew. He would laugh, probably.

Groszinger's secretary was dusting off his desk when he walked in. "You could use some sleep, couldn't you?" she said. "Honestly, why you men don't take better care of yourselves I just don't know. If you had a wife, she'd make you—"

"Never felt better in my life," said Groszinger. "Any word from General Dane?"

"He was looking for you about ten minutes ago. He's back in the radio room now. He's been on the phone with Washington for half an hour."

She had only the vaguest notion of what the project was about. Again, Groszinger felt the urge to tell about Major Rice and the voices, to see what effect the news would have on someone else. Perhaps his secretary would react as he himself had reacted, with a shrug. Maybe that was the spirit of this era of the atom bomb, H-bomb, God-knows-what-next bomb—to be amazed at nothing. Science had given humanity forces enough to destroy the earth, and politics had given humanity a fair assurance that the forces would be used. There could be no cause for awe to top *that* one. But proof of a spirit world might at least equal it. Maybe that was the shock the world needed, maybe word from the spirits could change the suicidal course of history.

General Dane looked up wearily as Groszinger walked into the radio room. "They're bringing him down," he said. "There's nothing else we can do. He's no damn good to us now." The loudspeaker, turned low, sang the monotonous hum of the jamming signal. The radio operator slept before the set, his head resting on his folded arms.

"Did you try to get through to him again?"

"Twice. He's clear off his head now. Tried to tell him to change his frequency, to code his messages, but he just went on jabbering like he couldn't hear me—talking about that woman's voice."

"Who's the woman? Did he say?"

The General looked at him oddly. "Says it's his wife, Margaret. Guess that's enough to throw anybody, wouldn't you say? Pretty bright, weren't we, sending up a guy with no family ties." He arose and stretched. "I'm going out for a minute. Just make sure you keep your hands off that set." He slammed the door behind him.

The radio operator stirred. "They're bringing him down," he said.

"I know," said Groszinger.

"That'll kill him, won't it?"

"He has controls for gliding her in, once he hits the atmosphere."

"If he wants to."

"That's right—if he wants to. They'll get him out of his orbit and back to the atmosphere under rocket power. After that, it'll be up to him to take over and make the landing."

They fell silent. The only sound in the room was the muted jamming signal in the loudspeaker.

"He don't want to live, you know that?" said the radio operator suddenly. "Would you want to?"

"Guess that's something you don't know until you come up against it," said Groszinger. He was trying to imagine the world of the future—a world in constant touch with the spirits, the living inseparable from the dead. It was bound to come. Other men, probing into space, were certain to find out. Would it make life heaven or hell? Every bum and genius, criminal and hero, average man and madman, now and forever part of humanity—advising, squabbling, conniving, placating . . .

The radio operator looked furtively toward the door. "Want to hear him again?"

Groszinger shook his head. "Everybody's listening to that frequency now. We'd all be in a nice mess if you stopped jamming." He didn't want to hear more. He was baffled, miserable. Would Death unmasked drive men to suicide, or bring new hope? he was asking himself. Would the living desert their leaders and turn to the dead for guidance? To Caesar . . . Charlemagne . . . Peter the Great . . . Napoleon . . . Bismarck . . . Lincoln . . . Roosevelt? To Jesus Christ? Were the dead wiser than—

Before Groszinger could stop him, the sergeant switched off the oscillator that was jamming the frequency.

Major Rice's voice came through instantly, high and giddy. ". . . thousands of them, thousands of them, all around me, standing on nothing, shimmering like northern lights—beautiful, curving off in space, all around the earth like a glowing fog. I can see them, do you hear? I can see them now. I can see Margaret. She's waving and smiling, misty, heavenly, beautiful. If only you could see it, if—"

The radio operator flicked on the jamming signal. There was a footfall in the hallway.

General Dane stalked into the radio room, studying his watch. "In five minutes they'll start him down," he said. He plunged his hands deep into his pockets and slouched dejectedly. "We failed this time. Next time, by God, we'll make it. The next man who goes up will know what he's up against—he'll be ready to take it."

He put his hand on Groszinger's shoulder. "The most important job you'll ever have to do, my friend, is to keep your mouth shut about those spirits out there, do you understand? We don't want the enemy to know we've had a ship out there, and we don't want them to know what they'll come across if they try it. The security of this country depends on that being our secret. Do I make myself clear?"

"Yes, sir," said Groszinger, grateful to have no choice but to be quiet. He didn't want to be the one to tell the world. He wished he had had nothing to do with sending Rice out into space. What discovery of the dead would do to humanity he didn't know, but the impact would be terrific. Now, like the rest, he would have to wait for the next wild twist of history.

The General looked at his watch again. "They're bringing him down," he said.

At 1:39 p.m., on Friday, July 28th, the British liner *Capricorn*, two hundred eighty miles out of New York City, bound for Liverpool, radioed that an unidentified object had crashed into the sea, sending up a towering geyser on the horizon to starboard of the ship. Several passengers were said to have seen something glinting as the thing fell from the sky. Upon reaching the scene of the crash, the *Capricorn* reported finding dead and stunned fish on the surface, and turbulent water, but no wreckage.

Newspapers suggested that the *Capricorn* had seen the crash of an experimental rocket fired out to sea in a test of range. The Secretary of Defense promptly denied that any such tests were being conducted over the Atlantic.

In Boston, Dr. Bernard Groszinger, young rocket consultant for the Air Force, told newsmen that what the *Capricorn* had observed might well have been a meteor.

"That seems quite likely," he said. "If it was a meteor, the fact that it reached the earth's surface should, I think, be one of the year's most important science news stories. Usually meteors burn to nothing before they're even through the stratosphere."

"Excuse me, sir," interrupted a reporter. "Is there anything out beyond the stratosphere—I mean, is there any name for it?"

"Well, actually the term 'stratosphere' is kind of arbitrary. It's the outer shell of the atmosphere. You can't say definitely where it stops. Beyond it is just, well—dead space."

"Dead space—that's the right name for it, eh?" said the reporter.

"If you want something fancier, maybe we could put it into Greek," said Groszinger playfully. *"Thanatos,* that's Greek for 'death,' I think. Maybe instead of 'dead space' you'd prefer 'Thanasphere.' Has a nice scientific ring to it, don't you think?"

The newsmen laughed politely.

"Dr. Groszinger, when's the first rocket ship going to make it into space?" asked another reporter.

"You people read too many comic books," said Groszinger. "Come back in twenty years, and maybe I'll have a story for you."

Mnemonics

Alfred Moorhead dropped the report into his *Out* basket, and smiled to think that he had been able to check something for facts without referring to records and notes. Six weeks before, he couldn't have done it. Now, since he had attended the company's two-day Memory Clinic, names, facts, and numbers clung to his memory like burdocks to an Airedale. The clinic had, in fact, indirectly cleared up just about every major problem in his uncomplicated life, save one—his inability to break the ice with his secretary, Ellen, whom he had silently adored for two years. . . .

"Mnemonics is the art of improving the memory," the clinic's instructor had begun. "It makes use of two elementary psychological facts: You remember things that interest you longer than things that don't, and pictures stick in your mind better than isolated facts do. I'll show you what I mean. We'll use Mr. Moorhead for our guinea pig."

Alfred had shifted uncomfortably as the man read off a nonsensical list and told him to memorize it: "Smoke, oak tree, sedan, bottle, oriole." The instructor had talked about something else, then pointed to Alfred. "Mr. Moorhead, the list."

"Smoke, oriole, uh—" Alfred had shrugged.

"Don't be discouraged. You're perfectly normal," the instructor had said. "But let's see if we can't help you do a little better. Let's build an image, something pleasant, something we'd like to remember. Smoke, oak tree, sedan—I see a man relaxing under a leafy oak tree. He is smoking a pipe, and in the background is his car, a yellow sedan. See it, Mr. Moorhead?"

"Uh-huh." Alfred *had* seen it.

"Good. Now for 'bottle' and 'oriole.' By the man's side is a vacuum bottle of iced coffee, and an oriole is singing on a branch overhead. There, we can remember that happy picture without any trouble, eh?" Alfred had nodded uncertainly. The instructor had gone on to other matters, then challenged him again.

"Smoke, sedan, bottle, uh—" Alfred had avoided the instructor's eyes.

When the snickering of the class had subsided, the instructor had said, "I suppose you think Mr. Moorhead has proved that mnemonics is bunk. Not at all. He has helped me to make another important point. The images used to help memory vary widely from person to person. Mr. Moorhead's personality is clearly different from mine. I shouldn't have forced my images on him. I'll repeat the list, Mr. Moorhead, and this time I want you to build a picture of your own."

At the end of the class, the instructor had called on Alfred again. Alfred had rattled the list off as though it were the alphabet.

The technique was so good, Alfred had reflected, that he would be able to recall the meaningless list for the rest of his life. He could still see himself and Rita Hayworth sharing a cigarette beneath a giant oak. He filled her glass from a bottle of excellent wine, and as she drank, an oriole brushed her cheek with its wing. Then Alfred kissed her. As for "sedan," he had lent it to Aly Khan.

Rewards for his new faculty had been splendid and immediate. The promotion had unquestionably come from his filing-cabinet command of business details. His boss, Ralph L. Thriller, had said, "Moorhead, I didn't know it was possible for a man to change as much as you have in a few weeks. Wonderful!"

His happiness was unbroken—except by his melancholy relationship with his secretary. While his memory worked like a mousetrap, paralysis still gripped him whenever he thought of mentioning love to the serene brunette.

Alfred sighed and picked up a sheaf of invoices. The first was addressed to the Davenport Spot-welding Company. He closed his eyes and a shimmering tableau appeared. He had composed it two days previous, when Mr. Thriller had given him special instructions. Two davenports faced each other. Lana Turner, sheathed in a tight-fitting leopard skin, lay on one. On the other was Jane Russell, in a sarong made of telegrams. Both of them blew kisses to Alfred, who contemplated them for a moment, then reluctantly let them fade.

He scribbled a note to Ellen: *Please make sure Davenport Spot-welding Company and Davenport Wire and Cable Com-*

pany have not been confused in our billing. Six weeks before, the matter would certainly have slipped his mind. *I love you,* he added, and then carefully crossed it out with a long black rectangle of ink.

In one way, his good memory was a curse. By freeing him from hours of searching through filing cabinets, it gave him that much more time to worry about Ellen. The richest moments in his life were and had been—even before the Memory Clinic—his daydreams. The most delicious of these featured Ellen. Were he to give her the opportunity to turn him down, and she almost certainly would, she could never appear in his fantasies again. Alfred couldn't bring himself to risk that.

The telephone rang. "It's Mr. Thriller," said Ellen.

"Moorhead," said Mr. Thriller, "I've got a lot of little stuff piled up on me. Could you take some of it over?"

"Glad to, chief. Shoot."

"Got a pencil?"

"Nonsense, chief," said Alfred.

"No, I mean it," said Mr. Thriller grimly. "I'd feel better if you wrote this down. There's an awful lot of stuff."

Alfred's pen had gone dry, and he couldn't lay his hands on a pencil without getting up, so he lied. "Okay, got one. Shoot."

"First of all, we're getting a lot of subcontracts on big defense jobs, and a new series of code numbers is going to be used for these jobs. Any number beginning with Sixteen A will designate that it's one of them. Better wire all our plants about it."

In Alfred's mind, Ava Gardner executed a smart manual of arms with a rifle. Emblazoned on her sweater was a large 16A. "Right, chief."

"And I've got a memo here from . . ."

Fifteen minutes later, Alfred, perspiring freely, said, "Right, chief," for the forty-third time and hung up. Before his mind's eye was a pageant to belittle the most flamboyant dreams of Cecil B. DeMille. Ranged about Alfred was every woman motion picture star he had ever seen, and each brandished or wore or carried or sat astride something Alfred could be fired for forgetting. The image was colossal, and the slightest disturbance might knock it to smithereens. He had to get to pencil and paper before tragedy struck. He crossed the room like a game-stalker, hunched, noiselessly.

"Mr. Moorhead, are you all right?" said Ellen, alarmed.

"Mmm. Mmm!" said Alfred, frowning.

He reached the pencil and pad, and exhaled. The picture was fogging, but it was still there. Alfred considered the ladies one by one, wrote down their messages, and allowed them to dissolve.

As their numbers decreased, he began to slow their exits in order to savor them. Now Ann Sheridan, the next-to-the-last in line, astride a western pony, tapped him on the forehead with a lightbulb to remind him of the name of an important contact at General Electric—Mr. Bronk. She blushed under his gaze, dismounted, and dissolved.

The last stood before him, clutching a sheaf of papers. Alfred was stumped. The papers seemed to be the only clue, and they recalled nothing. He reached out and clasped her to him. "Now, baby," he murmured, "what's on *your* mind?"

"Oh, Mr. Moorhead," sighed Ellen.

"Oh, gosh!" said Alfred, freeing her. "Ellen—I'm sorry, I forgot myself."

"Well, praise be, you finally remembered *me*."

Any Reasonable Offer

A few days ago, just before I came up here to Newport on a vacation, in spite of being broke, it occurred to me there isn't any profession—or racket, or whatever—that takes more of a beating from its clients than real estate. If you stand still, they club you. If you run, they shoot.

Maybe dentists have rougher client relationships, but I doubt it. Give a man a choice between having his teeth or a real estate salesman's commission extracted, and he'll choose the pliers and novocaine every time.

Consider Delahanty. Two weeks ago, Dennis Delahanty asked me to sell his house for him, said he wanted twenty thousand for it.

That afternoon I took a prospect out to see the house. The

prospect walked through it once, said that he liked it and he'd take it. That evening he closed the deal. With Delahanty. Behind my back.

Then I sent Delahanty a bill for my commission—five percent of the sale price, one thousand dollars.

"What the hell are you?" he wanted to know. "A busy movie star?"

"You knew what my commission was going to be."

"Sure, I knew. But you only worked an hour. A thousand bucks an hour! Forty thousand a week, two million a year! I just figured it out."

"Some years I make ten million," I said.

"I work six days a week, fifty weeks a year, and then turn around and pay some young squirt like you a thousand for one hour of smiles and small talk and a pint of gas. I'm going to write my congressman. If it's legal, it sure as hell shouldn't be."

"He's my congressman, too, and you signed a contract. You read it, didn't you?"

He hung up on me. He still hasn't paid me.

Old Mrs. Hellbrunner called right after Delahanty. *Her* house has been on the market for three years, and it represents about all that's left of the Hellbrunner family's fortune. Twenty-seven rooms, nine baths, ballroom, den, study, music room, solarium, turrets with slits for crossbowmen, simulated drawbridge and portcullis, and a dry moat. Somewhere in the basement, I suppose, are racks and gibbets for insubordinate domestics.

"Something is very wrong," said Mrs. Hellbrunner. "Mr. Delahanty sold that awful little cracker-box of his in one day, and for four thousand more than he paid for it. Good heavens, I'm asking only a quarter of the replacement price for my house."

"Well—it's a very *special* sort of person who would want your place, Mrs. Hellbrunner," I said, thinking of an escaped maniac. "But someday he'll come along. They say there's a house for every person, and a person for every house. It isn't every day I get someone in here who's looking for something in the hundred-thousand-dollar range. But sooner or later—"

"When you accepted Mr. Delahanty as a client, you went right to work and earned your commission," she said. "Why can't you do the same for me?"

"We'll just have to be patient. It's—"

She, too, hung up, and then I saw the tall, gray-haired gentleman standing in the office doorway. Something about him— or maybe about me—made me want to jump to attention and suck in my sagging gut.

"Yessir!" I said.

"Is this yours?" he said, handing me an ad clipped from the morning paper. He held it as though he were returning a soiled handkerchief that had fallen from my pocket.

"Yessir—the Hurty place. That's mine, all right."

"This is the place, Pam," he said, and a tall, somberly dressed woman joined him. She didn't look directly at me, but at an imaginary horizon over my left shoulder, as though I were a headwaiter or some other minor functionary.

"Perhaps you'd like to know what they're asking for the place before we go out there," I said.

"The swimming pool is in order?" said the woman.

"Yes, ma'am. Just two years old."

"And the stables are usable?" said the man.

"Yessir. Mr. Hurty has his horses in them now. They're all newly whitewashed, fireproof, everything. He's asking eighty-five thousand for the place, and it's a firm price. Is that within your price range, sir?"

He curled his lip.

"I said that about price range, because some people—"

"Do we look like any of them?" said the woman.

"No, you certainly don't." And they didn't, either, and every second they were looking more like a four-thousand-two-hundred-fifty-dollar commission. "I'll call Mr. Hurty right away."

"Tell him that Colonel and Mrs. Bradley Peckham are interested in his property."

The Peckhams had come by cab, so I drove them to the Hurty estate in my old two-door sedan, for which I apologized, and, to judge from their expression, rightly so.

Their town car, they related, had developed an infuriating little squeak, and was in the hands of a local dealer, who had staked his reputation on getting the squeak out.

"What is it you do, Colonel?" I asked, making small talk.

His eyebrows went up. "Do? Why, whatever amuses me. Or in time of crisis, whatever my country needs most."

"Right now he's straightening things out at National Steel Foundry," said Mrs. Peckham.

"Rum show, that," said the Colonel, "but coming along, coming along."

At the Hurty threshold, Mr. Hurty himself came to the door, tweedy, booted, and spurred. His family was in Europe. The Colonel and his wife, once I had made the formal introductions, ignored me. The Peckhams had some distance to go, however, before offending four thousand dollars' worth of my pride.

I sat quietly, like a Seeing Eye dog or overnight bag, and listened to the banter of those who bought and sold eighty-five-thousand-dollar estates with urbane negligence.

There were none of your shabby questions about how much the place cost to heat or keep up, or what the taxes were, or whether the cellar was dry. Not on your life.

"I'm so glad there's a greenhouse," said Mrs. Peckham. "I had such high hopes for the place, but the ad didn't mention a greenhouse, and I just prayed there was one."

"Never underestimate the power of prayer," I said to myself.

"Yes, I think you've done well with it," the Colonel said to Hurty. "I'm glad to see you've got an honest-to-God swimming pool, and not one of these cement-lined puddles."

"One thing you may be interested in," said Hurty, "is that the water isn't chlorinated. It's passed under ultraviolet light."

"I should hope so," said the Colonel.

"Um," said Hurty.

"Have you a labyrinth?" said Mrs. Peckham.

"How's that?" said Hurty.

"A labyrinth made of box hedge. They're awfully picturesque."

"No, sorry," said Hurty, pulling on his mustache.

"Well, no matter," said the Colonel, making the best of it. "We can put one in."

"Yes," said his wife. "Oh, dear," she murmured, and placed her hand over her heart. Her eyes rolled, and she started to sink to the floor.

"Darling!" The Colonel caught her about the waist.

"Please—" she gasped.

"A stimulant!" commanded the Colonel. "Brandy! Anything!"

Hurty, unnerved, fetched a decanter and poured a shot.

The Colonel's wife forced some between her lips, and the roses returned to her cheeks.

"More, darling?" the Colonel asked.

"A sip," she whispered.

When she'd finished it off, the Colonel sniffed the glass. "By George, but that's got a lovely bouquet!" He held out the glass to Hurty, and Hurty filled it.

"Jove!" said the Colonel, savoring, sniffing. "First-rate. Mmm. You know, it's a vanishing race that has the patience really to know the exquisite things in life. With most, it's gulp, gulp, and they're off on some mad chase again."

"Sure," said Hurty.

"Better, dear?" the Colonel asked his wife.

"Much. You know how it is. It comes and goes."

I watched the Colonel take a book from the shelves. He looked in the front, possibly to make sure it was a first edition. "Well, Mr. Hurty," he said, "I think it must show in our eyes how much we like the place. There are some things we'd change, of course, but by and large—"

Hurty looked to me.

I cleared my throat. "Well," I lied, "there are a number of people very interested in this property, as you might expect. I think you'd better make your offer official as soon as possible, if it's really to your liking."

"You aren't going to sell it to just *anybody*, are you?" said the Colonel.

"Certainly not!" lied Hurty, trying to recapture some of the élan he had lost during the labyrinth and brandy episodes.

"Well," said the Colonel, "the legal end can be handled quickly enough when the time comes. But first, if you don't mind, we'd like to get the feel of the place—get the newness out of it."

"Yes, of course, certainly," said Hurty, slightly puzzled.

"Then you don't mind if we sort of wander about a bit, as though it were already ours?"

"No, I guess not. I mean, certainly not. Go right ahead."

And the Peckhams did, while I waited, fidgeting in the living room, and Hurty locked himself in his study. They made themselves at home all afternoon, feeding the horses carrots, loosening the earth about the roots of plants in the greenhouse, drowsing in the sun by the swimming pool.

Once or twice I tried to join them, to point out this feature or that, but they received me as though I were an impertinent butler, so I gave it up.

At four, they asked a maid for tea, and got it—with little cakes. At five, Hurty came out of his study, found them still there, covered his surprise admirably, and mixed us all cocktails.

The Colonel said he always had *his* man rub the inside of martini glasses with garlic. He asked if there was a level spot for polo.

Mrs. Peckham discussed the parking problems of large parties, and asked if there was anything in the local air that was damaging to oil paintings.

At seven, Hurty, fighting yawns, excused himself, and telling the Peckhams to go on making themselves at home, he went to his supper. At eight, the Peckhams, having eddied about Hurty and his meal on their way to one place or another, announced that they were leaving.

They asked me to drop them off at the town's best restaurant.

"I take it you're interested?" I said.

"We'll want to talk a little," said the Colonel. "The price is certainly no obstacle. We'll let you know."

"How can I reach you, Colonel, sir?"

"I'm here for a rest. I prefer not to have anyone know my whereabouts, if you don't mind. I'll call you."

"Fine."

"Tell me," said Mrs. Peckham. "How did Mr. Hurty make his money?"

"He's the biggest used-car salesman in this part of the state."

"Aha!" said the Colonel. "I knew it! The whole place had the air of new money about it."

"Does that mean you don't want it after all?" I asked.

"No, not exactly. We'll simply have to live with it a little while to see what can be done about it, if anything."

"Could you tell me specifically what it was you didn't like?" I asked.

"If you can't see it," said Mrs. Peckham, "no one could possibly point it out to you."

"Oh."

"We'll let you know," said the Colonel.

Three days passed, with their normal complement of calls from Delahanty and Mrs. Hellbrunner, but without a sign from Colonel Peckham and his lady.

As I was closing my office on the afternoon of the fourth day, Hurty called me.

"When the hell," he said, "are those Peckham people going to come to a boil?"

"Lord knows," I said. "There's no way I can get in touch with them. He said he'd call me."

"You can get in touch with them anytime of night or day."

"How?"

"Just call my place. They've been out here for the past three days, taking the newness out of it. They've damn well taken something out of me, too. Do the liquor and cigars and food come out of your commission?"

"If there is a commission."

"You mean there's some question about it? He goes around here as though he has the money in his pocket and is just waiting for the right time to give it to me."

"Well, since he won't talk with me, you might as well do the pressuring. Tell him I've just told you a retired brewer from Toledo has offered seventy-five thousand. That ought to get action."

"All right. I'll have to wait until they come in from swimming, for cocktails."

"Call me back when you've got a reaction, and I'll toot out with an offer form all ready to go."

Ten minutes later he did. "Guess what, brain-box?"

"He bit?"

"I'm getting a brand-new real estate agent."

"Oh?"

"Yes indeed. I took the advice of the last one I had, and a red-hot prospect and his wife walked out with their noses in the air."

"No! Why?"

"Colonel and Mrs. Peckham wish you to know that they couldn't possibly be interested in anything that would appeal to a retired brewer from Toledo."

. . . . .

It was a lousy estate anyhow, so I gaily laughed and gave my attention to more substantial matters, such as the Hellbrunner mansion. I ran a boldface advertisement describing the joys of life in a fortified castle.

The next morning, I looked up from my work to see the ad, torn from the paper, in the long, clean fingers of Colonel Peckham.

"Is this yours?"

"Good morning, Colonel. Yessir, it is."

"It sounds like *our* kind of place," said the voice of Mrs. Peckham.

We crossed the simulated drawbridge and passed under the rusty portcullis of their kind of place.

Mrs. Hellbrunner liked the Peckhams immediately. For one thing, they were, I'm pretty sure, the first people in several generations to admire the place. More to the point, they gave every indication of being about to buy it.

"It would cost about a half-million to replace," said Mrs. Hellbrunner.

"Yes," said the Colonel. "They don't build houses like this anymore."

"Oh!" gasped Mrs. Peckham, and the Colonel caught her as she headed for the floor.

"Quick! Brandy! Anything!" cried Colonel Peckham.

When I drove the Peckhams back to the center of town, they were in splendid spirits.

"Why on earth didn't you show us this place first?" said the Colonel.

"Just came on the market yesterday," I said, "and priced the way it is, I don't expect it'll be on the market very long."

The Colonel squeezed his wife's hand. "I don't expect so, do you, dear?"

Mrs. Hellbrunner still called me every day, but now her tone was cheery and flattering. She reported that the Peckhams arrived shortly after noon each day, and that they seemed more in love with the house on each visit.

"I'm treating them just like Hellbrunners," she said craftily.

"That's the ticket."

"I even got cigars for him."

"Pour it on. It's all tax-deductible," I cheered.

Four nights later, she called me again to say that the Peckhams were coming to dinner. "Why don't you sort of casually drop in afterward, and just happen to have an offer form with you?"

"Have they mentioned any figures?"

"Only that it's perfectly astonishing what you can get for a hundred thousand."

I set my briefcase down in the Hellbrunner music room after dinner that evening. I said, "Greetings."

The Colonel, on the piano bench, rattled the ice in his drink.

"And how are *you*, Mrs. Hellbrunner?" I said. One glance told me she had never in all her life been worse.

"I'm fine," she said hoarsely. "The Colonel has just been speaking very interestingly. The State Department wants him to do some troubleshooting in Bangkok."

The Colonel shrugged sadly. "Once more to the colors, as a civilian this time."

"We leave tomorrow," said Mrs. Peckham, "to close our place in Philadelphia—"

"And finish up at National Steel Foundry," said the Colonel.

"Then off to Bangkok they go," quavered Mrs. Hellbrunner.

"Men must work, and women must weep," said Mrs. Peckham.

"Yup," I said.

The next morning, the telephone was ringing when I unlocked my office door.

It was Mrs. Hellbrunner. Shrill. Not like old family at all. "I don't *believe* he's going to Bangkok," she raged. "It was the price. He was too polite to bargain."

"You'll take less?" Up to now, she'd been very firm about the hundred-thousand figure.

"Less?" Her voice became prayerful. "Lord—I'd take fifty to get rid of the monster!" She was silent for a moment. "Forty. Thirty. Sell it!"

So I sent a telegram to the Colonel, care of National Steel Foundry, Philadelphia.

There was no reply, and then I tried the telephone.

"National Steel Foundry," said a woman in Philadelphia.

"Colonel Peckham, please."

"Who?"

"Peckham. Colonel Bradley Peckham. *The* Peckham."

"We have a Peckham, B. C., in Drafting."

"Is he an executive?"

"I don't know, sir. You can ask him."

There was a click in my ear as she switched my call to Drafting.

"Drafting," said a woman.

The first operator broke in: "This gentleman wishes to speak to Mr. Peckham."

"*Colonel* Peckham," I specified.

"Mr. Melrose," called the second woman, "is Peckham back yet?"

"Peckham!" Mr. Melrose shouted. "Shag your tail. Telephone!"

Above the sound of room noises, I heard someone ask, "Have a good time?"

"So-so," said a vaguely familiar, faraway voice. "Think we'll try Newport next time. Looked pretty good from the bus."

"How the hell do you manage tony places like that on your salary?"

"Takes a bit of doing." And then the voice became loud, and terribly familiar. "Peckham speaking. Drafting."

I let the receiver fall into its cradle.

I was awfully tired. I realized that I hadn't had a vacation since the end of the war. I had to get away from it all for a little while, or I would go mad. But Delahanty hadn't come through yet, so I was stone broke.

And then I thought about what Colonel Bradley Peckham had said about Newport. There *were* a lot of nice houses there—all beautifully staffed, furnished, stocked, overlooking the sea, and for sale.

For instance, take this place—the Van Tuyl estate. It has almost everything: private beach *and* swimming pool, polo field, two grass tennis courts, nine-hole golf course, stables, paddocks, French chef, at least three exceptionally attractive Irish parlor maids, English butler, cellar full of vintage stuff—

The labyrinth is an interesting feature, too. I get lost in it almost every day. Then the real estate agent comes looking for me, and he gets lost just as I find my way out. Believe me, the property is worth every penny of the asking price. I'm not going to haggle about it, not for a minute. When the time comes, I'll either take it or leave it.

But I've got to live with the place a little longer—to get the newness out—before I tell the agent what I'm going to do. Meanwhile, I'm having a wonderful time. Wish you were here.

The Package

"What do you know about that?" said Earl Fenton. He unslung his stereoscopic camera, took off his coat, and laid the coat and the camera on top of the television-radio-phonograph console. "Here we go on a trip clean around the world, Maude, and two minutes after we come back to our new house, the telephone rings. That's civilization."

"For you, Mr. Fenton," said the maid.

"Earl Fenton speaking . . . Who? . . . You got the right Fenton? There's a *Brudd* Fenton on San Bonito Boulevard. . . . Yes, that's right, I did. Class of 1910 . . . Wait! No! Sure I do! Listen, you tell the hotel to go to hell, Charley, you're my guest. . . . Have we got room?"

Earl covered the mouthpiece and grinned at his wife. "He

wants to know if we've got room!" He spoke into the telephone again. "Listen, Charley, we've got rooms I've never been in. No kidding. We just moved in today—five minutes ago. . . . No, it's all fixed up. Decorator furnished the place nice as you please weeks ago, and the servants got everything going like a dollar watch, so we're ready. Catch you a cab, you hear? . . .

"No, I sold the plant last year. Kids are grown up and on their own and all—young Earl's a doctor now, got a big house in Santa Monica, and Ted's just passed his bar exams and gone in with his Uncle George— Yeah, and Maude and I, we've just decided to sit back and take a well-earned— But the hell with talking on the phone. You come right on out. Boy! Have we got a lot of catching up to do!" Earl hung up and made clucking sounds with his tongue.

Maude was examining a switch panel in the hallway. "I don't know if this thingamajig works the air-conditioning or the garage doors or the windows or what," she said.

"We'll get Lou Converse out here to show us how everything works," said Earl. Converse was the contractor who had put up the rambling, many-leveled "machine for living" during their trip abroad.

Earl's expression became thoughtful as he gazed through a picture window at the flagstone terrace and grill, flooded with California sunshine, and at the cartwheel gate that opened onto the macadam driveway, and at the garage, with its martin house, weathercock, and two Cadillacs. "By golly, Maude," he said, "I just finished talking to a ghost."

"Um?" said Maude. "Aha! See, the picture window goes up, and down comes the screen. Ghost? Who on earth?"

"Freeman, Charley Freeman. A name from the past, Maude. I couldn't believe it at first. Charley was a fraternity brother and just about the biggest man in the whole class of 1910. Track star, president of the fraternity, editor of the paper, Phi Beta Kappa."

"Goodness! What's he doing coming here to see poor little us?" said Maude.

Earl was witnessing a troubling tableau that had been in the back of his mind for years: Charley Freeman, urbane, tastefully clothed, was having a plate set before him by Earl, who wore a waiter's jacket. When he'd invited Charley to come on out, Earl's enthusiasm had been automatic, the reflex of a man who prided himself on being a plain, ordinary, friendly fellow, for all of his success. Now, remembering their college relationship, Earl found that the prospect of Charley's arrival was making him uncomfortable. "He was a rich kid," Earl said. "One of those guys"—and his voice was tinged with bitterness—"who had everything. You know?"

"Well, hon," said Maude, "you weren't exactly behind the door when they passed out the looks and brains."

"No—but when they passed out the money, they handed me a waiter's jacket and a mop." She looked at him sympathetically, and he was encouraged to pour out his heart on the subject. "By golly, Maude, it does something to a man to go around having to wait on guys his same age, cleaning up after 'em, and seeing them with nice clothes and all the money in the world, going off to some resort in the summer when I had to go to work to pay next year's tuition." Earl was surprised at the emotion in his voice. "And all the time they're looking down on you, like there was something wrong with people who weren't handed their money on a silver platter."

"Well, that makes me good and mad!" Maude said, squaring her shoulders indignantly, as though to protect Earl from those who'd humiliated him in college. "If this great Charley Freeman snooted you in the old days, I don't see why we should have him in the house now."

"Oh, heck—forgive and forget," Earl said gloomily. "Doesn't throw me anymore. He seemed to want to come out, and I try to be a good fellow, no matter what."

"So what's the high-and-mighty Freeman doing now?"

"Don't know. Something big, I guess. He went to med school, and I came back here, and we kind of lost touch." Experimentally, Earl pressed a button on the wall. From the basement came muffled whirs and clicks, as machines took control of the temperature and humidity and purity of the atmosphere about him. "But I don't expect Charley's doing a bit better than this."

"What were some of the things he did to you?" Maude pursued, still indignant.

Earl waved the subject away with his hand. There weren't any specific incidents that he could tell Maude about. People like Charley Freeman hadn't come right out and said anything to humiliate Earl when he'd waited on them. But just the same, Earl was sure that he'd been looked down on, and he was willing to bet that when he'd been out of earshot, they'd talked about him, and . . .

He shook his head in an effort to get rid of his dour mood, and he smiled. "Well, Mama, what say we have a little drinkie, and then take a tour of the place? If I'm going to show it to Charley, I'd better find out how a few of these gimcracks work, or he'll think old Earl is about as at home in a setup like this as a retired janitor or waiter or something. By golly, there goes the phone again! That's civilization for you."

"Mr. Fenton," the maid said, "it's Mr. Converse."

"Hello, Lou, you old horse thief. Just looking over your

handiwork. Maude and I are going to have to go back to college for a course in electrical engineering, ha ha. . . . Eh? Who? . . . No kidding. They really want to? . . . Well, I guess that's the kind of thing you have to expect to go through. If they've got their heart set on it, okay. Maude and I go clean around the world, and two minutes after we're home, it's like the middle of Grand Central Station."

Earl hung up and scratched his head in mock wonderment and weariness. In reality, he was pleased with the activity, with the bell-ringing proof that his life, unlike his ownership of the plant and the raising of his kids and the world cruise, was barely begun.

"What now?" said Maude.

"Aw, Converse says some fool home magazine wants to do a story on the place, and they want to get the pictures this afternoon."

"What fun!"

"Yeah—I guess. I dunno. I don't want to be standing around in all the pictures like some stuffed shirt." To show how little he cared, he interested himself in another matter. "I don't know why she wouldn't, considering what we paid her, but that decorator really thought of everything, you know?" He'd opened a closet next to the terrace doors and found an apron, a chef's hat, and asbestos gloves inside. "By golly, you know, that's pretty rich. See what it says on the apron, Maude?"

"Cute," said Maude, and she read the legend aloud: "'Don't shoot the cook, he's doing the best he can.' Why, you look like a regular Oscar of the Waldorf, Earl. Now let me see you in the hat."

He grinned bashfully and fussed with the hat. "Don't know exactly how one of the fool things is supposed to go. Feel kind of like a man from Mars."

"Well, you look wonderful to me, and I wouldn't trade you for a hundred stuck-up Charley Freemans."

They wandered arm in arm over the flagstone terrace to the grill, a stone edifice that might have been mistaken from a distance for a branch post office. They kissed, as they had kissed beside the Great Pyramid, the Colosseum, and the Taj Mahal.

"You know something, Maude?" said Earl, a great emotion ballooning in his breast. "You know, I used to wish my old man was rich, so you and I could have had a place like this right off— bing!—the minute I got out of college and we got married. But you know, we couldn't have had this moment looking back and knowing, by God, we made every inch of the way on our own. And we understand the little guy, Maude, because we were little guys once. By gosh, nobody born with a silver spoon in their mouth can buy that understanding. A lot of people on the cruise didn't want to look at all that terrible poverty in Asia, like their consciences bothered them. But us—well, seeing as how we'd come up the hard way, I don't guess we had much on our consciences, and we could look out at those poor people and kind of understand."

"Uh-huh," said Maude.

Earl worked his fingers in the thick gloves. "And tonight I'm going to broil you and me and Charley a sirloin steak as thick as a Manhattan phone book, and deserve every ounce of it, if I do say so myself."

"We aren't even unpacked."

"So what? I'm not tired. Got a lot of living to do, and the quicker I get at it, the more I'll get done."

Earl and Maude were in the living room, Earl still in his chef's outfit, when Charley Freeman was ushered in by the maid.

"By golly!" said Earl. "If it isn't Charley!"

Charley was still thin and erect, and the chief mark of age upon him was the graying of his thick hair. While his face was lined, it was still confident and wise-looking, was still, in Earl's opinion, subtly mocking. There was so much left of the old Charley, in fact, that the college relationship, dead for forty years, came alive again in Earl's mind. In spite of himself, Earl felt resentfully servile, felt crude and dull. His only defense was the old one—hidden resentment, with a promise that things would be very different before long.

"Been a long time, hasn't it, Earl?" Charley said, his voice still deep and virile. "You're looking fine."

"Lot of water can go under the bridge in forty years," said Earl. He was running his finger nervously over the rich fabric of the sofa. And then he remembered Maude, who was standing rigid, thin-lipped behind him. "Oh, excuse me, Charley, this is my wife, Maude."

"This is a pleasure I've had to put off for a long time," said Charley. "I feel I know you, Earl spoke of you so much in college."

"How do you do?" said Maude.

"Far better than I had any reason to expect six months ago," said Charley. "What a handsome house!" He laid his hand on the television-radio-phonograph console. "Now, what the devil do you call this?"

"Huh?" said Earl. "TV set. What's it look like?"

"TV?" said Charley, frowning. "TV? Oh—abbreviation for 'television.' That it?"

"You kidding me, Charley?"

"No, really. There must be more than a billion and a half poor souls who've never seen one of the things, and I'm one of them. Does it hurt to touch the glass part?"

"The tube?" Earl laughed uneasily. "Hell, no—go ahead."

"Mr. Freeman's probably got a tube five times as big as this one at home," said Maude, smiling coldly, "and he's kidding us along like he doesn't even know this is a TV set, the tube's so small."

"Well, Charley," said Earl, cutting briskly into the silence that followed Maude's comment, "and to what do we owe the honor of this visit?"

"For old times' sake," said Charley. "I happened to be in town, and I remem—"

Before Charley could elaborate, he was interrupted by a party composed of Lou Converse, a photographer from *Home Beautiful*, and a young, pretty woman writer.

The photographer, who introduced himself simply as Slotkin, took command of the household, and as he was to do for the whole of his stay, he quashed all talk and activities not related to getting the magazine pictures taken. "Zo," said Slotkin, "und de gimmick is de pagatch, eh?"

"Baggage?" said Earl.

"*Package*," said the writer. "See, the angle on the story is that you come home from a world cruise to a complete package for living—everything anybody could possibly want for a full life."

"Oh."

"It's complete," said Lou Converse, "complete right down to a fully stocked wine cellar and a pantry filled with gourmet specialties. Brand-new cars, brand-new everything but wine."

"Aha! Dey vin a condezt."

"He sold his factory and retired," said Converse.

"Maude and I figured we owed ourselves a little something," said Earl. "We held back all these years, putting money back into the business and all, and then, when the kids were grown up and the big offer came for the plant, we all of a sudden felt kind of crazy, and said, 'Why not?' And we just went ahead and ordered everything we'd ever wanted."

Earl glanced at Charley Freeman, who stood apart and in the background, half smiling, seeming to be fascinated by the scene. "We started out, Maude and I," said Earl, "in a two-room apartment down by the docks. Put that in the story."

"We had love," said Maude.

"Yes," said Earl, "and I don't want people to think I'm just another stuffed shirt who was born with a wad of money and blew himself to this setup. No, sir! This is the end of a long, hard road. Write that down. Charley remembers me back in the old days, when I had to work my way through school."

"Rugged days for Earl," said Charley.

Now the center of attention, Earl felt his self-confidence returning, and he began to see Charley's coming back into his life at this point as a generous act of fate, a fine opportunity to settle the old scores once and for all. "It wasn't the work that made it rugged," Earl said pointedly.

Charley seemed surprised by Earl's vehemence. "All right," he said, "then the work wasn't rugged. It was so long ago I can remember it either way."

"I mean it was tough being looked down on because I wasn't born with a silver spoon in my mouth," said Earl.

"Earl!" said Charley, smiling in his incredulity. "As many fat-heads as we had for fraternity brothers, not one of them for a minute looked down—"

"Make ready for de pigdures," Slotkin said. "Stardt mit de grill—breadt, saladt, und a big, bloody piece of meadt."

The maid brought a five-pound slab of steak from the freezer, and Earl held it over the grill. "Hurry up," he said. "Can't hold a cow at arm's length all day." Behind his smile, however, he was nettled by Charley's bland dismissal of his college grievances.

"Hold it!" said Slotkin. The flashbulbs went off. "Good!"

And the party moved indoors. There, Earl and Maude posed in room after room, watering a plant in the solarium, reading the latest book before the living room fireplace, working push-button windows, chatting with the maid over the laundry console, planning menus, having a drink at the rumpus room bar, sawing a plank in the workshop, dusting off Earl's gun collection in the den.

And always, there was Charley Freeman at the rear of the entourage, missing nothing, obviously amused as Maude and Earl demonstrated their packaged good life. Under Charley's gaze, Earl became more and more restless and self-conscious as he performed, and Slotkin berated him for wearing such a counterfeit smile.

"By God, Maude," said Earl, perspiring in the master bedroom, "if I ever have to come out of retirement—knock on wood—I can go on television as a quick-change artist. This better be the last picture, by golly. Feel like a darn clotheshorse."

But the feeling didn't prevent his changing once more at Slotkin's command, this time into a tuxedo. Slotkin wanted a picture of dinner by candlelight. The dining room curtains would be drawn, electrically, to hide the fact of midafternoon outdoors.

"Well, I guess Charley's getting an eyeful," said Earl, distorting his face as he punched a collar button into place. "I think he's pretty darn impressed." His voice lacked conviction, and he turned hopefully to Maude for confirmation.

She was sitting at her dressing table, staring mercilessly at her image in the mirror, trying on different bits of jewelry. "Hmm?"

"I said I guess Charley's pretty impressed."

"*Him,*" she said flatly. "He's just a little *too* smooth, if you ask me. After the way he used to snoot you, and then he comes here all smiles and good manners."

"Yeah," said Earl, with a sigh. "Doggone it, he used to make me feel like two bits, and he still does, looking at us like we were showing off instead of just trying to help a magazine out. And did you hear what he said when I came right out and told him what I didn't like about college?"

"He acted like you just made it up, like it was just in your mind. Oh, he's a slick article, all right. But I'm not going to let him get my goat," said Maude. "This started out as the happiest day of our lives, and it's going to go on being that. And you want to know something else?"

"What's that?" Backed by Maude, Earl felt his morale rising. He hadn't been absolutely sure that Charley was inwardly making fun of them, but Maude was, and she was burned up about it, too.

Her voice dropped to a whisper. "For all his superior ways, and kidding us about our TV set and everything, I don't think the great Charley Freeman amounts to a hill of beans. Did you see his suit—up close?"

"Well, Slotkin kept things moving so fast, I don't guess I got a close look."

"You can bet *I* did, Earl," said Maude. "It's all worn and shiny, and the cuffs are a sight! I'd die of shame if you went around in a suit like that."

Earl was startled. He had been so on the defensive that it hadn't occurred to him that Charley's fortunes could be anything but what they'd been in college. "Maybe a favorite old suit he hates to chuck out," he said at last. "Rich people are funny about things like that sometimes."

"He's got on a favorite old shirt and a favorite old pair of shoes, too."

"I can't believe it," murmured Earl. He pulled aside a curtain for a glimpse of the fairyland of the terrace and grill, where Charley Freeman stood chatting with Slotkin and Converse and the writer. The cuffs of Charley's trousers, Earl saw with amazement, were indeed frayed, and the heels of his shoes were worn thin. Earl touched a button, and a bedroom window slithered open.

"It's a pleasant town," Charley was telling them. "I might as well settle here as anywhere, since I haven't very strong reasons for living in any particular part of the country."

"Zo eggspensif!" said Slotkin.

"Yes," said Charley, "I'd probably be smart to move inland, where my money'd go a little farther. Lord, it's incredible what things cost these days!"

Maude laid her hand on Earl's shoulder. "Seems kind of fishy, doesn't it?" she whispered. "You don't hear from him for forty years, and all of a sudden he shows up, down-and-out, to pay us a big, friendly call. What's he after?"

"Said he just wanted to see me for old times' sake," said Earl. Maude sniffed. "You believe that?"

The dining room table looked like an open treasure chest, with the flames of the candelabra caught in a thousand perfect surfaces—the silver, the china, the facets of the crystal, Maude's rubies, and Maude's and Earl's proud eyes. The maid set steaming soup, prepared for the sake of the picture, before them.

"Perfect!" said Slotkin. "So! Now talk."

"What about?" said Earl.

"Anything," said the woman writer. "Just so the picture won't look posed. Talk about your trip. How does the situation in Asia look?"

It was a question Earl wasn't inclined to chat about lightly.

"You've been to Asia?" said Charley.

Earl smiled. "India, Burma, the Philippines, Japan. All in all, Maude and I must have spent two months looking the situation over."

"Earl and I took every side trip there was," said Maude. "He just had to see for himself what was what."

"Trouble with the State Department is they're all up in an ivory tower," said Earl.

Beyond the glittering camera lens and the bank of flashbulb reflectors, Earl saw the eyes of Charley Freeman. Expert talk on large affairs had been among Charley's many strong points in college, and Earl had been able only to listen and nod and wonder.

"Yes, sir," said Earl, summing up, "the situation looked just about hopeless to everybody on the cruise but Maude and me, and it took us a while to figure out why that was. Then we realized that we were about the only ones who'd pulled themselves up by their bootstraps—that we were the only ones who really understood that no matter how low a man is, if he's got what it takes, he can get clean to the top." He paused. "There's nothing wrong with Asia that a little spunk and common sense and know-how won't cure."

"I'm glad it's that easy," said Charley. "I was afraid things were more complicated than that."

Earl, who rightly considered himself one of the easiest men on earth to get along with, found himself in the unfamiliar position of being furious with a fellow human being. Charley Freeman, who evidently had failed as Earl had risen in the world, was openly belittling one of Earl's proudest accomplishments, his knowledge of Asia. "I've seen it, Charley!" said Earl. "I'm not talking as just one more darn fool armchair strategist who's never been outside his own city limits!"

Slotkin fired his flashbulbs. "One more," he said.

"Of course you're not, Earl," said Charley. "That was rude of me. What you say is very true, in a way, but it's such an over-simplification. Taken by itself, it's a dangerous way of thinking. I shouldn't have interrupted. It's simply that the subject is one I have a deep interest in."

Earl felt his cheeks reddening, as Charley, with his seeming apology, set himself up as a greater authority on Asia than Earl. "Think maybe I'm entitled to some opinions on Asia, Charley. I actually got out and rubbed elbows with the people over there, finding out how their minds work and all."

"You should have seen him jawing away with the Chinese bellboys in Manila," said Maude, challenging Charley with her eyes to top *that*.

"Now then," said the writer, checking a list, "the last shot we want is of you two coming in the front door with your suitcases, looking surprised, as though you've just arrived. . . ."

In the master bedroom again, Earl and Maude obediently changed back into the clothes they'd been wearing when they first arrived. Earl was studying his face in a mirror, practicing looks of pleased surprise and trying not to let the presence of Charley Freeman spoil this day of days.

"He's staying for supper and the night?" asked Maude.

"Oh heck, I was just trying to be a good fellow on the phone.

Wasn't even thinking when I asked him to stay here instead of at the hotel. I could kick myself around the block."

"Lordy. Maybe he'll stay a week."

"Who knows? Slotkin hasn't given me a chance to ask Charley much of anything."

Maude nodded soberly. "Earl, what does it all add up to?"

"All what?"

"I mean, have you tried to put any of it together—the old clothes, and his paleness, and that crack about doing better now than he'd had any right to expect six months ago, and the books, and the TV set? Did you hear him ask Converse about the books?"

"Yeah, that threw me, too, because Charley was the book kind."

"All best-sellers, and he hadn't heard of a one! And he wasn't kidding about television, either. He really hasn't seen it before. He's been out of circulation for a while, and that's for sure."

"Sick, maybe," said Earl.

"Or in jail," whispered Maude.

"Good gosh! You don't suppose—"

"I suppose something's rotten in the state of Denmark," said Maude, "and I don't want him around much longer, if we can help it. I keep trying to figure out what he's doing here, and the only thing that makes sense is that he's here with his fancy ways to bamboozle you out of money, one way or another."

"All right, all right," said Earl, signaling with his hands for her to lower her voice. "Let's keep things as friendly as we can, and ease him out gently."

"How?" said Maude, and between them they devised what

they considered a subtle method for bringing Charley's visit to an end before supper.

"Zo . . . zo much for dis," the photographer said. He winked at Earl and Maude warmly, as though noticing them as human beings for the first time. "Denk you. Nice pagatch you live." He had taken the last picture. He packed his equipment, bowed, and left with Lou Converse and the writer.

Putting off the moment when he would have to sit down with Charley, Earl joined the maid and Maude in the hunt for flashbulbs, which Slotkin had thrown everywhere. When the last bulb was found, Earl mixed martinis and sat down on a couch that faced another, on which Charley sat.

"Well, Charley, here we are."

"And you've come a distance, too, haven't you, Earl?" said Charley, turning his palms upward to indicate the wonder of the dream house. "I see you've got a lot of science fiction on your shelves. Earl, this house *is* science fiction."

"I suppose," said Earl. The flattery was beginning, building up to something—a big touch, probably. Earl was determined not to be spellbound by Charley's smooth ways. "About par for the course in America, maybe, for somebody who isn't afraid of hard work."

"What a course—with this for par, eh?"

Earl looked closely at his guest, trying to discover if Charley was belittling him again. "If I seemed to brag a little when those fool magazine people were here," he said, "I think maybe I've got a little something to brag about. This house is a lot more'n a house. It's the story of my life, Charley—my own personal pyramid, sort of."

Charley lifted his glass in a toast. "May it last as long as the Great Pyramid at Gizeh."

"Thanks," said Earl. It was high time, he decided, that Charley be put on the defensive. "You a doctor, Charley?"

"Yes. Got my degree in 1916."

"Uh-huh. Where you practicing?"

"Little old to start practicing medicine again, Earl. Medicine's changed so much in this country in recent years, that I'm afraid I'm pretty much out of it."

"I see." Earl went over in his mind a list of things that might get a doctor in trouble with the law. He kept his voice casual. "How come you suddenly got the idea of coming to see me?"

"My ship docked here, and I remembered that this was your hometown," said Charley. "Haven't any family left, and trying to start life all over on this side again, I thought I'd look up some of my old college friends. Since the boat landed here, you were the first."

That was going to be Charley's tale, then, Earl thought—that he had been out of the country for a long time. Next would come the touch. "Don't pay much attention to the college gang, myself," he said, unable to resist a small dig. "Such a bunch of snobs there that I was glad to get away and forget 'em."

"God help them if they didn't outgrow the ridiculous social values of college days," said Charley.

Earl was taken aback by the sharpness in Charley's voice, and not understanding it, he hastily changed the subject. "Been overseas, eh? Where, exactly, Charley?"

"Earl!" Maude called from the dining room, according to the plan. "The most awful thing has happened."

"Oh?"

Maude appeared in the doorway. "Angela"—she turned to

Charley to explain—"my sister. Earl, Angela just called to say she was coming here with Arthur and the children before dinner, and could we put them up for the night."

"Gosh," said Earl, "don't see how we can. There're five of them, and we've only got two guest rooms, and Charley here—"

"No, no," said Charley. "See here, tell them to come ahead. I planned to stay at the hotel, anyway, and I have some errands to run, so I couldn't possibly stay."

"Okay, if you say so," said Earl.

"If he's got to go, he's got to go," said Maude.

"Yes, well, got a lot to do. Sorry." Charley was on his way to the door, having left his drink half finished. "Thanks. It's been pleasant seeing you. I envy you your package."

"Be good," said Earl, and he closed the door with a shudder and a sigh.

While Earl was still in the hallway, wondering at what could become of a man in forty years, the door chimes sounded, deep and sweet. Earl opened the door cautiously to find Lou Converse, the contractor, standing on the doorstep. Across the street, Charley Freeman was getting into a taxi.

Lou waved to Charley, then turned to face Earl. "Hello! Not inviting myself to dinner. Came back after my hat. Think I left it in the solarium."

"Come on in," said Earl, watching Charley's taxi disappear toward the heart of town. "Maude and I are just getting set to celebrate. Why not stay for dinner and, while you're at it, show us how some of the gadgets work?"

"Thanks, but I'm expected home. I can stick around a little while and explain whatever you don't understand. Too bad you couldn't get Freeman to stay, though."

Maude winked at Earl. "We asked him, but he said he had a lot of errands to run."

"Yeah, he seemed like he was in kind of a hurry just now. You know," Converse said thoughtfully, "guys like Freeman are funny. They make you feel good and bad at the same time."

"What do you know about that, Maude?" said Earl. "Lou instinctively felt the same way we did about Charley! How do you mean that, exactly, Lou, about feeling good and bad at the same time?"

"Well, good because you're glad to know there are still some people like that in the world," said Converse. "And bad—well, when you come across a guy like that, you can't help wondering where the hell your own life's gone to."

"I don't get you," said Earl.

Converse shrugged. "Oh, Lord knows we couldn't all dedicate our lives the way he did. Can't all be heroes. But thinking about Freeman makes me feel like maybe I could have done a little more'n I have."

Earl exchanged glances with Maude. "What did Charley tell you he'd been doing, Lou?"

"Slotkin and I didn't get much out of him. We just had a few minutes there while you and Maude were changing, and I figured I'd get the whole story from you sometime. All he told us was, he'd been in China for the last thirty years. Then I remembered there was a big piece about him in the paper this morning, only I'd forgotten his name. That's where I found out about how he sunk all his money in a hospital over there and ran it until the Commies locked him up and finally threw him out. Quite a story."

"Yup," Earl said bleakly, ending a deathly silence, "quite a story, all right." He put his arm around Maude, who was staring through the picture window at the grill. He squeezed her gently. "I said it's quite a story, isn't it, Mama?"

"We really did ask him to stay," she said.

"That's not like us, Maude, or if it is, I don't want it to be anymore. Come on, hon, let's face it."

"Call him up at the hotel!" said Maude. "That's what we'll do. We'll tell him it was all a mistake about my sister, that—" The impossibility of any sort of recovery made her voice break. "Oh, Earl, honey, why'd he have to pick today? All our life we worked for today, and then he had to come and spoil it."

"He couldn't have tried any harder not to," Earl sighed. "But the odds were too stiff."

Converse looked at them with incomprehension and sympathy. "Well, heck, if he had errands he had errands," he said. "That's no reflection on your hospitality. Good gosh, there isn't another host in the country who's got a better setup for entertaining than you two. All you have to do is flick a switch or push a button for anything a person could want."

Earl walked across the thick carpet to a cluster of buttons by the bookshelves. Listlessly, he pressed one, and floodlights concealed in shrubbery all around the house went on. "That isn't it." He pressed another, and a garage door rumbled shut. "Nope." He pressed another, and the maid appeared in the doorway.

"You ring, Mr. Fenton?"

"Sorry, a mistake," said Earl. "That wasn't the one I wanted."

Converse frowned. "What is it you're looking for, Earl?"

"Maude and I'd like to start today all over again," said Earl. "Show us which button to push, Lou."

The No-Talent Kid

It was autumn, and the leaves outside Lincoln High School were turning the same rusty color as the bare brick walls in the band rehearsal room. George M. Helmholtz, head of the music department and director of the band, was ringed by folding chairs and instrument cases, and on each chair sat a very young man, nervously prepared to blow through something or, in the case of the percussion section, to hit something, the instant Mr. Helmholtz lowered his white baton.

Mr. Helmholtz, a man of forty, who believed that his great belly was a sign of health, strength, and dignity, smiled angelically, as though he were about to release the most exquisite sounds ever heard by human beings. Down came his baton.

Blooooomp! went the big sousaphones.

Blat! Blat! echoed the French horns, and the plodding, shrieking, querulous waltz was begun.

Mr. Helmholtz's expression did not change as the brasses lost their places, as the woodwinds' nerve failed and they became inaudible rather than have their mistakes heard, while the percussion section sounded like the Battle of Gettysburg.

"A-a-a-a-ta-ta, a-a-a-a-a-a, ta-ta-ta-ta!" In a loud tenor, Mr. Helmholtz sang the first-cornet part when the first cornetist, florid and perspiring, gave up and slouched in his chair, his instrument in his lap.

"Saxophones, let me hear you," called Mr. Helmholtz. "Good!"

This was the C Band, and for the C Band, the performance was good. It couldn't have been more polished for the fifth session of the school year. Most of the youngsters were just starting out as bandsmen, and in the years ahead of them they would acquire artistry enough to move into the B Band, which met the next hour. And finally the best of them would gain positions in the pride of the city, the Lincoln High School Ten Square Band.

The football team lost half its games and the basketball team lost two-thirds of theirs, but the band, in the ten years Mr. Helmholtz had been running it, had been second to none until the past June. It had been the first in the state to use flag twirlers, the first to use choral as well as instrumental numbers, the first to use triple-tonguing extensively, the first to march in breathtaking double time, the first to put a light in its bass drum. Lincoln High School awarded letter sweaters to the members of the A Band, and the sweaters were deeply respected, and properly so. The band had won every statewide

high school band competition for ten years—save the show-
down in June.

While members of the C Band dropped out of the waltz,
one by one, as though mustard gas were coming out of the ven-
tilation, Mr. Helmholtz continued to smile and wave his baton
for the survivors, and to brood inwardly over the defeat his
band had sustained in June, when Johnstown High School had
won with a secret weapon, a bass drum seven feet in diameter.
The judges, who were not musicians but politicians, had had
eyes and ears for nothing but this Eighth Wonder of the World,
and since then Mr. Helmholtz had thought of little else. But
the school budget was already lopsided with band expenses.
When the school board had given him the last special appropri-
ation he'd begged so desperately—money to wire the plumes of
the bandsmen's hats with flashlight bulbs and batteries for
night games—the board had made him swear like a habitual
drunkard that, so help him God, this was the last time.

Only two members of the C Band were playing now, a clarinetist and a snare drummer, both playing loudly, proudly,
confidently, and all wrong. Mr. Helmholtz, coming out of his
wistful dream of a bass drum bigger than the one that had
beaten him, administered the coup de grâce to the waltz by
clattering his stick against his music stand. "All righty, all
righty," he said cheerily, and he nodded his congratulations to
the two who had persevered to the bitter end.

Walter Plummer, the clarinetist, responded gravely, like a
concert soloist receiving an ovation led by the director of a symphony orchestra. He was small, but with a thick chest developed in summers spent at the bottom of swimming pools, and
he could hold a note longer than anyone in the A Band, much

longer, but that was all he could do. He drew back his tired, reddened lips, showing the two large front teeth that gave him the look of a squirrel, adjusted his reed, limbered his fingers, and awaited the next challenge to his virtuosity.

This would be Plummer's third year in the C Band, Mr. Helmholtz thought, with a mixture of pity and fear. Nothing could shake Plummer's determination to earn the right to wear one of the sacred letters of the A Band, so far, terribly far away.

Mr. Helmholtz had tried to tell Plummer how misplaced his ambitions were, to recommend other fields for his great lungs and enthusiasm, where pitch would be unimportant. But Plummer was in love, not with music, but with the letter sweaters. Being as tone-deaf as boiled cabbage, he could detect nothing in his own playing about which to be discouraged.

"Remember," said Mr. Helmholtz to the C Band, "Friday is challenge day, so be on your toes. The chairs you have now were assigned arbitrarily. On challenge day it'll be up to you to prove which chair you really deserve." He avoided the narrowed, confident eyes of Plummer, who had taken the first clarinetist's chair without consulting the seating plan posted on the bulletin board. Challenge day occurred every two weeks, and on that day any bandsman could challenge anyone ahead of him to a contest for his position, with Mr. Helmholtz as judge.

Plummer's hand was raised, its fingers snapping.

"Yes, Plummer?" said Mr. Helmholtz. He had come to dread challenge day because of Plummer. He had come to think of it as Plummer's day. Plummer never challenged anybody in the C Band or even the B Band, but stormed the organization at the very top, challenging, as was unfortunately the privilege of all, only members of the A Band. The waste of the A Band's time was troubling enough, but infinitely more painful for Mr. Helmholtz were Plummer's looks of stunned disbelief when he heard Mr. Helmholtz's decision that he hadn't outplayed the men he'd challenged.

"Mr. Helmholtz," said Plummer, "I'd like to come to A Band session that day."

"All right—if you feel up to it." Plummer always felt up to it, and it would have been more of a surprise if Plummer had announced that he wouldn't be at the A Band session.

"I'd like to challenge Flammer."

The rustling of sheet music and clicking of instrument case latches stopped. Flammer was the first clarinetist in the A Band, a genius whom not even members of the A Band would have had the gall to challenge.

Mr. Helmholtz cleared his throat. "I admire your spirit, Plummer, but isn't that rather ambitious for the first of the year? Perhaps you should start out with, say, challenging Ed Delaney." Delaney held down the last chair in the B Band.

"You don't understand," said Plummer. "You haven't noticed I have a new clarinet."

"Hmm? Oh—well, so you do."

Plummer stroked the satin-black barrel of the instrument as though it were King Arthur's sword, giving magical powers to whoever possessed it. "It's as good as Flammer's," said Plummer. "Better, even."

There was a warning in his voice, telling Mr. Helmholtz that the days of discrimination were over, that nobody in his right mind would dare to hold back a man with an instrument like this.

"Um," said Mr. Helmholtz. "Well, we'll see, we'll see."

After practice, he was forced into close quarters with Plummer again in the crowded hallway. Plummer was talking darkly to a wide-eyed freshman bandsman.

"Know why the band lost to Johnstown High last June?" asked Plummer, seemingly ignorant of the fact that he was back-to-back with Mr. Helmholtz. "Because they stopped running the band on the merit system. Keep your eyes open on Friday."

Mr. George M. Helmholtz lived in a world of music, and even the throbbing of his headache came to him musically, if painfully, as the deep-throated boom of a bass drum seven feet in diameter. It was late afternoon on the first challenge day of the new school year. He was sitting in his living room, his eyes covered, awaiting another sort of thump—the impact of the evening paper, hurled against the clapboards of the front of the house by Walter Plummer, the delivery boy.

As Mr. Helmholtz was telling himself that he would rather not have his newspaper on challenge day, since Plummer came with it, the paper was delivered with a crash.

"Plummer!" he cried.

"Yes, sir?" said Plummer from the sidewalk.

Mr. Helmholtz shuffled to the door in his carpet slippers. "Please, my boy," he said, "can't we be friends?"

"Sure—why not?" said Plummer. "Let bygones be bygones, is what I say." He gave a bitter imitation of an amiable chuckle. "Water over the dam. It's been two hours now since you stuck the knife in me."

Mr. Helmholtz sighed. "Have you got a moment? It's time we had a talk, my boy."

Plummer hid his papers under the shrubbery, and walked in. Mr. Helmholtz gestured at the most comfortable chair in the room, the one in which he'd been sitting. Plummer chose to sit on the edge of a hard one with a straight back instead.

"My boy," said the bandmaster, "God made all kinds of people: some who can run fast, some who can write wonderful stories, some who can paint pictures, some who can sell anything, some who can make beautiful music. But He didn't make anybody who could do everything well. Part of the growing-up process is finding out what we can do well and what we can't do well." He patted Plummer's shoulder. "The last part, finding out what we can't do, is what hurts most about growing up. But everybody has to face it, and then go in search of his true self."

Plummer's head was sinking lower and lower on his chest, and Mr. Helmholtz hastily pointed out a silver lining. "For instance, Flammer could never run a business like a paper route, keeping records, getting new customers. He hasn't that kind of a mind, and couldn't do that sort of thing if his life depended on it."

"You've got a point," said Plummer with unexpected brightness. "A guy's got to be awful one-sided to be as good at one thing as Flammer is. I think it's more worthwhile to try to be better rounded. No, Flammer beat me fair and square today, and I don't want you to think I'm a bad sport about that. It isn't that that gets me."

"That's mature of you," said Mr. Helmholtz. "But what I was trying to point out to you was that we've all got weak points, and—"

Plummer waved him to silence. "You don't have to explain to me, Mr. Helmholtz. With a job as big as you've got, it'd be a miracle if you did the whole thing right."

"Now, hold on, Plummer!" said Mr. Helmholtz.

"All I'm asking is that you look at it from my point of view," said Plummer. "No sooner'd I come back from challenging A Band material, no sooner'd I come back from playing my heart out, than you turned those C Band kids loose on me. You and I know we were just giving 'em the feel of challenge days, and that I was all played out. But did you tell them that? Heck, no, you didn't, Mr. Helmholtz, and those kids all think they can play better than me. That's all I'm sore about, Mr. Helmholtz. They think it means something, me in the last chair of the C Band."

"Plummer," said Mr. Helmholtz, "I have been trying to tell you something as kindly as possible, but the only way to get it across to you is to tell it to you straight."

"Go ahead and quash criticism," said Plummer, standing.

"Quash?"

"Quash," said Plummer with finality. He headed for the door. "I'm probably ruining my chances for getting into the A Band by speaking out like this, Mr. Helmholtz, but frankly, it's incidents like what happened to me today that lost you the band competition last June."

"It was a seven-foot bass drum!"

"Well, get one for Lincoln High and see how you make out then."

"I'd give my right arm for one!" said Mr. Helmholtz, forgetting the point at issue and remembering his all-consuming dream.

Plummer paused on the threshold. "One like the Knights of Kandahar use in their parades?"

"That's the ticket!" Mr. Helmholtz imagined the Knights of Kandahar's huge drum, the showpiece of every local parade. He tried to think of it with the Lincoln High School black panther painted on it. "Yes, sir!" When the bandmaster returned to earth, Plummer was astride his bicycle.

Mr. Helmholtz started to shout after Plummer, to bring him back and tell him bluntly that he didn't have the remotest chance of getting out of C Band ever, that he would never be able to understand that the mission of a band wasn't simply to make noises but to make special kinds of noises. But Plummer was off and away.

Temporarily relieved until next challenge day, Mr. Helmholtz sat down to enjoy his paper, to read that the treasurer of the Knights of Kandahar, a respected citizen, had disappeared with the organization's funds, leaving behind and unpaid the Knights' bills for the past year and a half. "We'll pay a hundred cents on the dollar, if we have to sell everything but the Sacred Mace," the Sublime Chamberlain of the Inner Shrine had said.

Mr. Helmholtz didn't know any of the people involved, and he yawned and turned to the funnies. He gasped, turned to the front page again. He looked up a number in the phone book and dialed.

"Zum-zum-zum-zum," went the busy signal in his ear. He dropped the telephone into its cradle. Hundreds of people, he thought, must be trying to get in touch with the Sublime Chamberlain of the Inner Shrine of the Knights of Kandahar at this moment. He looked up at his flaking ceiling in prayer. But none of them, he prayed, was after a bargain in a cart-borne bass drum.

He dialed again and again, and always got the busy signal. He walked out on his porch to relieve some of the tension building up in him. He would be the only one bidding on the drum, he told himself, and he could name his price. Good Lord! If he offered fifty dollars for it, he could probably have it! He'd put up his own money, and get the school to pay him back in three years, when the plumes with the electric lights in them were paid for in full.

He was laughing like a department store Santa Claus, when his gaze dropped from heaven to his lawn and he espied Plummer's undelivered newspapers lying beneath the shrubbery.

He went inside and called the Sublime Chamberlain again, with the same results. He then called Plummer's home to let him know where the papers were mislaid. But that line was busy, too.

He dialed alternately the Plummers' number and the Sublime Chamberlain's number for fifteen minutes before getting a ringing signal.

"Yes?" said Mrs. Plummer.

"This is Mr. Helmholtz, Mrs. Plummer. Is Walter there?"

"He was here a minute ago, telephoning, but he just went out of here like a shot."

"Looking for his papers? He left them under my spirea."

"He did? Heavens, I have no idea where he was going. He didn't say anything about his papers, but I thought I overheard something about selling his clarinet." She sighed, and then laughed. "Having money of their own makes them awfully independent. He never tells me anything."

"Well, you tell him I think maybe it's for the best, his selling his clarinet. And tell him where his papers are."

It was unexpected good news that Plummer had at last seen the light about his musical career. The bandmaster now called the Sublime Chamberlain's home again for more good news.

He got through this time, but was disappointed to learn that the man had just left on some sort of lodge business.

For years, Mr. Helmholtz had managed to smile and keep his wits about him in C Band practice sessions. But on the day after his fruitless efforts to find out anything about the Knights of Kandahar's bass drum, his defenses were down, and the poisonous music penetrated to the roots of his soul.

"No, no, no!" he cried in pain. He threw his white baton against the brick wall. The springy stick bounded off the bricks and fell into an empty folding chair at the rear of the clarinet section—Plummer's empty chair.

As Mr. Helmholtz retrieved the baton, he found himself unexpectedly moved by the symbol of the empty chair. No one else, he realized, no matter how untalented, could fill the last chair in the organization as well as Plummer had. Mr. Helmholtz looked up to find many of the bandsmen contemplating the chair with him, as though they, too, sensed that something great, in a fantastic way, had disappeared, and that life would be a good bit duller on account of that.

During the ten minutes between the C Band and B Band sessions, Mr. Helmholtz hurried to his office and again tried to get in touch with the Sublime Chamberlain of the Knights of Kandahar. No luck! "Lord knows where he's off to now," Mr. Helmholtz was told. "He was in for just a second, but went right out again. I gave him your name, so I expect he'll call you when he gets a minute. You're the drum gentleman, aren't you?"

"That's right—the drum gentleman."

The buzzers in the hall were sounding, marking the beginning of another class period. Mr. Helmholtz wanted to stay by the phone until he'd caught the Sublime Chamberlain and closed the deal, but the B Band was waiting—and after that it would be the A Band.

An inspiration came to him. He called Western Union and sent a telegram to the man, offering fifty dollars for the drum and requesting a reply collect.

But no reply came during B Band practice. Nor had one come by the halfway point of the A Band session. The bandsmen, a sensitive, high-strung lot, knew immediately that their director was on edge about something, and the rehearsal went badly. Mr. Helmholtz stopped a march in the middle because somebody outside was shaking the large double doors at one end of the rehearsal room.

"All right, all right, let's wait until the racket dies down so we can hear ourselves," Mr. Helmholtz said.

At that moment, a student messenger handed him a telegram. Mr. Helmholtz tore open the envelope, and this is what he read:

DRUM SOLD STOP COULD YOU USE A STUFFED CAMEL ON
WHEELS STOP

The wooden doors opened with a shriek of rusty hinges. A snappy autumn gust showered the band with leaves. Plummer stood in the great opening, winded and perspiring, harnessed to a drum as big as a harvest moon!

"I know this isn't challenge day," said Plummer, "but I thought you might make an exception in my case."

He walked in with splendid dignity, the huge apparatus grumbling along behind him.

Mr. Helmholtz rushed to meet him. He crushed Plummer's right hand between both of his. "Plummer, boy! You got it for us. Good boy! I'll pay you whatever you paid for it," he cried, and in his joy he added rashly, "And a nice little profit besides. Good boy!"

"Sell it?" said Plummer. "I'll give it to you when I graduate. All I want to do is play it in the A Band as long as I'm here."

"But Plummer," said Mr. Helmholtz, "you don't know anything about drums."

"I'll practice hard," said Plummer. He backed his instrument into an aisle between the tubas and the trombones, toward the percussion section, where the amazed musicians were hastily making room.

"Now, just a minute," said Mr. Helmholtz, chuckling as though Plummer were joking, and knowing full well he wasn't. "There's more to drum playing than just lambasting the thing whenever you take a notion to, you know. It takes years to be a drummer."

"Well," said Plummer, "the quicker I get at it, the quicker I'll get good."

"What I meant was that I'm afraid you won't be quite ready for the A Band for a little while."

Plummer stopped his backing. "How long?" he asked.

"Oh, sometime in your senior year, perhaps. Meanwhile, you could let the band have your drum to use until you're ready."

Mr. Helmholtz's skin began to itch all over as Plummer stared at him coldly. "Until hell freezes over?" Plummer said at last.

Mr. Helmholtz sighed. "I'm afraid that's about right." He shook his head. "It's what I tried to tell you yesterday afternoon: Nobody can do everything well, and we've all got to face up to our limitations. You're a fine boy, Plummer, but you'll never be a musician—not in a million years. The only thing to do is what we all have to do now and then: smile, shrug, and say, 'Well, that's just one of those things that's not for me.'"

Tears formed on the rims of Plummer's eyes. He walked slowly toward the doorway, with the drum tagging after him. He paused on the doorsill for one more wistful look at the A Band that would never have a chair for him. He smiled feebly and shrugged. "Some people have eight-foot drums," he said, "and others don't, and that's just the way life is. You're a fine man, Mr. Helmholtz, but you'll never get this drum in a million years, because I'm going to give it to my mother for a coffee table."

"Plummer!" cried Mr. Helmholtz. His plaintive voice was drowned out by the rumble and rattle of the big drum as it followed its small master down the school's concrete driveway.

Mr. Helmholtz ran after him. Plummer and his drum had stopped at an intersection to wait for a light to change. Mr. Helmholtz caught him there and seized his arm. "We've got to have that drum," he panted. "How much do you want?"

"Smile," said Plummer. "Shrug! That's what I did." Plummer did it again. "See? So I can't get into the A Band, so you can't have the drum. Who cares? All part of the growing-up process."

"The situations aren't the same!" said Mr. Helmholtz. "Not at all the same!"

"You're right," said Plummer. "I'm growing up, and you're not."

The light changed, and Plummer left Mr. Helmholtz on the corner, stunned.

Mr. Helmholtz had to run after him again. "Plummer," he wheedled, "you'll never be able to play it well."

"Rub it in," said Plummer.

"But look at what a swell job you're doing of pulling it," said Mr. Helmholtz.

"Rub it in," Plummer repeated.

"No, no, no," said Mr. Helmholtz. "Not at all. If the school gets that drum, whoever's pulling it will be as crucial and valued a member of the A Band as the first-chair clarinet. What if it capsized?"

"He'd win a band letter if it didn't capsize?" said Plummer.

And Mr. Helmholtz said this: "I don't see why not."

Poor Little
Rich Town

Newell Cady had the polish, the wealth, the influence, and the middle-aged good looks of an idealized Julius Caesar. Most of all, though, Cady had know-how, know-how of a priceless variety that caused large manufacturing concerns to bid for his services like dying sultans offering half their kingdoms for a cure.

Cady could stroll through a plant that had been losing money for a generation, glance at the books, yawn and tell the manager how he could save half a million a year in materials, reduce his staff by a third, triple his output, and sell the stuff he'd been throwing out as waste for more than the cost of installing air-conditioning and continuous music throughout the plant.

And the air-conditioning and music would increase individual productivity by as much as ten percent and cut union grievances by a fifth.

The latest firm to hire him was the Federal Apparatus Corporation, which had given him the rank of vice-president and sent him to Ilium, New York, where he was to see that the new company headquarters were built properly from the ground up. When the buildings were finished, hundreds of the company's top executives would move their offices from New York City to Ilium, a city that had virtually died when its textile mills moved south after the Second World War.

There was jubilation in Ilium when the deep, thick foundations for the new headquarters were poured, but the exultation was possibly highest in the village of Spruce Falls, nine miles from Ilium, for it was there that Newell Cady had rented, with an option to buy, one of the mansions that lined the shaded main street.

Spruce Falls was a cluster of small businesses and a public school and a post office and a police station and a firehouse serving surrounding dairy farms. During the second decade of the century it experienced a real estate boom. Fifteen mansions were built back then, in the belief that the area, because of its warm mineral springs, was becoming a spa for rich invalids and hypochondriacs and horse people, as had Saratoga, not far away.

In 1922, though, it was determined that bathing in the waters of the spring, while fairly harmless, was nonetheless responsible for several cases of a rash that a Manhattan dermatologist, with no respect for upstate real estate values, named "Spruce Falls disease."

In no time at all the mansions and their stables were as

vacant as the abandoned palaces and temples of Angkor Thom in Cambodia. Banks foreclosed on those mansions that were mortgaged. The rest became property of the town in lieu of unpaid taxes. Nobody arrived from out of town to bid for them at any price, as though Spruce Falls disease were leprosy or cholera or bubonic plague.

Nine mansions were eventually bought from the banks or the town by locals, who could not resist getting so much for so little. They set up housekeeping in maybe six rooms at most, while dry rot and termites and mice and rats and squirrels and kids wrought havoc with the rest of the property.

"If we can make Newell Cady taste the joys of village life," said Fire Chief Stanley Atkins, speaking before an extraordinary meeting of the volunteer firemen on a Saturday afternoon, "he'll *use* that option to buy, and Spruce Falls will become *the* fashionable place for Federal Apparatus executives to live. Without further ado," said Chief Atkins expansively, "I move that Mr. Newell Cady be elected to full membership in the fire department and be named head judge of the annual Hobby Show."

"*Audaces fortuna juvat!*" said Upton Beaton, who was a tall, fierce-seeming sixty-five. He was the last of what had been the first family of Spruce Falls. "Fortune," he translated after a pause, "favors the bold, that's true. But gentlemen—" and he paused again, portentously, while Chief Atkins looked worried and the other members of the fire department shifted about on their folding chairs. Like his forebears, Beaton had an ornamental education from Harvard, and like them, he lived in Spruce Falls because it took little effort for a Beaton to feel superior to his neighbors there. He survived on money his family had made during the short-lived boom.

"But," Beaton said again, as he stood up, "is this the kind of fortune we want? We are being asked to waive the three-year residence requirement for membership in the fire department in Mr. Cady's case, and thereby all our memberships are cheapened. If I may say so, the post of judge of the Hobby Show is of far greater significance than it would seem to an outsider. In our small village, we have only small ways of honoring our great, but we, for generations now, have taken pains to reserve those small honors for those of us who have shown such greatness as it is possible to achieve in the eyes of a village. I hasten to add that those honors that have come to me are marks of respect for my family and my age, not for myself, and are exceptions that should probably be curtailed."

He sighed. "If we waive this proud tradition, then that one, and then another, all for money, we will soon find ourselves with nothing left to wave but the white flag of an abject surrender of all we hold dear!" He sat, folded his arms, and stared at the floor.

Chief Atkins had reddened during the speech, and he avoided looking at Beaton. "The real estate people," he mumbled, "swear property values in Spruce Falls will quadruple if Cady stays."

"What is a village profited if it shall gain a real estate boom and lose its own soul?" Beaton asked.

Chief Atkins cleared his throat. "There's a motion on the floor," he said. "Is there a second?"

"Second," said someone who kept his head down.

"All in favor?" said Atkins.

There was a scuffling of chair legs, and faint voices, like the sounds of a playground a mile away.

"Opposed?"

Beaton was silent. The Beaton dynasty of Spruce Falls had come to an end. Its paternal guidance, unopposed for four generations, had just been voted down.

"Carried," said Atkins. He started to say something, then motioned for silence. "Shhh!" The post office was next door to the meeting hall, in the same building, and on the other side of the thin partition, Mr. Newell Cady was asking for his mail.

"That's all, is it, Mrs. Dickie?" Cady was saying to the post-mistress.

"That's more'n some people get around here in a year," said Mrs. Dickie. "There's still a little second-class to put around. Maybe some for you."

"Mmm," said Cady. "That the way the government teaches its people to sort?"

"Them teach me?" said Mrs. Dickie. "I'd like to see anybody teach me anything about this business. I been postmistress for twenty-five years now, ever since my husband passed on."

"Um," said Cady. "Here—do you mind if I come back there and take a look at the second-class for just a minute?"

"Sorry—regulations, you know," said Mrs. Dickie.

But the door of Mrs. Dickie's cage creaked open anyway. "Thank you," said Cady. "Now, suppose, instead of holding these envelopes the way you were, suppose you took them like this, and uh—ah—putting that rubber cap on your thumb instead of your index finger—"

"My land!" cried Mrs. Dickie. "Look at you go!"

"It would be even faster," said Cady, "if it weren't for that tier of boxes by the floor. Why not move them over here, at eye level, see? And what on earth is this table doing back here?"

"For my children," said Mrs. Dickie.

"Your children play back here?"

"Not real children," said Mrs. Dickie. "That's what I call the plants on the table—the wise little cyclamen, the playful little screw pine, the temperamental little sansevieria, the—"

"Do you realize," said Cady, "that you must spend twenty man-minutes and heaven knows how many foot-pounds a day just detouring around it?"

"Well," said Mrs. Dickie, "I'm sure it's awfully nice of you to take such an interest, but you know, I'd just feel kind of lost without—"

"I can't help taking an interest," said Cady. "It causes me actual physical pain to see things done the wrong way, when it's so easy to do them the right way. Oops! Moved your thumb right back to where I told you not to put it!"

"Chief Atkins," whispered Upton Beaton in the meeting hall.

"Eh?"

"Don't you scratch your head like that," said Beaton. "Spread your fingers like this, see? *Then* dig in. Cover twice as much scalp in half the time."

"All due respect to you, sir," said Atkins, "this village could do with a little progress and perking up."

"I'd be the last to stand in its way," said Beaton. After a moment he added, "'Ill fares the land, to hastening ills a prey, where wealth accumulates, and men decay.'"

"Cady's across the street, looking at the fire truck," said Ed Newcomb, who had served twenty years as secretary of the fire department. The Ilium real estate man, who had put stars in every eye except Beaton's, had assured Newcomb that his twenty-six-room Georgian colonial, with a little paper and paint, would look like a steal to a corporation executive at fifty thousand dollars. "Let's tell him the good news!" Newcomb's father had bought the ark at a bank foreclosure sale. He was the only bidder.

The fire department joined its newest member by the fire truck and congratulated him on his election.

"Thanks," said Cady, tinkering with the apparatus strapped to the side of the big red truck. "By George, but there's a lot of chrome on one of these things," he said.

"Wait till you see the new one!" said Ed Newcomb.

"They make the damn things as ornamental as a merry-go-round," said Cady. "You'd think they were playthings. Lord! What all this plating and gimcrackery must add to the cost! New one, you say?"

"Sure," said Newcomb. "It hasn't been voted on yet, but it's sure to pass." The joy of the prospect showed on every face.

"Fifteen hundred gallons a minute!" said a fireman.

"Two floodlights!" said another.

"Closed cab!"

"Eighteen-foot ladders!"

"Carbon dioxide tank!"

"And a swivel-mounted nozzle in the turret smack-spang in the middle!" cried Atkins above them all.

After the silence that followed the passionate hymn to the new truck, Cady spoke. "Preposterous," he said. "This is a perfectly sound, adequate truck here."

"Mr. Cady is absolutely right," said Upton Beaton. "It's a sensible, sturdy truck, with many years of dependable service ahead of it. We were foolish to think of putting the fire district into debt for the next twenty years, just for an expensive play-thing for the fire department. Mr. Cady has cut right to the heart of the matter."

"It's the same sort of thing I've been fighting in industry for half my life," said Cady. "Men falling in love with show instead of the job to be done. The sole purpose of a fire department should be to put out fires and to do it as economically as possible."

Beaton clapped Chief Atkins on the arm. "Learn something every day, don't we, Chief?"

Atkins smiled sweetly, as though he'd just been shot in the stomach.

The Spruce Falls annual Hobby Show took place in the church basement three weeks after Newell Cady's election to the fire department. During the intervening twenty-one days, Hal Brayton, the grocer, had stopped adding bills on paper sacks and bought an adding machine, and had moved his counters around so as to transform his customer space from a jammed box canyon into a racetrack. Mrs. Dickie, the postmistress, had moved her leafy children and their table out of her cage and had had the lowest tier of mailboxes raised to eye level. The fire department had voted down scarlet and blue capes for the band as unnecessary for firefighting. And startling figures had been produced in a school meeting proving beyond any doubt that it would cost seven dollars, twenty-nine cents, and six mills more per student per year to maintain the Spruce Falls Grade School than it would to ship the children to the big, efficient, central-ized school in Ilium.

The whole populace looked as though it had received a powerful stimulant. People walked and drove faster, concluded business more quickly, and every eye seemed wider and brighter—even frenzied. And moving proudly through this brave new world were the two men who were shaping it, constant companions after working hours now. Newell Cady and Upton Beaton. Beaton's function was to provide Cady with the facts and figures behind village activities and then to endorse outrageously Cady's realistic suggestions for reforms, which followed facts and figures as the night the day.

The judges of the Hobby Show were Newell Cady, Upton Beaton, and Chief Stanley Atkins, and they moved slowly along the great assemblage of tables on which the entries were displayed. Atkins, who had lost weight and grown listless since informed public opinion had turned against the new fire truck, carried a shoe box in which lay neat stacks of blue prize ribbons.

"Surely we won't need all these ribbons," said Cady.

"Wouldn't do to run out," said Atkins. "We did one year, and there was hell to pay."

"There are a lot of classes of entries," explained Beaton, "with first prizes in each." He held out his hand to Atkins. "One with a pin, please, Chief." He pinned a ribbon to a dirty gray ball four feet in diameter.

"See here," said Cady. "I mean, aren't we going to talk this over? I mean, we shouldn't all merrily go our own ways, should we, sticking ribbons wherever we happen to take a notion to? Heavens, here you're giving first prize to this frightful blob, and I don't even know what it is."

"String," said Atkins. "It's Ted Batsford's string. Can you believe it—the very first bit he ever started saving, right in the center of this ball, he picked up during the second Cleveland administration."

"Um," said Cady. "And he decided to enter it in the show this year."

"Every show since I can remember," said Beaton. "I knew this thing when it was no bigger than a bowling ball."

"So for brute persistence, I suppose we should at last award him a first prize, eh?" Cady said wearily.

"At last?" said Beaton. "He's always gotten first prize in the string-saving class."

Cady was about to say something caustic about this, when his attention was diverted. "Good Lord in heaven!" he said. "What is that mess of garbage you're giving first prize to now?"

Atkins looked bewildered. "Why, it's Mrs. Dickie's flower arrangement, of course."

"*That* jumble is a flower arrangement?" said Cady. "I could do better with a rusty bucket and a handful of toadstools. And you're giving it first prize. Where's the competition?"

"Nobody enters anybody else's class," said Beaton, laying a ribbon across the poop deck of a half-finished ship model.

Cady snatched the ribbon away from the model. "Hold on! Everybody gets a prize—am I right?"

"Why, yes, in his or her own class," said Beaton.

"So what's the point of the show?" demanded Cady.

"Point?" said Beaton. "It's a show, is all. Does it have to have a point?"

"Damn it all," said Cady. "I mean that it should have some sort of mission—to foster an interest in the arts and crafts, or something like that. Or to improve skills and refine tastes." He gestured at the displays. "Junk, every bit of it junk—and for years these misguided people have been getting top honors, as though they didn't have a single thing more to learn, or as though all it takes to gain acclaim in this world is the patience to have saved string since the second Cleveland administration."

Atkins looked shocked and hurt.

"Well," said Beaton, "you're head judge. Let's do it your way."

"Listen, Mr. Cady, sir," Atkins said hollowly, "we just can't not give—"

"You're standing in the way of progress," said Beaton.

"Now then, as I see it," said Cady, "there's only one thing in this whole room that shows the slightest glimmer of real creativity and ambition."

There were few lights in Spruce Falls that went off before midnight on the night of the Hobby Show opening, though the town was usually dark by ten. Those few nonparticipants who dropped in at the church to see the exhibits, and who hadn't heard about the judging, were amazed to find one lonely object, a petit-point copy of the cover of a woman's magazine, on view. Pinned to it was the single blue ribbon awarded that day. The other exhibitors had angrily hauled home their rejected offerings, and the sole prizewinner appeared late in the evening, embarrassed and furtive, to take her entry home, leaving the blue ribbon behind.

Only Newell Cady and Upton Beaton slept peacefully that night, with feelings of solid, worthwhile work behind them. But when Monday came again, there was a dogged cheerfulness in the town, for on Sunday, as though to offset the holocaust of the Hobby Show, the real estate man had been around. He had been writing to Federal Apparatus Corporation executives in New York, telling them of the mansions in Spruce Falls that could virtually be stolen from the simple-hearted natives and that were but a stone's throw from the prospective home of their esteemed colleague Mr. Newell Cady. What the real estate man had to show on Sunday were letters from executives who believed him.

By late afternoon on Monday, the last bitter word about the Hobby Show had been spoken, and talk centered now on the computation of capital gains taxes, the ruthless destruction of profit motives by the state and federal governments, the outrageous cost of building small houses—

"But I tell you," said Chief Atkins, "under this new law, you don't have to pay *any* tax on the profit you make off of selling your house. All that profit is just a paper profit, just plain, ordinary inflation, and they don't tax you on that, because it wouldn't be fair." He and Upton Beaton and Ed Newcomb were talking in the post office, while Mrs. Dickie sorted the late-afternoon mail.

"Sorry," said Beaton, "but you have to buy another house for at least as much as you got for your old one, in order to come under that law."

"What would I want with a fifty-thousand-dollar house?" said Newcomb, awed.

"You can have mine for that, Ed," said Atkins. "That way, you wouldn't have to pay any tax at all." He lived in three rooms of an eighteen-room white elephant his own father had bought for peanuts.

"And have twice as many termites and four times as much rot as I've got to fight now," said Newcomb.

Atkins didn't smile. Instead, he kicked shut the post office door, which was ajar. "You big fool! You can't tell who might of been walking past and heard that, what you said about my house."

Beaton stepped between them. "Calm down! Nobody out there but old Dave Mansfield, and he hasn't heard anything since his boiler blew up. Lord, if the little progress we've had so far is making everybody that jumpy, what's it going to be like when we've got a Cady in every big house?"

"He's a fine gentleman," said Atkins.

Mrs. Dickie was puffing and swearing quietly in her cage. "I've bobbed up and down for that bottom tier of boxes for twenty-five years, and I can't make myself stop it, now that they're not there anymore. Whoops!" The mail in her hands fell to the floor. "See what happens when I put my thumb the way he told me to?"

"Makes no difference," said Beaton. "Put it where he told you to, because here he comes."

Cady's black Mercedes came to a stop before the post office.

"Nice day, Mr. Cady, sir," said Atkins.

"Hmmm? Oh yes, I suppose it is. I was thinking about something else." Cady went to Mrs. Dickie's cage for his mail, but continued to talk to the group over his shoulder, not looking at Mrs. Dickie at all. "I just figured out that I go eight-tenths of a mile out of my way every day to pick up my mail."

"Good excuse to get out and pass the time of day with people," said Newcomb.

"And that's two hundred forty-nine point six miles per year, roughly," Cady went on earnestly, "which at eight cents a mile comes out to nineteen dollars and ninety-seven cents a year."

"I'm glad to hear you can still buy something worthwhile for nineteen dollars and ninety-seven cents," said Beaton.

Cady was in a transport of creativeness, oblivious of the tension mounting in the small room. "And there must be at least a hundred others who drive to get their mail, which means an annual expenditure for the hundred of one thousand, nine hundred and ninety-seven dollars, not to mention man-hours. Think of it!"

"Huh," said Beaton, while Atkins and Newcomb shuffled their feet, eager to leave. "I'd hate to think what we spend on shaving cream." He took Cady's arm. "Come on over to my house a minute, would you? I've something I think you'd—"

Cady stayed put before Mrs. Dickie's cage. "It's not the same thing as shaving cream at all," he said. "Men have to shave, and shaving cream's the best thing there is to take whiskers off. And we have to get our mail, certainly, but I've found out something apparently nobody around here knows."

"Come on over to my house," said Beaton, "and we'll talk about it."

"It's so perfectly simple, there's no need to talk about it," said Cady. "I found out that Spruce Falls can get rural free delivery, just by telling the Ilium post office and sticking out mailboxes in front of our houses the way every other village around here does. And that's been true for years!" He smiled, and glanced absently at Mrs. Dickie's hands. "Ah, ah, ah!" he chided. "Slipping back to your old ways, aren't you, Mrs. Dickie?"

Atkins and Newcomb were holding open the door, like a pair of guards at the entrance to an execution chamber, while Upton Beaton hustled Cady out.

"It's a great advantage, coming into situations from the outside, the way I do," said Cady. "People inside of situations are so blinded by custom. Here you people were, supporting a post of-fice, when you could get much better service for just a fraction of the cost and trouble." He chuckled modestly, as Atkins shut the post office door behind him. "One-eyed man in the land of the blind, you might say."

"A one-eyed man might as well be blind," declared Upton Beaton, "if he doesn't watch people's faces and doesn't give the blind credit for the senses they do have."

"What on earth are you talking about?" said Cady.

"If you'd looked at Mrs. Dickie's face instead of how she was doing her work, you would have seen she was crying," said Beaton. "Her husband died in a fire, saving some of these people around the village you call blind. You talk a lot about wasting time, Mr. Cady—for a really big waste of time, walk around the village someday and try to find somebody who doesn't know he can have his mail brought to his door anytime he wants to."

The second extraordinary meeting of the volunteer firemen within a month finished its business, and the full membership, save one fireman who had not been invited, seemed relaxed and contented for the first time in weeks. The business of the meeting had gone swiftly, with Upton Beaton, the patriarch of Spruce Falls, making motions, and the membership seconding in chorus. Now they waited for the one absent member, Newell Cady, to arrive at the post office on the other side of the thin wall to pick up his Saturday-afternoon mail.

"Here he is," whispered Ed Newcomb, who had been stand-ing watch by the window.

A moment later, the rich voice came through the wall. "Good heavens, you've got all those plants in there with you again!"

"Just got lonesome," said Mrs. Dickie.

"But my dear Mrs. Dickie," said Cady, "think of—"

"The motion's been carried, then," said Chief Atkins in a loud voice. "Mr. Beaton is to be a committee of one to inform Mr. Cady that his fire department membership, unfortunately, is in violation of the by-laws, which call for three years' residence in the village prior to election."

"I will make it clear to him," said Beaton, also speaking loudly, "that this is in no way a personal affront, that it's simply a matter of conforming to our by-laws, which have been in effect for years."

"Make sure he understands that we all like him," said Ed Newcomb, "and tell him we're proud an important man like him would want to live here."

"I will," said Beaton. "He's a brilliant man, and I'm sure he'll see the wisdom in the residence requirement. A village isn't like a factory, where you can walk in and see what's being made at a glance, and then look at the books and see if it's a good or bad operation. We're not manufacturing or selling anything. We're trying to live together. Every man's got to be his own expert at that, and it takes years."

The meeting was adjourned.

The Ilium real estate man was upset, because everyone he wanted to see in Spruce Falls was out. He stood in Hal Brayton's grocery store, looking at the deserted street and fiddling with his fountain pen.

"They're *all* with the fire engine salesman?" he said.

"They're all going to be paying for the truck for the next twenty years," said Upton Beaton. He was tending Brayton's store while Brayton went for a ride on the fire engine.

"Red-hot prospects are going to start coming through here in a week, and everybody goes out joy-riding," said the real estate man bitterly. He opened the soft drink cooler and let the lid fall shut again. "What's the matter—this thing broken? Everything's warm."

"No, Brayton just hasn't gotten around to plugging it in since he moved things back the way they used to be."

"You said he's the one who doesn't want to sell his place?"

"One of the ones," said Beaton.

"Who else?"

"Everybody else."

"Go on!"

"Really," said Beaton. "We've decided to wait and see how Mr. Cady adapts himself, before we put anything else on the market. He's having a tough time, but he's got a good heart, I think, and we're all rooting for him."

Souvenir

Joe Bane was a pawnbroker, a fat, lazy, bald man, whose features seemed pulled to the left by his lifetime of looking at the world through a jeweler's glass. He was a lonely, untalented man and would not have wanted to go on living had he been prevented from playing every day save Sunday the one game he played brilliantly—the acquiring of objects for very little, and the selling of them for a great deal more. He was obsessed by the game, the one opportunity life offered him to best his fellow men. The game was the thing, the money he made a secondary matter, a way of keeping score.

When Joe Bane opened his shop Monday morning, a black ceiling of rainclouds had settled below the valley's rim, holding the city in a dark pocket of dead, dank air. Autumn thunder grumbled along the misty hillsides. No sooner had Bane hung up his coat and hat and umbrella, taken off his rubbers, turned on the lights, and settled his great bulk on a stool behind a counter than a lean young man in overalls, shy and dark as an Indian, plainly poor and awed by the city, walked in to offer him a fantastic pocketwatch for five hundred dollars.

"No, sir," said the young farmer politely. "I don't want to borrow money on it. I want to sell it, if I can get enough for it." He seemed reluctant to hand it to Bane, and cupped it tenderly in his rough hands for a moment before setting it down on a square of black velvet. "I kind of hoped to hang on to it, and pass it on to my oldest boy, but we need the money a whole lot worse right now."

"Five hundred dollars is a lot of money," said Bane, like a man who had been victimized too often by his own kindness. He examined the jewels studding the watch without betraying anything of his inner amazement. He turned the watch this way and that, catching the glare of the ceiling light in four diamonds marking the hours three, six, nine, and twelve, and the ruby crowning the winder. The jewels alone, Bane reflected, were worth at least four times what the farmer was asking.

"I don't get much call for a watch like this," said Bane. "If I tied up five hundred dollars in it, I might be stuck with it for years before the right man came along." He watched the farmer's sunburned face and thought he read there that the watch could be had for a good bit less.

"There ain't another one like it in the whole county," said the farmer, in a clumsy attempt at salesmanship.

"That's my point," said Bane. "Who wants a watch like this?" Bane, for one, wanted it, and was already regarding it as his own. He pressed a button on the side of the case and listened to the whirring of tiny machinery striking the nearest hour on sweet, clear chimes.

"You want it or not?" said the farmer.

"Now, now," said Bane, "this isn't the kind of deal you just dive headfirst into. I'd have to know more about this watch before I bought it." He pried open the back and found inside an engraved inscription in a foreign language. "What does this say? Any idea?"

"Showed it to a schoolteacher back home," said the young man, "and all she could say was it looked a whole lot like German."

Bane laid a sheet of tissue paper over the inscription, and rubbed a pencil back and forth across it until he'd picked up a legible copy. He gave the copy and a dime to a shoeshine boy loitering by the door and sent him down the block to ask a German restaurant proprietor for a translation.

The first drops of rain were spattering clean streaks on the sooty glass when Bane said casually to the farmer, "The cops keep pretty close check on what comes in here."

The farmer reddened. "That watch is mine, all right. I got it in the war," he said.

"Uh-huh. And you paid duty on it?"

"Duty?"

"Certainly. You can't bring jewelry into this country without paying taxes on it. That's smuggling."

"Just tucked it in my barracks bag and brought her on home, the way everybody done," said the farmer. He was as worried as Bane had hoped.

"Contraband," said Bane. "Just about the same as stolen goods." He held up his hands placatingly. "I don't mean I can't buy it, I just want to point out to you that it'd be a tricky thing to handle. If you were willing to let it go for, oh, say a hundred dollars, maybe I'd take a chance on it to help you out. I try to give veterans a break here whenever I can."

"A hundred dollars! That's all?"

"That's all it's worth, and I'm probably a sucker to offer that," said Bane. "What the hell—that's an easy hundred bucks for you, isn't it? What'd you do—cop it off some German prisoner or find it lying around in the ruins?"

"No, sir," said the farmer, "it was a little tougher'n that."

Bane, who was keenly sensitive to such things, saw that the farmer, as he began to tell how he'd gotten the watch, was regaining the stubborn confidence that had deserted him when he'd left his farm for the city to make the sale.

"My best buddy Buzzer and me," said the farmer, "were prisoners of war together in some hills in Germany—in Sudetenland, somebody said it was. One morning, Buzzer woke me up and said the war was over, the guards were gone, the gates were open."

Joe Bane was impatient at first with having to listen to the tale. But it was a tale told well and proudly, and long a fan of others' adventures for want of any of his own, Bane began to see, enviously, the two soldiers walking through the open gates of their prison, and down a country road in the hills early on a bright spring morning in 1945, on the day the Second World War ended in Europe.

The young farmer, whose name was Eddie, and his best buddy Buzzer walked out into peace and freedom skinny, ragged, dirty, and hungry, but with no ill will toward anyone. They'd gone to war out of pride, not bitterness. Now the war was over, the job done, and they wanted only to go home. They were a year apart, but as alike as two poplars in a windbreak.

Their notion was to take a brief sightseeing tour of the neighborhood near the camp, then to come back and wait with the rest of the prisoners for the arrival of some official liberators. But the plan evaporated when a pair of Canadian prisoners invited the buddies to toast victory with a bottle of brandy they'd found in a wrecked German truck.

Their shrunken bellies gloriously hot and tingling, their heads light and full of trust and love for all mankind, Eddie and Buzzer found themselves swept along by a jostling, plaintive parade of German refugees that jammed the main road through the hills, refugees fleeing from the Russian tanks that growled monotonously and unopposed in the valley behind and below them. The tanks were coming to occupy this last undefended bit of German soil.

"What're we runnin' from?" said Buzzer. "The war's over, ain't it?"

"Everybody else is runnin'," said Eddie, "so I guess maybe we better be runnin', too."

"I don't even know where we are," said Buzzer.

"Them Canadians said it's Sudetenland."

"Where's that?"

"Where we're at," said Eddie. "Swell guys, them Canadians."

"I'll tell the world! Man," said Buzzer, "I love everybody today. Whoooooey! I'd like to get me a bottle of that brandy, put a nipple on it, and go to bed with it for a week."

Eddie touched the elbow of a tall, worried-looking man with close-cropped black hair, who wore a civilian suit too small for him. "Where we runnin' to, sir? Ain't the war over?"

The man glared, grunted something, and pushed by roughly.

"He don't understand English," said Eddie.

"Why, hell, man," said Buzzer, "why'n't you talk to these folks in their native tongue? Don't hide your candle under a bushel. Let's hear you sprecken some Dutch to this man here."

They'd come alongside a small, low black roadster, which was stalled on the shoulder of the road. A heavily muscled square-faced young man was tinkering with the dead motor. On the leather front seat of the car sat an older man whose face was covered with dust and several days' growth of black beard, and shaded by a hat with the brim pulled down.

Eddie and Buzzer stopped. "All right," said Eddie. "Just listen to this: *Wie geht's?*" he said to the blond man, using the only German he knew.

"*Gut, gut,*" muttered the young German. Then, realizing the absurdity of his automatic reply to the greeting, he said with terrible bitterness, "*Ja! Geht's gut!*"

"He says everything's just fine," said Eddie.

"Oh, you're fluent, mighty fluent," said Buzzer.

"Yes, I've traveled extensively, you might say," said Eddie.

The older man came to life and yelled at the man who was working on the motor, yelled shrilly and threateningly.

The blond seemed frightened. He went to work on the motor with redoubled desperation.

The older man's eyes, bleary a moment before, were wide and bright now. Several refugees turned to stare as they passed.

The older man glanced challengingly from one face to the next, and filled his lungs to shout something at them. But he changed his mind, sighed instead, and his spirits collapsed. He thrust his face in his hands.

"Wha'd he say?" said Buzzer.

"He don't speak my particular dialect," said Eddie.

"Speaks low-class German, huh?" said Buzzer. "Well, I'm not goin' another step till we find somebody who can tell us what's goin' on. We're Americans, boy. Our side won, didn't it? What we doin' all tangled up with these Jerries?"

"You—you Americans," said the blond, surprisingly enough in English. "Now you will have to fight them."

"Here's one that talks English!" said Buzzer.

"Talks it pretty good, too," said Eddie.

"Ain't bad, ain't bad at all," said Buzzer. "Who we got to fight?"

"The Russians," said the young German, seeming to relish the idea. "They'll kill you, too, if they catch you. They're killing everybody in their path."

"Hell, man," said Buzzer, "we're on their side."

"For how long? Run, boys, run." The blond swore and hurled his wrench at the motor. He turned to the old man and spoke, scared to death of him.

The older man released a stream of German abuse, tired of it quickly, got out of the car, and slammed the door behind him. The two looked anxiously in the direction from which the tanks would come, and started down the road on foot.

"Where you guys headed?" said Eddie.

"Prague—the Americans are in Prague."

Eddie and Buzzer fell in behind them. "Sure gettin' a mess of geography today, ain't we, Eddie?" said Buzzer. He stumbled, and Eddie caught him. "Oh, oh, Eddie, that old booze is sneakin' up on me."

"Yeah," said Eddie, whose own senses were growing fuzzier. "I say to hell with Prague. If we don't ride, we don't go, and that's that."

"Sure. We'll just find us some shady spot, and sit and wait for the Russians. We'll just show 'em our dog tags," said Buzzer. "And when they see 'em, bet they give us a big banquet." He dipped a finger inside his collar and brought out the tags on their string.

"Oh my, yes," said the blond German, who had been listening carefully, "a wonderful big banquet they'll give you."

The column had been moving more and more slowly, growing more packed. Now it came to a muttering halt.

"Must be a woman up front, tryin' to read a road map," said Buzzer.

From far down the road came an exchange of shouts like a distant surf. Restless, anxious moments later, the cause of the trouble was clear: The column had met another, fleeing in terror from the opposite direction. The Russians had the area surrounded. Now the two columns merged to form an aimless whirlpool in the heart of a small village, flooding out into side lanes and up the slopes on either side.

"Don't know nobody in Prague, anyhow," said Buzzer, and he wandered off the road and sat by the gate of a walled farmyard.

Eddie followed his example. "By God," he said, "maybe we oughta stay right here and open us up a gun shop, Buzzer." He included in a sweep of his hand the discarded rifles and pistols that were strewn over the grass. "Bullets and all."

"Swell place to open a gun shop, Europe is," said Buzzer. "They're just crazy about guns around here."

Despite the growing panic of the persons milling about them, Buzzer dropped off into a brandy-induced nap. Eddie had trouble keeping his eyes open.

"Aha!" said a voice from the road. "Here our American friends are."

Eddie looked up to see the two Germans, the husky young man and the irascible older one, grinning down at them.

"Hello," said Eddie. The cheering edge of the brandy was wearing off, and queasiness was taking its place.

The young German pushed open the gate to the farmyard. "Come in here, would you?" he told Eddie. "We have something important to say to you."

"Say it here," said Eddie.

The blond leaned down. "We've come to surrender to you."

"You've come to what?"

"We surrender," said the blond. "We are your prisoners—prisoners of the United States Army."

Eddie laughed.

"Seriously!"

"Buzzer!" Eddie nudged his buddy with the toe of his boot. "Hey, Buzzer—you gotta hear this."

"Hmmmm?"

"We just captured some people."

Buzzer opened his eyes and squinted at the pair. "You're drunker'n I am, by God, Eddie, goin' out capturin' people," he said at last. "You damn fool—the war's over." He waved his hand magnanimously. "Turn 'em loose."

"Take us through the Russian lines to Prague as American prisoners, and you'll be heroes," said the blond. He lowered his voice. "This is a famous German general. Think of it—you two can bring him in as your prisoner!"

"He really a general?" said Buzzer. "Heil Hitler, Pop."

The older man raised his arm in an abbreviated salute.

"Got a little pepper left in him, at that," said Buzzer.

"From what I heard," said Eddie, "me and Buzzer'll be heroes if we get just us through the Russian lines, let alone a German general."

The noise of a tank column of the Red Army grew louder.

"All right, all right," said the blond, "sell us your uniforms, then. You'll still have your dog tags, and you can take our clothes."

"I'd rather be poor than dead," said Eddie. "Wouldn't you, Buzzer?"

"Just a minute, Eddie," said Buzzer, "just hold on. What'll you give us?"

"Come in the farmyard. We can't show you here," said the blond.

"I even heard there was some Nazis in the neighborhood," said Buzzer. "Come on, give us a little peek here."

"Now who's a damn fool?" said Eddie.

"Just want to be able to tell my grandchildren what I passed up," said Buzzer.

The blond was going through his pockets. He pulled out a fat roll of German currency.

"Confederate money!" said Buzzer. "What else you got?"

It was then that the old man showed them his pocketwatch, four diamonds, a ruby, and gold. And there, in the midst of a mob of every imaginable sort of refugee, the blond told Buzzer and Eddie that they could have the watch if they would go behind a wall and exchange their ragged American uniforms for the Germans' civilian clothes. They thought Americans were so dumb!

This was all so funny and crazy! Eddie and Buzzer were so drunk! What a story they would have to tell when they got home! They didn't want the watch. They wanted to get home alive. There, in the midst of a mob of every imaginable sort of refugee, the blond was showing them a small pistol, as though they could have that, too, along with the watch.

But it was now impossible for anybody to say any more funny stuff and still be heard. The earth shook, and the air was ripped to shreds as armored vehicles from the victorious Soviet Union, thundering and backfiring, came up the road. Everybody who could got out of the way of the juggernaut. Some were not so lucky. They were mangled. They were squashed.

Eddie and Buzzer and the old man and the blond found themselves behind the wall where the blond had said the Americans could swap their uniforms for the watch and civilian clothes. In the uproar, during which anybody could do anything, and nobody cared what anybody else did, the blond shot Buzzer in the head. He aimed his pistol at Eddie. He fired. He missed.

That had evidently been the plan all along, to kill Eddie and Buzzer. But what chance did the old man, who spoke no English, have to pass himself off to his captors as an American? None. It was the blond who was going to do that. And they were both about to be captured. All the old man could do was commit suicide.

Eddie went back over the wall, putting it between himself and the blond. But the blond didn't care what had become of him. Everything the blond needed was on Buzzer's body. When Eddie peered over the wall to see if Buzzer was still alive, the blond was stripping the body. The old man now had the pistol. He put its muzzle in his mouth and blew his brains out.

The blond walked off with Buzzer's clothes and dog tags. Buzzer was in his GI underwear and dead, without ID. On the ground between the old man and Buzzer, Eddie found the watch. It was running. It told the right time. Eddie picked it up and put it in his pocket.

The rainstorm outside Joe Bane's pawnshop had stopped. "When I got home," said Eddie, "I wrote Buzzer's folks. I told 'em he'd been killed in a fight with a German, even though the war was over. I told the Army the same thing. I didn't know the name of the place where he'd died, so there was no way they could look for his body and give him a decent funeral. I had to leave him there. Whoever buried him, unless they could recognize GI underwear, wouldn't have known he was American. He could have been a German. He could have been anything."

Eddie snatched the watch from under the pawnbroker's nose. "Thanks for letting me know what it's worth," he said. "Makes more sense to keep it for a souvenir."

"Five hundred," said Bane, but Eddie was already on his way out the door.

Ten minutes later, the shoeshine boy returned with a translation of the inscription inside the watch. This was it:

"To General Heinz Guderian, Chief of the Army General Staff, who cannot rest until the last enemy soldier is driven from the sacred soil of the Third German Reich. ADOLF HITLER."

The Cruise of
The Jolly Roger

During the Great Depression, Nathan Durant was homeless until he found a home in the United States Army. He spent seventeen years in the Army, thinking of the earth as terrain, of the hills and valleys as enfilade and defilade, of the horizon as something a man should never silhouette himself against, of the houses and woods and thickets as cover. It was a good life, and when he got tired of thinking about war, he got himself a girl and a bottle, and the next morning he was ready to think about war some more.

When he was thirty-six, an enemy projectile dropped into a command post under thick green cover in defilade in the terrain of Korea, and blew Major Durant, his maps, and his career through the wall of his tent.

He had always assumed that he was going to die young and gallantly. But he didn't die. Death was far, far away, and Durant faced unfamiliar and frightening battalions of peaceful years.

In the hospital, the man in the next bed talked constantly of the boat he was going to own when he was whole again. For want of exciting peacetime dreams of his own, for want of a home or family or civilian friends, Durant borrowed his neighbor's dream.

With a deep scar across his cheek, with the lobe of his right ear gone, with a stiff leg, he limped into a boatyard in New London, the port nearest the hospital, and bought a secondhand cabin cruiser. He learned to run it in the harbor there, christened the boat *The Jolly Roger* at the suggestion of some children who haunted the boatyard, and set out arbitrarily for Martha's Vineyard.

He stayed on the island but a day, depressed by the tranquility and permanence, by the feeling of deep, still lakes of time, by men and women so at one with the peace of the place as to have nothing to exchange with an old soldier but a few words about the weather.

Durant fled to Chatham, at the elbow of Cape Cod, and found himself beside a beautiful woman at the foot of a lighthouse there. Had he been in his old uniform, seeming as he'd liked to seem in the old days, about to leave on a dangerous mission, he and the woman might have strolled off together. Women had once treated him like a small boy with special permission to eat icing off cakes. But the woman looked away without interest. He was nobody and nothing. The spark was gone.

His former swashbuckling spirits returned for an hour or two during a brief blow off the dunes of Cape Cod's east coast, but there was no one aboard to notice. When he reached the sheltered harbor at Provincetown and went ashore, he was a hollow man again, who didn't have to be anywhere at any time, whose life was all behind him.

"Look up, please," commanded a gaudily dressed young man with a camera in his hands and a girl on his arm.

Surprised, Durant did look up, and the camera shutter clicked. "Thank you," said the young man brightly.

"Are you a painter?" asked his girl.

"Painter?" said Durant. "No—retired Army officer."

The couple did a poor job of covering their disappointment.

"Sorry," said Durant, and he felt dull and annoyed.

"Oh!" said the girl. "There's some real painters over there."

Durant glanced at the artists, three men and one woman, probably in their late twenties, who sat on the wharf, their backs to a silvered splintering pile, sketching. The woman, a tanned brunette, was looking right at Durant.

"Do you mind being sketched?" she said.

"No—no, I guess not," said Durant bearishly. Freezing in his pose, he wondered what it was he'd been thinking about that had made him interesting enough to draw. He realized that he'd been thinking about lunch, about the tiny galley aboard *The Jolly Roger*, about the four wrinkled wieners, the half-pound of cheese, and the flat remains of a quart of beer that awaited him there.

"There," said the woman, "you see?" She held out the sketch.

What Durant saw was a big, scarred, hungry man, hunched over and desolate as a lost child. "Do I really look that bad?" he said, managing to laugh.

"Do you really feel that awful?"

"I was thinking of lunch. Lunch can be pretty terrible."

"Not where we eat it," she said. "Why not come with us?"

Major Durant went with them, with the three men, Ed, Teddy, and Lou, who danced through a life that seemed full of funny secrets, and with the girl, Marion. He found he was relieved to be with others again, even with these others, and his step down the walk was jaunty.

At lunch, the four spoke of painting, ballet, and drama. Durant grew tired of counterfeiting interest, but he kept at it.

"Isn't the food good here?" said Marion, in a casual and polite aside.

"Um," said Durant. "But the shrimp sauce is flat. Needs—" He gave up. The four were off again in their merry whirlwind of talk.

"Did you just drive here?" said Teddy, when he saw Durant staring at him disapprovingly.

"No," said Durant. "I came in my boat."

"A boat!" they echoed, excited, and Durant found himself center stage.

"What kind?" said Marion.

"Cabin cruiser," said Durant.

Their faces fell. "Oh," said Marion, "one of those floating tourist cabins with a motor."

"Well," said Durant, tempted to tell them about the blow he'd weathered, "it's certainly no picnic when—"

"What's its name?" said Lou.

"*The Jolly Roger*," said Durant.

The four exchanged glances, and then burst into laughter, repeating the boat's name, to Durant's consternation and bafflement.

"If you had a dog," said Marion, "I'll bet you'd call it Spot."

"Seems like a perfectly good name for a dog," said Durant, reddening.

Marion reached across the table and patted his hand. "Aaaaaah, you lamb, you musn't mind us." She was an irresponsibly affectionate woman, and appeared to have no idea how profoundly her touch was moving the lonely Durant, in spite of his resentment. "Here we've been talking away and not letting you say a word," she said. "What is it you do in the Army?"

Durant was startled. He hadn't mentioned the Army, and there were no insignia on his faded khakis. "Well, I was in Korea for a little while," he said, "and I'm out of the Army now because of wounds."

The four were impressed and respectful. "Do you mind talking about it?" said Ed.

Durant sighed. He did mind talking about it to Ed, Teddy, and Lou, but he wanted very much for Marion to hear about it—wanted to show her that while he couldn't speak her language, he could speak one of his own that had life to it. "No," he said, "there are some things that would just as well stay unsaid, but for the most part, why not talk about it?" He sat back and lit a cigarette, and squinted into the past as though through a thin screen of shrubs in a forward observation post.

"Well," he said, "we were over on the east coast, and . . ." He had never tried to tell the tale before, and now, in his eagerness to be glib and urbane, he found himself including details, large and small, as they occurred to him, until his tale was no tale at all, but a formless, unwieldy description of war as it had really seemed: a senseless, complicated mess that in the telling was first-rate realism but miserable entertainment.

He had been talking for twenty minutes now, and his audience had finished coffee and dessert, and two cigarettes apiece, and the waitress was getting restive about the check. Durant, florid and irritated with himself, was trying to manage a cast of thousands spread over the forty thousand square miles of South Korea. His audience was listening with glazed eyes, brightening at any sign that the parts were about to be brought together into a whole and thence to an end. But the signs were always false, and at last, when Marion swallowed her third yawn, Durant blew himself in his story through the wall of his tent and fell silent.

"Well," said Teddy, "it's hard for us who haven't seen it to imagine."

"Words can hardly convey it," said Marion. She patted Durant's hand again. "You've been through so much, and you're so modest about it."

"Nothing, really," said Durant.

After a moment of silence, Marion stood. "It's certainly been pleasant and interesting, Major," she said, "and we all wish you bon voyage on *The Jolly Roger*."

And there it ended.

Back aboard *The Jolly Roger*, Durant finished the stale quart of beer and told himself he was ready to give up—to sell the boat, return to the hospital, put on a bathrobe, and play cards and thumb through magazines until doomsday.

Moodily he studied his charts for a course back to New London. It was then he realized that he was only a few miles from the home village of a friend who had been killed in the Second World War. It struck him as wryly fitting that he should call on this ghost on his way back.

He arrived at the village through an early-morning mist, the day before Memorial Day, feeling ghostlike himself. He made a bad landing that shook the village dock, and tied up *The Jolly Roger* with a clumsy knot.

When he reached the main street, he found it quiet but lined with flags. Only two other people were abroad to glance at the dour stranger.

He stepped into the post office and spoke to the brisk old woman who was sorting mail in a rickety cage.

"Pardon me," said Durant, "I'm looking for the Pefko family."

"Pefko? Pefko?" said the postmistress. "That doesn't sound like any name around here. Pefko? They summer people?"

"No—I don't think so. I'm sure they're not. They may have moved away a while ago."

"Well, if they lived here, you'd think I'd know. They'd come here for their mail. There's only four hundred of us year around, and I never heard of any Pefko."

The secretary from the law office across the street came in and knelt by Durant, and worked the combination lock of her mailbox.

"Annie," said the postmistress, "you know about anybody named Pefko around here?"

"No," said Annie, "unless they had one of the summer cottages out on the dunes. It's hard to keep track of who is in those. They're changing hands all the time."

She stood, and Durant saw that she was attractive in a determinedly practical way, without wiles or ornamentation. But Durant was now so convinced of his own dullness that his manner toward her was perfunctory.

"Look," he said, "my name is Durant, Major Nathan Durant, and one of my best friends in the Army was from here. George Pefko—I know he was from here. He said so, and so did all his records. I'm sure of it."

"Ohhhhhh," said Annie. "Now wait, wait, wait. That's right—certainly. Now I remember."

"You knew him?" said Durant.

"I knew *of* him," said Annie. "I know now who you're talking about: the one that got killed in the war."

"I was with him," said Durant.

"Still can't say as I remember him," said the postmistress.

"You don't remember him, probably, but you remember the family," said Annie. "And they *did* live out on the dunes, too. Goodness, that was a long time ago—ten or fifteen years. Remember that big family that talked Paul Eldredge into letting them live in one of his summer cottages all winter? About six kids or more. That was the Pefkos. A wonder they didn't freeze to death, with nothing but a fireplace for heat. The old man came out here to pick cranberries, and stayed on through the winter."

"Wouldn't exactly call this their hometown," said the postmistress.

"George did," said Durant.

"Well," said Annie, "I suppose one hometown was as good as another for young George. Those Pefkos were wanderers."

"George enlisted from here," said Durant. "I suppose that's how he settled on it." By the same line of reasoning, Durant had chosen Pittsburgh as his hometown, though a dozen other places had as strong a claim.

"One of those people who found a home in the Army," said the postmistress. "Scrawny, tough boy. I remember now. His family never got any mail. That was it, and they weren't church people. That's why I forgot. Drifters. He must have been about your brother's age, Annie."

"I know. But I tagged after my brother all the time in those days, and George Pefko never had anything to do with his gang. They kept to themselves, the Pefkos did."

"There must be somebody who remembers him well," said Durant. "Somebody who—" He let the sentence die on a note of urgency. It was unbearable that every vestige of George had disappeared, unmissed.

"Now that I think about it," said Annie, "I'm almost sure there's a square named after him."

"A square?" said Durant.

"Not really a square," said Annie. "They just call it a square. When a man from around here gets killed in a war, the town names some little plot of town property after him—a traffic circle or something like that. They put up a plaque with his name on it. That triangle down by the village dock—I'm almost sure that was named for your friend."

"It's hard to keep track of them all, *these* days," said the postmistress.

"Would you like to go down and see it?" said Annie. "I'll be glad to show you."

"A plaque?" said Durant. "Never mind." He dusted his hands. "Well, which way is the restaurant—the one with a bar?"

"After June fifteenth, any way you want to go," said the postmistress. "But right now everything is closed and shuttered. You can get a sandwich at the drugstore."

"I might as well move on," said Durant.

"As long as you've come, you ought to stay for the parade," said Annie.

"After seventeen years in the Army, that would be a real treat," said Durant. "What parade?"

"Memorial Day," said Annie.

"That's tomorrow, I thought," said Durant.

"The children march today. School is closed tomorrow," said Annie. She smiled. "I'm afraid you're going to have to endure one more parade, Major, because here it comes."

Durant followed her apathetically out onto the sidewalk. He could hear the sound of a band, but the marchers weren't yet in sight. There were no more than a dozen people waiting for the parade to pass.

"They go from square to square," said Annie. "We really ought to wait for them down by George's."

"Whatever you say," said Durant. "I'll be closer to the boat."

They walked down the slope toward the village dock and *The Jolly Roger*.

"They keep up the squares very nicely," said Annie.

"They always do, they always do," said Durant.

"Are you in a hurry to get somewhere else today?"

"Me?" said Durant bitterly. "Me? Nothing's waiting for me anywhere."

"I see," said Annie, startled. "Sorry."

"It isn't your fault."

"I don't understand."

"I'm an Army bum like George. They should have handed me a plaque and shot me. I'm not worth a dime to anybody."

"Here's the square," said Annie gently.

"Where? Oh—that." The square was a triangle of grass, ten feet on a side, an accident of intersecting lanes and a footpath. In its center was a low boulder on which was fixed a small metal plaque, easily overlooked.

"George Pefko Memorial Square," said Durant. "By golly, I wonder what George would make of that?"

"He'd like it, wouldn't he?" said Annie.

"He'd probably laugh."

"I don't see that there's anything to laugh about."

"Nothing, nothing at all—except that it doesn't have much to do with anything, does it? Who cares about George? Why should anyone care about George? It's just what people are expected to do, put up plaques."

The bandsmen were in sight now, all eight of them, teenagers, out of step, rounding a corner with confident, proud, sour, and incoherent noise intended to be music.

Before them rode the town policeman, fat with leisure, authority, leather, bullets, pistol, handcuffs, club, and a badge. He was splendidly oblivious to the smoking, backfiring motorcycle beneath him as he swept slowly back and forth before the parade.

Behind the band came a cloud of purple, seeming to float a few feet above the street. It was lilacs carried by children. Along the curb, teachers looking as austere as New England churches called orders to the children.

"The lilacs came in time this year," said Annie. "Sometimes they don't. It's touch-and-go."

"That so?" said Durant.

A teacher blew a whistle. The parade halted, and Durant found a dozen children bearing down on him, their eyes large, their arms filled with flowers, their knees lifted high.

Durant stepped aside.

A bugler played taps badly.

The children laid their flowers before the plaque on George Pefko Memorial Square.

"Lovely?" whispered Annie.

"Yes," said Durant. "It would make a statue want to cry. But what does it mean?"

"Tom," called Annie to a small boy who had just laid down his flowers, "why did you do that?"

The boy looked around guiltily. "Do what?"

"Put the flowers down there," said Annie.

"Tell them you're paying homage to one of the fallen valiant who selflessly gave his life," prompted a teacher.

Tom looked at her blankly, and then back at the flowers.

"Don't you know?" said Annie.

"Sure," said Tom at last. "He died fighting so we could be safe and free. And we're thanking him with flowers, because it was a nice thing to do." He looked up at Annie, amazed that she should ask. "Everybody knows that."

The policeman raced his motorcycle engine. The teacher shepherded the children back into line. The parade moved on.

"Well," said Annie, "are you sorry you had to endure one more parade, Major?"

"It's true, isn't it," murmured Durant. "It's so damn simple, and so easy to forget." Watching the innocent marchers under the flowers, he was aware of life, the beauty and importance of a village at peace. "Maybe I never knew—never had any way of knowing. This *is* what war is about, isn't it. This."

Durant laughed. "George, you homeless, horny, wild old rummy," he said to George Pefko Memorial Square, "damned if you didn't turn out to be a saint."

The old spark was back. Major Durant, home from the wars, was somebody.

"I wonder," he said to Annie, "if you'd have lunch with me, and then, maybe, we could go for a ride in my boat."

Custom-Made Bride

I am a customer's man for an investment counseling firm. I'm starting to build a clientele and to see my way clear to take, in a modest way, the good advice I sell. My uniform—gray suit, Homburg hat, and navy blue overcoat—is paid for, and after I get a half-dozen more white shirts, I'm going to buy some stock.

We in the investment counseling business have a standard question, which goes, "Mr. X, sir, before we can make our analyses and recommendations, we'd like to know just what it is you want from your portfolio: income or growth?" A portfolio is a nest egg in the form of stocks and bonds. What the question tries to get at is, does the client want to put his nest egg where it will grow, not paying much in dividends at first, or does he want the nest egg to stay about the same size but pay nice dividends?

The usual answer is that the client wants his nest egg to grow *and* pay a lot of dividends. He wants to get richer fast. But I've had plenty of unusual answers, particularly from clients who, because of some kind of mental block, can't take money in the abstract seriously. When asked what they want from their portfolio, they're likely to name something they're itching to blow money on—a car, a trip, a boat, a house.

When I put the question to a client named Otto Krummbein, he said he wanted to make two women happy: Kitty and Falloleen.

Otto Krummbein is a genius, designer of the Krummbein Chair, the Krummbein Di-Modular Bed, the body of the Marittima-Frascati Sports Racer, and the entire line of Mercury Kitchen Appliances.

He is so engrossed in beauty that his mental development in money matters is that of a chickadee. When I showed him the first stock certificate I bought for his portfolio, he wanted to sell it again because he didn't like the artwork.

"What difference do the looks of the certificate make, Otto?" I said, bewildered. "The point is that the company behind it is well managed, growing, and has a big cash reserve."

"Any company," said Otto, "that would choose as its symbol this monstrosity at the top of the certificate, this fat Medusa astride a length of sewer pipe and wrapped in cable, is certainly insensitive, vulgar, and stupid."

When I got Otto as a client, he was in no condition to start building a portfolio. I got him through his lawyer, Hal Murphy, a friend of mine.

"I laid eyes on him for the first time two days ago," said Hal. "He came wandering in here, and said in a casual, fogbound way that he thought he might need a little help." Hal chuckled. "They tell me this Krummbein is a genius, but I say he belongs on Skid Row or in a laughing academy. He's made over two hundred and thirty-five thousand dollars in the past seven years, and—"

"Then he is a genius," I said.

"He's blown every dime of it on parties, nightclubbing, his house, and clothes for his wife," said Hal.

"Hooray," I said. "That's the investment advice I always wanted to give, but nobody would pay for it."

"Well, Krummbein is perfectly happy with his investments," said Hal. "What made him think he might just possibly need a little help was a call from the Internal Revenue Service."

"Oh, oh," I said. "I'll bet he forgot to file a declaration of estimated income for the coming year."

"You lose," said Hal. "This genius has never paid a cent of income taxes—ever! He said he kept expecting them to send him a bill, and they never did." Hal groaned. "Well, brother, they finally got around to it. Some bill!"

"What can I do?" I asked.

"He's got bundles of money coming in all the time—and insists on being paid in cashier's checks," said Hal. "You take care of them while I try to keep him out of prison. I've told him all about you, and he says for you to come out to his house right away."

"What bank does he use?" I said.

"He doesn't use a bank, except to cash the checks, which he keeps in a wicker basket under his drafting table," said Hal. "Get that basket!"

. . . .

Otto's home and place of business is thirty miles from town, in a wilderness by a waterfall. It looks, roughly, like a matchbox resting on a spool. The upper story, the matchbox, has glass walls all the way around, and the lower story, the spool, is a windowless brick cylinder.

There were four other cars in the guest parking area when I arrived. A small cocktail party was in progress. As I was skirting the house, wondering how to get into it, I heard somebody tapping on the inside of a glass wall above. I looked up to see the most startling and, in a bizarre way, one of the most beautiful women of my experience.

She was tall and slender, with a subtly muscled figure sheathed in a zebra-striped leotard. Her hair was bleached silver and touched with blue, and in the white and perfect oval of her face were eyes of glittering green, set off by painted eyebrows, jet black and arched. She wore one earring, a barbaric gold hoop. She was making spiral motions with her hand, and I understood at last that I was to climb the spiral ramp that wound around the brick cylinder.

The ramp brought me up to a catwalk outside the glass walls. A towering, vigorous man in his early thirties slid back a glass panel and invited me in. He wore lavender nylon coveralls and sandals. He was nervous, and there was tiredness in his deep-set eyes.

"Mr. Krummbein?" I said.

"Who else would I be?" said Otto. "And you must be the wizard of high finance. We can go into my studio, where we'll have more privacy, and then"—pointing to the woman—"you can join us in a drink."

His studio was inside the brick cylinder, and he led me through a door and down another spiral ramp into it. There were no windows. All light was artificial.

"Guess this is the most modern house I've ever been in," I said.

"Modern?" said Otto. "It's twenty years behind the times, but it's the best my imagination can do. Everything else is at least a hundred years behind the times, and that is why we have all the unrest, this running to psychiatrists, broken homes, wars. We haven't learned to design our living for our own times. Our lives clash with our times. Look at your clothes! Shades of 1910. You're not dressed for 1954."

"Maybe not," I said, "but I'm dressed for helping people handle money."

"You are being suffocated by tradition," said Otto. "Why don't you say, 'I am going to build a life for myself, for my time, and make it a work of art'? Your life isn't a work of art—it's a thirdhand Victorian whatnot shelf, complete with someone else's collection of seashells and hand-carved elephants."

"Yup," I said, sitting down on a twenty-foot couch. "That's my life, all right."

"Design your life like that Finnish carafe over there," said Otto, "clean, harmonious, alive with the cool, tart soul of truth in our time. Like Falloleen."

"I'll try," I said. "Mostly it's a question of getting my head above water first. What is Falloleen, a new miracle fiber?"

"My wife," said Otto. "She's hard to miss."

"In the leotard," I said.

"Did you ever see a woman who fitted so well into surroundings like this—who seems herself to be designed for contemporary living?" said Otto. "A rare thing, believe me. I've had many famous beauties out here, but Falloleen is the only one who doesn't look like a piece of 1920-vintage overstuffed furniture."

"How long have you been married?" I said.

"The party upstairs is in celebration of one month of blissful marriage," said Otto, "of a honeymoon that will never end."

"How nice," I said. "And now, about your financial picture—"

"Just promise me one thing," he said, "don't be depressing. I can't work if I'm depressed. The slightest thing can throw me off—that tie of yours, for instance. It jars me. I can't think straight when I look at it. Would you mind taking it off? Lemon yellow is your color, not that gruesome maroon."

Half an hour later, tieless, I felt like a man prowling through a city dump surrounded by smoldering tire casings, rusting bed-springs, and heaps of tin cans, for that was the financial picture of Otto Krummbein. He kept no books, bought whatever caught his fancy, without considering the cost, owed ruinous bills all over town for clothes for Falloleen, and didn't have a cent in a savings account, insurance, or a portfolio.

"Look," said Otto, "I'm scared. I don't want to go to prison, I didn't mean to do anything wrong. I've learned my lesson. I promise to do anything you say. Anything! Just don't depress me."

"If you can be cheerful about this mess," I said, "the Lord knows I can. The thing to do, I think, is to save you from your-self by letting me manage your income, putting you on an al-lowance."

"Excellent," said Otto. "I admire a bold approach to prob-lems. And that will leave me free to work out an idea I got on my honeymoon, an idea that is going to make millions. I'll wipe out all this indebtedness in one fell swoop!"

"Just remember," I said, "you're going to have to pay taxes on that, too. You're the first man I ever heard of who got a profitable idea on his honeymoon. Is it a secret?"

"Moonlight-engineered cosmetics," said Otto, "designed expressly, according to the laws of light and color, to make a woman look her best in the moonlight. Millions, zillions!"

"That's swell," I said, "but in the meantime, I'd like to go over your bills to see exactly how deep in you are, and also to figure out what allowance you could get by on at a bare minimum."

"You could go out to supper with us tonight," said Otto, "and then come back and work undisturbed here in the studio. I'm sorry we have to go out, but it's the cook's day off."

"That would suit me fine," I said. "That way I'll have you around to answer questions. There ought to be plenty of those. For instance, how much is in the basket?"

Otto paled. "Oh, you know about the basket?" he said. "I'm afraid we can't use that. That's special."

"In what way?" I said.

"I need it—not for me, for Falloleen," said Otto. "Can't I keep that much, and send you all the royalty checks that come in from now on? It isn't right to make Falloleen suffer because of my mistakes. Don't force me to do that, don't strip me of my self-respect as a husband."

I was fed up, and I stood irritably. "I won't strip you of anything, Mr. Krummbein," I said. "I've decided I don't want the job. I'm not a business manager, anyway. I offered to help as a favor to Hal Murphy, but I didn't know how bad working conditions were. You say I'm trying to strip you, when the truth is that your bones were bleached white on the desert of your own prodigality before I arrived. Is there a secret exit out of this silo," I said, "or do I go out the way I came in?"

"No, no, no," said Otto apologetically. "Please, sit down. You've got to help me. It's just that it's a shock for me to get used to how bad things really are. I thought you'd tell me to give up cigarettes or something like that." He shrugged. "Take the basket and give me my allowance." He covered his eyes. "Entertaining Falloleen on an allowance is like running a Mercedes on Pepsi-Cola."

In the basket was five thousand—odd dollars in royalty checks from manufacturers and about two hundred dollars in cash. As I was making out a receipt for Otto, the studio door opened above us, and Falloleen, forever identified in my mind with a Finnish carafe, came down the ramp gracefully, carrying a tray on which were three martinis.

"I thought your throats might be getting parched," said Falloleen.

"A voice like crystal chimes," said Otto.

"Must I go, or can I stay?" said Falloleen. "It's such a dull party without you, Otto, and I get self-conscious and run out of things to say."

"Beauty needs no tongue," said Otto.

I dusted my hands. "I think we've got things settled for the time being. I'll get down to work in earnest this evening."

"I'm awfully dumb about finances," said Falloleen. "I just leave all that to Otto—he's so brilliant. Isn't he!"

"Yup," I said.

"I was thinking what fun it would be to take our whole party to Chez Armando for dinner," said Falloleen.

Otto looked askance at me.

"We were just talking about love and money," I said to Falloleen, "and I was saying that if a woman loves a man, how much or how little money the man spends on her makes no difference to her. Do you agree?"

Otto leaned forward to hear her answer.

"Where were you brought up?" said Falloleen to me. "On a chicken farm in Saskatchewan?"

Otto groaned.

Falloleen looked at him in alarm. "There's more going on here than I know about," she said. "I was joking. Was that so awful, what I said? It seemed like such a silly question about love and money." Comprehension bloomed on her face. "Otto," she said, "are you broke?"

"Yes," said Otto.

Falloleen squared her lovely shoulders. "Then tell the others to go to Chez Armando without us, that you and I want to spend a quiet evening at home for a change."

"You belong where there are people and excitement," said Otto.

"I get tired of it," said Falloleen. "You've taken me out every night since God knows when. People must wonder if maybe we're afraid to be alone with each other."

Otto went up the ramp to send the guests on their way, leaving Falloleen and me alone on the long couch. Fuddled by her perfume and beauty, I said, "Were you in show business, Mrs. Krummbein?"

"Sometimes I feel like I am," said Falloleen. She looked down at her blue fingernails. "I certainly put on a show wherever I go, don't I?"

"A marvelous show," I said.

She sighed. "I guess it should be a good show," she said. "I've been designed by the greatest designer in the world, the father of the Krummbein Di-Modular Bed."

"Your husband designed you?"

"Didn't you know?" said Falloleen. "I'm a silk purse made out of a sow's ear. He'll design you, too, if he gets the chance. I see he's already made you take off your tie. I'll bet he's told you what your color is, too."

"Lemon yellow," I said.

"Each time he sees you," said Falloleen, "he'll make some suggestion about how to improve your appearance." She ran her hands dispassionately over her spectacular self. "Step by step, one goes a long way."

"You were never any sow's ear," I said.

"One year ago," she said, "I was a plain, brown-haired, dowdy thing, fresh out of secretarial school, starting to work as secretary to the Great Krummbein."

"Love at first sight?" I said.

"For me," murmured Falloleen. "For Otto it was a design problem at first sight. There were things about me that jarred him, that made it impossible for him to think straight when I was around. We changed those things one by one, and what became of Kitty Cahoun, nobody knows."

"Kitty Cahoun?" I said.

"The plain, brown-haired, dowdy thing, fresh out of secretarial school," said Falloleen.

"Then Falloleen isn't your real name?" I said.

"It's a Krummbein original," said Falloleen. "Kitty Cahoun didn't go with the decor." She hung her head. "Love—" she said, "don't ask me any more silly questions about love."

"They're off to Chez Armando," said Otto, returning to the studio. He handed me a yellow silk handkerchief. "That's for you," he said. "Put it in your breast pocket. That dark suit needs it like a forest needs daffodils."

I obeyed, and saw in a mirror that the handkerchief really did give me a little dash, without being offensive. "Thanks very much," I said. "Your wife and I've been having a pleasant time talking about the mysterious disappearance of Kitty Cahoun."

"What ever did become of her?" said Otto earnestly. A look of abject stupidity crossed his face as he realized what he'd said. He tried to laugh it off. "An amazing and amusing demonstration of how the human mind works, wasn't it?" he said. "I'm so used to thinking of you as Falloleen, darling." He changed the subject. "Well, now the maestro is going to cook supper." He laid his hand on my shoulder. "I absolutely insist that you stay. Chicken à la Krummbein, asparagus tips à la Krummbein, potatoes à la—"

"I think I ought to cook supper," said Falloleen. "It's high time the bride got her first meal."

"Won't hear of it," said Otto. "I won't have you suffering for my lack of financial acumen. It would make me feel terrible. Falloleen doesn't belong in a kitchen."

"I know what," said Falloleen, "we'll both get supper. Wouldn't that be cozy, just the two of us?"

"No, no, no, no," said Otto. "I want everything to be a surprise. You stay down here with J. P. Morgan, until I call you. No fair peeking."

"I refuse to worry about it," said Otto, as he, Falloleen, and I cleared away the supper dishes. "If I worry, I can't work, and if I can't work, I can't get any money to bail me out of this mess."

"The important thing is for somebody to worry," I said, "and I guess I'm it. I'll leave you two lovebirds alone up here in the greenhouse while I go to work."

"Man must spend half his time at one with Nature," said Otto, "and half at one with himself. Most houses provide only a muddy, murky in-between." He caught my sleeve. "Listen, don't rush off. All work and no play make Jack a dull boy. Why don't the three of us just have a pleasant social evening, so you can get to know us, and then tomorrow you can start getting down to brass tacks?"

"That's nice of you," I said. "But the quicker I get to work, the quicker you'll be out of the woods. Besides, newlyweds don't want to entertain on their first evening at home."

"Heavens!" said Otto. "We're not newlyweds anymore."

"Yes we are," said Falloleen meekly.

"Of course you are," I said, opening my briefcase. "And you must have an awful lot to say to each other."

"Um," said Otto.

There followed an awkward silence in which Otto and Falloleen stared out into the night through the glass walls, avoiding each other's eyes.

"Didn't Falloleen put on one too many earrings for supper?" said Otto.

"I felt lopsided with just one," said Falloleen.

"Let me be the judge of that," said Otto. "What you don't get is a sense of the whole composition—something a little off-balance here, but lo and behold, a perfect counterbalance down there."

"So you won't capsize," I said, opening the studio door. "Have fun."

"It didn't really jar you, did it, Otto?" said Falloleen guiltily. I closed the door.

The studio was soundproofed, and I could hear nothing of the Krummbeins' first evening at home as I picked over the wreckage of their finances.

I intruded once, with a long list of questions, and found the upstairs perfectly quiet, save for soft music from the phonograph and the rustle of rich, heavy material. Falloleen was turning around in a lazy sort of ballet, wearing a magnificent evening gown. Otto, lying on the couch, watched her through narrowed lids and blew smoke rings.

"Fashion show?" I said.

"We thought it would be fun for me to try on all the things Otto's bought me that I haven't had a chance to wear," said Falloleen. Despite her heavy makeup, her face had taken on a haggard look. "Like it?" she said.

"Very much," I said, and I roused Otto from his torpor to answer my questions.

"Shouldn't I come down and work with you?" he asked.

"Thanks," I said, "but I'd rather you wouldn't. The perfect quiet is just what I need."

Otto was disappointed. "Well, please don't hesitate to call me for anything."

. . . .

An hour later, Falloleen and Otto came down into the studio with cups and a pot of coffee. They smiled, but their eyes were glazed with boredom.

Falloleen had on a strapless gown of blue velveteen, with ermine around the hem and below her white shoulders. She slouched and shuffled. Otto hardly glanced at her.

"Ah-h-h!" I said. "Coffee! Just the thing! Style show all over?"

"Ran out of clothes," said Falloleen. She poured the coffee, kicked off her shoes, and lay down at one end of the couch. Otto lay down at the other end, grunting. The peace of the scene was deceptive. Neither Otto nor Falloleen was relaxed. Falloleen was clenching and unclenching her hands. Every few seconds Otto would click his teeth like castanets.

"You certainly look very lovely, Falloleen," I said. "Are those by any chance moonlight-engineered cosmetics you're wearing?"

"Yes," said Falloleen. "Otto had some samples made up, and I'm a walking laboratory. Fascinating work."

"You're not in moonlight," I said, "but I'd say the experiment was a smashing success."

Otto sat up, refreshed by praise of his work. "You really think so? We had moonlight for most of our honeymoon, and the idea practically forced itself on me."

Falloleen sat up as well, sentimentally interested in the subject of the honeymoon. "I loved going out to glamorous places every evening," she said, "but the evening I liked best was the one when we went canoeing, just the two of us, and the lake and the moon."

"I kept looking at her lips there in the moonlight," said Otto, "and—"

"I was looking at your eyes," said Falloleen.

Otto snapped his fingers. "And then it came to me! By heaven, something was all wrong with ordinary cosmetics in the moonlight. The wrong colors came out, blues and greens. Falloleen looked like she'd just swum the English Channel."

Falloleen slapped him with all her might.

"Whatja do that for?" bellowed Otto, his face crimson from the blow. "You think I've got no sense of pain?"

"You think I haven't?" seethed Falloleen. "You think I'm striated plywood and plastic?"

Otto gasped.

"I'm sick of being Falloleen and the style show that never ends!" Her voice dropped to a whisper. "She's dull and shallow, scared and lost, unhappy and unloved."

She twitched the yellow handkerchief from my breast pocket and wiped it across her face dramatically, leaving a smear of red, pink, white, blue, and black. "You designed her, you deserve her, and here she is!" She pressed the stained handkerchief into Otto's limp hand. Up the ramp she went. "Good-bye!"

"Falloleen!" cried Otto.

She paused in the doorway. "My name is Kitty Cahoun Krummbein," she said. "Falloleen is in your hand."

Otto waved the handkerchief at her. "She's as much yours as she is mine," he said. "You wanted to be Falloleen. You did everything you could to be Falloleen."

"Because I loved you," said Kitty. She was weeping. "She was all your design, all for you."

Otto turned his palms upward. "Krummbein is not infallible," he said. "There was widespread bloodshed when the

American housewife took the Krummbein Vortex Can Opener to her bosom. I thought being Falloleen would make you happy, and it's made you unhappy instead. I'm sorry. No matter how it turned out, it was a work of love."

"You love Falloleen," said Kitty.

"I love the way she looked," said Otto. He hesitated. "Are you really Kitty again?"

"Would Falloleen show her face looking like this?"

"Never," said Otto. "Then I can tell you, Kitty, that Falloleen was a crashing bore when she wasn't striking a pose or making a dramatic entrance or exit. I lived in terror of being left alone with her."

"Falloleen didn't know who she was or what she was," Kitty sobbed. "You didn't give her any insides."

Otto went up to her and put his arms around her. "Sweetheart," he said, "Kitty Cahoun was supposed to be inside, but she disappeared completely."

"You didn't like anything about Kitty Cahoun," said Kitty.

"My dear, sweet wife," said Otto, "there are only four things on earth that don't scream for redesigning, and one of them is the soul of Kitty Cahoun. I thought it was lost forever."

She put her arms around him tentatively. "And the other three?" she said.

"The egg," said Otto, "the Model-T Ford, and the exterior of Falloleen.

"Why don't you freshen up," said Otto, "slip into your lavender negligee, and put a white rose behind your ear, while I straighten things out here with the Scourge of Wall Street?"

"Oh, dear," she said. "I'm starting to feel like Falloleen again."

"Don't be afraid of it," said Otto. "Just make sure this time that Kitty shines through in all her glory."

She left, supremely happy.

"I'll get right out," I said. "Now I know you want to be alone with her."

"Frankly, I do," said Otto.

"I'll open a checking account and hire a safe-deposit box in your name tomorrow," I said.

And Otto said, "Sounds like your kind of thing. Enjoy, enjoy."

Ambitious Sophomore

George M. Helmholtz, head of the music department and director of the band of Lincoln High School, was a good, fat man who saw no evil, heard no evil, and spoke no evil, for wherever he went, the roar and boom and blast of a marching band, real or imagined, filled his soul. There was room for little else, and the Lincoln High School Ten Square Band he led was, as a consequence, as fine as any band on earth.

Sometimes, when he heard muted, wistful passages, real or imagined, Helmholtz would wonder if it wasn't indecent of him to be so happy in such terrible times. But then the brasses and percussion section would put sadness to flight, and Mr. Helmholtz would see that his happiness and its source could only be good and rich and full of hope for everyone.

Helmholtz often gave the impression of a man lost in dreams, but there was a side to him that was as tough as a rhinoceros. It was that side that raised money for the band, that hammered home to the school board, the Parent Teacher Association, Chamber of Commerce, Kiwanis, Rotary, and Lions that the goodness and richness and hope that his band inspired cost money. In his fund-raising harangues, he would recall for his audiences black days for the Lincoln High football team, days when the Lincoln stands had been silent, hurt, and ashamed.

"Half-time," he would murmur, and hang his head.

He would twitch a whistle from his pocket and blow a shrill blast. "Lincoln High School Ten Square Band!" he'd shout. "Forward—harch! Boom! Ta-ta-ta-taaaaaa!" Helmholtz, singing, marching in place, would become flag twirlers, drummers, brasses, woodwinds, glockenspiel and all. By the time he'd marched his one-man band up and down the imaginary football field once, his audience was elated and wringing wet, ready to buy the band anything it wanted.

But no matter how much money came in, the band was always without funds. Helmholtz was a spender when it came to band equipment, and was known among rival bandmasters as "The Plunger" and "Diamond Jim."

Among the many duties of Stewart Haley, Assistant Principal of Lincoln High, was keeping an eye on band finances. Whenever it was necessary for Haley to discuss band finances with Helmholtz, Haley tried to corner the bandmaster where he couldn't march and swing his arms.

Helmholtz knew this, and felt trapped when Haley appeared in the door of the bandmaster's small office, brandishing a bill for ninety-five dollars. Following Haley was a delivery boy from a tailor shop, who carried a suit box under his arm. As Haley closed the office door from inside, Helmholtz hunched over a drawing board, pretending deep concentration.

"Helmholtz," said Haley, "I have here an utterly unexpected, utterly unauthorized bill for—"

"Sh!" said Helmholtz. "I'll be with you in a moment." He drew a dotted line across a diagram that was already a black thicket of lines. "I'm just putting the finishing touches on the Mother's Day formation," he said. "I'm trying to make an arrow pierce a heart and then spell 'Mom.' It isn't easy."

"That's very sweet," said Haley, rattling the bill, "and I'm as fond of mothers as you are, but you've just put a ninety-five-dollar arrow through the public treasury."

Helmholtz did not look up. "I was going to tell you about it," he said, drawing another line, "but what with getting ready for the state band festival and Mother's Day, it seemed unimportant. First things first."

"Unimportant!" said Haley. "You hypnotize the community into buying you one hundred new uniforms for the Ten Square Band, and now—"

"Now?" said Helmholtz mildly.

"This boy brings me a bill for the hundred-and-first uniform!" said Haley. "Give you an inch and—"

Haley was interrupted by a knock. "Come in," said Helmholtz. The door opened, and there stood Leroy Duggan, a shy, droll, slope-shouldered sophomore. Leroy was so self-conscious that when anyone turned to look at him he did a sort of fan dance with his piccolo case and portfolio, hiding himself as well as he could behind them.

"Come right in, Leroy," said Helmholtz.

"Wait outside a moment, Leroy," said Haley. "This is rather urgent business."

Leroy backed out, mumbling an apology, and Haley closed the door again.

"My door is always open to my musicians," said Helmholtz.

"It will be," said Haley, "just as soon as we clear up the mystery of the hundred-and-first uniform."

"I'm frankly surprised and hurt at the administration's lack of faith in my judgment," said Helmholtz. "Running a precision organization of a hundred highly talented young men isn't the simple operation everyone seems to think."

"Simple!" said Haley. "Who thinks it's simple! It's plainly the most tangled, mysterious, expensive mess in the entire school system. You say a hundred young men, but this boy here just delivered the hundred-and-first uniform. Has the Ten Square Band added a tail gunner?"

"No," said Helmholtz. "It's still a hundred, much as I'd like to have more, much as I need them. For instance, I was just trying to figure out how to make *Whistler's Mother* with a hundred men, and it simply can't be done." He frowned. "If we could throw in the girls' glee club we might make it. You're intelligent and have good taste. Would you give me your ideas on the band festival and this Mother's Day thing?"

Haley lost his temper. "Don't try to fuddle me, Helmholtz! What's the extra uniform for?"

"For the greater glory of Lincoln High School!" barked Helmholtz. "For the third leg and permanent possession of the state band festival trophy!" His voice dropped to a whisper, and he glanced furtively at the door. "Specifically, it's for Leroy Duggan, probably the finest piccoloist in this hemisphere. Let's keep our voices down, because we can't discuss the uniform without discussing Leroy."

The conversation became tense whispers.

"And what's the matter with Leroy's wearing one of the uniforms you've already got?" said Haley.

"Leroy is bell-shaped," said Helmholtz. "We don't have a uniform that doesn't bag or bind on him."

"This is a public school, not a Broadway musical!" said Haley. "Not only have we got students shaped liked bells, we've got them shaped like telephone poles, pop bottles, chimpanzees, and Greek gods. There's going to have to be a certain amount of bagging and binding."

"My duty," said Helmholtz, standing, "is to bring the best music out of whoever chooses to come to me. If a boy's shape prevents him from making the music he's capable of making, then it's my duty to get him a shape that will make him play like an angel. This I did, and here we are." He sat down. "If I could be made to feel sorry for this, then I wouldn't be the man for my job."

"A special uniform is going to make Leroy play better?" said Haley.

"In rehearsals, with nobody but fellow musicians around," said Helmholtz, "Leroy has brilliance and feeling that would make you weep and faint. But when Leroy marches, with strangers watching, particularly girls, he gets out of step, stumbles, and can't even play 'Row, Row, Row Your Boat.'" Helmholtz brought his fist down on the desk. "And that's not going to happen at the state band festival!"

The bill in Haley's hand was rumpled and moist now. "The message I came to deliver today," he said, "remains unchanged: You can't get blood out of a turnip. The total cash assets of the band are seventy-five dollars, and there is absolutely no way for the school to provide the remaining twenty—absolutely none."

He turned to the delivery boy. "That is my somber message to you, as well," he said.

"Mr. Kornblum said he was losing money on it as it was," said the delivery boy. "He said Mr. Helmholtz came in and started talking, and before he knew it—"

"Don't worry about a thing," said Helmholtz. He brought out his checkbook and, with a smile and a flourish, wrote a check for twenty dollars.

Haley was ashen. "I'm sorry it has to turn out this way," he said.

Helmholtz ignored him. He took the parcel from the delivery boy and called to Leroy, "Would you come in, please?"

Leroy came in slowly, shuffling, doing his fan dance with the piccolo case and portfolio, apologizing as he came.

"Thought you might like to try on your new uniform for the band festival, Leroy," said Helmholtz.

"I don't think I'd better march," said Leroy. "I'd get all mixed up and ruin everything."

Helmholtz opened the box dramatically. "This uniform's special, Leroy."

"Every time I see one of those uniforms," said Haley, "all I can think of is a road company of *The Chocolate Soldier*. That's the uniform the stars wear, but you've got a hundred of the things—a hundred and one."

Helmholtz removed Leroy's jacket. Leroy stood humbly in his shirtsleeves, relieved of his piccolo case and portfolio, comical, seeing nothing at all comical in being bell-shaped.

Helmholtz slipped the new jacket over Leroy's narrow shoulders. He buttoned the great brass buttons and fluffed up the gold braid cascading from the epaulets. "There, Leroy."

"Zoot!" exclaimed the delivery boy. "Man, I mean zoot!"

Leroy looked dazedly from one massive, jutting shoulder to the other, and then down at the astonishing taper to his hips.

"Rocky Marciano!" said Haley.

"Walk up and down the halls, Leroy," said Helmholtz. "Get the feel of it."

Leroy blundered through the door, catching his epaulets on the frame.

"Sideways," said Helmholtz, "you'll have to learn to go through doors sideways."

"Only about ten percent of what's under the uniform is Leroy," said Haley, when Leroy was out of hearing.

"It's all Leroy," said Helmholtz. "Wait and see—wait until we swing past the reviewing stand at the band festival and Leroy does his stuff."

When Leroy returned to the office, he was marching, knees high. He halted and clicked his heels. His chin was up, his breathing shallow.

"You can take it off, Leroy," said Helmholtz. "If you don't feel up to marching in the band festival, just forget it." He reached across his desk and undid a brass button.

Leroy's hand came up quickly to protect the rest of the buttons. "Please," he said, "I think maybe I could march after all."

"That can be arranged," said Helmholtz. "I have a certain amount of influence in band matters."

Leroy buttoned the button. "Gee," he said, "I walked past the athletic office, and Coach Jorgenson came out like he was shot out of a cannon."

"What did the silent Swede have to say?" said Helmholtz.

"He said that only in this band-happy school would they make a piccolo player out of a man built like a locomotive," said Leroy. "His secretary came out, too."

"Did Miss Bearden like the uniform?" said Helmholtz.

"I don't know," said Leroy. "She didn't say anything. She just looked and looked."

Late that afternoon, George M. Helmholtz appeared in the office of Harold Crane, head of the English Department. Helmholtz was carrying a heavy, ornate gold picture frame and looking embarrassed.

"I hardly know how to begin," said Helmholtz. "I—I thought maybe I could sell you a picture frame." He turned the frame this way and that. "It's a nice frame, isn't it?"

"Yes, it is," said Crane. "I've admired it often in your office. That is the frame you had around John Philip Sousa, isn't it?"

Helmholtz nodded. "I thought maybe you'd like to frame some John Philip Sousa in your line—Shakespeare, Edgar Rice Burroughs."

"That might be nice," said Crane. "But frankly, the need hasn't made itself strongly felt."

"It's a thirty-nine-dollar frame," said Helmholtz. "I'll let it go for twenty."

"Look here," said Crane, "if you're in some sort of jam, I can let you have—"

"No, no, no," said Helmholtz, holding up his hand. Fear crossed his face. "If I started on credit, heaven only knows where it would end."

Crane shook his head. "That's a nice frame, all right, and a real bargain. Sad to say, though, I'm in no shape to lay out twenty dollars for something like that. I've got to buy a new tire for twenty-three dollars this afternoon and—"

"What size?" said Helmholtz.

"Size?" said Crane. "Six-seventy, fifteen. Why?"

"I'll sell you one for twenty dollars," said Helmholtz. "Never been touched."

"Where would you get a tire?" said Crane.

"By a stroke of luck," said Helmholtz, "I have an extra one."

"You don't mean your spare, do you?" said Crane.

"Yes," said Helmholtz, "but I'll never need it. I'll be careful where I drive. Please, you've got to buy it. The money isn't for me, it's for the band."

"What else would it be for?" said Crane helplessly. He took out his billfold.

When Helmholtz got back to his office, and was restoring John Philip Sousa to the frame, Leroy walked in, whistling. He wore the jacket with the boulder shoulders.

"You still here, Leroy?" said Helmholtz. "Thought you went home hours ago."

"Can't seem to take the thing off," said Leroy. "I was trying a kind of experiment with it."

"Oh?"

"I'd walk down the hall past a bunch of girls," said Leroy, "whistling the piccolo part of 'The Stars and Stripes Forever.'"

"And?" said Helmholtz.

"Kept step and didn't miss a note," said Leroy.

The city's main street was cleared of traffic for eight blocks, swept, and lined with bunting for the cream of the state's youth, its high school bands. At one end of the line of march was a great square with a reviewing stand. At the other end were the bands, hidden in alleys, waiting for orders to march.

The band that looked and sounded best to the judges in the reviewing stand would receive a great trophy, donated by the Chamber of Commerce. The trophy was two years old, and bore the name of Lincoln High School as winner twice.

In the alleys, twenty-five bandmasters were preparing secret weapons with which they hoped to prevent Lincoln's winning a third time—special effects with flash powder, flaming batons, pretty cowgirls, and at least one three-inch cannon. But everywhere hung the smog of defeat, save over the bright plumage of the ranks of Lincoln High.

Beside those complacent ranks stood Stewart Haley, Assistant Principal, and, wearing what Haley referred to privately as the uniform of a Bulgarian rear admiral, George M. Helmholtz, Director of the Band.

Lincoln High shared the alley with bands from three other schools, and the blank walls on either side echoed harshly with the shrieks and growls of bands tuning up.

Helmholtz was lighting pieces of punk with Haley's lighter, blowing on them, and passing them in to every fourth man, who had a straight, cylindrical firework under his sash.

"First will come the order 'Prepare to light!'" said Helmholtz. "Ten seconds later, 'Light!' When your left foot strikes the ground, touch your punk to the end of the fuse. The rest of you, when we hit the reviewing stand, I want you to stop playing as though you'd been shot in the heart. And Leroy—"

Helmholtz craned his neck to find Leroy. As he did so, he became aware of a rival drum major, seedy and drab by comparison with Lincoln's peacocks, who had been listening to everything he said.

"What can I do for you?" said Helmholtz.

"Is this the Doormen's Convention?" said the drum major.

Helmholtz did not smile. "You'd do well to stay with your own organization," he said crisply. "You're plainly in need of practice and sprucing up, and time is short."

The drum major walked away, sneering, insolently spinning his baton.

"Now, where's Leroy got to, this time?" said Helmholtz. "He's a disciplinary problem whenever he puts on that uniform. A new man."

"You mean Blabbermouth Duggan?" said Haley. He pointed to Leroy's broad back in the midst of another band. Leroy was talking animatedly to a fellow piccoloist, who happened to be a very pretty girl with golden curls tucked under her cap. "You mean Casanova Duggan?" said Haley.

"Everything's built around Leroy," said Helmholtz. "If anything went wrong with Leroy, we'd be lucky to place second. . . . Leroy!"

Leroy paid no attention.

Leroy was too engrossed to hear Helmholtz. He was too engrossed to notice that the insolent drum major, who had lately called Helmholtz's band a Doormen's Convention, was now examining his broad back with profound curiosity.

The drum major prodded one of Leroy's shoulder pads with the rubber tip of his baton. Leroy gave no sign that he felt it. The drum major laid his hand on Leroy's shoulder and dug his fingers several inches into it. Leroy went on talking.

With an audience gathering, the drum major began a series

of probings with his baton, starting from the outside of Leroy's shoulder and moving in toward the middle, trying to locate the point where padding stopped and Leroy began.

The baton at last found flesh, and Leroy turned in surprise. "What's the idea?" he said.

"Making sure your stuffing's all in place, General," said the drum major. "Spring a leak, and we'll be up to our knees in sawdust."

Leroy reddened. "I don't know what you're talking about," he said.

"Ask your boyfriend to take off his jacket so we can all see his rippling muscles," the drum major said to Leroy's new girl. He challenged Leroy, "Go on, take it off."

"Make me," said Leroy.

"All righty, all righty," said Helmholtz, stepping between the two.

"You think I can't?" said the drum major.

Leroy swallowed and thought for a long time. "I know you can't," he said at last.

The drum major pushed Helmholtz aside and seized Leroy's jacket by its shoulders. Off came the epaulets, then the citation cord, then the sash. Buttons popped off, and Leroy's undershirt showed.

"Now," said the drum major, "we'll simply undo this, and—"

Leroy exploded. He hit the drum major's nose, stripped off his buttons, medals, and braid, hit him in the stomach, and went over to get his baton, with the apparent intention of beating him to death with it.

"Leroy! Stop!" cried Helmholtz in anguish. He wrenched the baton from Leroy. "Just look at you! Look at your new uniform—wrecked!" Trembling, he touched the rents, the threads of missing buttons, the misshapen padding. He raised his hands in a gesture of surrender. "It's all over. We concede—Lincoln High concedes."

Leroy was wild-eyed, unrepentant. "I don't care!" he yelled. "I'm glad!"

Helmholtz called over another bandsman and gave him the keys to his car. "There's a spare uniform in the back," he said numbly. "Go get it for Leroy."

The Lincoln High School Ten Square Band swung smartly along the street, moving toward the bright banners of the reviewing stand. George M. Helmholtz smiled as he marched along the curb beside it. Inside he was ill, angry, and full of dread. With one cruel stroke, Fate had transformed his plan for winning the trophy into the most preposterous anticlimax in band history.

He couldn't bear to look at the young man on whom he had staked everything. He could imagine Leroy with appalling clarity, slouching along, slovenly, lost in a misfit uniform, a jumble of neuroses and costly fabrics. Leroy was to play alone when the band passed in review. Leroy, Helmholtz reflected, would be incapable even of recalling his own name at that point.

Ahead was the first of a series of chalk marks Helmholtz had made on the curb earlier in the day, carefully measured distances from the reviewing stand.

Helmholtz blew his whistle as he passed the mark, and the band struck up "The Stars and Stripes Forever," full-blooded, throbbing, thrilling. It raised the crowd on its toes and put roses in its cheeks. The judges leaned out of the reviewing stand in happy anticipation of the coming splendor.

Helmholtz passed another mark. "Prepare to light!" he shouted. And a moment later, "Light!"

Helmholtz smiled glassily. In five seconds the band would be before the reviewing stand, the music would stop, the fireworks would send American flags into the sky. And then, playing alone, Leroy would tootle pathetically, ridiculously, if he played at all.

The music stopped. Fireworks banged, and up went the parachutes. The Lincoln High School Ten Square Band passed in review, lines straight, plumes high, brass flashing.

Helmholtz almost cried as American flags hung in air from parachutes. Among them, like a cloudburst of diamonds, was the Sousa piccolo masterpiece. Leroy! Leroy!

The bands were massed before the reviewing stand. George M. Helmholtz stood at parade rest before his band, between the great banner bearing the Lincoln High Black Panther on a scarlet field and Old Glory.

When he was called forward to receive the trophy, the bandmaster crossed the broad square to the accompaniment of a snare drum and a piccolo. As he returned with thirty pounds of bronze and walnut, the band played "Lincoln's Foes Shall Wail Tonight," words and music by George M. Helmholtz.

When the parade was dismissed, Assistant Principal Haley hurried from the crowd to shake Helmholtz's hand.

"Shake Leroy's hand," said Helmholtz. "He's the hero." He looked around for Leroy, beaming, and saw the boy was with the pretty blond piccolo player again, more animated than ever. She was responding warmly.

"She doesn't seem to miss the shoulders, does she?" said Helmholtz.

"That's because *he* doesn't miss them anymore," said Haley. "He's a man now, bell-shaped or not."

"He certainly gave his all for Lincoln High," said Helmholtz. "I admire school spirit in a boy."

Haley laughed. "That wasn't school spirit—that was the love song of a full-bodied American male. Don't you know anything about love?"

Helmholtz thought about love as he walked back to his car alone, his arms aching with the weight of the great trophy. If love was blinding, obsessing, demanding, beyond reason, and all the other wild things people said it was, then he had never known it, Helmholtz told himself. He sighed, and supposed he was missing something, not knowing romance.

When he got to his car, he found that the left front tire was flat. He remembered that he had no spare. But he felt nothing more than mild inconvenience. He boarded a streetcar, sat down with the trophy on his lap, and smiled. He was hearing music again.

Bagombo
Snuff Box

This place is new, isn't it?" said Eddie Laird.

He was sitting in a bar in the heart of the city. He was the only customer, and he was talking to the bartender.

"I don't remember this place," he said, "and I used to know every bar in town."

Laird was a big man, thirty-three, with a pleasantly impudent moon face. He was dressed in a blue flannel suit that was plainly a very recent purchase. He watched his image in the bar mirror as he talked. Now and then, one of his hands would stray from the glass to stroke a soft lapel.

"Not so new," said the bartender, a sleepy, fat man in his fifties. "When was the last time you were in town?"

"The war," Laird said.

"Which war was that?"

"Which war?" Laird repeated. "I guess you have to ask people that nowadays, when they talk about war. The second one—the Second *World* War. I was stationed out at Cunningham Field. Used to come to town every weekend I could."

A sweet sadness welled up in him as he remembered his reflection in other bar mirrors in other days, remembered the reflected flash of captain's bars and silver wings.

"This place was built in 'forty-six, and been renovated twice since then," the bartender said.

"Built—and renovated twice," Laird said wonderingly. "Things wear out pretty fast these days, don't they? Can you still get a plank steak at Charley's Steak House for two dollars?"

"Burned down," the bartender said. "There's a J. C. Penney there now."

"So what's the big Air Force hangout these days?" Laird said.

"Isn't one," the bartender said. "They closed down Cunningham Field."

Laird picked up his drink, and walked over to the window to watch the people go by. "I halfway expected the women here to be wearing short skirts still," he said. "Where are all the pretty pink knees?" He rattled his fingernails against the window. A woman glanced at him and hurried on.

"I've got a wife out there somewhere," Laird said. "What do you suppose has happened to *her* in eleven years?"

"A wife?"

"An ex-wife. One of those war things. I was twenty-two, and she was eighteen. Lasted six months."

"What went wrong?"

"Wrong?" Laird said. "I just didn't want to be owned, that's all. I wanted to be able to stick my toothbrush in my hip pocket and take off whenever I felt like it. And she didn't go for that. So . . ." He grinned. "Adiós. No tears, no hard feelings."

He walked over to the jukebox. "What's the most frantically popular song of the minute?"

"Try number seventeen," the bartender said. "I guess I could stand it one more time."

Laird played number seventeen, a loud, tearful ballad of lost love. He listened intently. And at the end, he stamped his foot and winked, just as he had done years before.

"One more drink," Laird said, "and then, by heaven, I'm going to call up my ex-wife." He appealed to the bartender. "That's all right, isn't it? Can't I call her up if I want to?" He laughed. "'Dear Emily Post: I have a slight problem in etiquette. I haven't seen or exchanged a word with my ex-wife for eleven years. Now I find myself in the same city with her—'"

"How do you know she's still around?" the bartender said.

"I called up an old buddy when I blew in this morning. He said she's all set—got just what she wants: a wage slave of a husband, a vine-covered cottage with expansion attic, two kids, and a quarter of an acre of lawn as green as Arlington National Cemetery."

Laird strode to the telephone. For the fourth time that day, he looked up his ex-wife's number, under the name of her second husband, and held a dime an inch above the slot. This time, he let the coin fall. "Here goes nothing," Laird said. He dialed.

A woman answered. In the background, a child shrieked and a radio blabbed.

"Amy?" Laird said.

"Yes?" She was out of breath.

A silly grin spread over Laird's face. "Hey—guess what? This is Eddie Laird."

"Who?"

"Eddie Laird—Eddie!"

"Wait a minute, would you, please?" Amy said. "The baby is making such a terrible racket, and the radio's on, and I've got brownies in the oven, just ready to come out. I can't hear a thing. Would you hold on?"

"Sure."

"Now then," she said, winded, "who did you say this was?"

"Eddie Laird."

She gasped. "Really?"

"Really," Laird said merrily. "I just blew in from Ceylon, by way of Baghdad, Rome, and New York."

"Good heavens," said Amy. "What a shock. I didn't even know if you were alive or dead."

Laird laughed. "They can't kill me, and by heaven, they've sure tried."

"What have you been up to?"

"Ohhhhh—a little bit of everything. I just quit a job flying for a pearling outfit in Ceylon. I'm starting a company of my own, prospecting for uranium up around the Klondike region. Before the Ceylon deal, I was hunting diamonds in the Amazon rain forest, and before that, flying for a sheik in Iraq."

"Like something out of *The Arabian Nights*," said Amy. "My head just swims."

"Well, don't get any glamorous illusions," Laird said. "Most of it was hard, dirty, dangerous work." He sighed. "And how are you, Amy?"

"Me?" said Amy. "How is any housewife? Harassed."

The child began to cry again.

"Amy," said Laird huskily, "is everything all right—between us?"

Her voice was very small. "Time heals all wounds," she said. "It hurt at first, Eddie—it hurt very much. But I've come to understand it was all for the best. You can't help being restless. You were born that way. You were like a caged eagle, mooning, molting."

"And you, Amy, are *you* happy?"

"Very," said Amy, with all her heart. "It's wild and it's messy with the children. But when I get a chance to catch my breath, I can see it's sweet and good. It's what *I* always wanted. So in the end, we both got our way, didn't we? The eagle and the homing pigeon."

"Amy," Laird said, "could I come out to see you?"

"Oh, Eddie, the house is a horror and I'm a witch. I couldn't stand to have you see me like this—after you've come from Ceylon by way of Baghdad, Rome, and New York. What a hideous letdown for someone like you. Stevie had the measles last week, and the baby has had Harry and me up three times a night, and—"

"Now, now," Laird said, "I'll see the real you shining through it all. I'll come out at five, and say hello, and leave again right away. Please?"

On the cab ride out to Amy's home, Laird encouraged himself to feel sentimental about the coming reunion. He tried to daydream about the best of his days with her, but got only fantasies of movie starlet–like nymphs dancing about him with red lips and vacant eyes. This shortcoming of his imagination, like everything else about the day, was a throwback to his salad days in the Air Force. All pretty women had seemed to come from the same mold.

Laird told the cab to wait for him. "This will be short and sweet," he said.

As he walked up to Amy's small, ordinary house, he managed a smile of sad maturity, the smile of a man who has hurt and been hurt, who has seen everything, who has learned a great deal from it all, and who, incidentally, has made a lot of money along the way.

He knocked and, while he waited, picked at the flaking paint on the door frame.

Harry, Amy's husband, a blocky man with a kind face, invited Larry in.

"I'm changing the baby," Amy called from inside. "Be there in two shakes."

Harry was clearly startled by Laird's size and splendor, and Laird looked down on him and clapped his arm in comradely fashion.

"I guess a lot of people would say this is pretty irregular," Laird said. "But what happened between Amy and me was a long time ago. We were just a couple of crazy kids, and we're all older and wiser now. I hope we can all be friends."

Harry nodded. "Why, yes, of course. Why not?" he said. "Would you like something to drink? I'm afraid I don't have much of a selection. Rye or beer?"

"Anything at all, Harry," Laird said. "I've had kava with the Maoris, scotch with the British, champagne with the French, and cacao with the Tupi. I'll have a rye or a beer with you. When in Rome . . ." He dipped into his pocket and brought out a snuff box encrusted with semiprecious gems. "Say, I brought you and Amy a little something." He pressed the box into Harry's hand. "I picked it up for a song in Bagombo."

"Bagombo?" said Harry, dazzled.

"Ceylon," Laird said easily. "Flew for a pearling outfit out there. Pay was fantastic, the mean temperature was seventy-three, but I didn't like the monsoons. Couldn't stand being bottled up in the same rooms for weeks at a time, waiting for the rain to quit. A man's got to get out, or he just goes to pot— gets flabby and womanly."

"Um," said Harry.

Already the small house and the smells of cooking and the clutter of family life were crowding in on Laird, making him want to be off and away. "Nice place you have here," he said.

"It's a little small," Harry said. "But—"

"Cozy," said Laird. "Too much room can drive you nuts. I know. Back in Bagombo, I had twenty-six rooms, and twelve servants to look after them, but they didn't make me happy. They mocked me, actually. But the place rented for seven dollars a month, and I couldn't pass it up, could I?"

Harry started to leave for the kitchen, but stopped in the doorway, thunderstruck. "Seven dollars a month for twenty-six rooms?" he said.

"Turned out I was being taken. The tenant before me got it for three."

"Three," Harry murmured. "Tell me," he said hesitantly, "are there a lot of jobs waiting for Americans in places like that? Are they recruiting?"

"You wouldn't want to leave your family, would you?"

Harry was conscience-stricken. "Oh, no! I thought maybe I could take them."

"No soap," said Laird. "What they want is bachelors. And

anyway, you've got a nice setup here. And you've got to have a specialty, too, to qualify for the big money. Fly, handle a boat, speak a language. Besides, most of the recruiting is done in bars in Singapore, Algiers, and places like that. Now, I'm taking a flier at uranium prospecting on my own, up in the Klondike, and I need a couple of good Geiger counter technicians. Can you repair a Geiger counter, Harry?"

"Nope," said Harry.

"Well, the men I want are going to have to be single, anyway," said Laird. "It's a beautiful part of the world, teeming with moose and salmon, but rugged. No place for women or children. What *is* your line?"

"Oh," said Harry, "credit manager for a department store."

"Harry," Amy called, "would you please warm up the baby's formula, and see if the lima beans are done?"

"Yes, dear," said Harry.

"What did you say, honey?"

"I said yes!" Harry bellowed.

A shocked silence settled over the house.

And then Amy came in, and Laird had his memory refreshed. Laird stood. Amy was a lovely woman, with black hair, and wise brown affectionate eyes. She was still young, but obviously very tired. She was prettily dressed, carefully made-up, and quite self-conscious.

"Eddie, how nice," she said with brittle cheerfulness. "Don't you look well!"

"You, too," Laird said.

"Do I really?" Amy said. "I feel so ancient."

"You shouldn't," Laird said. "This life obviously agrees with you."

"We *have* been very happy," Amy said.

"You're as pretty as a model in Paris, a movie star in Rome."

"You don't mean it." Amy was pleased.

"I do," Laird said. "I can see you now in a Mainbocher suit, your high heels clicking smartly along the Champs-Élysées, with the soft winds of the Parisian spring ruffling your black hair, and with every eye drinking you in—and a gendarme salutes!"

"Oh, Eddie!" Amy cried.

"Have you been to Paris?" said Laird.

"Nope," said Amy.

"No matter. In many ways, there are more exotic thrills in New York. I can see you there, in a theater crowd, with each man falling silent and turning to stare as you pass by. When was the last time you were in New York?"

"Hmmmmm?" Amy said, staring into the distance.

"When were you last in New York?"

"Oh, I've never been there. Harry has—on business."

"Why didn't he take you?" Laird said gallantly. "You can't let your youth slip away without going to New York. It's a young person's town."

"Angel," Harry called from the kitchen, "how can you tell if lima beans are done?"

"Stick a lousy fork into 'em!" Amy yelled.

Harry appeared in the doorway with drinks, and blinked in hurt bewilderment. "Do you have to yell at me?" he said.

Amy rubbed her eyes. "I'm sorry," she said. "I'm tired. We're both tired."

"We haven't had much sleep," Harry said. He patted his wife's back. "We're both a little tense."

Amy took her husband's hand and squeezed it. Peace settled over the house once more.

Harry passed out the drinks, and Laird proposed a toast.

"Eat, drink, and be merry," Laird said, "for tomorrow we could die."

Harry and Amy winced, and drank thirstily.

"He brought us a snuff box from Bagombo, honey," said Harry. "Did I pronounce that right?"

"You've Americanized it a little," said Laird. "But that's about it." He pursed his lips. "*Bagombo.*"

"It's very pretty," said Amy. "I'll put it on my dressing table, and not let the children near it. Bagombo."

"There!" Laird said. "*She* said it just right. It's a funny thing. Some people have an ear for languages. They hear them once, and they catch all the subtle sounds immediately. And some people have a tin ear, and never catch on. Amy, listen, and then repeat what I say: '*Toli! Pakka sahn nebul rokka ta. Si notte loni gin ta tonic.*'"

Cautiously Amy repeated the sentence.

"Perfect! You know what you just said in Buhna-Simca? 'Young woman, go cover the baby, and bring me a gin and tonic on the south terrace.' Now then, Harry, you say, '*Pilla! Sibba tu bang-bang. Libbin hru donna steek!*'"

Harry, frowning, repeated the sentence.

Laird sat back with a sympathetic smile for Amy. "Well, I don't know, Harry. That might get across, except you'd earn a laugh from the natives when you turned your back."

Harry was stung. "What did I say?"

"'Boy!'" Laird translated. "'Hand me the gun. The tiger is in the clump of trees just ahead.'"

"*Pilla!*" Harry said imperiously. "*Sibba tu bang-bang. Libbin hru donna steek!*" He held out his hand for the gun, and the hand twitched like a fish dying on a riverbank.

"Better—much better!" Laird said.

"That *was* good," Amy said.

Harry brushed off their adulation. He was grim, purposeful. "Tell me," he said, "are tigers a problem around Bagombo?"

"Sometimes, when game gets scarce in the jungles, tigers come into the outskirts of villages," Laird said. "And then you have to go out and get them."

"You had servants in Bagombo, did you?" Amy said.

"At six cents a day for a man, and four cents a day for a woman? I guess!" Laird said.

There was the sound of a bicycle bumping against the outside of the house.

"Stevie's home," Harry said.

"I want to go to Bagombo," Amy said.

"It's no place to raise kids," Laird said. "That's the big drawback."

The front door opened, and a good-looking, muscular nine-year-old boy came in, hot and sweaty. He threw his cap at a hook in the front closet and started upstairs.

"Hang up your hat, Stevie!" Amy said. "I'm not a servant who follows you around, gathering things wherever you care to throw them."

"And pick up your feet!" said Harry.

Stevie came creeping down the stairway, shocked and perplexed. "What got into you two all of a sudden?" he said.

"Don't be fresh," Harry said. "Come in here and meet Mr. Laird."

"*Major* Laird," said Laird.

"Hi," said Stevie. "How come you haven't got a uniform on, if you're a Major?"

"Reserve commission," Laird said. The boy's eyes, frank, irreverent, and unromantic, scared him. "Nice boy you have here."

"Oh," Stevie said, "*that* kind of a Major." He saw the snuff box, and picked it up.

"Stevie," Amy said, "put that down. It's one of Mother's treasures, and it's not going to get broken like everything else. Put it down."

"Okay, okay, okay," said Stevie. He set the box down with elaborate gentleness. "I didn't know it was such a treasure."

"Major Laird brought it all the way from Bagombo," Amy said.

"Bagombo, Japan?" Stevie said.

"Ceylon, Stevie," Harry said. "Bagombo is in Ceylon."

"Then how come it's got 'Made in Japan' on the bottom?"

Laird paled. "They export their stuff to Japan, and the Japanese market it for them," he said.

"There, Stevie," Amy said. "You learned something today."

"Then why don't they say it was made in Ceylon?" Stevie wanted to know.

"The Oriental mind works in devious ways," said Harry.

"Exactly," said Laird. "You've caught the whole spirit of the Orient in that one sentence, Harry."

"They ship these things all the way from Africa to Japan?" Stevie asked.

A hideous doubt stabbed Laird. A map of the world swirled in his mind, with continents flapping and changing shape and with an island named Ceylon scuttling through the seven seas. Only two points held firm, and these were Stevie's irreverent blue eyes.

"I always thought it was off India," Amy said.

"It's funny how things leave you when you start thinking about them too hard," Harry said. "Now I've got Ceylon all balled up with Madagascar."

"And Sumatra and Borneo," Amy said. "That's what we get for never leaving home."

Now four islands were sailing the troubled seas in Laird's mind.

"What's the answer, Eddie?" Amy said. "Where *is* Ceylon?"

"It's an island off Africa," Stevie said firmly. "We studied it."

Laird looked around the room and saw doubt on every face but Stevie's. He cleared his throat. "The boy is right," he croaked.

"I'll get my atlas and show you," Stevie said with pride, and ran upstairs.

Laird stood up, weak. "Must dash."

"So soon?" Harry said. "Well, I hope you find lots of uranium." He avoided his wife's eyes. "I'd give my right arm to go with you."

"Someday, when the children are grown," Amy said, "maybe we'll still be young enough to enjoy New York and Paris, and all those other places—and maybe retire in Bagombo."

"I hope so," said Laird. He blundered out the door, and down the walk, which now seemed endless, and into the waiting taxicab. "Let's go," he told the driver.

"They're all yelling at you," said the driver. He rolled down his window so Laird could hear.

"Hey, Major!" Stevie was shouting. "Mom's right, and we're wrong. Ceylon *is* off India."

The family that Laird had so recently scattered to the winds was together again, united in mirth on the doorstep.

"*Pilla!*" called Harry gaily. "*Sibba tu bang-bang. Libbin hru donna steek!*"

"*Toli!*" Amy called back. "*Pakka sahn nebul rokka ta. Si notte loni gin ta tonic.*"

The cab pulled away.

That night, in his hotel room, Laird put in a long-distance call to his second wife, Selma, in a small house in Levittown, Long Island, New York, far, far away.

"Is Arthur doing any better with his reading, Selma?" he asked.

"The teacher says he isn't dull, he's lazy," Selma said. "She says he can catch up with the class anytime he makes up his mind to."

"I'll talk to him when I get home," Laird said. "And the twins? Are they letting you sleep at all?"

"Well, I'm getting two of them out of the way at one crack. Let's look at it that way." Selma yawned agonizingly. "How's the trip going?"

"You remember how they said you couldn't sell potato chips in Dubuque?"

"Yes."

"Well, *I* did," said Laird. "I'm going to make history in this territory. I'll stand *this* town on its ear."

"Are you—" Selma hesitated. "Are you going to call *her* up, Eddie?"

"Naaaaah," Laird said. "Why open old graves?"

"You're not even curious about what's happened to her?"

"Naaaaah. We'd hardly know each other. People change, people change." He snapped his fingers. "Oh, I almost forgot. What did the dentist say about Dawn's teeth?"

Selma sighed. "She needs braces."

"Get them. I'm clicking, Selma. We're going to start living. I bought a new suit."

"It's about time," Selma said. "You've needed one for *so* long. Does it look nice on you?"

"I think so," Laird said. "I love you, Selma."

"I love you, Eddie. Good night."

"Miss you," Laird said. "Good night."

The Powder-Blue Dragon

A thin young man with big grimy hands crossed the sun-softened asphalt of the seaside village's main street, went from the automobile dealership where he worked to the post office. The village had once been a whaling port. Now its natives served the owners and renters of mansions on the beachfront.

The young man mailed some letters and bought stamps for his boss. Then he went to the drugstore next door on business of his own. Two summer people, a man and a woman his age, were coming out as he was going in. He gave them a sullen glance, as though their health and wealth and lazy aplomb were meant to mock him.

He asked the druggist, who knew him well, to cash his own

personal check for five dollars. It was drawn on his account at a bank in the next town. There was no bank in the village. His name was Kiah.

Kiah had moved his money, which was quite a lot, from a savings account into checking. The check Kiah handed the druggist was the first he had ever written. It was in fact numbered 1. Kiah didn't need the five dollars. He worked off the books for the automobile dealer, and was paid in cash. He wanted to make sure a check written by him was really money, would really work.

"My name is written on top there," he said.

"I see that," said the druggist. "You're certainly coming up in the world."

"Don't worry," said Kiah, "it's good." Was it ever good! Kiah thought maybe the druggist would faint if he knew how good that check was.

"Why would I worry about a check from the most honest, hardworking boy in town?" The druggist corrected himself. "A checking account makes you a big man now, just like J. P. Morgan."

"What kind of a car does he drive?" asked Kiah.

"Who?"

"J. P. Morgan."

"He's dead. Is that how you judge people, by the cars they drive?" The druggist was seventy years old, very tired, and looking for somebody to buy his store. "You must have a very low opinion of me, driving a secondhand Chevy." He handed Kiah five one-dollar bills.

Kiah named the Chevy's model instantly: "Malibu."

"I think maybe working for Daggett has made you car-crazy." Daggett was the dealer across the street. He sold foreign sports cars there, and had another showroom in New York City. "How many jobs you got now, besides Daggett?"

"Wait tables at the Quarterdeck weekends, pump gas at Ed's nights." Kiah was an orphan who lived in a boardinghouse. His father had worked for a landscape contractor, his mother as a chambermaid at the Howard Johnson's out on the turnpike. They were killed in a head-on collision in front of the Howard Johnson's when Kiah was sixteen. The police had said the crash was their fault. His parents had no money, and their second-hand Plymouth Fury was totaled, so they didn't even have a car to leave him.

"I worry about you, Kiah," said the druggist. "All work and no play. Still haven't saved enough to buy a car?" It was generally known in the village that Kiah worked such long hours so he could buy a car. He had no girl.

"Ever hear of a Marittima-Frascati?"

"No. And I don't believe anybody else ever heard of one, either."

Kiah looked at the druggist pityingly. "Won the Avignon road race two years in a row—over Jaguars, Mercedes, and everything. Guaranteed to do a hundred and thirty on an open stretch. Most beautiful car in the world. Daggett's got one in his New York place." Kiah went up on his tiptoes. "Nobody's ever seen anything like it around here. Nobody."

"Why don't you ever talk about Fords or Chevrolets or something I've heard of? Marittima-Frascati!"

"No class. That's why I don't talk about them."

"Class! Listen who's talking about class all the time. He sweeps floors, polishes cars, waits tables, pumps gas, and he's got to have class or nothing."

"You dream your dreams, I'll dream mine," Kiah said.

"I dream of being young like you in a village that's as pretty and pleasant as this one is," said the druggist. "You can take class and—"

Daggett, a portly New Yorker who operated his branch show-room only in the summer, was selling a car to an urbane and tweedy gentleman as Kiah walked in.

"I'm back, Mr. Daggett," Kiah said.

Daggett paid no attention to him. Kiah sat down on a chair to wait and daydream. His heart was beating hard.

"It's not for me, understand," the customer was saying. He looked down in amazement at the low, boxy MG. "It's for my boy. He's been talking about one of these things."

"A fine young-man's car," Daggett said. "And reasonably priced for a sports car."

"Now he's raving about some other car, a Mara-something."

"Marittima-Frascati," said Kiah.

Daggett and the customer seemed surprised to find him in the same room.

"Mmmm, yes, that's the name," the customer said.

"Have one in the city. I could get it out here early next week," said Daggett.

"How much?"

"Fifty-six hundred and fifty-one dollars," said Kiah.

Daggett gave a flat, unfriendly laugh. "You've got a good memory, Kiah."

"Fifty-six hundred!" the customer said. "I love my boy, but love's got to draw the line somewhere. I'll take this one." He took a checkbook from his pocket.

Kiah's long shadow fell across the receipt Daggett was making out.

"Kiah, please. You're in the light." Kiah didn't move. "Kiah, what is it you want? Why don't you sweep out the back room or something?"

"I just wanted to say," Kiah said, his breathing shallow, "that when this gentleman is through, I'd like to order the Marittima-Frascati."

"You what?" Daggett stood angrily.

Kiah took out his own checkbook.

"Beat it!" Daggett said.

The customer laughed.

"Do you want my business?" Kiah asked.

"I'll take care of your business, kid, but good. Now sit down and wait."

Kiah sat down until the customer left.

Daggett then walked toward Kiah slowly, his fists clenched. "Now, young man, your funny business almost lost me a sale."

"I'll give you two minutes, Mr. Daggett, to call up the bank and find out if I've got the money, or I'll get my car someplace else."

Daggett called the bank. "George, this is Bill Daggett." He interjected a supercilious laugh. "Look, George, Kiah Higgins wants to write me a check for fifty-six hundred dollars. . . . That's what I said. I swear he does. . . . Okay, I'll wait." He drummed on the desktop and avoided looking at Kiah.

"Fine, George. Thanks." He hung up.

"Well?" Kiah said.

"I made that call to satisfy my curiosity," said Daggett. "Congratulations. I'm very impressed. Back to work."

"It's my money. I earned it," Kiah said. "I worked and saved for four years—four lousy, long years. Now I want that car."

"You've got to be kidding."

"That car is all I can think about, and now it's going to be mine, the damnedest car anybody around here ever saw."

Daggett was exasperated. "The Marittima-Frascati is a plaything for maharajas and Texas oil barons. Fifty-six hundred dollars, boy! What would that leave of your savings?"

"Enough for insurance and a few tanks of gas." Kiah stood. "If you don't want my business . . ."

"You must be sick," said Daggett.

"You'd understand if you'd been brought up here, Mr. Daggett, and your parents had been dead broke."

"Baloney! Don't tell me what it is to be broke till you've been broke in the city. Anyway, what's the car going to do for you?"

"It's going to give me one hell of a good time—and about time. I'm going to do some living, Mr. Daggett. The first of next week, Mr. Daggett?"

The midafternoon stillness of the village was broken by the whir of a starter and the well-bred grumble of a splendid engine.

Kiah sat deep in the lemon-yellow leather cushions of the powder-blue Marittima-Frascati, listening to the sweet thunder that followed each gentle pressure of his toe. He was scrubbed pink, and his hair was freshly cut.

"No fast stuff, now, for a thousand miles, you hear?" Daggett said. He was in a holiday mood, resigned to the bizarre wonder Kiah had wrought. "That's a piece of fine jewelry under the hood, and you'd better treat it right. Keep it under sixty for the first thousand miles, under eighty until three thousand." He laughed. "And don't try to find out what she can really do until you've put five thousand on her." He clapped Kiah on the shoulder. "Don't get impatient, boy. Don't worry—she'll do it!"

Kiah switched on the engine again, seeming indifferent to the crowd gathered around him.

"How many of these you suppose are in the country?" Kiah asked Daggett.

"Ten, twelve." Daggett winked. "Don't worry. All the others are in Dallas and Hollywood."

Kiah nodded judiciously. He hoped to look like a man who had made a sensible purchase and, satisfied with his money's worth, was going to take it home now. The moment for him was beautiful and funny, but he did not smile.

He put the car in gear for the first time. It was so easy. "Pardon me," he said to those in his way. He raced his engine rather than blow his brass choir of horns. "Thank you."

When Kiah got the car onto the six-lane turnpike, he ceased feeling like an intruder in the universe. He was as much a part of it as the clouds and the sea. With the mock modesty of a god traveling incognito, he permitted a Cadillac convertible to pass him. A pretty girl at its wheel smiled down on him.

Kiah touched the throttle lightly and streaked around her. He laughed at the speck she became in his rearview mirror. The temperature gauge climbed, and Kiah slowed the Marittima-Frascati, forgiving himself this one indulgence. Just this once—it had been worth it. This was the life!

The girl and the Cadillac passed him again. She smiled, and

gestured disparagingly at the expanse of hood before her. She loved his car. She hated hers.

At the mouth of a hotel's circular driveway, she signaled with a flourish and turned in. As though coming home, the Marittima-Frascati followed, purred beneath the porte cochere and into the parking lot. A uniformed man waved, smiled, admired, and directed Kiah into the space next to the Cadillac. Kiah watched the girl disappear into the cocktail lounge, each step an invitation to follow.

As he crossed the deep white gravel, a cloud crossed the sun, and in the momentary chill, Kiah's stride shortened. The universe was treating him like an intruder again. He paused on the cocktail lounge steps and looked over his shoulder at the car. There it waited for its master, low, lean, greedy for miles—Kiah Higgins's car.

Refreshed, Kiah walked into the cool lounge. The girl sat alone in a corner booth, her eyes down. She amused herself by picking a wooden swizzle stick to bits. The only other person in the room was the bartender, who read a newspaper.

"Looking for somebody, sonny?"

Sonny? Kiah felt like driving the Marittima-Frascati into the bar. He hoped the girl hadn't heard. "Give me a gin and tonic," he said coldly, "and don't forget the lime."

She looked up. Kiah smiled with the camaraderie of privilege, horsepower, and the open road.

She nodded back, puzzled, and returned her attention to the swizzle stick.

"Here you are, sonny," said the bartender, setting the drink before him. He rattled his newspaper and resumed his reading.

Kiah drank, cleared his throat, and spoke to the girl. "Nice weather," he said.

She gave no sign that he'd said anything. Kiah turned to the bartender, as though it were to him he'd been speaking. "You like to drive?"

"Sometimes," the bartender said.

"Weather like this makes a man feel like really letting his car go full-bore." The bartender turned a page without comment. "But I'm just breaking her in, and I've got to keep her under fifty."

"I guess."

"Big temptation, knowing she's guaranteed to do a hundred and thirty."

The bartender put down his paper irritably. "What's guaranteed?"

"My new car, my Marittima-Frascati."

The girl looked up, interested.

"Your what?" the bartender said.

"My Marittima-Frascati. It's an Italian car."

"It sure don't sound like an American one. Who you driving it for?"

"Who'm I driving it for?"

"Yeah. Who owns it?"

"Who you think owns it? *I* own it."

The bartender picked up his paper again. "*He* owns it. He owns it, and it goes a hundred and thirty. Lucky boy."

Kiah replied by turning his back. "Hello," he said to the girl, with more assurance than he thought possible. "How's the Cad treating you?"

She laughed. "My car, my fiancé, or my father?"

"Your car," Kiah said, feeling stupid for not having a snappier retort.

"Cads always treat me nicely. I remember you now. You were

in that darling little blue thing with yellow seats. I somehow
didn't connect you with the car. You look different. What did
you call it?"

"A Marittima-Frascati."

"Mmmmmm. I could never learn to say that."

"It's a very famous car in Europe," Kiah said. Everything was
going swimmingly. "Won the Avignon road race two years running, you know."

She smiled a bewitching smile. "No! I *didn't* know that."

"Guaranteed to go a hundred and thirty."

"Goodness. I didn't think a car could go that fast."

"Only about twelve in the country, if *that.*"

"Certainly isn't many, is it? Do you mind my asking how
much one of those wonderful cars costs?"

Kiah leaned back against the bar. "No, I don't mind. Seems
to me it was somewhere between five and six."

"Oh, between *those*, is it? Quite something to be between."

"Oh, I think it's well worth it. I certainly don't feel I've
thrown any money down a sewer."

"That's the important thing."

Kiah nodded happily, and stared into the wonderful eyes,
whose admiration seemed bottomless. He opened his mouth
to say more, to keep the delightful game going forever and
ever, when he realized he had nothing more to say. "Nice
weather."

A glaze of boredom formed on her eyes. "Have you got the
time?" she asked the bartender.

"Yes, ma'am. Seven after four."

"What did you say?" asked Kiah.

"Four, sonny."

A ride, Kiah thought, maybe she'd like to go for a ride.

The door swung open. A handsome young man in tennis shorts blinked and grinned around the room, poised, vain, and buoyant. "Marion!" he cried. "Thank heaven you're still here. What an angel you are for waiting for me!"

Her face was stunning with adoration. "You're not very late, Paul, and I forgive you."

"Like a fool, I let myself get into a game of doubles, and it just went on and on. I finally threw the game. I was afraid I'd lose you forever. What've you been up to while you've been waiting?"

"Let me see. Well, I tore up a swizzle stick, and I, uh— Ohhhhhh! I met an extremely interesting gentleman who has a car that will go a hundred and thirty miles an hour."

"Well, you've been slickered, dear, because the man was lying about his car."

"Those are pretty strong words," Marion said.

Paul looked pleased. "They are?"

"Considering that the man you called a liar is right here in this room."

"Oh, my." Paul looked around the room with a playful expression of fear. His eyes passed over Kiah and the bartender. "There are only four of us here."

She pointed to Kiah. "That boy there. Would you mind telling Paul about your Vanilla Frappé?"

"Marittima-Frascati," Kiah said, his voice barely audible. He repeated it, louder. "Marittima-Frascati."

"Well," Paul said, "I must say it sounds like it'd go two hundred a second. Have you got it here?"

"Outside," Kiah said.

"That's what I meant," Paul said. "I must learn to express myself with more precision." He looked out over the parking lot. "Oho, I see. The little blue jobbie. Ver-ry nice, scary but gorgeous. And that's yours?"

"I said it was."

"Might be the second-fastest car in these parts. Probably is."

"Is that a fact?" Kiah said sarcastically. "I'd like to see the first."

"Would you? It's right outside, too. There, the green one."

The car was a British Hampton. Kiah knew the car well. It was the one he'd begun saving for before Daggett showed him pictures of the Marittima-Frascati.

"It'll do," Kiah said.

"Do, will it?" Paul laughed. "It'll do yours in, and I'll bet anything you like."

"Listen," said Kiah, "I'd bet the world on my car against yours, if mine was broken in."

"Pity," said Paul. "Another time, then." He explained to Marion, "Not broken in, Marion. Shall we go?"

"I'm ready, Paul," she said. "I'd better tell the attendant I'll be back for the Cadillac, or he'll think I've been kidnapped."

"Which is exactly what is about to happen," said Paul. "Be seeing you, Ralph," he said to the bartender. They knew each other.

"Always glad to see you, Paul," said Ralph.

So Kiah now knew the names of all three, but they didn't know what his name was. Nobody had asked. Nobody cared. What could matter less than what his name was?

Kiah watched through a window as Marion spoke to the parking attendant, and then eased herself down into the passenger seat of the low-slung Hampton.

Ralph asked the nameless one this: "You a mechanic? Somebody left that car with you, and you took it out for a road test? Better put the top up, because it's gonna rain."

The rear wheels of the powder-blue dragon with the lemon-yellow leather bucket seats sprayed gravel at the parking attendant's legs. A doorman beneath the porte cochere signaled for it to slow down, then jumped for his life.

Kiah was encouraging it softly, saying, "That's good, let's go, let's go. I love yah," and so on. He steered, and shifted the synchromesh gears so the car could go ever faster smoothly, but he felt doing all that was really unnecessary, that the car itself knew better than he did where to go and how to do what it had been born to do.

The only Marittima-Frascati for thousands of miles swept past cars and trucks as though they were standing still. The needle of the temperature gauge on the padded dashboard was soon trembling against the pin at the extreme end of the red zone.

"Good girl," said Kiah. He talked to the car sometimes as though it were a girl, sometimes as though it were a boy.

It overtook the Hampton, which was going only a hair over the speed limit. The Marittima-Frascati had to slow a lot, so it could run alongside the Hampton and Kiah could give Marion and Paul the finger.

Paul shook his head and waved Kiah on, then applied his brakes to drop far behind. There would be no race.

"He's got no guts, baby," said Kiah. "Let's show the world what guts are." He pressed the accelerator to the floor. As blurs loomed before him and vanished, he kept it there.

The engine was shrieking in agony now, and Kiah said in a matter-of-fact tone, "Explode, explode."

But the engine didn't explode or catch fire. Its precious jewels simply merged with one another, and the engine ceased to be an engine. Nor was the clutch a clutch anymore. That allowed the car to roll into the breakdown lane of the highway, powered by nothing but the last bit of momentum it would ever have on its own.

The Hampton, with Paul and Marion aboard, never passed. They must have gotten off at some exit far behind, Kiah thought.

Kiah left the car where it died. He thumbed a ride back to the village, without having to give his lift a story of any kind. He returned to Daggett's showroom and acted as though he was there to work. The MG was still on the floor. The man who said he would buy it for his son had changed his mind.

"I gave you the whole day off," said Daggett.

"I know," said Kiah.

"So where's the car?"

"I killed it."

"You what?"

"I got it up to one forty-four, when they said it could only do one thirty-five."

"You're joking."

"Wait'll you see," said Kiah. "That's one dead sports vehicle. You'll have to send the tow truck."

"My God, boy, why would you do such a thing?"

"Call me Kiah."

"Kiah," echoed Daggett, convinced he was dealing with a lunatic.

"Who knows why anybody does anything?" said Kiah. "I don't know why I killed it. All I know is I'm glad it's dead."

A Present for
Big Saint Nick

Big Nick was said to be the most recent heir to the power of Al Capone. He refused to affirm or deny it, on the grounds that he might tend to incriminate himself.

He bought whatever caught his fancy, a twenty-three-room house outside Chicago, a seventeen-room house in Miami, racehorses, a ninety-foot yacht, one hundred fifteen suits, and among other things, controlling interest in a middleweight boxer named Bernie O'Hare, the Shenandoah Blaster.

When O'Hare lost sight in one eye on his way to the top of his profession, Big Nick added him to his squad of bodyguards.

Big Nick gave a party every year, a little before Christmas, for the children of his staff, and on the morning of the day of the party, Bernie O'Hare, the Shenandoah Blaster, went shopping in downtown Chicago with his wife, Wanda, and their four-year-old son, Willy.

The three were in a jewelry store when young Willy began to complain and cling to his father's trousers like a drunken bell-ringer.

Bernie, a tough, scarred, obedient young thug, set down a velvet-lined tray of watches and grabbed the waist of his trousers. "Let go my pants, Willy! Let go!" He turned to Wanda. "How'm I supposed to pick a Christmas present for Big Nick with Willy pulling my pants down? Take him off me, Wan. What ails the kid?"

"There must be a Santa Claus around," said Wanda.

"There ain't no Santy Clauses in jewelry stores," said Bernie. "You ain't got no Santy Claus in here, have you?" he asked the clerk.

"No, sir," said the clerk. His face bloomed, and he leaned over the counter to speak to Willy. "But if the little boy would like to talk to old Saint Nick, I think he'll find the jolly old elf right next—"

"Can it," said Bernie.

The clerk paled. "I was just going to say, sir, that the department store next door has a Santa Claus, and the little—"

"Can'tcha see you're making the kid worse?" said Bernie. He knelt by Willy. "Willy boy, there ain't no Santy Clauses around for miles. The guy is full of baloney. There ain't no Santy next door."

"There, Daddy, there," said Willy. He pointed a finger at a tiny red figure standing by a clock behind the counter.

"Cripes!" said Bernie haggardly, slapping his knee. "The kid's got a eye like a eagle for Santy Clauses." He gave a fraudulent laugh. "Why, say, Willy boy, I'm surprised at you. That's just a little *plastic* Santy. He can't hurt you."

"I hate him," said Willy.

"How much you want for the thing?" said Ernie.

"The plastic Santa Claus, sir?" said the bewildered clerk. "Why, it's just a little decoration. I think you can get one at any five-and-ten-cent store."

"I want that one," said Bernie. "Right now."

The clerk gave it to him. "No charge," he said. "Be our guest."

Bernie dropped the Santa Claus on the terrazzo floor. "Watch what Daddy's going to do to Old Whiskers, Willy," he said. He brought his heel down. "Keeeeee-runch!"

Willy smiled faintly, then began to laugh as his father's heel came down again and again.

"Now you do it, Willy," said Bernie. "Who's afraid of *him*, eh?"

"I'll bust his ol' head off," said Willy gleefully. "Crunch him up!" He himself trampled Father Christmas.

"That was *real* smart," said Wanda. "You make me spend all year trying to get him to like Santa Claus, and then you pull a stunt like that."

"I hadda do something to make him pipe down, didn't I?" said Bernie. "Okay, okay. Now maybe we can have a little peace and quiet so I can look at the watches. How much is this one with the diamonds for numbers?"

"Three hundred dollars, sir, including tax," said the clerk.

"Does it glow in the dark? It's gotta glow in the dark."

"Yes, sir, the face is luminous."

"I'll take it," said Bernie.

"Three hundred bucks!" said Wanda, pained. "Holy smokes, Bernie."

"Whaddya mean, holy smokes?" said Bernie. "I'm ashamed to give him a little piece of junk like this. What's a lousy three-hundred-dollar watch to Big Nick? You kick about this, but I don't hear you kicking about the way the savings account keeps going up. Big Nick *is* Santy Claus, whether you like it or not."

"I don't like it," said Wanda. "And neither does Willy. Look at the poor kid—Christmas is ruined for him."

"Aaaaah, now," said Bernie, "it ain't that bad. It's real warm-hearted of Big Nick to wanna give a party for the kids. I mean, no matter how it comes out, he's got the right idea."

"Some heart!" said Wanda. "Some idea! He gets dressed up in a Santa Claus suit so all the kids'll worship him. And he tops that off by makin' the kids squeal on their parents."

Bernie nodded in resignation. "What can I do?"

"Quit," said Wanda. "Work for somebody else."

"What else I know how to do, Wan? All I ever done was fight, and where else am I gonna make money like what Big Nick pays me? Where?"

A tall, urbane gentleman with a small mustache came up to the adjoining counter, trailed by a wife in mink and a son. The son was Willy's age, and was snuffling and peering apprehensively over his shoulder at the front door.

The clerk excused himself and went to serve the genteel new arrivals.

"Hey," said Bernie, "there's Mr. and Mrs. Pullman. You remember them from last Christmas, Wan."

"Big Nick's accountant?" said Wanda.

"Naw, his lawyer." Bernie saluted Pullman with a wave of his hand. "Hi, Mr. Pullman."

"Oh, hello," said Pullman without warmth. "Big Nick's bodyguard," he explained to his wife. "You remember him from the last Christmas party."

"Doing your Christmas shopping late like everybody else, I see," said Bernie.

"Yes," said Pullman. He looked down at his child, Richard. "Can't you stop snuffling?"

"It's psychosomatic," said Mrs. Pullman. "He snuffles every time he sees a Santa Claus. You can't bring a child downtown at Christmastime and not have him see a Santa Claus *somewhere*. One came out of the cafeteria next door just a minute ago. Scared poor Richard half to death."

"I won't have a snuffling son," said Pullman. "Richard! Stiff upper lip! Santa Claus is your friend, my friend, everybody's friend."

"I wish he'd stay at the North Pole," said Richard.

"And freeze his nose off," said Willy.

"And get ate up by a polar bear," said Richard.

"*Eaten* up by a polar bear," Mrs. Pullman corrected.

"Are you encouraging the boy to hate Santa Claus?" said Mr. Pullman.

"Why pretend?" said Mrs. Pullman. "*Our* Santa Claus *is* a dirty, vulgar, prying, foulmouthed, ill-smelling fake."

The clerk's eyes rolled.

"Sometimes, dear," said Pullman, "I wonder if you remember what we were like before we met that jolly elf. Quite broke."

"Give me integrity or give me death," said Mrs. Pullman.

"Shame comes along with the money," said Pullman. "It's a package deal. And we're in this thing together." He addressed the clerk. "I want something terribly overpriced and in the worst possible taste, something, possibly, that glows in the dark and has a barometer in it." He pressed his thumb and forefinger together in a symbol of delicacy. "Do you sense the sort of thing I'm looking for?"

"I'm sorry to say you've come to the right place," said the clerk. "We have a model of the *Mayflower* in chromium, with a red light that shines through the portholes," he said. "However, *that* has a clock instead of a barometer. We have a silver statuette of Man o' War with rubies for eyes, and *that's* got a barometer. Ugh."

"I wonder," said Mrs. Pullman, "if we couldn't have Man o' War welded to the poop deck of the *Mayflower*?"

"You're on the right track," said Pullman. "You surprise me. I didn't think you'd ever get the hang of Big Nick's personality." He rubbed his eyes. "Oh Lord, what does he need, what does he need? Any ideas, Bernie?"

"Nothing," said Bernie. "He's got seven of everything. But he says he still likes to get presents, just to remind him of all the friends he's got."

"He *would* think that was the way to count them," said Pullman.

"Friends are important to Big Nick," said Bernie. "He's gotta be told a hunnerd times a day everybody loves him, or he starts bustin' up the furniture an' the help."

Pullman nodded. "Richard," he said to his son, "do you remember what you are to tell Santa Claus when he asks what Mommy and Daddy think of Big Nick?"

"Mommy and Daddy love Big Nick," said Richard. "Mommy and Daddy think he's a real gentleman."

"What're you gonna say, Willy?" Bernie asked his own son.

"Mommy and Daddy say they owe an awful lot to Big Nick," said Willy. "Big Nick is a kind, generous man."

"Ev-ry-bo-dy loves Big Nick," said Wanda.

"Or they wind up in Lake Michigan with cement overshoes," said Pullman. He smiled at the clerk, who had just brought him the *Mayflower* and Man o' War. "They're fine as far as they go," he said. "But do they glow in the dark?"

Bernie O'Hare was the front-door guard at Big Nick's house on the day of the party. Now he admitted Mr. and Mrs. Pullman and their son.

"Ho ho ho," said Bernie softly.

"Ho ho ho," said Pullman.

"Well, Richard," said Bernie to young Pullman, "I see you're all calmed down."

"Daddy gave me half a sleeping tablet," said Richard.

"Has the master of the house been holding high wassail?" said Mrs. Pullman.

"I beg your pardon?" said Bernie.

"Is he drunk?" said Mrs. Pullman.

"Do fish swim?" said Bernie.

"Did the sun rise?" said Mr. Pullman.

A small intercom phone on the wall buzzed. "Yeah. Nick?" said Bernie.

"They all here yet?" said a truculent voice.

"Yeah, Nick. The Pullmans just got here. They're the last. The rest are sitting in the living room."

"Do your stuff." Nick hung up.

Bernie sighed, took a string of sleighbells from the closet, turned off the alarm system, and stepped outside into the shrubbery.

He shook the sleighbells and shouted. "Hey! It's Santy

Claus! And Dunder and Blitzen and Dancer and Prancer! Oh, boy! They're landing on the roof! Now Santy's coming in through an upstairs bedroom window!"

He went back inside, hid the bells, bolted and chained the door, reset the alarm system, and went into the living room, where twelve children and eight sets of parents sat silently.

All the men in the group worked for Nick. Bernie was the only one who looked like a hoodlum. The rest looked like ordinary, respectable businessmen. They labored largely in Big Nick's headquarters, where brutality was remote. They kept his books and gave him business and legal advice, and applied the most up-to-date management methods to his varied enterprises. They were a fraction of his staff, the ones who had children young enough to believe in Santa Claus.

"Merry Christmas!" said Santa Claus harshly, his big black boots clumping down the stairs.

Willy squirmed away from his mother and ran to Bernie for better protection.

Santa Claus leaned on the newel post, a cigar jutting from his cotton beard, his beady eyes traveling malevolently from one face to the next. Santa Claus was fat and squat and pasty-faced. He reeked of booze.

"I just got down from me workshop at the Nort' Pole," he said challengingly. "Ain't nobody gonna say hi to ol' Saint Nick?"

All around the room parents nudged children who would not speak.

"Talk it up!" said Santa. "This ain't no morgue." He pointed a blunt finger at Richard Pullman. "You been a good boy, heh?"

Mr. Pullman squeezed his son like a bagpipe.

"Yup," piped Richard.

"Ya sure?" said Santa suspiciously. "Ain't been fresh wit' grown-ups?"

"Nope," said Richard.

"Okay," said Santa. "Maybe I got a electric train for ya, an' maybe I don't." He rummaged through a pile of parcels under the tree. "Now, where'd I put that stinkin' train?" He found the parcel with Richard's name on it. "Want it?"

"Yup," said Richard.

"Well, *act* like you want it," said Santa Claus.

Young Richard could only swallow.

"Ya know what it cost?" said Santa Claus. "Hunnerd and twenny-four fifty." He paused dramatically. "*Wholesale.*" He leaned over Richard. "Lemme hear you say t'anks."

Mr. Pullman squeezed Richard.

"T'anks," said Richard.

"T'anks. I guess," said Santa Claus with heavy irony. "You never got no hunnerd-and-twenny-four-fifty train from your old man, I'll tell you that. Lemme tell you, kid, he'd still be chasin' ambulances an' missin' payments on his briefcase if it wasn't for me. An' don't nobody forget it."

Mr. Pullman whispered something to his son.

"What was that?" said Santa. "Come on, kid, wha'd your old man say?"

"He said sticks and stones could break his bones, but words would never hurt him." Richard seemed embarrassed for his father. So did Mrs. Pullman, who was hyperventilating.

"Ha!" said Santa Claus. "That's a hot one. I bet he says that one a hunnerd times a day. What's he say about Big Nick at home, eh? Come on, Richard, this is Santa Claus you're talkin' to, and I keep a book about kids that don't tell the trut' up at the Nort' Pole. What's he really t'ink of Big Nick?"

Pullman looked away as though Richard's reply couldn't concern him less.

"Mommy and Daddy say Big Nick is a real gentleman," recited Richard. "Mommy and Daddy love Big Nick."

"Okay, kid," said Santa, "here's your train. You're a good boy."

"T'anks," said Richard.

"Now I got a big doll for little Gwen Zerbe," said Santa, taking another parcel from under the tree. "But first come over here, Gwen, so you and me can talk where nobody can hear us, eh?"

Gwen, propelled by her father, Big Nick's chief accountant, minced over to Santa Claus. Her father, a short, pudgy man, smiled thinly, strained his ears to hear, and turned green. At the end of the questioning, Zerbe exhaled with relief and got some of his color back. Santa Claus was smiling. Gwen had her doll.

"Willy O'Hare!" thundered Santa Claus. "Tell Santy the trut', and ya get a swell boat. What's your old man and old lady say about Big Nick?"

"They say they owe him a lot," said Willy dutifully.

Santa Claus guffawed. "I guess they do, boy! Willy, you know where your old man'd be if it wasn't for Big Nick? He'd be dancin' aroun' in little circles, talking to hisself, wit'out nuttin' to his name but a flock of canaries in his head. Here, kid, here's your boat, an' Merry Christmas."

"Merry Christmas to you," said Willy politely. "Please, could I have a rag?"

"A rag?" said Santa.

"Please," said Willy. "I wanna wipe off the boat."

"Willy!" said Bernie and Wanda together.

"Wait a minute, wait a minute," said Santa. "Let the kid talk. *Why* you wanna wipe it off, Willy?"

"I want to wipe off the blood and dirt," said Willy.

"Blood!" said Santa. "Dirt!"

"Willy!" cried Bernie.

"Mama says everything we get from Santa's got blood on it," said Willy. He pointed at Mrs. Pullman. "And that lady says he's dirty."

"No I didn't, no I didn't," said Mrs. Pullman.

"Yes you did," said Richard. "I heard you."

"My father," said Gwen Zerbe, breaking the dreadful silence, "says kissing Santa Claus isn't any worse than kissing a dog."

"Gwen!" cried her father.

"I kiss the dog all the time," said Gwen, determined to complete her thought, "and I never get sick."

"I guess we can wash off the blood and dirt when we get home," said Willy.

"Why, you fresh little punk!" roared Santa Claus, bringing his hand back to hit Willy.

Bernie stood quickly and clasped Santa's wrists. "Please," he said, "the kid don't mean nothing."

"Take your filt'y hands off me!" roared Santa. "You wanna commit suicide?"

Bernie let go of Santa.

"Ain't you gonna say nuttin'?" said Santa. "I t'ink I got a little apology comin'."

"I'm very sorry, Santa Claus," said Bernie. His big fist smashed Santa's cigar all over his face. Santa went reeling into the Christmas tree, clawing down ornaments as he fell.

Childish cheers filled the room. Bernie grinned broadly and clasped his hands over his head, a champ!

"Shut them kids up!" Santa Claus sputtered. "Shut them up, or you're all dead!"

Parents scuffled with their children, trying to muzzle them, and the children twisted free, hooting and jeering and booing Santa Claus.

"Make him eat his whiskers, Bernie!"

"Feed him to the reindeers!"

"You're all t'rough! You're all dead!" shouted Santa Claus, still on his back. "I get bums like you knocked off for twenty-five bucks, five for a hunnerd. Get out!"

The children were so happy! They danced out of the house without their coats, saying things like, "Jingle bells, you old poop," and "Eat tinsel, Santy," and so on. They were too innocent to realize that nothing had changed in the economic structure in which their parents were still embedded. In so many movies they'd seen, one punch to the face of a bad guy by a good guy turned hell into an earthly paradise.

Santa Claus, flailing his arms, drove their parents after them. "I got ways of findin' you no matter where you go! I been good to you, and this is the thanks I get. Well, you're gonna get thanks from me, in spades. You bums are all gonna get rubbed out."

"My dad knocked Santa on his butt!" crowed Willy.

"I'm a dead man," said O'Hare to his wife.

"I'm a dead woman," she said, "but it was almost worth it. Look how happy the children are."

They could expect to be killed by a hit man, unless they fled to some godforsaken country where the Mafia didn't have a chapter. So could the Pullmans.

Saint Nicholas disappeared inside the house, then reappeared with another armload of packages in Christmas wrappings. His white cotton beard was stained red from a nosebleed. He stripped the wrappings from one package, held up a cigarette lighter in the form of a knight in armor. He read the enclosed card aloud: "'To Big Nick, the one and only. Love you madly.'" The signature was that of a famous movie star out in Hollywood.

Now Saint Nicholas showed off another pretty package. "Here's one comes all the way from a friend in Italy." He gave its red ribbon a mighty yank. The explosion not only blew off his bloody beard and fur-trimmed red hat, but removed his chin and nose as well. What a mess! What a terrible thing for the young to see, one would think, but they wouldn't have missed it for the world.

After the police left, and the corpse was carted off to the morgue, dressed like Kris Kringle from the neck down, O'Hare's wife said this: "I don't think this is a Christmas the children are going to forget very soon. I know I won't."

Their son Willy had a souvenir that would help him remember. He had found the greeting card that came with the bomb. It was in the shrubbery. It said, "Merry Christmas to the greatest guy in the world." It was signed "The Family."

There would be a rude awakening, of course. The fathers were going to have to find new jobs, ho ho.

Unpaid Consultant

Most married women won't meet an old beau for cocktails, send him a Christmas card, or even look him straight in the eye. But if they happen to need something an old beau sells—anything from an appendectomy to venetian blinds—they'll come bouncing back into his life, all pink and smiling, to get it for wholesale or less.

If a Don Juan were to go into the household appliance business, his former conquests would ruin him inside of a year.

What I sell is good advice on stocks and bonds. I'm a contact man for an investment counseling firm, and the girls I've lost, even by default, never hesitate to bring their investment problems to me.

I am a bachelor, and in return for my services, which after all cost me nothing, they sometimes offer me that jewel beyond price—the home-cooked meal.

The largest portfolio I ever examined, in return for nostalgia and chicken, country style, was the portfolio of Celeste Divine. I lost Celeste in high school, and we didn't exchange a word for seventeen years, until she called me at my office one day to say, "Long time no see."

Celeste Divine is a singer. Her hair is black and curly, her eyes large and brown, her lips full and glistening. Painted and spangled and sheathed in gold lamé, Celeste is before the television cameras for one hour each week, making love to all the world. For this public service she gets five thousand dollars a week.

"I've been meaning to have you out for a long time," said Celeste to me. "What would you say to home-cooked chicken, Idaho potatoes, and strawberry shortcake?"

"Mmmmmmmmm," I said.

"And after supper," said Celeste, "you and Harry and I can sit before a roaring fire and talk about old times and old friends back home."

"Swell," I said. I could see the firelight playing over the columns of figures, *The Wall Street Journal*, the prospectuses and graphs. I could hear Celeste and her husband Harry murmuring about the smell of new-mown hay, American Brake Shoe preferred, moonlight on the Wabash, Consolidated Edison three-percent bonds, cornbread, and Chicago, Milwaukee, St. Paul, and Pacific common.

"We've only been away from here for two years," said Celeste, "but it seems like a lifetime, so much has happened. It'll be good to see somebody from back home."

"You really came up fast, didn't you, Celeste," I said.

"I feel like Cinderella," said Celeste. "One day, Harry and I were struggling along on his pay from Joe's Greasing Palace, and the next day, everything I touched seemed to turn to gold."

It wasn't until I'd hung up that I began wondering how Harry felt.

Harry was the man I'd lost Celeste to. I remembered him as a small, good-looking, sleepy boy, who asked nothing more of life than the prettiest wife in town and a decent job as an automobile mechanic. He got both one week after graduation.

When I went to the Divine home for supper, Celeste herself, with the body of a love goddess and the face of a Betsy Wetsy, let me in.

The nest she'd bought for herself and her mate was an old mansion on the river, as big and ugly as the Schenectady railroad station.

She gave me her hand to kiss, and befuddled by her beauty and perfume, I kissed it.

"Harry? Harry!" she called. "Guess who's here."

I expected to see either a cadaver or a slob, the remains of Harry, come shuffling in.

But there was no response from Harry.

"He's in his study," said Celeste. "How that man can concentrate! When he gets something on his mind, it's just like he was in another world." She opened the study door cautiously. "You see?"

Lying on his back on a tiger-skin rug was Harry. He was staring at the ceiling. Beside him was a frosty pitcher of martinis, and in his fingers he held a drained glass. He rolled the olive in it around and around and around.

"Darling," said Celeste to Harry, "I hate to interrupt, dear."

"What? What's that?" said Harry, startled. He sat up. "Oh! I beg your pardon. I didn't hear you come in." He stood and shook my hand forthrightly, and I saw that the years had left him untouched.

Harry seemed very excited about something, but underneath his excitement was the sleepy contentment I remembered from high school. "I haven't any right to relax," he said. "Everybody in the whole damn industry is relaxing. If I relax, down comes the roof. Ten thousand men out of jobs." He seized my arm. "Count their families, and you've got a city the size of Terre Haute hanging by a thread."

"I don't understand," I said. "Why are they hanging by a thread?"

"The industry!" said Harry.

"What industry?" I said.

"The catchup industry," said Celeste.

Harry looked at me. "What do *you* call it? Catchup? Ketchup? Catsup?"

"I guess I call it different things at different times," I said.

Harry slammed his hand down on the coffee table. "There's the story of the catchup-ketchup-catsup industry in a nutshell! They can't even get together on how to spell the name of the product. If we can't even hang together that much," he said, "we'll all hang separately. Does one automobile manufacturer call automobiles 'applemobiles,' and another one 'axlemobiles,' and another one 'urblemowheels'?"

"Nope," I said.

"You bet they don't," said Harry. He filled his glass, motioned us to chairs, and lay down again on the tiger skin.

"Harry's found himself," said Celeste. "Isn't it marvelous?

He was at loose ends so long. We had some terrible scenes after we moved here, didn't we, Harry?"

"I was immature," said Harry. "I admit it."

"And then," said Celeste, "just when things looked blackest, Harry blossomed! I got a brand-new husband!"

Harry plucked tufts of hair from the rug, rolled them into little balls, and flipped them into the fireplace. "I had an inferiority complex," he said. "I thought all I could ever be was a mechanic." He waved away Celeste's and my objections. "Then I found out plain horse sense is the rarest commodity in the business world. Next to most of the guys in the catchup industry, I look like an Einstein."

"Speaking of people blossoming," I said, "your wife gets more gorgeous by the minute."

"Hmmmmm?" said Harry.

"I said, Celeste is really something—one of the most beautiful and famous women in the country. You're a lucky man," I said.

"Yeah, yeah—sure," said Harry, his mind elsewhere.

"You knew what you wanted, and you got it, didn't you?" I said to Celeste.

"I—" Celeste began.

"Tell me, Celeste," I said, "what's your life like now? Pretty wild, I'll bet, with the program and the nightclub appearances, publicity, and all that."

"It is," said Celeste. "It's the most—"

"It's a lot like the industry," said Harry. "Keep the show moving, keep the show moving—keep the catchup moving, keep the catchup moving. There are millions of people who take television for granted, and there are millions of people taking catchup for granted. They want it when they want it. It's got to be there—and it's got to be right. They don't stop to think about how it got there. They aren't interested." He dug his fingers into his thighs. "But they wouldn't get television, and they wouldn't get catchup if there weren't people tearing their hearts out to get it to 'em."

"I liked your record of 'Solitude' very much, Celeste," I said. "The last chorus, where you—"

Harry clapped his hands together. "Sure she's good. Hell, I said we'd sponsor her, if the industry'd ever get together on anything." He rolled over and looked up at Celeste. "What's the story on chow, Mother?" he said.

At supper, conversation strayed from one topic to another, but always settled, like a ball in a crooked roulette wheel, on the catchup industry.

Celeste tried to bring up the problem of her investments, but the subject, ordinarily a thriller, fizzled and sank in a sea of catchup again and again.

"I'm making five thousand a week now," said Celeste, "and there are a million people ready to tell me what to do with it. But I want to ask a friend—an old friend."

"It all depends on what you want from your investments," I said. "Do you want growth? Do you want stability? Do you want a quick return in dividends?"

"Don't put it in the catchup industry," said Harry. "If they wake up, if I can wake 'em up, OK. I'd say get in catchup and stay in catchup. But the way things are now, you might as well sink your money in Grant's Tomb, for all the action you'll get."

"Um," I said. "Well, Celeste, with your tax situation, I don't think you'd want dividends as much as you'd want growth."

"It's just crazy about taxes," said Celeste. "Harry figured out it was actually cheaper for him to work for nothing."

"For love," said Harry.

"What company are you with, Harry?" I said.

"I'm in a consulting capacity for the industry as a whole," said Harry.

The telephone rang, and a maid came in to tell Celeste that her agent was on the line.

I was left alone with Harry, and I found it hard to think of anything to say—anything that wouldn't be trivial in the face of the catchup industry's impending collapse.

I glanced around the room, humming nervously, and saw that the wall behind me was covered with impressive documents, blobbed with sealing wax, decked with ribbons, and signed with big black swirling signatures. The documents were from every conceivable combination of human beings, all gathered in solemn assembly to declare something nice about Celeste. She was a beacon to youth, a promoter of Fire Prevention Week, the sweetheart of a regiment, the television discovery of the year.

"Quite a girl," I said.

"See how they get those things up?" said Harry. "They really look like something, don't they?"

"Like nonaggression pacts," I said.

"When someone gets one of these, they think they've got something—even if what it says is just plain hogwash and not even good English. Makes 'em feel good," said Harry. "Makes 'em feel important."

"I suppose," I said. "But all these citations are certainly evidence of affection and respect."

"That's what a suggestion award should look like," said

Harry. "It's one of the things I'm trying to put through. When a guy in the industry figures out a better way to do something, he ought to get some kind of certificate, a booby-dazzler he can frame and show off."

Celeste came back in, thrilled about something. "Honey," she said to Harry.

"I'm telling him about suggestion awards," said Harry. "Will it keep a minute?" He turned back to me. "Before you can understand a suggestion a guy made the other day," he said, "you've got to understand how catchup is made. You start with the tomatoes out on the farms, see?"

"Honey," said Celeste plaintively, "I hate to interrupt, but they want me to play Dolley Madison in a movie."

"Go ahead, if you want to," said Harry. "If you don't, don't. Now where was I?"

"Catchup," I said.

As I left the Divine home, I found myself attacked by a feeling of doom. Harry's anxieties about the catchup industry had become a part of me. An evening with Harry was like a year of solitary confinement in a catchup vat. No man could come away without a strong opinion about catchup.

"Let's have lunch sometime, Harry," I said as I left. "What's your number at the office?"

"It's unlisted," said Harry. He gave me the number very reluctantly. "I'd appreciate it if you'd keep it to yourself."

"People would always be calling him up to pick his brains, if the number got around," said Celeste.

"Good night, Celeste," I said. "I'm glad you're such a success. How could you miss with that face, that voice, and the name Celeste Divine? You didn't have to change a thing, did you?"

"It's just the opposite with catchup," said Harry. "The original catchup wasn't anything like what we call catchup or ketchup or catsup. The original stuff was made out of mushrooms, walnuts, and a lot of other things. It all started in Malaya. *Catchup* means 'taste' in Malaya. Not many people know that."

"I certainly didn't," I said. "Well, good night."

I didn't get around to calling Harry until several weeks later, when a prospective client, a Mr. Arthur J. Bunting, dropped into my office shortly before noon. Mr. Bunting was a splendid old gentleman, stout, over six feet tall, with the white mustache and fierce eyes of an old Indian fighter.

Mr. Bunting had sold his factory, which had been in his family for three generations, and he wanted my suggestions as to how to invest the proceeds. His factory had been a catchup factory.

"I've often wondered," I said, "how the original catchup would go over in this country—made the way they make it in Malaya."

A moment before, Mr. Bunting had been a sour old man, morbidly tidying his life. Now he was radiant. "You know catchup?" he said.

"As an amateur," I said.

"Was your family in catchup?" he said.

"A friend," I said.

Mr. Bunting's face clouded over with sadness. "I and my father," he said hoarsely, "and my father's father made the finest catchup this world has ever known. Never once did we cut corners on quality." He gave an anguished sigh. "I'm sorry I sold out!" he said. "There's a tragedy for someone to write: A man sells something priceless for a price he can't resist."

"There's a lot of that going on, I guess," I said.

"Being in the catchup business was ridiculous to a lot of people," said Mr. Bunting. "But by glory, if everybody did his job as well as my grandfather did, my father did, and I did, it would be a perfect world! Let me tell you that!"

I nodded, and dialed Harry's unlisted telephone number. "I've got a friend I'd like very much to have you meet, Mr. Bunting," I said. "I hope he can have lunch with us."

"Good, fine," said Mr. Bunting. "And now the work of three generations is in the hands of strangers," he said.

A man with a tough voice answered the telephone. "Yeah?"

"Mr. Harry Divine, please," I said.

"Out to lunch. Back at one," said the man.

"Gee, that's too bad. Mr. Bunting," I said, hanging up, "it would have been wonderful to get you two together."

"Who is this person?"

"Who is he?" I said. I laughed. "Why, my friend Harry is Mr. Catchup himself!"

Mr. Bunting looked as though he'd been shot in the belly. "Mr. Catchup?" he said hollowly. "That's what they used to call me. Who's he with?"

"He's a consultant for the whole industry," I said.

The corners of Mr. Bunting's mouth pulled down. "I never even heard of him," he said. "My word, things happen fast these days!"

As we sat down to lunch, Mr. Bunting was still very upset.

"Mr. Bunting, sir," I said, "I was using the term 'Mr. Catchup' loosely. I'm sure Harry doesn't claim the title. I just mean that catchup was a big thing in *his* life, too."

Mr. Bunting finished his drink grimly. "New names, new faces," he said. "These sharp youngsters, coming up fast, still wet behind the ears, knowing all the answers, taking over—do they know they've got a heritage to respect and protect?" His voice quivered. "Or are they going to tear everything down, without even bothering to ask why it was built that way?"

There was a stir in the restaurant. In the doorway stood Celeste, a bird of paradise, creating a sensation.

Beside her, talking animatedly, demanding her full attention, was Harry.

I waved to them, and they crossed the room to join us at our table. The headwaiter escorted them, flattering the life out of Celeste. And every face turned toward her, full of adoration.

Harry, seemingly blind to it all, was shouting at Celeste about the catchup industry.

"You know what I said to them?" said Harry, as they reached our table.

"No, dear," said Celeste.

"I told them there was only one thing to do," said Harry, "and that was burn the whole damn catchup industry down to the ground. And next time, when we build it, by heaven, let's *think!*"

Mr. Bunting stood, snow white, every nerve twanging.

Uneasily I made the introductions.

"How do you do?" said Mr. Bunting.

Celeste smiled warmly. Her smile faded as Mr. Bunting looked at Harry with naked hate.

Harry was too wound up to notice. "I am now making a historical study of the catchup industry," he announced, "to determine whether it never left the Dark Ages, or whether it left and then scampered back."

I chuckled idiotically. "Mr. Bunting, sir," I said, "you've no doubt seen Celeste on television. She's—"

"The communications industry," said Harry, "has reached the point where it can send the picture of my wife through the air to forty million homes. And the catchup industry is still bogged down, trying to lick thixotropy."

Mr. Bunting blew up. "Maybe the public doesn't *want* thixotropy licked!" he bellowed. "Maybe they'd rather have good catchup, and thixotropy be damned! It's flavor they want! It's quality they want! Lick thixotropy, and you'll have some new red bilge sold under a proud old name!" He was trembling all over.

Harry was staggered. "You know what thixotropy is?" he said.

"Of course I know!" said Bunting, furious. "And I know what good catchup is. And I know what you are—an arrogant, enterprising, self-serving little pipsqueak!" He turned to me. "And a man is judged by the company he keeps. Good day!" He strode out of the restaurant, grandly.

"There were tears in his eyes," said Celeste, bewildered.

"His life, his father's life, and his grandfather's life have been devoted to catchup," I said. "I thought Harry knew that. I thought everybody in the industry knew who Arthur J. Bunting was."

Harry was miserable. "I really hurt him, didn't I?" he said. "God knows, I didn't want to do that."

Celeste laid her hand on Harry's. "You're like Louis Pasteur, darling," she said. "Pasteur must have hurt the feelings of a lot of old men, too."

"Yeah," said Harry. "Like Louis Pasteur—that's me."

"The old collision between youth and age," I said.

"Big client, was he?" said Harry.

"Yes, I'm afraid so," I said.

"I'm sorry," said Harry. "I can't tell you how sorry. I'll call him up and make things right."

"I don't want you to say anything that will go against your integrity, Harry," I said. "Not on my account."

Mr. Bunting called the next day to say that he had accepted Harry's apology.

"He made a clean breast of how he got into catchup," said Mr. Bunting, "and he promised to get out. As far as I'm concerned, the matter is closed."

I called up Harry immediately. "Harry, boy, listen!" I said. "Mr. Bunting's business isn't *that* important to me. If you're right about catchup and the Buntings are wrong, stick with it and fight it out!"

"It's all right," said Harry, "I was getting sick of catchup. I was about to move on, anyway." He hung up. I called him back, and was told that he had gone to lunch.

"Do you know where he's eating?"

"Yeah, right across the street. I can see him going in."

I got the address of the restaurant and hailed a cab.

The restaurant was a cheap, greasy diner, across the street from a garage. I looked around for Harry for some time before realizing that he was on a stool at the counter, watching me in the cigarette machine mirror.

He was wearing coveralls. He turned on his stool, and held out a hand whose nails were edged in black. "Shake hands with the new birdseed king," he said. His grip was firm.

"Harry, you're working as a mechanic," I said.

"Not half an hour ago," said Harry, "a man with a broken fuel pump thanked God for me. Have a seat."

"What about the catchup business?" I said.

"It saved my marriage and it saved my life," said Harry. "I'm grateful to the pioneers, like the Buntings, who built it."

"And now you've quit, just like that?" I snapped my fingers.

"I was never in it," said Harry. "Bunting has promised to keep that to himself, and I'd appreciate it if you'd do the same."

"But you know so much about catchup!" I said.

"For eighteen months after Celeste struck it rich and we moved here," said Harry, "I walked the streets, looking for a job suitable for the husband of the famous and beautiful Celeste."

Remembering those dark days, he rubbed his eyes, reached for the catchup. "When I got tired, cold, or wet," he said, "I'd sit in the public library, and study all the different things men could do for a living. Making catchup was one of them."

He shook the bottle of catchup over his hamburger, violently. The bottle was almost full, but nothing came out. "There—you see?" he said. "When you shake catchup one way, it behaves like a solid. You shake it another way, and it behaves like a liquid." He shook the bottle gently, and catchup poured over his hamburger. "Know what that's called?"

"No," I said.

"Thixotropy," said Harry. He hit me playfully on the upper arm. "There—you learned something new today."

Der Arme
Dolmetscher

I was astonished one day in 1944, in the midst of front-line hell-raising, to learn that I had been made interpreter, *Dolmetscher* if you please, for a whole battalion, and was to be billeted in a Belgian burgomaster's house within artillery range of the Siegfried Line.

It had never entered my head that I had what it took to dolmetsch. I qualified for the position while waiting to move from France into the front lines. While a student, I had learned the first stanza of Heinrich Heine's "Die Lorelei" by rote from a college roommate, and I happened to give those lines a dogged rendition while working within earshot of the battalion commander. The Colonel (a hotel detective from Mobile) asked his Executive Officer (a dry-goods salesman from Knoxville) in what language the lyrics were. The Executive withheld judgment until I had bungled through "*Der Gipfel des Berges foounk-kelt im Abendsonnenschein.*"

"Ah believes tha's Kraut, Cuhnel," he said.

My understanding in English of the only German I knew was this: "I don't know why I am so sad. I can't get an old legend out of my head. The air is cool and it's getting dark, and quiet flows the Rhine. The peak of the mountain twinkles in evening sunshine."

The Colonel felt his role carried with it the obligation to make quick, headstrong decisions. He made some dandies before the Wehrmacht was whipped, but the one he made that day was my favorite. "If tha's Kraut, whassat man doin' on the honey-dippin' detail?" he wanted to know. Two hours later, the company clerk told me to lay down the buckets, for I was now battalion interpreter.

Orders to move up came soon after. Those in authority were too harried to hear my declarations of incompetence. "You talk Kraut good enough foah us," said the Executive Officer. "Theah ain't goin' to be much talkin' to Krauts where weah goin'." He patted my rifle affectionately. "Heah's what's goin' to do most of youah interpretin' fo' ya," he said. The Executive, who had learned everything he knew from the Colonel, had the idea that the American Army had just licked the Belgians, and that I was to be stationed with the burgomaster to make sure he didn't try to pull a fast one. "Besides," the Executive concluded, "theah ain't nobody else can talk Kraut at all."

I rode to the burgomaster's farm on a truck with three disgruntled Pennsylvania Dutchmen who had applied for interpreters' jobs months earlier. When I made it clear that I was no competition for them, and that I hoped to be liquidated within twenty-four hours, they warmed up enough for me to furnish the interesting information that I was a *Dolmetscher*. They also decoded "Die Lorelei" at my request. This gave me command of about forty words (par for a two-year-old), but no combination of them would get me so much as a glass of cold water.

Every turn of the truck's wheels brought a new question: "What's the word for 'army'? . . . How do I ask for the bathroom? . . . What's the word for 'sick'? . . . 'well'? . . . 'dish'? . . . 'brother'? . . . 'shoe'?" My phlegmatic instructors tired, and one handed me a pamphlet purporting to make German easy for the man in the foxhole.

"Some of the first pages are missing," the donor explained as I jumped from the truck before the burgomaster's stone farmhouse. "Used 'em for cigarette papers," he said.

It was early morning when I knocked at the burgomaster's door. I stood on the step like a bit player in the wings, with the one line I was to deliver banging around an otherwise empty head. The door swung open. "*Dolmetscher*," I said.

The burgomaster himself, old, thin, and nightshirted, ushered me into the first-floor bedroom that was to be mine. He pantomimed as well as spoke his welcome, and a sprinkling of "*Danke schön*" was adequate dolmetsching for the time being. I was prepared to throttle further discussion with "*Ich weiss nicht, was soll es bedeuten, dass ich so traurig bin.*" This would have sent him padding off to bed, convinced that he had a fluent, albeit shot-full-of-*Weltschmerz*, *Dolmetscher*. The stratagem wasn't necessary. He left me alone to consolidate my resources.

Chief among these was the mutilated pamphlet. I examined each of its precious pages in turn, delighted by the simplicity of transposing English into German. With this booklet, all I had to do was run my finger down the left-hand column until I found the English phrase I wanted, and then rattle off the nonsense syllables printed opposite in the right-hand column. "How many grenade launchers have you?" for instance, was *Vee feel grenada vairfair habben zee?* Impeccable German for "Where are your tank columns?" proved to be nothing more troublesome than *Vo zint eara pantzer shpitzen?* I mouthed the phrases: "Where are your howitzers? How many machine guns have you? Surrender! Don't shoot! Where have you hidden your motorcycle? Hands up! What unit are you from?"

The pamphlet came to an abrupt end, toppling my spirits from manic to depressive. The Pennsylvania Dutchman had smoked up all the rear-area pleasantries, the pamphlet's first half, leaving me with nothing to work with but the repartee of hand-to-hand fighting.

As I lay sleepless in bed, the one drama in which I could play took shape in my mind. . . .

DOLMETSCHER (*to* BURGOMASTER'S DAUGHTER): I don't know what will become of me, I am so sad. (*Embraces her.*)

BURGOMASTER'S DAUGHTER (*with yielding shyness*): The air is cool, and it's getting dark, and the Rhine is flowing quietly.

(DOLMETSCHER *seizes* BURGOMASTER'S DAUGHTER, *carries her bodily into his room.*)

DOLMETSCHER (*softly*): Surrender.

BURGOMASTER (*brandishing Luger*): Ach! Hands up!

DOLMETSCHER and BURGOMASTER'S DAUGHTER: Don't shoot!

(A *map, showing disposition of American First Army, falls from* BURGOMASTER'S *breast pocket.*)

DOLMETSCHER (*aside, in English*): What is this supposedly pro-Ally burgomaster doing with a map showing the disposition of the American First Army? And why am I supposed to be dolmetsching with a Belgian in German? (*He snatches .45 automatic pistol from beneath pillow and aims at* BURGOMASTER.)

BURGOMASTER and BURGOMASTER'S DAUGHTER: Don't shoot! (BURGOMASTER *drops Luger, cowers, sneers.*)

DOLMETSCHER: What unit are you from? (BURGOMASTER *remains sullen, silent.* BURGOMASTER'S DAUGHTER *goes to his side, weeps softly.* DOLMETSCHER *confronts* BURGOMASTER'S DAUGHTER.) Where have *you* hidden your motorcycle? (*Turns again to* BURGOMASTER.) Where are your howitzers, eh? Where are your tank columns? How many grenade launchers have you?

BURGOMASTER (*cracking under terrific grilling*): I—I surrender.

BURGOMASTER'S DAUGHTER: I am so sad.

(*Enter* GUARD DETAIL *composed of Pennsylvania Dutchmen, making a routine check just in time to hear* BURGOMASTER *and* BURGOMASTER'S DAUGHTER *confess to being Nazi agents parachuted behind American lines.*)

Johann Christoph Friedrich von Schiller couldn't have done any better with the same words, and they were the only words I had. There was no chance of my muddling through, and no pleasure in being interpreter for a full battalion in December and not being able to say so much as "Merry Christmas."

I made my bed, tightened the drawstrings on my duffel bag, and stole through the blackout curtains and into the night.

Wary sentinels directed me to Battalion Headquarters, where I found most of our officers either poring over maps or loading their weapons. There was a holiday spirit in the air, and the Executive Officer was honing an eighteen-inch bowie knife and humming "Are You from Dixie?"

"Well, bless mah soul," he said, noticing me in the doorway, "here's old 'Sprecken Zee Dutch.' Speak up, boy. Ain't you supposed to be ovah at the mayah's house?"

"It's no good," I said. "They all speak Low German, and I speak High."

The executive was impressed. "Too good foah 'em, eh?" He ran his index finger down the edge of his murderous knife. "Ah think we'll be runnin' into some who can talk the high-class Kraut putty soon," he said, and then added, "Weah surrounded."

"We'll whomp 'em the way we whomped 'em in Nawth Ca'lina and Tennessee," said the Colonel, who had never lost on maneuvers back home. "You stay heah, son. Ah'm gonna want you foah mah pussnel intupretah."

Twenty minutes later I was in the thick of dolmetsching again. Four Tiger tanks drove up to the front door of Headquarters, and two dozen German infantrymen dismounted to round us up with submachine guns.

"Say sumpin'," ordered the Colonel, spunky to the last.

I ran my eye down the left-hand columns of my pamphlet until I found the phrase that most fairly represented our sentiments. "Don't shoot," I said.

A German tank officer swaggered in to have a look at his catch. In his hand was a pamphlet, somewhat smaller than mine. "Where are your howitzers?" he said.

The Boy Who
Hated Girls

George M. Helmholtz, head of the music department and director of the band of Lincoln High School, could sound like any musical instrument. He could shriek like a clarinet, mumble like a trombone, bawl like a trumpet. He could swell his big belly and roar like a sousaphone, could purse his lips sweetly, close his eyes, and whistle like a piccolo.

At eight o'clock one Wednesday night, he was marching around the band rehearsal room at the school, shrieking, mumbling, bawling, roaring, and whistling "Semper Fidelis."

It was easy for Helmholtz to do. For almost half of his forty years, he'd been forming bands from the river of boys that flowed through the school. He'd sung along with them all. He'd sung so long and wished so hard for his bands that he dealt with life in terms of them alone.

Marching beside the lusty pink bandmaster, his face now white with awe and concentration, was a gangly sixteen-year-old named Bert Higgens. He had a big nose, and circles under his eyes. Bert marched flappingly, like a mother flamingo pretending to be injured, luring alligators from her nest.

"*Rump-yump, tiddle-tiddle, rump-yump, burdle-burdle,*" sang Helmholtz. "Left, right, *left*, Bert! El-bows *in*, Bert! Eyes off *feet*, Bert! Keep on *line*, Bert! Don't turn *head*, Bert! Left, right, *left*, Bert! Halt—one, *two!*"

Helmholtz smiled. "I think maybe there was some improvement there."

Bert nodded. "It's sure been a help to practice with you, Mr. Helmholtz."

"As long as you're willing to work at it, so am I," said Helmholtz. He was bewildered by the change that had come over Bert in the past week. The boy seemed to have lost two years, to become what he'd been in his freshman year: awkward, cowering, lonely, dull.

"Bert," said Helmholtz, "are you sure you haven't had any injury, any sickness recently?" He knew Bert well, had given him trumpet lessons for two years. He had watched Bert grow into a proud, straight figure. The collapse of the boy's spirits and co-ordination was beyond belief.

Bert puffed out his cheeks childishly as he thought hard. It was a mannerism Helmholtz had talked him out of long before. Now he was doing it again. Bert let out the air. "Nope," he said.

"I've taught a thousand boys to march," said Helmholtz, "and you're the first one who ever forgot how to do it." The thousand passed in review in Helmholtz's mind—ranks stretching to infinity, straight as sunbeams. "Maybe we ought to talk this over with the school nurse," said Helmholtz. A cheerful thought struck him. "Unless this is girl trouble."

Bert raised one foot, then the other. "Nope," he said. "No trouble like that."

"Pretty little thing," said Helmholtz.

"Who?" said Bert.

"That dewy pink tulip I see you walking home with," said Helmholtz.

Bert grimaced. "Ah-h-h-h—her," he said. "Charlotte."

"Charlotte isn't much good?" said Helmholtz.

"I dunno. I guess she's all right. I suppose she's OK. I haven't got anything against her. I dunno."

Helmholtz shook Bert gently, as though hoping to jiggle a loose part into place. "Do you remember it at all—the feeling you used to have when you marched so well, before this relapse?"

"I think it's kind of coming back," said Bert.

"Coming up through the C and B bands, you learned to march fine," said Helmholtz. These were the training bands through which the hundred men of the Lincoln High School Ten Square Band came.

"I dunno what the trouble is," said Bert, "unless it's the excitement of getting in the Ten Square Band." He puffed his cheeks. "Maybe it's stopping my lessons with you."

When Bert had qualified for the Ten Square Band three months before, Helmholtz had turned him over to the best trumpet teacher in town, Larry Fink, for the final touches of grace and color.

"Say, Fink isn't giving you a hard time, is he?" said Helmholtz.

"Nope," said Bert. "He's a nice gentleman." He rolled his

eyes. "Mr. Helmholtz—if we could practice marching just a couple more times, I think I'll be fine."

"Gee, Bert," said Helmholtz, "I don't know when I can fit you in. When you went to Fink, I took on another boy. It just so happened he was sick tonight. But next week—"

"Who is he?" said Bert.

"Norton Shakely," said Helmholtz. "Little fellow—kind of green around the gills. He's just like you were when you started out. No faith in himself. Doesn't think he'll ever make the Ten Square Band, but he will, he will."

"He will," agreed Bert. "No doubt about it."

Helmholtz clapped Bert on the arm, to put some heart into him. "Chin up!" he sang. "Shoulders back! Go get your coat, and I'll take you home."

As Bert put on his coat, Helmholtz thought of the windows of Bert's home—windows as vacant as dead men's eyes. Bert's father had wandered away years before—and his mother was seldom there. Helmholtz wondered if that was where the trouble was.

Helmholtz was depressed. "Maybe we can stop somewhere and get a soda, and maybe play a little table tennis afterward in my basement," he said. When he'd given Bert trumpet lessons, they'd always stopped somewhere for a soda, and then played table tennis afterward.

"Unless you'd rather go see Charlotte or something," said Helmholtz.

"Are you kidding?" said Bert. "I hate the way she talks sometimes."

The next morning, Helmholtz talked with Miss Peach, the school nurse. It was a symposium between two hearty, plump people, blooming with hygiene and common sense. In the background, rickety and confused, stripped to the waist, was Bert.

"By 'blacked out,' you mean Bert fainted?" said Miss Peach.

"You didn't see him do it at the Whitestown game last Friday?" said Helmholtz.

"I missed that game," said Miss Peach.

"It was right after we'd formed the block L, when we were marching down the field to form the pinwheel that turned into the Lincoln High panther and the Whitestown eagle," said Helmholtz. The eagle had screamed, and the panther had eaten it.

"So what did Bert do?" said Miss Peach.

"He was marching along with the band, fine as you please," said Helmholtz. "And then he just drifted out of it. He wound up marching by himself."

"What did it feel like, Bert?" said Miss Peach.

"Like a dream at first," said Bert. "Real good, kind of. And then I woke up, and I was alone." He gave a sickly smile. "And everybody was laughing at me."

"How's your appetite, Bert?" said Miss Peach.

"He polished off a soda and a hamburger last night," said Helmholtz.

"What about your coordination when you play games, Bert?" said Miss Peach.

"I'm not in sports," said Bert. "The trumpet takes all the time I've got."

"Don't you and your father throw a ball sometimes?" said Miss Peach.

"I don't have a father," said Bert.

"He beat me at table tennis last night," said Helmholtz.

"All in all, it was quite a binge last night, wasn't it?" Miss Peach said.

"It's what we used to do every Wednesday night," said Bert.

"It's what I do with all the boys I give lessons to," said Helmholtz.

Miss Peach cocked her head. "You used to do it with Bert?"

"I take lessons from Mr. Fink now," said Bert.

"When a boy reaches the Ten Square Band," said Helmholtz, "he's beyond me, as far as individual lessons are concerned. I don't treat him like a boy anymore. I treat him like a man. And he's an artist. Only an artist like Fink can teach him anything from that point on."

"Ten Square Band," mused Miss Peach. "That's ten on a side—a hundred in all? All dressed alike, all marching like parts of a fine machine?"

"Like a block of postage stamps," said Helmholtz proudly.

"Uh-huh," said Miss Peach. "And all of them have had lessons from you?"

"Heavens, no," said Helmholtz. "I've only got time to give five boys individual lessons."

"A lucky, lucky five," said Miss Peach. "For a little while."

The door of the office opened, and Stewart Haley, the Assistant Principal, came in. He had begun his career as a bright young man. But now, after ten years of dealing with oversize spirits on undersize salaries, his brightness had mellowed to the dull gloss of pewter. A lot of his luster had been lost in verbal scuffles with Helmholtz over expenses of the band.

In Haley's hand was a bill. "Well, Helmholtz," he said, "if I'd known you were going to be here, I'd have brought another interesting bill with me. Five war-surplus Signal Corps wire-laying reels, complete with pack frames? Does that ring a bell?"

"It does," said Helmholtz, unabashed. "And may I say—"

"Later," said Haley. "Right now I have a matter to take up with Miss Peach—one that makes your peculation look like peanuts." He rattled the bill at Miss Peach. "Miss Peach—have you ordered a large quantity of bandages recently?"

Miss Peach paled. "I—I ordered thirty yards of sterile gauze," she said. "It came this morning. And it's thirty yards, and it's gauze."

Haley sat down on a white stool. "According to this bill," he said, "somebody in this grand institution has ordered and received two hundred yards of silver nylon ribbon, three inches wide—treated to glow in the dark."

He was looking blankly at Helmholtz when he said it. He went on looking at Helmholtz, and color crept into his cheeks. "Hello again, Helmholtz."

"Hi," said Helmholtz.

"Down for your daily shot of cocaine?" said Haley.

"Cocaine?" said Helmholtz.

"How else," said Haley, "could a man get dreams of cornering the world output of nylon ribbon treated to glow in the dark?"

"It costs much less to make things glow in the dark than most people realize," said Helmholtz.

Haley stood. "So it was you!"

Helmholtz laid his hand on Haley's shoulder and looked him in the eye. "Stewart," he said, "the question on everybody's lips is, How can the Ten Square Band possibly top its performance at the Westfield game last year?"

"The big question is," said Haley, "How can a high school with a modest budget like ours afford such a vainglorious, Cecil B. DeMille machine for making music? And the answer is," said Haley, "We can't!" He jerked his head from side to side. "Ninety-five-dollar uniforms! Biggest drum in the state! Batons and hats that light up! Everything treated to glow in the dark! Holy smokes!" he said wildly. "The biggest jukebox in the world!"

The inventory brought nothing but joy to Helmholtz. "You love it," he said. "Everybody loves it. And wait till you hear what we're going to do with those reels and that ribbon!"

"Waiting," said Haley. "Waiting."

"Now then," said Helmholtz, "any band can form block letters. That's about the oldest stuff there is. As of this moment our band is the only band, as far as I know, equipped to write longhand."

In the muddled silence that followed, Bert, all but forgotten, spoke up. He had put his shirt back on. "Are you all through with me?" he said.

"You can go, Bert," said Miss Peach. "I didn't find anything wrong with you."

"Bye," said Bert, his hand on the doorknob. "Bye, Mr. Helmholtz."

"So long," said Helmholtz. "Now what do you think of that?" he said to Haley. "Longhand!"

Just outside the door, Bert bumped into Charlotte, the dewy pink tulip of a girl who often walked home with him.

"Bert," said Charlotte, "they told me you were down here. I thought you were hurt. Are you all right?"

Bert brushed past her without a word, leaning, as though into a cold, wet gale.

. . . . .

"What do I think of the ribbon?" said Haley to Helmholtz. "I think this is where the spending of the Ten Square Band is finally stopped."

"That isn't the only kind of spree that's got to be stopped," said Miss Peach darkly.

"What do you mean by that?" said Helmholtz.

"I mean," said Miss Peach, "all this playing fast and loose with kids' emotions." She frowned. "George, I've been watching you for years—watching you use every emotional trick in the books to make your kids march and play."

"I try to be friends," said Helmholtz, untroubled.

"You try to be a lot more than that," said Miss Peach. "Whatever a kid needs, you're it. Father, mother, sister, brother, God, slave, or dog—you're it. No wonder we've got the best band in the world. The only wonder is that what's happened with Bert hasn't happened a thousand times."

"What's eating Bert?" said Helmholtz.

"You won him," said Miss Peach. "That's what. Lock, stock, and barrel—he's yours, all yours."

"Sure he likes me," said Helmholtz. "Hope he does, anyway."

"He likes you like a son likes a father," said Miss Peach. "There's a casual thing for you."

Helmholtz couldn't imagine what the argument was about. Everything Miss Peach had said was obvious. "That's only natural, isn't it?" he said. "Bert doesn't have a father, so he's going to look around for one, naturally, until he finds some girl who'll take him over and—"

"Will you please open your eyes, and see what you've done to Bert's life?" said Miss Peach. "Look what he did to get your attention, after you stuck him in the Ten Square Band, then

sent him off to Mr. Fink and forgot all about him. He was willing to have the whole world laugh at him, just to get you to look
at him again."

"Growing up isn't supposed to be painless," said Helmholtz.
"A baby's one thing, a child's another, and a man's another.
Changing from one thing to the next is a famous mess." He
opened his eyes wide. "If we don't know that, who does?"

"Growing up isn't supposed to be hell!" said Miss Peach.

Helmholtz was stunned by the word. "What do you want
me to do?"

"It's none of my business," said Miss Peach. "It's a highly
personal affair. That's the way you made it. That's the way you
work. I'd think the least you could do would be to learn the difference between getting yourself tangled up in a boy and getting yourself tangled up in ribbon. You can cut the ribbon. You
can't do that to a boy."

"About that ribbon—" said Haley.

"We'll pack it up and send it back," said Helmholtz. He
didn't care about the ribbon anymore. He walked out of the office, his ears burning.

Helmholtz carried himself as though he'd done nothing
wrong. But guilt rode on his back like a chimpanzee. In his tiny
office off the band rehearsal room, Helmholtz removed stacks
of sheet music from the washbasin in the corner and dashed
cold water in his face, hoping to make the chimpanzee go away
at least for the next hour. The next hour was the rehearsal period for the Ten Square Band.

Helmholtz telephoned his good friend Larry Fink, the trumpet teacher.

"What's the trouble this time, George?" said Fink.

"The school nurse just jumped all over me for being too nice to my boys. She says I get too involved, and that's a very dangerous thing."

"Oh?"

"Psychology's a wonderful science," said Helmholtz. "Without it, everybody'd still be making the same terrible mistake—being nice to each other."

"What brought this on?" said Fink.

"Bert," said Helmholtz.

"I finally let him go last week," said Fink. "He never practiced, came to the lessons unprepared. Frankly, George, I know you thought a lot of him, but he wasn't very talented. He wasn't even very fond of music, as near as I can tell."

Helmholtz protested with all his heart. "That boy went from the C Band to the Ten Square in two years! He took to music like a duck to water."

"Like a camel in quicksand, if you ask me," said Fink. "That boy busted his butt for you, George. And then you busted his heart when you handed him on to me. The school nurse is right: You've got to be more careful about who you're nice to."

"He's even forgotten how to march. He fell out of step and spoiled a formation, forgot where he was supposed to go, at half-time at the Findlay Tech game."

"He told me about it," said Fink.

"Did he have any explanation?"

"He was surprised you and the nurse didn't come up with it. Or maybe the nurse figured it out, but didn't want anybody else to know."

"I still can't imagine," said Helmholtz.

"He was drunk, George. He said it was his first time, and promised it would be his last. Unfortunately, I don't believe we can count on that."

"But he still can't march," said Helmholtz, shocked. "When just the two of us practice alone, with nobody watching, he finds it impossible to keep in step with me. Is he drunk all the time?"

"George," said Fink, "you and your innocence have turned a person who never should have been a musician into an actor instead."

From the rehearsal room outside Helmholtz's office came the cracks and slams of chairs being set up for the Ten Square Band. Bandsmen with a free period were doing that. The coming hour was ordinarily a perfect one for the bandmaster, in which he became weightless, as he sang the part of this instrument or that one, while his bandsmen played. But now he feared it.

He was going to have to face Bert again, having been made aware in the interim of how much he might have hurt the boy. And maybe others.

Would he be to blame, if Bert went on to become an alcoholic? He thought about the thousand or more boys with whom he had behaved like a father, whether they had a real father or not. To his knowledge, several had later become drunks. Two had been arrested for drugs, and one for burglary. He lost track of most. Few came back to see him after graduation. That was something else it was time to think about.

The rest of the band entered now, Bert among them. Helmholtz heard himself say to him, as privately as he could, "Could you see me in my office after school?" He hadn't a clue of what he would say then.

He went to his music stand in front, rapped his baton against it. The band fell silent. "Let's start off with 'Lincoln's Foes Shall Wail Tonight.'" The author of the words and music was Helmholtz himself. He had written them during his first year as bandmaster, when the school's bandsmen at athletic events and parades had numbered only fifty. Their uniforms fit them purely by chance, and in any case made them look, as Helmholtz himself had said at the time, like "deserters from Valley Forge." That was twenty years before.

"Everybody ready?" he said. "Good! Fortissimo! Con brio! A-one, a-two, a-three, a-four!" Helmholtz stayed earth-bound this time. He weighed a ton.

When Bert came to his office after school, Helmholtz had an agenda. He wanted the lonely boy to stop disliking Charlotte. She appeared to be a warm person, who could lead Bert into a social life apart from the band and Helmholtz. He thought it important, too, that the dangers of alcohol be discussed.

But the talk wouldn't go at all as planned, and Helmholtz sensed that it wouldn't as soon as Bert sat down. He had self-respect on a scale Helmholtz had never seen him exhibit before. Something big must have happened, thought Helmholtz. Bert was staring straight at him, challenging, as though they were equals, no longer man and boy.

"Bert," Helmholtz began, "I won't beat around the bush. I know you were drunk at the football game."

"Mr. Fink told you?"

"Yes, and it troubled me."

"Why didn't you realize it at the time?" said Bert. "Everybody else did. People were laughing at you because you thought I was sick."

"I had a lot on my mind," said Helmholtz.

"Music," said Bert, as though it were a dirty word.

"Certainly music," said Helmholtz, taken aback. "My goodness."

"*Nothin'* but music," said Bert, his gaze like laser beams.

"That's often the case, and why not?" Again Helmholtz added incredulously, "My goodness."

"Charlotte was right."

"I thought you hated her."

"I like her a lot, except for the things she said about you. Now I know how right she was, and I not only like her, I love her."

Helmholtz was scared now, and unused to that. This was a most unpleasant scene. "Whatever she said about me, I don't think I'd care to hear it."

"I won't tell you, because all you'd hear is music." Bert put his trumpet in its case on the bandmaster's desk. The trumpet was rented from the school. "Give this to somebody else, who'll love it more than I did," he said. "I only loved it because you were so good to me, and you told me to." He stood. "Goodbye."

Bert was at the door before Helmholtz asked him to stop, to turn around and look him in the eye again, and say what Charlotte had said about him.

Bert was glad to tell him. He was angry, as though Helmholtz had somehow swindled him. "She said you were completely disconnected from real life, and only pretended to be interested in people. She said all you paid attention to was music, and if people weren't playing it, you could still hear it in your head. She said you were nuts."

"Nuts?" echoed Helmholtz wonderingly.

"I told her to stop saying that," said Bert, "but then you showed me how really nutty you are."

"Please tell me how. I need to know," said Helmholtz. But a concert band in his head was striking up Tchaikovsky's *1812 Overture*, complete with the roar of cannons. It was all he could do not to sing along.

"When you gave me marching lessons," Bert was saying, "and I was acting drunk, you didn't even notice how crazy it was. You weren't even there!"

A brief silence followed a crescendo in the music in the bandmaster's head. Helmholtz asked this question: "How could that girl know anything about me?"

"She dates a lot of other bandsmen," said Bert. "She gets 'em to tell her the really funny stuff."

Before leaving for home at sunset that day, Helmholtz paid a visit to the school nurse. He said he needed to talk to her about something.

"Is it that Bert Higgens again?" she said.

"I'm afraid it's even closer to home than that," he said. "It's me this time. It's I. It's me."

This Son
of Mine

The factory made the best centrifugal pumps in the world,
and Merle Waggoner owned it. He'd started it. He'd just
been offered two million dollars for it by the General Forge and
Foundry Company. He didn't have any stockholders and he
didn't owe a dime. He was fifty-one, a widower, and he had one
heir—a son. The boy's name was Franklin. The boy was named
for Benjamin Franklin.

One Friday afternoon father and son went out of Merle's office and into the factory. They walked down a factory aisle to
Rudy Linberg's lathe.

"Rudy," said Merle, "the boy here's home from college for
three days, and I thought maybe you and him and your boy and

me might go out to the farm and shoot some clay pigeons to-morrow."

Rudy turned his sky-blue eyes to Merle and young Franklin. He was Merle's age, and he had the deep and narrow dignity of a man who had learned his limitations early—who had never tried to go beyond them. His limitations were those of his tools, his flute, and his shotgun.

"Might try crows," he said.

Rudy stood at attention like the good soldier he was. And like an old soldier, he did it without humility, managed to convey that he was the big winner in life, after all. He had been Merle's first employee. He might have been a partner way back then, for two thousand dollars. And Rudy'd had the cash. But the enter-prise had looked chancy to him. He didn't seem sorry now.

"We could set up my owl," said Rudy. He had a stuffed owl to lure crows. He and his son, Karl, had made it.

"Need a rifle to get at the crows out there," said Merle. "They know all about that owl of yours and Karl's. Don't think we could get any closer to 'em than half a mile."

"Might be sport, trying to get at 'em with a scope," said Franklin softly. He was tall and thin, in cashmere and gray flan-nel. He was almost goofy with shyness and guilt. He had just told his father that he wanted to be an actor, that he didn't want the factory. And shock at his own words had come so fast that he'd heard himself adding, out of control, the hideously empty phrase, "Thanks just the same."

His father hadn't reacted—yet. The conversation had gone blandly on to the farm, to shooting, to Rudy and Karl, to Rudy and Karl's new station wagon, and now to crows.

"Let's go ask my boy what he's got on tomorrow," said Rudy.

It was a formality. Karl always did what his father wanted him to do, did it with profound love.

Rudy, Merle, and Franklin went down the aisle to a lathe thirty feet from Rudy's. Merle's chin was up. Rudy looked straight ahead. Franklin looked down at the floor.

Karl was a carbon copy of his father. He was such a good mimic of Rudy that his joints seemed to ache a little with age. He seemed sobered by fifty-one years of life, though he'd lived only twenty. He seemed instinctively wary of safety hazards that had been eliminated from the factory by the time he'd learned to walk. Karl stood at attention without humility, just as his father had done.

"Want to go shooting tomorrow?" said Rudy.

"Shoot what?" said Karl.

"Crows. Clay pigeons," said Rudy. "Maybe a woodchuck."

"Don't mind," said Karl. He nodded briefly to Merle and Franklin. "Glad to."

"We could take some steaks and have supper out there," said Merle. "You make the steak sauce, Rudy?"

"Don't mind," said Rudy. He was famous for his steak sauce, and had taught the secret to his son. "Be glad to."

"Got a bottle of twenty-year-old bourbon I've been saving for something special," said Merle. "I guess tomorrow'll be special enough." He lit a cigar, and Franklin saw that his father's hand was shaking. "We'll have a ball," he said.

Clumsily Merle punched Franklin in the kidneys, man to man, trying to make him bubble. He regretted it at once. He laughed out loud to show it didn't matter, laughed through cigar smoke that stung his eyes. The laugh drove smoke into the walls of his lungs. Pleasure fled. On and on the laugh went.

"Look at him, Rudy!" said Merle, lashing the merriment onward. "Foot taller'n his old man, and president of what at Cornell?"

"Interfraternity Council," murmured Franklin, embarrassed. He and Karl avoided looking at each other. Their fathers had taken them hunting together maybe a hundred times. But the boys had hardly spoken to each other, had exchanged little more than humorless nods and head shakes for hits and misses.

"And how many fraternities at Cornell?" said Merle.

"Sixty-two," said Franklin, more softly than before.

"And how many men in a fraternity?" said Merle.

"Forty, maybe," said Franklin. He picked up a sharp, bright spiral shaving of steel from the floor. "There's a pretty thing," he said. He knew his father's reaction was coming now. He could hear the first warning tremors in his voice.

"Say sixty fraternities," said Merle. "Say forty men in each . . . Makes twenty-four hundred boys my boy's over, Rudy! When I was his age, I didn't have but six men under me."

"They aren't under me, Father," said Franklin. "I just run the meetings of the Council and—"

The explosion came. "You run the show!" roared Merle. "You can be as damn polite about it as you want to, but you still run the show!"

Nobody said anything.

Merle tried to smile, but the smile curdled, as though he were going to burst into tears. He took the strap of Rudy's overalls between his thumb and forefinger and rubbed the faded denim. He looked up into Rudy's sky-blue eyes.

"Boy wants to be an actor, Rudy," he said. And then he roared again. "That's what he said!" He turned away and ran back to his office.

In the moment before Franklin could make himself move, Rudy spoke to him as if nothing were wrong.

"You got enough shells?" said Rudy.

"What?" said Franklin.

"You got enough shells? You want us to pick up some?" said Rudy.

"No," said Franklin. "We've got plenty of shells. Half a case, last time I checked."

Rudy nodded. He examined the work in Karl's lathe and tapped his own temple. The tapping was a signal Franklin had seen many times on hunts. It meant that Karl was doing fine.

Rudy touched Karl's elbow lightly. It was the signal for Karl to get back to work. Rudy and Karl each held up a crooked finger and saluted with it. Franklin knew what that meant, too. It meant, "Good-bye, I love you."

Franklin put one foot in front of the other and went looking for his own father.

Merle was sitting at his desk, his head down, when Franklin came in. He held a steel plate about six inches square in his left hand. In the middle of the plate was a hole two inches square. In his right hand he held a steel cube that fitted the hole exactly.

On the desktop were two black bags of jeweler's velvet, one for the plate and one for the cube. About every ten seconds Merle put the cube through the hole.

Franklin sat down gingerly on a hard chair by the wall. The office hadn't changed much in the years he'd known it. It was one more factory room, with naked pipes overhead—the cold ones sweaty, the hot ones dry. Wires snaked from steel box to steel box. The green walls and cream trim were as rough as elephant hide in some places, with alternating coats of paint and grime, paint and grime.

There had never been time to scrape away the layers, and barely enough time, overnight, to slap on new paint. And there had never been time to finish the rough shelves that lined the room.

Franklin still saw the place through child's eyes. To him it had been a playroom. He remembered his father's rummaging through the shelves for toys to amuse his boy. The toys were still there: cutaway pumps, salesmen's samples, magnets, a pair of cracked safety glasses that had once saved Rudy Linberg's blue eyes.

And the playthings Franklin remembered best—remembered best because his father would show them to him, but never let him touch—were what Merle was playing with now.

Merle slipped the cube through the square hole once more. "Know what these are?" he said.

"Yes, sir," said Franklin. "They're what Rudy Linberg had to make when he was an apprentice in Sweden."

The cube could be slipped through the hole in twenty-four different ways, without letting the tiniest ray of light pass through with it.

"Unbelievable skill," said Franklin respectfully. "There aren't craftsmen like that coming along anymore." He didn't really feel much respect. He was simply saying what he knew his father wanted to hear. The cube and the hole struck him as criminal wastes of time and great bores. "Unbelievable," he said again.

"It's unbelievable, when you realize that Rudy didn't make

them," said Merle, "when you realize what generation the man who made them belongs to."

"Oh?" said Franklin. "Who did make them?"

"Rudy's boy," said Merle. "A member of your generation." He ground out his cigar. "He gave them to me on my last birthday. They were on my desk, boy, waiting for me when I came in—right beside the ones Rudy gave me so many years ago."

Franklin had sent a telegram on that birthday. Presumably, the telegram had been waiting on the desk, too. The telegram had said, "Happy Birthday, Father."

"I could have cried, boy, when I saw those two plates and those two cubes side by side," said Merle. "Can you understand that?" he asked. "Can you understand why I'd feel like crying?"

"Yes, sir," said Franklin.

Merle's eyes widened. "And then I guess I did cry—one tear, maybe two," he said. "Because—you know what I found out, boy?"

"No, sir," said Franklin.

"The cube of Karl's fitted through the hole of Rudy's!" said Merle. "They were interchangeable!"

"Gosh!" said Franklin. "I'll be darned. Really?"

And now he felt like crying, because he didn't care, couldn't care—and would have given his right arm to care. The factory whanged and banged and screeched in monstrous irrelevance— Franklin's, all Franklin's, if he just said the word.

"What'll you do with it—buy a theater in New York?" Merle said abruptly.

"Do with what, sir?" said Franklin.

"The money I'll get for the factory when I sell it—the money I'll leave to you when I'm dead," said Merle. He hit the word "dead" hard. "What's Waggoner Pump going to be converted into? Waggoner Theaters? Waggoner School of Acting? The Waggoner Home for Broken-Down Actors?"

"I—I hadn't thought about it," said Franklin. The idea of converting Waggoner Pump into something equally complicated hadn't occurred to him, and appalled him now. He was being asked to match his father's passion for the factory with an equal passion for something else. And Franklin had no such passion—for the theater or anything else.

He had nothing but the bittersweet, almost formless longings of youth. Saying he wanted to be an actor gave the longings a semblance of more fun than they really had. Saying it was poetry more than anything else.

"I can't help being a little interested," said Merle. "Do you mind?"

"No, sir," said Franklin.

"When Waggoner Pump becomes just one more division of General Forge and Foundry, and they send out a batch of bright young men to take over and straighten the place out, I'll want something else to think about—whatever it is you're going to do."

Franklin itched all over. "Yes, sir," he said. He looked at his watch and stood. "If we're going shooting tomorrow, I guess I'd better go see Aunt Margaret this afternoon." Margaret was Merle's sister.

"You do that," said Merle. "And I'll call up General Forge and Foundry, and tell them we accept their offer." He ran his finger down his calendar pad until he found a name and telephone number. "If we want to sell, I'm to call somebody named Guy Ferguson at something called extension five-oh-nine at something called the General Forge and Foundry Company at someplace called Ilium, New York." He licked his lips. "I'll tell him he and his friends can have Waggoner Pump."

"Don't sell on my account," said Franklin.

"On whose account would I keep it?" said Merle.

"Do you have to sell it today?" Franklin sounded horrified.

"Strike while the iron's hot, I always say," said Merle. "Today's the day you decided to be an actor, and as luck would have it, we have an excellent offer for what I did with my life."

"Couldn't we wait?"

"For what?" said Merle. He was having a good time now.

"Father!" cried Franklin. "For the love of heaven, Father, please!" He hung his head and shook it. "I don't know what I'm doing," he said. "I don't know for sure what I want to do yet. I'm just playing with ideas, trying to find myself. Please, Father, don't sell what you've done with your life, don't just throw it away because I'm not sure I want to do that with my life, too! Please!" Franklin looked up. "I'm not Karl Linberg," he said. "I can't help it. I'm sorry, but I'm not Karl Linberg."

Shame clouded his father's face, then passed. "I—I wasn't making any odious comparisons there," said Merle. He'd said exactly the same thing many times before. Franklin had forced him to it, just as he had forced him now, by apologizing for not being Karl Linberg.

"I wouldn't want you to be like Karl," said Merle. "I'm glad you're the way you are. I'm glad you've got big dreams of your own." He smiled. "Give 'em hell, boy—and be yourself! That's all I've ever told you to do with your life, isn't it?"

"Yes, sir," said Franklin. His last shred of faith in any dreams of his own had been twitched away. He could never dream two million dollars' worth, could never dream anything worth the death of his father's dreams. Actor, newspaperman, social

worker, sea captain—Franklin was in no condition to give anyone hell.

"I'd better get out to Aunt Margaret's," he said.

"You do that. And I'll hold off telling Ferguson or whatever-
his-name-is anything until Monday." Merle seemed at peace.

On his way through the factory parking lot to his car,
Franklin passed Rudy and Karl's new station wagon. His father
had raved about it, and now Franklin took a good look at it—
just as he took good looks at all the things his father loved.

The station wagon was German, bright blue, with white-
sidewall tires, its engine in the rear. It looked like a little bus—
no hood in front, a high, flat roof, sliding doors, and rows of
square windows on the sides.

The interior was a masterpiece of Rudy and Karl's orderli-
ness and cabinet work, of lockers and niches and racks. There
was a place for everything, and everything was in its place—
guns, fishing tackle, cooking utensils, stove, ice chest, blankets,
sleeping bags, lanterns, first-aid kit. There were even two
niches, side by side, in which were strapped the cases of Karl's
clarinet and Rudy's flute.

Looking inside admiringly, Franklin had a curious association of thoughts. His thoughts of the station wagon were mixed
with thoughts of a great ship that had been dug up in Egypt
after thousands of years. The ship had been fitted out with
every necessity for a trip to Paradise—every necessity save the
means of getting there.

"Mistuh Waggonuh, suh!" said a voice, and an engine raced.
Franklin turned to see that the parking lot guard had seen

him coming, had now brought him his car. Franklin had been spared the necessity of walking the last fifty feet to it.

The guard got out and saluted smartly. "This thing really go a hundred and twenty-five, like it says on the speedometer?" he said.

"Never tried," said Franklin, getting in. The car was a sports car, windy and skittish, with room for two. He had bought it secondhand, against his father's wish. His father had never ridden in it. It was fitted out for its trip to Paradise with three lipstick-stained tissues, a beer can opener, a full ashtray, and a road map of Illinois.

Franklin was embarrassed to see that the guard was cleaning the windshield with his handkerchief. "That's all right, that's all right," he said. "Forget it." He thought he remembered the guard's name, but he wasn't sure. He took a chance on it. "Thanks for everything, Harry," he said.

"George, suh!" said the guard. "George Miramar Jackson, suh!"

"Of course," said Franklin. "Sorry, George. Forgot."

George Miramar Jackson smiled brilliantly. "No offense, Mistuh Waggonuh, suh! Just remember next time—George Miramar Jackson, suh!" In George's eyes there blazed the dream of a future time, when Franklin would be boss, when a big new job would open up indoors. In that dream, Franklin would say to his secretary, "Miss So-and-So? Send for—" And out would roll the magical, magnificent, unforgettable name.

Franklin drove out of the parking lot without dreams to match even George Miramar Jackson's.

. . . . .

At supper, feeling no pain after two stiff cocktails and a whirlwind of mothering at Aunt Margaret's, Franklin told his father that he wanted to take over the factory in due time. He would become the Waggoner in Waggoner Pump when his father was ready to bow out.

Painlessly, Franklin moved his father as profoundly as Karl Linberg had with a steel plate, a steel cube, and heaven knows how many years of patient scree-scraw with a file.

"You're the only one—do you know that?" choked Merle. "The only one—I swear!"

"The only one what, sir?" said Franklin.

"The only son who's sticking with what his father or his grandfather or sometimes even his great-grandfather built." Merle shook his head mournfully. "No Hudson in Hudson Saw," he said. "I don't think you can even cut cheese with a Hudson saw these days. No Flemming in Flemming Tool and Die. No Warner in Warner Street. No Hawks, no Hinkley, no Bowman in Hawks, Hinkley, and Bowman."

Merle waved his hand westward. "You wonder who all the people are with the big new houses on the west side? Who can have a house like that, and we never meet them, never even meet anybody who knows them? They're the ones who are taking over instead of the sons. The town's for sale, and they buy. It's their town now—people named Ferguson from places called Ilium.

"What is it about the sons?" said Merle. "They're your friends, boy. You grew up with them. You know them better than their fathers do. What is it? All the wars? Drinking?"

"I don't know, Father," said Franklin, taking the easiest way out. He folded his napkin with a neat finality. He stood. "There's a dance out at the club tonight," he said. "I thought I'd go."

"You do that," said Merle.

But Franklin didn't. He got as far as the country club's parking lot, then didn't go in.

Suddenly he didn't want to see his friends—the killers of their fathers' dreams. Their young faces were the faces of old men hanging upside down, their expressions grotesque and unintelligible. Hanging upside down, they swung from bar to ballroom to crap game, and back to bar. No one pitied them in that great human belfry, because they were going to be rich, if they weren't already. They didn't have to dream, or even lift a finger.

Franklin went to a movie alone. The movie failed to suggest a way in which he might improve his life. It suggested that he be kind and loving and humble, and Franklin was nothing if he wasn't kind and loving and humble.

The colors of the farm the next day were the colors of straw and frost. The land was Merle's, and it was flat as a billiard table. The jackets and caps of Merle and Franklin, of Rudy and Karl, made a tiny cluster of bright colors in a field.

Franklin knelt in the stubble, cocking the trap that would send a clay pigeon skimming over the field. "Ready," he said.

Merle threw his gun to his shoulder, squinted down the barrel, grimaced, and lowered the gun once more. "Pull!" he said.

Franklin jerked the lanyard of the trap. Out flew the clay pigeon.

Merle fired one barrel and then, with the pigeon out of range, clowningly fired the other. He'd missed. He'd been missing all afternoon. He didn't seem to mind much. He was, after all, still the boss.

"Behind it," said Merle. "I'm trying too hard. I'm not leading." He broke down his gun and the empty shells popped out. "Next?" he said. "Karl?"

Franklin loaded another clay pigeon into the trap. It was a very dead pigeon. So would the next one be. Karl hadn't missed all afternoon, and after Karl came Rudy, who hadn't missed, either.

Surprisingly, neither had Franklin. Not giving a damn, he had come to be at one with the universe. With brainless harmony like that, he'd found that he couldn't miss.

If Merle's shots hadn't been going wild, the only words spoken might have been a steady rhythm of "Ready . . . Pull . . . Ready . . . Pull." Nothing had been said about the murder of Franklin's small dream—the dream of being an actor. Merle had made no triumphant announcement about the boy's definitely taking over the factory someday.

In the small world of a man hunched over, Franklin cocked the trap and had a nightmarish feeling that they had been shooting clay pigeons for years, that that was all there was to life, that only death could end it.

His feet were frozen.

"Ready," said Franklin.

"Pull!" said Karl.

Out went the clay pigeon. *Bang* went the gun, and the bird was dust.

Rudy tapped his temple, then saluted Karl with a crooked finger. Karl returned the salute. That had been going on all afternoon—without a trace of a smile. Karl stepped back and Rudy stepped up, the next cog in the humorless clay-pigeon-destroying machine.

It was now Karl's turn to work the trap. As he and Franklin changed places, Franklin hit him on the arm and gave him a cynical smile. Franklin put everything into that blow and the smile—fathers and sons, young dreams and old dreams, bosses and employees, cold feet, boredom, and gunpowder.

It was a crazy thing for Franklin to do. It was the most intimate thing that had ever passed between him and Karl. It was a desperate thing to do. Franklin had to know if there was a human being inside Karl and, if so, what the being was like.

Karl showed a little of himself—not much. He showed he could blush. And for a split second, he showed that there was something he'd like to explain to Franklin.

But all that vanished fast. He didn't smile back. "Ready," he said.

"Pull!" said Rudy.

Out went the clay pigeon. *Bang* went the gun, and the bird was dust.

"We're going to have to find something harder for you guys and easier for me," said Merle. "I can't complain about the gun, because the damn thing cost me six hundred dollars. What I need is a six-dollar gun I can hold responsible for everything."

"Sun's going down. Light's getting bad," said Rudy.

"Guess we better knock off," said Merle. "No question about who the old folks' champion is, Rudy. But the boys are neck-and-neck. Ought to have some kind of shoot-off."

"They could try the rifle," said Rudy. The rifle leaned against the fence, ready for crows. It had a telescope. It was Merle's.

Merle brought an empty cigarette pack from his pocket and stripped off the foil. He handed the foil to Karl. "You two boys hang this up about two hundred yards from here."

Franklin and Karl trudged along the fence line, trudged off two hundred yards. They were used to being sent together on errands one of them could have handled alone—were used to representing, ceremoniously, their generation as opposed to their fathers'.

Neither said anything until the foil was tacked to a fence post. And then, as they stepped back from the target, Karl said something so shyly that Franklin missed it.

"Beg your pardon?" said Franklin.

"I'm—I'm glad you're not gonna take over the factory," said Karl. "That's good—that's great. Maybe, when you come through town with a show, I'll come backstage and see you. That all right? You'll remember me?"

"Remember you?" said Franklin. "Good gosh, Karl!" For a moment he felt like the actor he'd dreamed briefly of being.

"Get out from under your old man," said Karl, "that's the thing to do. I just wanted to tell you—in case you thought I was thinking something else."

"Thanks, Karl," said Franklin. He shook his head weakly. "But I'm not going to be an actor. I'm going to take over when Father retires. I told him last night."

"Why?" said Karl. "Why?" He was angry.

"It makes the old man happy, and I don't have any better ideas."

"You can do it," Karl said. "You can go away. You can be anything you want!"

Franklin put his hands together, then opened them to form a flower of fatalism. "So can anybody."

Karl's eyes grew huge. "I can't," he said. "I can't! Your father doesn't just have you. He's got his big success." He turned away, so Franklin couldn't see his face. "All my old man's got is me."

"Oh, now, listen," said Franklin. "Hey, now!"

Karl faced him. "I'm what he'd rather have than the half of

Waggoner Pump he could have had for two thousand dollars!" he said. "Every day of my life he's told me so. Every day!"

"Well, my gosh, Karl," said Franklin, "it is a beautiful relationship you've got with your father."

"With my father?" said Karl incredulously. "With yours—with yours. It's him I'm supposed to get to love me. He's supposed to be eating his heart out for a son like me. That's the big idea." He waved his arms. "The station wagon, the duets, the guns that never miss, the damn-fool son that works on hand signals—that's all for your father to want."

Franklin was amazed. "Karl, that's all in your head. You are what your own father would rather have than half of Waggoner Pump or anything!"

"I used to think so," said Karl.

"The plate and cube you made," said Franklin, "you gave them to my father, but they were really a present for yours. And what perfect presents from a son to a father! I never gave my father anything like that—anything I'd put my heart and soul into. I couldn't!"

Karl reddened and turned away again. "I didn't make 'em," he said. He shivered. "I tried. How I tried!"

"I don't understand."

"My father had to make 'em!" said Karl bitterly. "And I found out it didn't make any difference to him who made 'em, just as long as your father thought I'd made 'em."

Franklin gave a sad, low whistle.

"When my old man did that, he rubbed my nose in what the big thing was to him." Karl actually wiped his nose on his jacket sleeve.

"But Karl—" said Franklin.

"Oh, hell," Karl said, tired. "I don't blame him. Sorry I said anything. I'm OK—I'm OK. I'll live." He flicked the foil target with a fingertip. "I'm gonna miss, and the hell with 'em."

Nothing more was said. The two trudged back to their fathers. It seemed to Franklin that they were leaving behind all they'd said, that the rising wind was whirling their dark thoughts away. By the time they had reached the firing line, Franklin was thinking only of whiskey, steak, and a red-hot stove.

When he and Karl fired at the foil, Franklin ticked a corner. Karl hit it in the middle. Rudy tapped his temple, then saluted Karl with a crooked finger. Karl returned the salute.

After supper, Rudy and Karl played duets for flute and clarinet. They played without sheet music, intricately and beautifully. Franklin and Merle could only keep time with their fingers, hoping that their tapping on the tabletop sounded like drums.

Franklin glanced at his father. When their eyes met, they decided that their drumming wasn't helping. Their drumming stopped.

With the moment to think about, to puzzle him pleasantly, Franklin found that the music wasn't speaking anymore of just Rudy and Karl. It was speaking of all fathers and sons. It was saying what they had all been saying haltingly, sometimes with pain and sometimes with anger and sometimes with cruelty and sometimes with love: that fathers and sons were one.

It was saying, too, that a time for a parting in spirit was near—no matter how close anyone held anyone, no matter what anyone tried.

A Night
for Love

Moonlight is all right for young lovers, and women never seem to get tired of it. But when a man gets older he usually thinks moonlight is too thin and cool for comfort. Turley Whitman thought so. Turley was in his pajamas at his bedroom window, waiting for his daughter Nancy to come home.

He was a huge, kind, handsome man. He looked like a good king, but he was only a company cop in charge of the parking lot at the Reinbeck Abrasives Company. His club, his pistol, his cartridges, and his handcuffs were on a chair by the bed. Turley was confused and upset.

His wife, Milly, was in bed. For about the first time since their three-day honeymoon, in 1936, Milly hadn't put up her hair in curlers. Her hair was all spread out on her pillow. It made her look young and soft and mysterious. Nobody had looked mysterious in that bedroom for years. Milly opened her eyes wide and stared at the moon.

Her attitude was what threw Turley as much as anything. Milly refused to worry about what was maybe happening to Nancy out in the moonlight somewhere so late at night. Milly would drop off to sleep without even knowing it, then wake up and stare at the moon for a while, and she would think big thoughts without telling Turley what they were, and then drop off to sleep again.

"You awake?" said Turley.

"Hm?" said Milly.

"You decided to be awake?"

"I'm staying awake," said Milly dreamily. She sounded like a girl.

"You think you've been staying awake?" said Turley.

"I must have dropped off without knowing it," she said.

"You've been sawing wood for an hour," said Turley.

He made her sound unattractive to herself because he wanted her to wake up more. He wanted her to wake up enough to talk to him instead of just staring at the moon. She hadn't really sawed wood while she slept. She'd been very beautiful and still.

Milly had been the town beauty once. Now her daughter was.

"I don't mind telling you, I'm worried sick," said Turley.

"Oh, honey," said Milly, "they're fine. They've got sense. They aren't crazy kids."

"You want to guarantee they're not cracked up in a ditch somewhere?" said Turley.

This roused Milly. She sat up, frowned, and blinked away her sleepiness. "You really think—"

"I really think!" said Turley. "He gave me his solemn promise he'd have her home two hours ago."

Milly pulled off her covers, put her bare feet close together on the floor. "All right," she said. "I'm sorry. I'm awake now. I'm worried now."

"About time," said Turley. He turned his back to her, and dramatized his responsible watch at the window by putting his big foot on the radiator.

"Do—do we just worry and wait?" said Milly.

"What do you suggest?" said Turley. "If you mean call the police to see if there's been an accident, I took care of that detail while you were sawing wood."

"No accidents?" said Milly in a small, small voice.

"No accidents they know of," said Turley.

"Well—that's—that's a little encouraging."

"Maybe it is to you," said Turley. "It isn't to me." He faced her, and he saw that she was now wide awake enough to hear what he had been wanting to say for some time. "If you'll pardon me saying so, you're treating this thing like it was some kind of holiday. You're acting like her being out with that rich young smart-aleck in his three-hundred-horsepower car was one of the greatest things that ever happened."

Milly stood, shocked and hurt. "Holiday?" she whispered. "Me?"

"Well—you left your hair down, didn't you, just so you'd look nice in case he got a look at you when he finally brought her home?"

Milly bit her lip. "I just thought if there was going to be a row, I didn't want to make it worse by having my hair up in curlers."

"You don't think there should be a row, do you?" said Turley.

"You're the head of the family. You—you do whatever you think is right." Milly went to him, touched him lightly. "Honey," she said, "I don't think it's good. Honest I don't. I'm trying just as hard as I can to think of things to do."

"Like what?" said Turley.

"Why don't you call up his father?" said Milly. "Maybe he knows where they are or what their plans were."

The suggestion had a curious effect on Turley. He continued to tower over Milly, but he no longer dominated the house, or the room, or even his little barefoot wife. "Oh, great!" he said. The words were loud, but they were as hollow as a bass drum.

"Why not?" said Milly.

Turley couldn't face her anymore. He took up his watch at the window again. "That would just be great," he said to the moonlit town. "Roust L. C. Reinbeck himself out of bed. 'Hello—L.C.? This is T.W. What the hell is your son doing with my daughter?'" Turley laughed bitterly.

Milly didn't seem to understand. "You've got a perfect right to call him or anybody else, if you really think there's an emergency," she said. "I mean, everybody's free and equal this time of night."

"Speak for yourself," Turley said, overacting. "Maybe you've been free and equal with the great L. C. Reinbeck, but I never have. And what's more, I never expect to be."

"All I'm saying is, he's human," said Milly.

"You're the expert on that," said Turley. "I'm sure I'm not. He never took me out dancing at the country club."

"He never took me out dancing at the country club, either. He doesn't like dancing." Milly corrected herself. "Or he didn't."

"Please, don't get technical on me this time of night," said Turley. "So he took you out and did whatever he likes to do. So whatever that was, you're the expert on him."

"Honey," said Milly, full of pain, "he took me out to supper once at the Blue Mill, and he took me to a movie once. He took me to *The Thin Man*. And all he did was talk, and all I did was listen. And it wasn't romantic talk. It was about how he was going to turn the abrasives company back into a porcelain company. And he was going to do the designing. And he never did anything of the kind, so that's how expert I am on the great Louis C. Reinbeck." She laid her hand on her bosom. "I'm the expert on you," she said, "if you want to know who I'm the expert on."

Turley made an animal sound.

"What, sweetheart?" said Milly.

"Me," said Turley, impatient. "What you're an expert on— me?"

Milly made helpless giving motions Turley didn't see.

He was standing stock-still, winding up tighter and tighter inside. Suddenly he moved, like a cumbersome windup man. He went to the telephone on the bedside table. "Why *shouldn't* I call him up?" he blustered. "Why shouldn't I?"

He looked up Louis C. Reinbeck's number in the telephone book clumsily, talked to himself about the times the Reinbeck company had gotten him up out of bed in the middle of the night.

He misdialed, hung up, got set to dial again. His courage was fading fast.

Milly hated to see the courage go. "He won't be asleep," she said. "They've been having a party."

"They've been having a what?" said Turley.

"The Reinbecks are having a party tonight—or it's just over."

"How you know that?" said Turley.

"It was in this morning's paper, on the society page. Besides," Milly continued, "you can go in the kitchen and look and see if their lights are on."

"You can see the Reinbeck house from our kitchen?" said Turley.

"Sure," said Milly. "You have to get your head down kind of low and over to one side, but then you can see their house in a corner of the window."

Turley nodded quizzically, watched Milly, thought about her, hard. He dialed again, let the Reinbecks' telephone ring twice. And then he hung up. He dominated his wife, his rooms, and his house again.

Milly knew that she had made a very bad mistake in the past thirty seconds. She was ready to bite off her tongue.

"Every time the Reinbecks do anything," said Turley, "you read every word about it in the paper?"

"Honey," said Milly, "all women read the society page. It doesn't mean anything. It's just a silly something to do when the paper comes. All women do it."

"Sure," said Turley. "Sure. But how many of 'em can say to theirselves, 'I could have been Mrs. Louis C. Reinbeck'?"

Turley made a great point of staying calm, of being like a father to Milly, of forgiving her in advance. "You want to face this thing about those two kids out there in the moonlight somewhere?" he said. "Or you want to go on pretending an accident's the only thing either one of us is thinking about?"

Milly stiffened. "I don't know what you mean," she said.

"You duck your head a hundred times a day to look at that big white house in the corner of the kitchen window, and you don't know what I mean?" said Turley. "Our girl is out in the moonlight somewhere with the kid who's going to get that house someday, and you don't know what I mean? You left your hair down and you stared at the moon and you hardly heard a word I said to you, and you don't know what I mean?" Turley shook his big, imperial head. "You just can't imagine?"

The telephone rang twice in the big white house on the hill. Then it stopped. Louis C. Reinbeck sat on a white iron chair on the lawn in the moonlight. He was looking out at the rolling lovely nonsense of the golf course and, beyond that and below, the town. All the lights in his house were out. He thought his wife, Natalie, was asleep.

Louis was drinking. He was thinking that the moonlight didn't make the world look any better. He thought the moonlight made the world look worse, made it look dead like the moon.

The telephone's ringing twice, then stopping, fitted in well with Louis's mood. The telephone was a good touch—urgency that could wait until hell froze over. "Shatter the night and then hang up," said Louis.

Along with the house and the Reinbeck Abrasives Company, Louis had inherited from his father and grandfather a deep and satisfying sense of having been corrupted by commerce. And like them, Louis thought of himself as a sensitive maker of porcelain, not grinding wheels, born in the wrong place at the wrong time.

Just as the telephone had rung twice at the right time, so did

Louis's wife appear as though on cue. Natalie was a cool, spare Boston girl. Her role was to misunderstand Louis. She did it beautifully, taking apart his reflective moods like a master mechanic.

"Did you hear the telephone ring, Louis?" she said.

"Hm? Oh—yes. Uh-huh," said Louis.

"It rang and then it stopped," said Natalie.

"I know," said Louis. He warned her with a sigh that he didn't want to discuss the telephone call or anything else in a flat, practical Yankee way.

Natalie ignored the warning. "Don't you wonder who it was?"

"No," said Louis.

"Maybe it was a guest who left something. You didn't see anything around, did you, that somebody left?"

"No," said Louis.

"An earring or something, I suppose," said Natalie. She wore a pale-blue cloudlike negligee that Louis had given her. But she made the negligee meaningless by dragging a heavy iron chair across the lawn, to set it next to Louis's. The arms of the chairs clicked together, and Louis jerked his fingers from between them just in time.

Natalie sat down. "Hi," she said.

"Hi," said Louis.

"See the moon?" said Natalie.

"Yup," said Louis.

"Think people had a nice time tonight?" said Natalie.

"I don't know," said Louis, "and I'm sure they don't, either." He meant by this that he was always the only artist and philosopher at his parties. Everybody else was a businessman.

Natalie was used to this. She let it pass. "What time did

Charlie get in?" she said. Charlie was their only son—actually Louis Charles Reinbeck, Junior.

"I'm sure I don't know," said Louis. "He didn't report in to me. Never does."

Natalie, who had been enjoying the moon, now sat forward uneasily. "He is home, isn't he?" she said.

"I haven't the remotest idea," said Louis.

Natalie bounded out of her chair.

She strained her eyes in the night, trying to see if Charlie's car was in the shadows of the garage. "Who did he go out with?" she asked.

"He doesn't talk with me," said Louis.

"Who is he with?" said Natalie.

"If he isn't by himself, then he's with somebody you don't approve of," said Louis.

But Natalie didn't hear him. She was running into the house. Then the telephone rang again, and went on ringing until Natalie answered.

She held the telephone out to Louis. "It's a man named Turley Whitman," she said. "He says he's one of your policemen."

"Something wrong at the plant?" said Louis, taking the phone. "Fire, I hope?"

"No," said Natalie, "nothing as serious as that." From her expression, Louis gathered that something a lot worse had happened. "It seems that our son is out with Mr. Turley's daughter somewhere, that they should have been back hours ago. Mr. Turley is naturally very deeply concerned about his daughter."

"Mr. Turley?" said Louis into the telephone.

"Turley's my first name, sir," said Turley. "Turley Whitman's my whole name."

"I'm going to listen on the upstairs phone," whispered Natalie. She gathered the folds of her negligee, ran manlike up the stairs.

"You probably don't know me except by sight," said Turley. "I'm the guard at the main-plant parking lot."

"Of course I know you—by sight and by name," said Louis. It was a lie. "Now what's this about my son and your daughter?"

Turley wasn't ready to get to the nut of the problem yet. He was still introducing himself and his family. "You probably know my wife a good deal better'n you know me, sir," he said.

There was a woman's small cry of surprise.

For an instant, Louis didn't know if it was the cry of his own wife or of Turley's. But when he heard sounds of somebody trying to hang up, he knew it had to be on Turley's end. Turley's wife obviously didn't want her name dragged in.

Turley was determined to drag it in, though, and he won out. "You knew her by her maiden name, of course," he said, "Milly—Mildred O'Shea."

All sounds of protest at Turley's end died. The death of protests came to Louis as a shocking thing. His shock was compounded as he remembered young, affectionate and pretty, mystifying Milly O'Shea. He hadn't thought of her for years, hadn't known what had become of her.

And yet at the mention of her name, it was as though Louis had thought of her constantly since she'd kissed him good-bye in the moonlight so long before.

"Yes—yes," said Louis. "Yes, I—I remember her well." He wanted to cry about growing old, about the shabby ends brave young lovers came to.

From the mention of Milly's name, Turley had his conversation with the great Louis C. Reinbeck all his own way. The miracle of equality had been achieved. Turley and Louis spoke man to man, father to father, with Louis apologizing, murmuring against his own son.

Louis thanked Turley for having called the police. Louis would call them, too. If he found out anything, he would call Turley at once. Louis addressed Turley as "sir."

Turley was exhilarated when he hung up. "He sends his regards," he said to Milly. He turned to find himself talking to air. Milly had left the room silently, on bare feet.

Turley found her heating coffee in the kitchen on the new electric stove. The stove was named the Globemaster. It had a ridiculously complicated control panel. The Globemaster was a wistful dream of Milly's come true. Not many of her dreams of nice things had come true.

The coffee was boiling, making the pot crackle and spit. Milly didn't notice that it was boiling, even though she was staring at the pot with terrible concentration. The pot spit, stung her hand. She burst into tears, put the stung hand to her mouth. And then she saw Turley.

She tried to duck past him and out of the kitchen, but he caught her arm.

"Honey," he said in a daze. He turned off the Globemaster's burner with his free hand. "Milly," he said.

Milly wanted desperately to get away. Big Turley had such an easy time holding her that he hardly realized he was doing it. Milly subsided at last, her sweet face red and twisted. "Won't— won't you tell me what's wrong, honey?" said Turley.

"Don't worry about me," said Milly. "Go worry about people dying in ditches."

Turley let her go. "I said something wrong?" He was sincerely bewildered.

"Oh, Turley, Turley," said Milly, "I never thought you'd hurt me this way—this much." She cupped her hands as though she were holding something precious. Then she let it fall from her hands, whatever her imagination thought it was.

Turley watched it fall. "Just because I told him your name?" he said.

"When—when you told him my name, there was so much else you told him." She was trying to forgive Turley, but it was hard for her. "I don't suppose you knew what else you were telling him. You couldn't have."

"All I told him was your name," said Turley.

"And all it meant to Louis C. Reinbeck," said Milly, "was that a woman down in the town had two silly little dates with him twenty years ago, and she's talked about nothing else since. And her husband knows about those two silly little dates, too—and he's just as proud of them as she is. Prouder!"

Milly put her head down and to one side, and she pointed out the kitchen window, pointed to a splash of white light in an upper corner of the window. "There," she said, "the great Louis C. Reinbeck is up in all that light somewhere, thinking I've loved him all these years." The floodlights on the Reinbeck house went out. "Now he's up there in the moonlight somewhere—thinking about the poor little woman and the poor little man and their poor little daughter down here." Milly shuddered. "Well, we're not poor! Or we weren't until tonight."

. . . . .

The great Louis C. Reinbeck returned to his drink and his white iron lawn chair. He had called the police, who had told him what they told Turley—that there were no wrecks they knew of.

Natalie sat down beside Louis again. She tried to catch his eye, tried to get him to see her maternal, teasing smile. But Louis wouldn't look.

"You—you know this girl's mother, do you?" she said.

"Knew," said Louis.

"You took her out on nights like this? Full moon and all that?"

"We could dig out a twenty-year-old calendar and see what the phases of the moon were," said Louis tartly. "You can't exactly avoid full moons, you know. You're bound to have one once a month."

"What was the moon on our wedding night?" said Natalie.

"Full?" said Louis.

"New," said Natalie. "Brand-new."

"Women are more sensitive to things like that," said Louis. "They notice things."

He surprised himself by sounding peevish. His conscience was doing funny things to his voice because he couldn't remember much of anything about his honeymoon with Natalie.

He could remember almost everything about the night he and Milly O'Shea had wandered out on the golf course. That night with Milly, the moon had been full.

Now Natalie was saying something. And when she was done, Louis had to ask her to say it all over again. He hadn't heard a word.

"I said, 'What's it like?'" said Natalie.

"What's what like?" said Louis.

"Being a young male Reinbeck—all hot-blooded and full of dreams, swooping down off the hill, grabbing a pretty little town girl and spiriting her into the moonlight." She laughed, teasing. "It must be kind of godlike."

"It isn't," said Louis.

"It isn't godlike?"

"Godlike? I never felt more human in all my life!" Louis threw his empty glass in the direction of the golf course. He wished he'd been strong enough to throw the glass straight to the spot where Milly had kissed him good-bye.

"Then let's hope Charlie marries this hot little girl from town," said Natalie. "Let's have no more cold, inhuman Reinbeck wives like me." She stood. "Face it, you would have been a thousand times happier if you'd married your Milly O'Shea."

She went to bed.

"Who's kidding anybody?" Turley Whitman asked his wife. "You would have been a million times happier if you'd married Louis Reinbeck." He was back at his post by the bedroom window, back with his big foot on the radiator.

Milly was sitting on the edge of the bed. "Not a million times, not two times, not the-smallest-number-there-is times happier," said Milly. She was wretched. "Turley—please don't say anything more like that. I can't stand it, it's so crazy."

"Well, you were kind of calling a spade a spade down there in the kitchen," said Turley, "giving me hell for telling the great Louis Reinbeck your name. Let me just call a spade a spade here, and say neither one of us wants our daughter to make the same mistake you did."

Milly went to him, put her arms around him. "Turley, please, that's the worst thing you could say to me."

He turned a stubborn red, was as unyielding as a statue. "I remember all the big promises I made you, all the big talk," he said. "Neither of us thinks company cop is one of the biggest jobs a man can hold."

Milly tried to shake him, with no luck. "I don't care what your job is," she said.

"I was gonna have more money than the great L. C. Reinbeck," said Turley, "and I was gonna make it all myself. Remember, Milly? That's what really sold you, wasn't it?"

Her arms dropped away from him. "No," she said.

"My famous good looks?" said Turley.

"They had a lot to do with it," said Milly. His looks had gone very well with the looks of the prettiest girl in town. "Most of all," she said, "it was the great Louis C. Reinbeck and the moon."

The great Louis C. Reinbeck was in his bedroom. His wife was in bed with the covers pulled up over her head. The room was cunningly contrived to give the illusion of romance and undying true love, no matter what really went on there.

Up to now, almost everything that had gone on in the room had been reasonably pleasant. Now it appeared that the marriage of Louis and Natalie was at an end. When Louis made her pull the covers away from her face, when Natalie showed him how swollen her face was with tears, this was plainly the case. This was the end.

Louis was miserable—he couldn't understand how things had fallen to pieces so fast. "I—I haven't thought of Milly O'Shea for twenty years," he said.

"Please—no. Don't lie. Don't explain," said Natalie. "I understand."

"I swear," said Louis. "I haven't seen her for twenty years."

"I believe you," said Natalie. "That's what makes it so much worse. I wish you had seen her—just as often as you liked. That would have been better, somehow, than all this—this—" She sat up, ransacked her mind for the right word. "All this horrible, empty, aching, nagging regret." She lay back down.

"About Milly?" said Louis.

"About Milly, about me, about the abrasives company, about all the things you wanted and didn't get, about all the things you got that you didn't want. Milly and me—that's as good a way of saying it as anything. That pretty well says it all."

"I—I don't love her. I never did," said Louis.

"You must have liked the one and only time in your life you felt human," said Natalie. "Whatever happened in the moonlight must have been nice—much nicer than anything you and I ever had."

Louis's nightmare got worse, because he knew Natalie had spoken the truth. There never had been anything as nice as that time in the moonlight with Milly.

"There was absolutely nothing there, no basis for love," said Louis. "We were perfect strangers then. I knew her as little as I know her now."

Louis's muscles knotted and the words came hard, because he thought he was extracting something from himself of terrible importance. "I—I suppose she is a symbol of my own disappointment in myself, of all I might have been," he said.

He went to the bedroom window, looked morbidly at the setting moon. The moon's rays were flat now, casting long shadows on the golf course, exaggerating the toy geography. Flags flew here and there, signifying less than nothing. This was where the great love scene had been played.

Suddenly he understood. "Moonlight," he murmured.

"What?" said Natalie.

"It had to be." Louis laughed, because the explanation was so explosively simple. "We had to be in love, with a moon like that, in a world like that. We owed it to the moon."

Natalie sat up, her disposition much improved.

"The richest boy in town and the prettiest girl in town," said Louis, "we couldn't let the moon down, could we?"

He laughed again, made his wife get out of bed, made her look at the moon with him. "And here I'd been thinking it really had been something big between Milly and me way back then." He shook his head. "When all it was was pure, beautiful, moonlit hokum."

He led his wife to bed. "You're the only one I ever loved. An hour ago, I didn't know that. I know that now."

So everything was fine.

"I won't lie to you," Milly Whitman said to her husband. "I loved the great Louis C. Reinbeck for a while. Out there on the golf course in the moonlight, I just had to fall in love. Can you understand that—how I would have to fall in love with him, even if we didn't like each other very well?"

Turley allowed as how he could see how that would be. But he wasn't happy about it.

"We kissed only once," said Milly. "And if he'd kissed me right, I think I might really be Mrs. Louis C. Reinbeck tonight." She nodded. "Since we're calling spades spades tonight, we might as well call that one a spade, too. And just before we kissed up there on the golf course, I was thinking what a poor little rich boy he was, and how much happier I could make him than any old cold, stuck-up country club girl. And then he kissed me, and I knew he wasn't in love, couldn't ever be in love. So I made that kiss good-bye."

"There's where you made your mistake," said Turley.

"No," said Milly, "because the next boy who kissed me kissed me right, showed me he knew what love was, even if there wasn't a moon. And I lived happily ever after, until tonight." She put her arms around Turley. "Now kiss me again the way you kissed me the first time, and I'll be all right tonight, too."

Turley did, so everything was all right there, too.

About twenty minutes after that, the telephones in both houses rang. The burden of the messages was that Charlie Reinbeck and Nancy Whitman were fine. They had, however, put their own interpretation on the moonlight. They'd decided that Cinderella and Prince Charming had as good a chance as anybody for really living happily ever after. So they'd married.

So now there was a new household. Whether everything was all right there remained to be seen. The moon went down.

Find Me
a Dream

If the Communists ever expect to overtake the democracies in sewer pipe production, they are certainly going to have to hump some—because just one factory in Creon, Pennsylvania, produces more pipe in six months than both Russia and China put together could produce in a year. That wonderful factory is the Creon Works of the General Forge and Foundry Company.

As Works manager, Arvin Borders told every rookie engineer, "If you don't like sewer pipe, you won't like Creon." Borders himself, a forty-six-year-old bachelor, was known throughout the industry as "Mr. Pipe."

Creon is the Pipe City. The high school football team is the Creon Pipers. The only country club is the Pipe City Golf and

Country Club. There is a permanent exhibit of pipe in the club lobby, and the band that plays for the Friday-night dances at the club is Andy Middleton and His Creon Pipe-Dreamers.

One Friday night in the summertime, Andy Middleton turned the band over to his piano player. He went out to the first tee for some peace and fresh air. He surprised a pretty young woman out there. She was crying. Andy had never seen her before. He was twenty-five at the time.

Andy asked if he could help her.

"I'm being very silly," she said. "Everything is fine. I'm just being silly."

"I see," said Andy.

"I cry very easily—and even when there's nothing at all to cry about, I cry," she said.

"That must be kind of confusing for people who are with you," he said.

"It's a mess," she said.

"It might come in handy in case you ever have to attend the funeral of someone you hate," he said.

"It isn't going to be very handy in the pipe industry," she said.

"Are you in the pipe industry?" he said.

"Isn't everybody in Creon in the pipe industry?" she said.

"I'm not," he said.

"How do you keep from starving to death?" she said.

"I wave a stick in front of a band . . . give music lessons . . . things like that," he said.

"Oh, God—a musician," she said, and she turned her back.

"That's against me?" he said.

"I never want to see another musician as long as I live," she said.

"In that case," he said, "close your eyes and I'll tiptoe away."
But he didn't leave.

"That's your band—playing tonight?" she said. They could
hear the music quite clearly.

"That's right," he said.

"You can stay," she said.

"Pardon me?" he said.

"You're no musician," she said, "or that band would have
made you curl up and die."

"You're the first person who ever listened to it," he said.

"I bet that's really the truth," she said. "Those people don't
hear anything that isn't about pipe. When they dance, do they
keep any kind of time to the music?"

"When they what?" he said.

"I said," she repeated, "when they dance."

"How can they dance," he said, "if the men spend the whole
evening in the locker room, drinking, shooting crap, and talking
sewer pipe, and all the women sit out on the terrace, talking about things they've overheard about pipe, about things
they've bought with money from pipe, about things they'd like
to buy with money from pipe?"

She started weeping again.

"Just being silly again?" he said. "Everything still fine?"

"Everything's fine," she said. The demoralized, ramshackle
little band in the empty ballroom ended a number with razz-
berries and squeals. "Oh God, but that band hates music!" she
said.

"They didn't always," he said.

"What happened?" she said.

"They found out they weren't ever going anywhere but
Creon—and they found out nobody in Creon would listen. If

I went and told them a beautiful woman was listening and weeping out here, they might get back a little of what they had once—and make a present of it to you."

"What's your instrument?" she said.

"Clarinet," he said. "Any special requests—any melodies you'd like to have us waft from the clubhouse while you weep alone?"

"No," she said. "That's sweet, but no music for me."

"Tranquilizers? Aspirin?" he said. "Cigarettes, chewing gum, candy?"

"A drink," she said.

Shouldering his way to the crowded bar, a bar called The Jolly Piper, Andy learned a lot of things about the sewer pipe business. Cleveland, he learned, had bought a lot of cheap pipe from another company, and Cleveland was going to be sorry about it in about twenty years. The Navy had specified Creon pipe for all buildings under construction, he learned, and nobody was going to be sorry. It was a little-known fact, he learned, that the whole world stood in awe of American pipe-making capabilities.

He also found out who the woman on the first tee was. She had been brought to the dance by Arvin Borders, bachelor manager of the Creon Works. Borders had met her in New York. She was a small-time actress, the widow of a jazz musician, the mother of two very young daughters.

Andy found out all this from the bartender. Arvin Borders, "Mr. Pipe" himself, came into the bar and craned his neck, looking for somebody. He was carrying two highballs. The ice in both glasses had melted.

"Still haven't seen her, Mr. Borders," the bartender called to him, and Borders nodded unhappily and left.

"Who haven't you seen?" Andy asked the bartender.

And the bartender told him all he knew about the widow. He also gave Andy the opinion, out of the corner of his mouth, that General Forge and Foundry Company headquarters in Ilium, New York, knew about the romance and took a very dim view of it. "You tell me where, in all of Creon," the bartender said to Andy, "a pretty, young New York actress could fit in."

The woman went by her stage name, which was Hildy Matthews, Andy learned. The bartender didn't have any idea who her husband had been.

Andy went into the ballroom to tell his Pipe-Dreamers to play a little better for a weeping lady on the golf course, and he found Arvin Borders talking to them. Borders, an earnest, thick-set man, was asking the band to play "Indian Love Call" very loud.

"Loud?" said Andy.

"So she'll hear it, wherever she is, and come," said Borders. "I can't imagine where she got to," he said. "I left her on the terrace, with the ladies, for a while—and she just plain evaporated."

"Maybe she got fed up with all the talk about pipe," said Andy.

"She's very interested in pipe," said Borders. "You wouldn't think a woman who looked like that would be, but she can listen to me talk shop for hours and never get tired of it."

"'Indian Love Call' will bring her back?" said Andy.

Borders mumbled something unintelligible.

"Pardon me, sir?" said Andy.

Borders turned red and pulled in his chin. "I said," he said gruffly, "'it's our tune.'"

"I see," said Andy.

"You boys might as well know now—I'm going to marry that girl," said Borders. "We're going to announce our engagement tonight."

Andy bowed slightly. "Congratulations," he said. He put his two highballs down on a chair, picked up his clarinet. "'Indian Love Call,' boys—real loud?" he said.

The band was slow to respond. Nobody seemed to want to play much, and everybody was trying to tell Andy something.

"What's the trouble?" said Andy.

"Before we play, Andy," said the pianist, "you ought to know just who we're playing for, whose *widow* we're playing for."

"Whose widow?" said Andy.

"I had no idea he was so famous," said Borders. "I mentioned him to your band here, and they almost fell off their chairs."

"Who?" said Andy.

"A dope fiend, an alcoholic, a wife-beater, and a woman-chaser who was shot dead last year by a jealous husband," said Borders indignantly. "Why anybody would think there was anything wonderful about a man like that I'll never know," he said. And then he gave the name of the man, a man who was probably the greatest jazz musician who had ever lived.

"I thought you weren't ever coming back," she said, out of the shadows on the first tee.

"I had to play a special request," said Andy. "Somebody wanted me to play 'Indian Love Call' as loud as I could."

"Oh," she said.

"You heard it and you didn't come running?" he said.

"Is that what he expected me to do?" she said.

"He said it was your tune," he said.

"That was his idea," she said. "He thinks it's the most beautiful song ever written."

"How did you two happen to meet?" he said.

"I was dead broke, looking for any kind of work at all," she said. "There was a General Forge and Foundry Company sales meeting in New York. They were going to put on a skit. They needed an actress. I got the part."

"What part did they give you?" he said.

"They dressed me in gold lamé, gave me a crown of pipe fittings, and introduced me as 'Miss Pipe Opportunities in the Golden Sixties,'" she said. "Arvin Borders was there," she said. She emptied her glass. "Kismet," she said.

"Kismet," he said.

She took his highball from him. "I'm sorry," she said, "I'm going to need this one, too."

"And ten more besides?" he said.

"If it takes ten more to get me back to all those people, all those lights, all that pipe," she said, "I'll drink ten more."

"The trip's that tough?" he said.

"If only I hadn't wandered out here," she said. "If only I'd stayed up there!"

"One of the worst mistakes a person can make, sometimes, I guess," he said, "is to try to get away from people and think. It's a great way to lose your forward motion."

"The band is playing so softly I can hardly hear the music," she said.

"They know whose widow's listening," he said, "and they'd just as soon you didn't hear them."

"Oh," she said. "They know. You know."

"He—he didn't leave you anything?" he said.

"Debts," she said. "Two daughters . . . for which I'm really very grateful."

"The horn?" he said.

"It's with him," she said. "Please—could I have one more drink?"

"One more drink," he said, "and you'll have to go back to your fiancé on your hands and knees."

"I'm perfectly capable of taking care of myself, thank you," she said. "It isn't up to you to watch out for me."

"Beg your pardon," he said.

She gave a small, melodious hiccup. "What a terrible time for that to happen," she said. "It doesn't have anything to do with drinking."

"I believe you," he said.

"You don't believe me," she said. "Give me some kind of a test. Make me walk a straight line or say something complicated."

"Forget it," he said.

"You don't believe I love Arvin Borders, either, do you?" she said. "Well, let me tell you that one of the things I do best is love. I don't mean pretending to love. I mean really loving. When I love somebody, I don't hold anything back. I go all the way, and right now I happen to love Arvin Borders."

"Lucky man," he said.

"Would you like to hear exactly how much I have already learned about pipe?" she said.

"Go ahead," he said.

"I read a whole book about pipe," she said. "I went to the public library and got down a book about pipe and nothing else but pipe."

"What did the book say?" he said.

From the tennis courts to the west came faint, crooning calls. Borders was now prowling the club grounds, looking for his Hildy. "Hildeee," he was calling. "Hildy?"

"You want me to yell yoo-hoo?" said Andy.

"Shhh!" she said. And she gave the small, melodious hiccup.

Arvin Borders wandered off into the parking lot, his cries fading away in the darkness that enveloped him.

"You were going to tell me about pipe," said Andy.

"Let's talk about you," she said.

"What would you like to know about me?" he said.

"People have to ask you questions or you can't talk?" she said.

He shrugged. "Small-time musician. Never married. Big dreams once. Big dreams all gone."

"Big dreams of what?" she said.

"Being half the musician your husband was," he said. "You want to hear more?"

"I love to hear other people's dreams," she said.

"All right—love," he said.

"You've never had that?" she said.

"Not that I've noticed," he said.

"May I ask you a very personal question?" she said.

"About my ability as a great lover?" he said.

"No," she said. "I think that would be a very silly kind of question. I think everybody young is basically a great lover. All anybody needs is the chance."

"Ask the *personal* question," he said.

"Do you make any money?" she said.

Andy didn't answer right away.

"Is that too personal?" she said.

"I don't guess it would kill me to answer," he said. He did some figuring in his head, gave her an honest report of his earnings.

"Why, that's very good," she said.

"More than a schoolteacher, less than a school janitor," he said.

"Do you live in an apartment or what?" she said.

"A big old house I inherited from my family," he said.

"You're really quite well off when you stop to think about it," she said. "Do you like little children—little girls?"

"Don't you think you'd better be getting back to your fiancé?" he said.

"My questions keep getting more and more personal," she said. "I can't help it, my own life has been so personal. Crazy, personal things happen to me all the time."

"I think we'd better break this up," he said.

She ignored him. "For instance," she said, "I pray for certain kinds of people to come to me, and they come to me. One time when I was very young, I prayed for a great musician to come and fall in love with me—and he did. And I loved him, too, even though he was the worst husband a woman could have. That's how good I am at loving."

"Hooray," he said quietly.

"And then," she said, "when my husband died and there was nothing to eat and I was sick of wild and crazy nights and days, I prayed for a solid, sensible, rich businessman to come along."

"And he did," said Andy.

"And then," she said, "when I came out here and ran away from all the people who liked pipe so much—do you know what I prayed for?"

"Nope," he said.

"A man to bring me a drink," she said. "That was all. I give you my word of honor, that was all."

"And I brought you two drinks," he said.

"And that isn't all, either," she said.

"Oh?" he said.

"I think that I could love you very much," she said.

"A pretty tough thing to do," he said.

"Not for me," she said. "I think you could be a very good musician if somebody encouraged you. And I could give you the big and beautiful love you want. You'd definitely have that."

"This is a proposal of marriage?" he said.

"Yes," she said. "And if you say no, I don't know what I'll do. I'll crawl under the shrubbery here and just die. I can't go back to all those pipe people, and there's no place else *to* go."

"I'm supposed to say yes?" he said.

"If you feel like saying yes, then say yes," she said.

"All right—" he said at last, "yes."

"We're both going to be so glad this happened," she said.

"What about Arvin Borders?" he said.

"We're doing him a favor," she said.

"We are?" he said.

"Oh, yes," she said. "On the terrace there, a woman came right out and said it would ruin Arvin's career if he married a woman like me—and you know, it probably would, too."

"That was the crack that sent you out here into the shadows?" he said.

"Yes," she said. "It was very upsetting. I didn't want to hurt anybody's career."

"That's considerate of you," he said.

"But you," she said, taking his arm, "I don't see how I could do anything for you but a world of good. You wait," she said. "You wait and see."

Runaways

They left a note saying teenagers were as capable of true love as anybody else—maybe more capable. And then they took off for parts unknown.

They took off in the boy's old blue Ford, with baby shoes dangling from the rearview mirror, with a pile of comic books on the burst backseat.

A police alarm went out for them right away, and their pictures were in the papers and on television. But they weren't caught for twenty-four hours. They got all the way to Chicago. A patrolman spotted them shopping together in a supermarket there, caught them buying what looked like a lifetime supply of candy, cosmetics, soft drinks, and frozen pizzas.

The girl's father gave the patrolman a two-hundred-dollar

reward. The girl's father was Jesse K. Southard, governor of the state of Indiana.

That was why they got so much publicity. It was exciting when an ex–reform school kid, a kid who ran a lawn mower at the governor's country club, ran off with the governor's daughter.

When the Indiana State Police brought the girl back to the Governor's Mansion in Indianapolis, Governor Southard announced that he would take immediate steps to get an annulment. An irreverent reporter pointed out to him that there could hardly be an annulment, since there hadn't been a marriage.

The governor blew up. "That boy never laid a finger on her," he roared, "because she wouldn't let him! And I'll knock the block off any man who says otherwise."

The reporters wanted to talk to the girl, naturally, and the governor said she would have a statement for them in about an hour. It wouldn't be her first statement about the escapade. In Chicago she and the boy had lectured reporters and police on love, hypocrisy, persecution of teenagers, the insensitivity of parents, and even rockets, Russia, and the hydrogen bomb.

When the girl came downstairs with her new statement, however, she contradicted everything she'd said in Chicago. Reading from a three-page typewritten script, she said the adventure had been a nightmare, said she didn't love the boy and never had, said she must have been crazy, and said she never wanted to see the boy again.

She said the only people she loved were her parents, said she didn't see how she could make it up to them for all the heartaches she had caused, said she was going to concentrate on schoolwork and getting into college, and said she didn't want to pose for pictures because she looked so awful after the ordeal.

She didn't look especially awful, except that she'd dyed her hair red, and the boy had given her a terrible haircut in an effort to disguise her. And she'd been crying some. She didn't look tired. She looked young and wild and captured—that was all.

Her name was Annie—Annie Southard.

When the reporters left, when they went to show the boy the girl's latest statement, the governor turned to his daughter and said to her, "Well, I certainly want to thank you. I don't see how I can ever thank you enough."

"You thank me for telling all those lies?" she said.

"I thank you for making a very small beginning in repairing the damage you've done," he said.

"My own father, the governor of the state of Indiana," said Annie, "ordered me to lie. I'll never forget that."

"That isn't the last of the orders you'll get from me," he said.

Annie said nothing out loud, but in her mind she placed a curse on her parents. She no longer owed them anything. She was going to be cold and indifferent to them for the rest of her days. The curse went into effect immediately.

Annie's mother, Mary, came down the spiral staircase. She had been listening to the lies from the landing above. "I think you handled that very well," she said to her husband.

"As well as I could, under the circumstances," he said.

"I only wish we could come out and say what there really is to say," said Annie's mother. "If we could only just come out and say we're not against love, and we're not against people who don't have money." She started to touch her daughter comfortingly, but was warned against it by Annie's eyes. "We're not snobs, darling—and we're not insensitive to love. Love is the most wonderful thing there is."

The governor turned away and glared out a window.

"We *believe* in love," said Annie's mother. "You've seen how much I love your father and how much your father loves me—and how much your father and I love you."

"If you're going to come out and say something, say it," said the governor.

"I thought I was," said his wife.

"Talk money, talk breeding, talk education, talk friends, talk interests," said the governor, "and then you can get back to love if you want." He faced his women. "Talk happiness, for heaven's sake," he said. "See that boy again, keep this thing going, marry him when you can do it legally, when we can't stop you," he said to Annie, "and not only will you be the unhappiest woman alive, but he'll be the unhappiest man alive. It will be a mess you can truly be proud of, because you will have married without having met a single condition for a happy marriage—and by single condition I mean one single, solitary thing in common.

"What did you plan to do for friends?" he said. "His gang at the poolroom or your gang at the country club? Would you start out by buying him a nice house and nice furniture and a nice automobile—or would you wait for him to buy those things, which he'll be just about ready to pay for when hell freezes over? Do you like comic books as well as he does? Do you like the same kind of comic books?" cried the governor.

"Who do you think you are?" he asked Annie. "You think you're Eve, and God only made one Adam for you?"

"Yes," said Annie, and she went upstairs to her room and

slammed the door. Moments later music came from her room. She was playing a record.

The governor and his wife stood outside the door and listened to the words of the song. These were the words:

They say we don't know what love is,
Boo-wah-wah, uh-huh, yeah.
But we know what the message in the stars above is,
Boo-wah-wah, uh-huh, yeah.
So hold me, hold me, baby,
And you'll make my poor heart sing,
Because everything they tell us, baby,
Why, it just don't mean a thing.

Eight miles away, eight miles due south, through the heart of town and out the other side, reporters were clumping onto the front porch of the boy's father's house.

It was old, cheap, a carpenter's special, a 1926 bungalow. Its front windows looked out into the perpetual damp twilight of a huge front porch. Its side windows looked into the neighbors' windows ten feet away. Light could reach the interior only through a window in the back. As luck would have it, the window let light into a tiny pantry.

The boy and his father and his mother did not hear the reporters knocking. The television set in the living room and the radio in the kitchen were both on, blatting away, and the family was having a row in the dining room, halfway between them.

The row was actually about everything in creation, but it had for its subject of the moment the boy's mustache. He had been growing it for a month and had just been caught by his father in the act of blacking it with shoe polish.

The boy's name was Rice Brentner. It was true, as the papers said, that Rice had spent time in reform school. That was three years behind him now. His crime had been, at the age of thirteen, the theft of sixteen automobiles within a period of a week. Except for the escapade with Annie, he hadn't been in any real trouble since.

"You march into the bathroom," said his mother, "and you shave that awful thing off."

Rice did not march. He stayed right where he was.

"You heard your mother," his father said. When Rice still didn't budge, his father tried to hurt him with scorn. "Makes him feel like a man, I guess—like a great big man," he said.

"Doesn't make him look like a man," said his mother. "It makes him look like an I-don't-know-what-it-is."

"You just named him," said his father. "That's exactly what he is: an I-don't-know-what-it-is." Finding a label like that seemed to ease the boy's father some. He was, as one newspaper and then all the newspapers had pointed out, an eighty-nine-dollar-and sixty-two-cent-a-week supply clerk in the main office of the public school system. He had reason to resent the thoroughness of the reporter who had dug that figure from the public records. The sixty-two cents galled him in particular. "An eighty-nine-dollar-and-sixty-two-cent-a-week supply clerk has an I-don't-know-what-it-is for a son," he said. "The Brentner family is certainly covered with glory today."

"Do you realize how lucky you are not to be in jail—rotting?" said Rice's mother. "If they had you in jail, they'd not only shave off your mustache, without even asking you about it—they'd shave off every hair on your head."

Rice wasn't listening much, only enough to keep himself smoldering comfortably. What he was thinking about was his car. He had paid for it with money he himself had earned. It hadn't cost his family a dime. Rice now swore to himself that if his parents tried to take his car away from him, he would leave home for good.

"He knows about jail. He's been there before," said his father.

"Let him keep his mustache if he wants to," said his mother. "I just wish he'd look in a mirror once to see how silly it makes him look."

"All right—let him keep it," said his father, "but I'll tell you one thing he isn't going to keep, and I give you my word of honor on that, and that's the automobile."

"Amen!" said his mother. "He's going to march down to a used-car lot, and he's going to sell the car, and then he's going to march over to the bank and put the money in his savings account, and then he's going to march home and give us the bankbook." As she uttered this complicated promise she became more and more martial until, at the end, she was marching in place like John Philip Sousa.

"You said a mouthful!" said her husband.

And now that the subject of the automobile had been introduced, it became the dominant theme and the loudest one of all. The old blue Ford was such a frightening symbol of disastrous freedom to Rice's parents that they could yammer about it endlessly.

And they just about did yammer about it endlessly this time.

"Well—the car is going," said Rice's mother, winded at last.

"That's the end of the car," said his father.

"And that's the end of me," said Rice. He walked out the back door, got into his car, turned on the radio, and drove away.

Music came from the radio. The song told of two teenagers who were going to get married, even though they were dead broke. The chorus of it went like this:

We'll have no fancy drapes—
No stove, no carpet, no refrigerator.
But our nest will look like a hunk of heaven,
Because love, baby, is our interior decorator.

Rice went to a phone booth a mile from the Governor's Mansion. He called the number that was the governor's family's private line.

He pitched his voice a half-octave higher, and he asked to speak to Annie.

It was the butler who answered. "I'm sorry, sir," he said, "but I don't think she's taking any calls just now. You want to leave your name?"

"Tell her it's Bob Counsel," said Rice. Counsel was the son of a man who had gotten very rich on coin-operated laundries. He spent most of his time at the country club. He was in love with Annie.

"I didn't recognize your voice for a minute there, Mr. Counsel," said the butler. "Please hold on, sir, if you'd be so kind."

Seconds later Annie's mother was on the phone. She wanted to believe so desperately that the caller was the polite and attractive and respectable Bob Counsel that she didn't even begin to suspect a fraud. And she did almost all the talking, so Rice had only to grunt from time to time.

"Oh Bob, oh Bob, oh Bob—you dear boy," she said. "How

nice, how awfully nice of you to call. It was what I was *praying* for! She *has* to talk to somebody her own age. Oh, her father and I have talked to her, and I guess she heard us, but there's such a gap between the generations these days.

"This thing—this thing Annie's been through," said Annie's mother, "it's more like a nervous breakdown than anything else. It isn't really a nervous breakdown, but she isn't herself—isn't the Annie we know. Do you understand what I'm trying to say?"

"Yup," said Rice.

"Oh, she'll be so glad to hear from you, Bob—to know she's still got her old friends, her real friends to fall back on. Hearing your voice," said the governor's wife, "our Annie will know everything's going to get back to normal again."

She went to get Annie—and had a ding-dong wrangle with her that Rice could hear over the telephone. Annie said she hated Bob Counsel, thought he was a jerk, a stuffed shirt, and a mamma's boy. Somebody thought to cover the mouthpiece at that point, so Rice didn't hear anything more until Annie came on the line.

"Hullo," she said emptily.

"I thought you might enjoy a ride—to kind of take your mind off your troubles," said Rice.

"What?" said Annie.

"This is Rice," he said. "Tell your mother you're going to the club to play tennis with good old Bob Counsel. Meet me at the gas station at Forty-sixth and Illinois."

So half an hour later, they took off again in the boy's old blue Ford, with baby shoes dangling from the rearview mirror, with a pile of comic books on the burst backseat.

The car radio sang as Annie and Rice left the city limits behind:

Oh, baby, baby, baby,
What a happy, rockin' day,
'Cause your sweet love and kisses
Chase those big, black blues away.

And the exhilarating chase began again.

Annie and Rice crossed the Ohio border on a back road and listened to the radio talk about them above the sound of gravel rattling in the fenders.

They had listened impatiently to news of a riot in Bangalore, of an airplane collision in Ireland, of a man who blew up his wife with nitroglycerine in West Virginia. The newscaster had saved the biggest news for last—that Annie and Rice, Juliet and Romeo, were playing hare and hounds again.

The newscaster called Rice "Rick," something nobody had ever called him, and Rice and Annie liked that.

"I'm going to call you Rick from now on," said Annie.

"That's all right with me," said Rice.

"You look more like a Rick than a Rice," said Annie. "How come they named you Rice?"

"Didn't I ever tell you?" said Rice.

"If you did," she said, "I've forgot."

The fact was that Rice had told her about a dozen times why he was named Rice, but she never really listened to him. For that matter, Rice never really listened to her, either. Both would have been bored stiff if they had listened, but they spared themselves that.

So their conversations were marvels of irrelevance. There

were only two subjects in common—self-pity and something called love.

"My mother had some ancestor back somewhere named Rice," said Rice. "He was a doctor, and I guess he was pretty famous."

"Dr. Siebolt is the only person who ever tried to understand me as a human being," said Annie. Dr. Siebolt was the governor's family physician.

"There's some other famous people back there somewhere, too—on my mother's side," said Rice. "I don't know what all they did, but there's good blood back there."

"Dr. Siebolt would hear what I was trying to say," said Annie. "My parents never had time to listen."

"That's why my old man always got burned up at me—because I've got so much of my mother's blood," said Rice. "You know—I want to do things and have things and live and take chances, and his side of the family isn't that way at all."

"I could talk to Dr. Siebolt about love—I could talk to him about anything," said Annie. "With my parents there were just all kinds of things I had to keep bottled up."

"Safety first—that's their motto," said Rice. "Well, that isn't my motto. They want me to end up the way they have, and I'm just not that kind of a person."

"It's a terrible thing to make somebody bottle things up," said Annie. "I used to cry all the time, and my parents never could figure out why."

"That's why I stole those cars," said Rice. "I just all of a sudden went crazy one day. They were trying to make me act like my father, and I'm just not that kind of man. They never understood me. They don't understand me yet."

"But the worst thing," said Annie, "was then my own father ordered me to lie. That was when I realized that my parents didn't care about truth. All they care about is what people think."

"This summer," said Rice, "I was actually making more money than my old man or any of his brothers. That really ate into him. He couldn't stand that."

"My mother started talking to me about love," said Annie, "and it was all I could do to keep from screaming, 'You don't know what love is! You never have known what it is!'"

"My parents kept telling me to act like a man," said Rice. "Then, when I really started acting like one, they went right through the roof. What's a guy supposed to do?" he said.

"Even if I screamed at her," said Annie, "she wouldn't hear it. She never listens. I think she's afraid to listen. Do you know what I mean?"

"My older brother was the favorite in our family," said Rice. "He could do no wrong, and I never could do anything right, as far as they were concerned. You never met my brother, did you?"

"My father killed something in me when he told me to lie," said Annie.

"We sure are lucky we found each other," said Rice.

"What?" said Annie.

"I said, 'We sure are lucky we found each other,'" said Rice.

Annie took his hand. "Oh yes, oh yes, oh yes," she said fervently. "When we first met out there on the golf course, I almost died because I knew how right we were for each other. Next to Dr. Siebolt, you're the first person I ever really felt close to."

"Dr. who?" said Rice.

. . . . .

In the study of the Governor's Mansion, Governor Southard had his radio on. Annie and Rice had just been picked up, twenty miles west of Cleveland, and Southard wanted to hear what the news services had to say about it.

So far he had heard only music, and was hearing it now:

Let's not go to school today,
Turtle dove, turtle dove.
Let's go out in the woods and play,
Play with love, play with love.

The governor turned the radio off. "How do they *dare* put things like that on the air?" he said. "The whole American entertainment industry does nothing but tell children how to kill their parents—and themselves in the bargain."

He put the question to his wife and to the Brentners, the parents of the boy, who were sitting in the study with him.

The Brentners shook their heads, meaning that they did not know the answer to the governor's question. They were appalled at having been called into the presence of the governor. They had said almost nothing—nothing beyond abject, rambling, ga-ga apologies at the very beginning. Since then they had been in numb agreement with anything the governor cared to say.

He had said plenty, wrestling with what he called the toughest decision of his life. He was trying to decide, with the concurrence of his wife and the Brentners, how to make the runaways grow up enough to realize what they were doing, how to fix them so they would never run away again.

"Any suggestions, Mr. Brentner?" he said to Rice's father.

Rice's father shrugged. "I haven't got any control over him, sir," he said. "If somebody'd tell me a way to get control of him, I'd be glad to try it, but . . ." He let the sentence trail off to nothing.

"But what?" said the governor.

"He's pretty close to being a man now, Governor," said Rice's father, "and he's just about as easy to control as any other man—and that isn't very easy." He murmured something else, which the governor didn't catch, and shrugged again.

"Beg your pardon?" said the governor.

Rice's father said it again, scarcely louder than the first time. "I said he doesn't respect me."

"By heaven, he would if you'd have the guts to lay down the law to him and make it stick!" said the governor with hot righteousness.

Rice's mother now did the most courageous thing in her life. She was boiling mad about having all the blame put on her son, and she now squared the governor of Indiana away. "Maybe if we'd raised our son the way you raised your daughter," she said, "maybe then we wouldn't have the trouble we have today."

The governor looked startled. He sat down at his desk. "Well said, madam," he said. He turned to his wife. "We should certainly give our child-rearing secret to the world."

"Annie isn't a bad girl," said his wife.

"Neither's our boy a bad boy," said Rice's mother, very pepped up, now that she'd given the governor the works.

"I—I'm sure he isn't," said the governor's wife.

"He isn't a bad boy anymore. That's the big thing," blurted Rice's father. And he took courage from his wife's example, and added something else. "And that little girl isn't what you'd call real little, either," he said.

"You recommend they get married?" said the governor, in-credulous.

"I don't know what I recommend," said Rice's father. "I'm not a recommending man. But maybe they really do love each other. Maybe they really were made for each other. Maybe they really would be happy for the rest of their lives together, starting right now, if we'd let 'em." He threw his hands up. "I don't know!" he said. "Do you?"

Annie and Rice were talking to reporters in a state police barracks outside of Cleveland. They were waiting to be hauled back home. They claimed to be unhappy, but they appeared to be having a pretty fine time. They were telling the report-ers about money now.

"People care too much about money," said Annie. "What is money, when you really stop to think about it?"

"We don't want money from her parents," said Rice. "I guess maybe her parents think I'm after their money. All I want is their daughter."

"It's all right with me, if they want to disinherit me," said Annie. "From what I've seen of the rich people I grew up with, money just makes people worried and unhappy. People with a lot of money get so worried about how maybe they'll lose it, they forget to live."

"I can always earn enough to keep a roof over our heads and keep from starving," said Rice. "I can earn more than my old man does. My car is completely paid for. It's all mine, free and clear."

"I can earn money, too," said Annie. "I would be a lot prouder of working than I would be of what my parents want me to do, which is hang around with a lot of other spoiled people and play games."

A state trooper now came in, told Annie her father was on the telephone. The governor of Indiana wanted to talk to her.

"What good will talk do?" said Annie. "Their generation doesn't understand our generation, and they never will. I don't want to talk to him."

The trooper left. He came back a few minutes later.

"He's still on the line?" said Annie.

"No, ma'am," said the trooper. "He gave me a message for you."

"Oh, boy," said Annie. "This should really be good."

"It's a message from your parents, too," the trooper said to Rice.

"I can hardly wait to hear it," said Rice.

"The message is this," said the trooper, keeping his face blankly official, "you are to come home in your own car whenever you feel like it. When you get home, they want you to get married and start being happy as soon as possible."

Annie and Rice crept home in the old blue Ford, with baby shoes dangling from the rearview mirror, with a pile of comic books on the burst backseat. They came home on the main highways. Nobody was looking for them anymore.

Their radio was on, and every news broadcast told the world the splendid news: Annie and Rice were to be married at once. True love had won another stunning victory.

By the time the lovers reached the Indiana border, they had heard the news of their indescribable happiness a dozen times. They were beginning to look like department store clerks on Christmas Eve, jangled and exhausted by relentless tidings of great joy.

Rice turned off the radio. Annie gave an involuntary sigh of relief. They hadn't talked much on the trip home. There didn't seem to be anything to talk about: everything was so settled— everything was so, as they say in business, finalized.

Annie and Rice got into a traffic jam in Indianapolis and were locked for stoplight after stoplight next to a car in which a baby was howling. The parents of the child were very young. The wife was scolding her husband, and the husband looked ready to uproot the steering wheel and brain her with it.

Rice turned on the radio again, and this is what the song on the radio said:

We certainly fooled them,
The ones who said our love wasn't true.
Now, forever and ever,
You've got me, and I've got you.

In almost a frenzy, with Annie's nerves winding ever tighter, Rice changed stations again and again. Every station bawled of either victories or the persecution of teenage love. And that's what the radio was bawling about when the old blue Ford stopped beneath the porte cochere of the Governor's Mansion.

Only one person came out to greet them, and that was the policeman who guarded the door. "Congratulations, sir . . . madam," he said blandly.

"Thank you," said Rice. He turned everything off with the ignition key. The last illusion of adventure died as the radio tubes lost their glow and the engine cooled.

The policeman opened the door on Annie's side. The door gave a rusty screech. Two loose jelly beans wobbled out the door and fell to the immaculate blacktop below.

Annie, still in the car, looked down at the jelly beans. One was green. The other was white. There were bits of lint stuck to them. "Rice?" she said.

"Hm?" he said.

"I'm sorry," she said, "I can't go through with it."

Rice made a sound like a faraway freight whistle. He was grateful for release.

"Could we talk alone, please?" Annie said to the policeman.

"Beg your pardon," said the policeman as he withdrew.

"Would it have worked?" said Annie.

Rice shrugged. "For a little while."

"You know what?" said Annie.

"What?" said Rice.

"We're too young," said Annie.

"Not too young to be in love," said Rice.

"No," said Annie, "not too young to be in love. Just too young for about everything else there is that goes with love." She kissed him. "Good-bye, Rice. I love you."

"I love you," he said.

She got out, and Rice drove away.

As he drove away, the radio came on. It was playing an old song now, and the words were these:

Now's the time for sweet good-bye
To what could never be,
To promises we ne'er could keep,
To a magic you and me.
If we should try to prove our love,
Our love would be in danger.
Let's put our love beyond all harm.
Good-bye—sweet, gentle stranger.

2BR02B

Everything was perfectly swell.

There were no prisons, no slums, no insane asylums, no cripples, no poverty, no wars.

All diseases were conquered. So was old age.

Death, barring accidents, was an adventure for volunteers.

The population of the United States was stabilized at forty million souls.

One bright morning in the Chicago Lying-In Hospital, a man named Edward K. Wehling, Jr., waited for his wife to give birth. He was the only man waiting. Not many people were born each day anymore.

Wehling was fifty-six, a mere stripling in a population whose average age was one hundred twenty-nine.

X rays had revealed that his wife was going to have triplets. The children would be his first.

Young Wehling was hunched in his chair, his head in his hands. He was so rumpled, so still and colorless as to be virtually invisible. His camouflage was perfect, since the waiting room had a disorderly and demoralized air, too. Chairs and ashtrays had been moved away from the walls. The floor was paved with spattered dropcloths.

The room was being redecorated. It was being redecorated as a memorial to a man who had volunteered to die.

A sardonic old man, about two hundred years old, sat on a stepladder, painting a mural he did not like. Back in the days when people aged visibly, his age would have been guessed at thirty-five or so. Aging had touched him that much before the cure for aging was found.

The mural he was working on depicted a very neat garden. Men and women in white, doctors and nurses, turned the soil, planted seedlings, sprayed bugs, spread fertilizer. Men and women in purple uniforms pulled up weeds, cut down plants that were old and sickly, raked leaves, carried refuse to trash burners.

Never, never, never—not even in medieval Holland or old Japan—had a garden been more formal, been better tended. Every plant had all the loam, light, water, air, and nourishment it could use.

A hospital orderly came down the corridor, singing under his breath a popular song:

If you don't like my kisses, honey,
Here's what I will do:
I'll go see a girl in purple,

Kiss this sad world toodle-oo.
If you don't want my lovin',
Why should I take up all this space?
I'll get off this old planet,
Let some sweet baby have my place.

The orderly looked in at the mural and the muralist. "Looks so real," he said, "I can practically imagine I'm standing in the middle of it."

"What makes you think you're not in it?" said the painter. He gave a satiric smile. "It's called *The Happy Garden of Life,* you know."

"That's good of Dr. Hitz," said the orderly.

He was referring to one of the male figures in white, whose head was a portrait of Dr. Benjamin Hitz, the hospital's chief obstetrician. Hitz was a blindingly handsome man.

"Lot of faces still to fill in," said the orderly. He meant that the faces of many of the figures in the mural were blank. All blanks were to be filled with portraits of important people either on the hospital staff or from the Chicago office of the Federal Bureau of Termination.

"Must be nice to be able to make pictures that look like something," said the orderly.

The painter's face curdled with scorn. "You think I'm proud of this drab? You think this is my idea of what life really looks like?"

"What's your idea of what life looks like?"

The painter gestured at a foul dropcloth. "There's a good picture of it," he said. "Frame that, and you'll have a picture a damn sight more honest than this one."

"You're a gloomy old duck, aren't you?" said the orderly.

"Is that a crime?" said the painter.

"If you don't like it here, Grandpa—" The orderly finished the thought with the trick telephone number that people who didn't want to live anymore were supposed to call. The zero in the telephone number he pronounced "naught."

The number was 2BR02B.

It was the telephone number of an institution whose fanciful sobriquets included "Automat," "Birdland," "Cannery," "Catbox," "Delouser," "Easy Go," "Good-bye, Mother," "Happy Hooligan," "Kiss Me Quick," "Lucky Pierre," "Sheepdip," "Waring Blender," "Weep No More," and "Why Worry?"

"To Be or Not to Be" was the telephone number of the municipal gas chambers of the Federal Bureau of Termination.

The painter thumbed his nose at the orderly. "When I decide it's time to go," he said, "it won't be at the Sheepdip."

"A do-it-yourselfer, eh?" said the orderly. "Messy business, Grandpa. Why don't you have a little consideration for the people who have to clean up after you?"

The painter expressed with an obscenity his lack of concern for the tribulations of his survivors. "The world could do with a good deal more mess, if you ask me," he said.

The orderly laughed and moved on.

Wehling, the waiting father, mumbled something without raising his head. And then he fell silent again.

A coarse, formidable woman strode into the waiting room on spike heels. Her shoes, stockings, trench coat, bag, and overseas cap were all purple, a purple the painter called "the color of grapes on Judgment Day."

The medallion on her purple musette bag was the seal of the Service Division of the Federal Bureau of Termination, an eagle perched on a turnstile.

The woman had a lot of facial hair—an unmistakable mustache, in fact. A curious thing about gas chamber hostesses was that no matter how lovely and feminine they were when recruited, they all sprouted mustaches within five years or so.

"Is this where I'm supposed to come?" she asked the painter.

"A lot would depend on what your business was," he said. "You aren't about to have a baby, are you?"

"They told me I was supposed to pose for some picture," she said. "My name's Leora Duncan." She waited.

"And you dunk people," he said.

"What?" she said.

"Skip it," he said.

"That sure is a beautiful picture," she said. "Looks just like heaven or something."

"Or something," said the painter. He took a list of names from his smock pocket. "Duncan, Duncan, Duncan," he said, scanning the list. "Yes—here you are. You're entitled to be immortalized. See any faceless body here you'd like me to stick your head on? We've got a few choice ones left."

She studied the mural. "Gee," she said, "they're all the same to me. I don't know anything about art."

"A body's a body, eh?" he said. "All righty. As a master of the fine art, I recommend this body here." He indicated the faceless figure of a woman who was carrying dried stalks to a trash burner.

"Well," said Leora Duncan, "that's more the disposal people, isn't it? I mean, I'm in service. I don't do any disposing."

The painter clapped his hands in mock delight. "You say you don't know anything about art, and then you prove in the next breath that you do know more about it than I do! Of course the sheaf carrier is wrong for a hostess! A snipper, a pruner—that's more your line." He pointed to a figure in purple who was sawing a dead branch from an apple tree. "How about her?" he said. "You like her at all?"

"Gosh—" she said, and she blushed and became humble. "That—that puts me right next to Dr. Hitz."

"That upsets you?" he said.

"Good gravy, no!" she said. "It's—it's just such an honor."

"Ah, you admire him, eh?" he said.

"Who doesn't admire him?" she said, worshipping the portrait of Hitz. It was the portrait of a tanned, white-haired, omnipotent Zeus, two hundred forty years old. "Who doesn't admire him?" she said again. "He was responsible for setting up the very first gas chamber in Chicago."

"Nothing would please me more," said the painter, "than to put you next to him for all time. Sawing off a limb—that strikes you as appropriate?"

"That is kind of like what I do," she said. She was demure about what she did. What she did was make people comfortable while she killed them.

And while Leora Duncan was posing for her portrait, into the waiting room bounded Dr. Hitz himself. He was seven feet tall, and he boomed with importance, accomplishments, and the joy of living.

"Well, Miss Duncan! Miss Duncan!" he said, and he made a joke. "What are you doing here? This isn't where the people leave. This is where they come in!"

"We're going to be in the same picture together," she said shyly.

"Good!" said Dr. Hitz. "And say, isn't that some picture?"

"I sure am honored to be in it with you," she said.

"Let me tell you, I'm honored to be in it with you. Without women like you, this wonderful world we've got wouldn't be possible."

He saluted her and moved toward the door that led to the delivery rooms. "Guess what was just born," he said.

"I can't," she said.

"Triplets!" he said.

"Triplets!" she said. She was exclaiming over the legal implications of triplets.

The law said that no newborn child could survive unless the parents of the child could find someone who would volunteer to die. Triplets, if they were all to live, called for three volunteers.

"Do the parents have three volunteers?" said Leora Duncan.

"Last I heard," said Dr. Hitz, "they had one, and were trying to scrape another two up."

"I don't think they made it," she said. "Nobody made three appointments with us. Nothing but singles going through today, unless somebody called in after I left. What's the name?"

"Wehling," said the waiting father, sitting up, red-eyed and frowzy. "Edward K. Wehling, Jr., is the name of the happy father-to-be."

He raised his right hand, looked at a spot on the wall, gave a hoarsely wretched chuckle. "Present," he said.

"Oh, Mr. Wehling," said Dr. Hitz, "I didn't see you."

"The invisible man," said Wehling.

"They just phoned me that your triplets have been born," said Dr. Hitz. "They're all fine, and so is the mother. I'm on my way in to see them now."

"Hooray," said Wehling emptily.

"You don't sound very happy," said Dr. Hitz.

"What man in my shoes wouldn't be happy?" said Wehling. He gestured with his hands to symbolize the carefree simplicity. "All I have to do is pick out which one of the triplets is going to live, then deliver my maternal grandfather to the Happy Hooligan, and come back here with a receipt."

Dr. Hitz became rather severe with Wehling, towered over him. "You don't believe in population control, Mr. Wehling?" he said.

"I think it's perfectly keen," said Wehling.

"Would you like to go back to the good old days, when the population of the earth was twenty billion—about to become forty billion, then eighty billion, then one hundred and sixty billion? Do you know what a drupelet is, Mr. Wehling?" said Hitz.

"Nope," said Wehling, sulking.

"A drupelet, Mr. Wehling, is one of the little knobs, one of the little pulpy grains, of a blackberry," said Dr. Hitz. "Without population control, human beings would now be packed on the surface of this old planet like drupelets on a blackberry! Think of it!"

Wehling continued to stare at the spot on the wall.

"In the year 2000," said Dr. Hitz, "before scientists stepped in and laid down the law, there wasn't even enough drinking water to go around, and nothing to eat but seaweed—and still people insisted on their right to reproduce like jackrabbits. And their right, if possible, to live forever."

"I want those kids," said Wehling. "I want all three of them."

"Of course you do," said Dr. Hitz. "That's only human."

"I don't want my grandfather to die, either," said Wehling.

"Nobody's really happy about taking a close relative to the Catbox," said Dr. Hitz sympathetically.

"I wish people wouldn't call it that," said Leora Duncan.

"What?" said Dr. Hitz.

"I wish people wouldn't call it the Catbox, and things like that," she said. "It gives people the wrong impression."

"You're absolutely right," said Dr. Hitz. "Forgive me." He corrected himself, gave the municipal gas chambers their official title, a title no one ever used in conversation. "I should have said 'Ethical Suicide Studios,'" he said.

"That sounds so much better," said Leora Duncan.

"This child of yours—whichever one you decide to keep, Mr. Wehling," said Dr. Hitz. "He or she is going to live on a happy, roomy, clean, rich planet, thanks to population control. In a garden like in that mural there." He shook his head. "Two centuries ago, when I was a young man, it was a hell that nobody thought could last another twenty years. Now centuries of peace and plenty stretch before us as far as the imagination cares to travel."

He smiled luminously.

The smile faded when he saw that Wehling had just drawn a revolver.

Wehling shot Dr. Hitz dead. "There's room for one—a great big one," he said.

And then he shot Leora Duncan. "It's only death," he said to her as she fell. "There! Room for two."

And then he shot himself, making room for all three of his children.

Nobody came running. Nobody, it seemed, had heard the shots.

The painter sat on the top of his stepladder, looking down reflectively on the sorry scene. He pondered the mournful puzzle of life demanding to be born and, once born, demanding to be fruitful . . . to multiply and to live as long as possible—to do all that on a very small planet that would have to last forever.

All the answers that the painter could think of were grim. Even grimmer, surely, than a Catbox, a Happy Hooligan, an Easy Go. He thought of war. He thought of plague. He thought of starvation.

He knew that he would never paint again. He let his paintbrush fall to the dropcloths below. And then he decided he had had about enough of the Happy Garden of Life, too, and he came slowly down from the ladder.

He took Wehling's pistol, really intending to shoot himself. But he didn't have the nerve.

And then he saw the telephone booth in a corner of the room. He went to it, dialed the well-remembered number: 2BR02B.

"Federal Bureau of Termination," said the warm voice of a hostess.

"How soon could I get an appointment?" he asked, speaking carefully.

"We could probably fit you in late this afternoon, sir," she said. "It might even be earlier, if we get a cancellation."

"All right," said the painter, "fit me in, if you please." And he gave her his name, spelling it out.

"Thank you, sir," said the hostess. "Your city thanks you, your country thanks you, your planet thanks you. But the deepest thanks of all is from future generations."

Lovers
Anonymous

Herb White keeps books for the various businesses around our town, and he makes out practically everybody's income tax. Our town is North Crawford, New Hampshire. Herb never got to college, where he would have done well. He learned about bookkeeping and taxes by mail. Herb fought in Korea, came home a hero. And he married Sheila Hinckley, a very pretty, intelligent woman practically all the men in my particular age group had hoped to marry. My particular age group is thirty-three, thirty-four, and thirty-five years old, these days.

On Sheila's wedding day we were twenty-one, twenty-two, and twenty-three. On Sheila's wedding night we all went down to North Crawford Manor and drank. One poor guy got up on the bar and spoke approximately as follows:

"Gentlemen, friends, brothers, I'm sure we wish the newly-weds nothing but happiness. But at the same time I have to say that the pain in our hearts will never die. And I propose that we form a permanent brotherhood of eternal sufferers, to aid each other in any way we can, though Lord knows there's very little anybody can do for pain like ours."

The crowd thought that was a fine idea.

Hay Boyden, who later became a house mover and wrecker, said we ought to call ourselves the Brotherhood of People Who Were Too Dumb to Realize That Sheila Hinckley Might Actually Want to Be a Housewife. Hay had boozy, complicated reasons for suggesting that. Sheila had been the smartest girl in high school, and had been going like a house afire at the University of Vermont, too. We'd all assumed there wasn't any point in serious courting until she'd finished college.

And then, right in the middle of her junior year, she'd quit and married Herb.

"Brother Boyden," said the drunk up on the bar, "I think that is a sterling suggestion. But in all humility I offer another title for our organization, a title in all ways inferior to yours except that it's about ten thousand times easier to say. Gentlemen, friends, brothers, I propose we call ourselves 'Lovers Anonymous.'"

The motion carried. The drunk up on the bar was me.

And like a lot of crazy things in small, old-fashioned towns, Lovers Anonymous lived on and on. Whenever several of us from that old gang happen to get together, somebody is sure to say, "Lovers Anonymous will please come to order." And it is still a standard joke in town to tell anybody who's had his heart broken lately that he should join LA. Don't get me wrong. Nobody in LA still pines for Sheila. We've all more or less got

Sheilas of our own. We think about Sheila more than we think about some of our other old girls, I suppose, mainly because of that crazy LA. But as Will Battola, the plumber, said one time, "Sheila Hinckley is now a spare whitewall tire on the Thunderbird of my dreams."

Then about a month ago my good wife served a sordid little piece of news along with the after-dinner coffee and macaroons. She said that Herb and Sheila weren't speaking to each other anymore.

"Now, what are you doing spreading idle gossip like that for?" I said.

"I thought it was my duty to tell you," she said, "since you're the lover-in-chief of Lovers Anonymous."

"I was merely present at the founding," I said, "and as you well know, that was many, many years ago."

"Well, I think you can start *un*-founding," she said.

"Look," I said, "there aren't many laws of life that stand up through the ages, but this is one of the few: People who are contemplating divorce do not buy combination aluminum storm windows and screens for a fifteen-room house." That is my business—combination aluminum storm windows and screens, and here and there a bathtub enclosure. And it was a fact that very recently Herb had bought thirty-seven Fleetwood windows, which is our first-line window, for the fifteen-room ark he called home.

"Families that don't even eat together don't keep together very long," she said.

"What do you know about their eating habits?" I wanted to know.

"Nothing I didn't find out by accident," she said. "I was collecting money for the Heart Fund yesterday." Yesterday was

Sunday. "I happened to get there just when they were having Sunday dinner, and there were the girls and Sheila at the dinner table, eating—and no Herb."

"He was probably out on business somewhere," I said.

"That's what I told myself," she said. "But then on my way to the next house I had to go by their old ell—where they keep the firewood and the garden tools."

"Go on."

"And Herb was in there, sitting on a box and eating lunch off a bigger box. I never saw anybody look so sad."

The next day Kennard Pelk, a member of LA in good standing and our chief of police, came into my showroom to complain about a bargain storm window that he had bought from a company that had since gone out of business. "The glass part is stuck halfway up and the screen is rusted out," he said, "and the aluminum is covered with something that looks like blue sugar."

"That's a shame," I said.

"The reason I turn to you is, I don't know where else I can get service."

"With your connections," I said, "couldn't you find out which penitentiary they put the manufacturers in?"

I finally agreed to go over and do what I could, but only if he understood that I wasn't representing the entire industry. "The only windows I stand behind," I said, "are the ones I sell."

And then he told me a screwy thing he'd seen in Herb White's rotten old ell the night before. Kennard had been on his way home in the police cruiser at about two a.m. The thing he'd seen in Herb White's ell was a candle.

"I mean, that old house has fifteen rooms, not counting the ell," said Kennard, "and a family of four—five, if you count the dog. And I couldn't understand how anybody, especially at that time of night, would want to go out to the ell. I thought maybe it was a burglar."

"The only thing worth stealing in that house is the Fleetwood windows."

"Anyway, it was my duty to investigate," said Kennard. "So I snook up to a window and looked in. And there was Herb on a mattress on the floor. He had a bottle of liquor and a glass next to him, and he had a candle stuck in another bottle, and he was reading a magazine by candlelight."

"That was a fine piece of police work," I said.

"He saw me outside the window, and I came closer so he could see who I was. The window was open, so I said to him, 'Hi—I was just wondering who was out here,' and he said, 'Robinson Crusoe.'"

"Robinson Crusoe?" I said.

"Yeah. He was very sarcastic with me," said Kennard. "He asked me if I had the rest of Lovers Anonymous with me. I told him no. And then he asked me if a man's home was still his castle, as far as the police were concerned, or whether that had been changed lately."

"So what did you say, Kennard?"

"What was there *to* say? I buttoned up my holster and went home."

Herb White himself came into my showroom right after Kennard left. Herb had the healthy, happy, excited look people sometimes get when they come down with double pneumonia. "I want to buy three more Fleetwood windows," he said.

"The Fleetwood is certainly a product that everybody can be enthusiastic about," I said, "but I think you're overstepping the bounds of reason. You've got Fleetwoods all around right now."

"I want them for the ell," he said.

"Do you feel all right, Herb?" I asked. "You haven't even got furniture in half the rooms we've already made wind-tight. Besides, you look feverish."

"I've just been taking a long, hard look at my life, is all," he said. "Now, do you want the business or not?"

"The storm window business is based on common sense, and I'd just as soon keep it that way," I replied. "That old ell of yours hasn't had any work done on it for I'll bet fifty years. The clapboards are loose, the sills are shot, and the wind whistles through the gaps in the foundation. You might as well put storm windows on a shredded wheat biscuit."

"I'm having it restored," he said.

"Is Sheila expecting a baby?"

He narrowed his eyes. "I sincerely hope not," he said, "for her sake, for my sake, and for the sake of the child."

I had lunch that day at the drugstore. About half of Lovers Anonymous had lunch at the drugstore. When I sat down, Selma Deal, the woman back of the counter, said, "Well, you great lover, got a quorum now. What you gonna vote about?"

Hay Boyden, the house mover and wrecker, turned to me. "Any new business, Mr. President?"

"I wish you people would quit calling me Mr. President," I said. "My marriage has never been one hundred percent ideal, and I wouldn't be surprised that was the fly in the ointment."

"Speaking of ideal marriages," said Will Battola, the plumber, "you didn't by chance sell some more windows to Herb White, did you?"

"How did you know?"

"It was a guess," he said. "We've been comparing notes here, and as near as we can figure, Herb has managed to give a little piece of remodeling business to every member of LA."

"Coincidence," I said.

"I'd say so, too," said Will, "if I could find anybody who wasn't a member and who still got a piece of the job."

Between us, we estimated Herb was going to put about six thousand dollars into the ell. That was a lot of money for a man in his circumstances to scratch up.

"The job wouldn't have to run more than three thousand if Herb didn't want a kitchen and a bathroom in the thing," said Will. "He's already got a kitchen and a bathroom ten feet from the door between the ell and the house."

Al Tedler, the carpenter, said, "According to the plans Herb gave me this morning, there ain't gonna *be* no door between the ell and the house. There's gonna be a double-studded wall with half-inch Sheetrock, packed with rockwood batts."

"How come double studding?" I asked.

"Herb wants it soundproof."

"How's a body supposed to get from the house to the ell?" I said.

"The body has to go outside, cross about sixty feet of lawn, and go in through the ell's own front door," said Al.

"Kind of a shivery trip on a cold winter's night," I said. "Not many bodies would care to make it barefoot."

And that was when Sheila Hinckley White walked in.

You often hear somebody say that So-and-So is a very well preserved woman. Nine times out of ten So-and-So turns out to be a scrawny woman with pink lipstick who looks as if she had been boiled in lanolin. But Sheila really is well preserved. That day in the drugstore she could have passed for twenty-two.

"By golly," Al Tedler said, "if I had that to cook for me, I wouldn't be any two-kitchen man."

Usually when Sheila came into a place where several members of LA were sitting, we would make some kind of noise to attract her attention and she would do something silly like wiggle her eyebrows or give us a wink. It didn't mean a thing.

But that day in the drugstore we didn't try to catch her eye and she didn't try to catch ours. She was all business. She was carrying a big red book about the size of a cinder block. She returned it to the lending library in the store, paid up, and left.

"Wonder what the book's about," said Hay.

"It's red," I said. "Probably about the fire engine industry."

That was a joke that went a long way back—clear back to what she'd put under her picture in the high school yearbook the year she graduated. Everybody was supposed to predict what kind of work he or she would go into in later life. Sheila put down that she would discover a new planet or be the first woman justice of the Supreme Court or president of a company that manufactured fire engines.

She was kidding, of course, but everybody—including Sheila, I guess—had the idea that she could be anything she set her heart on being.

At her wedding to Herb, I remember, I asked her, "Well now, what's the fire engine industry going to do?"

And she laughed and said, "It's going to have to limp along without me. I'm taking on a job a thousand times as important—keeping a good man healthy and happy, and raising his young."

"What about the seat they've been saving for you on the Supreme Court?"

"The happiest seat for me, and for any woman worthy of the name of woman," she said, "is a seat in a cozy kitchen, with children at my feet."

"You going to let somebody else discover that planet, Sheila?"

"Planets are stones, stone-dead stones," she said. "What I want to discover are my husband, my children, and through them, myself. Let somebody else learn what she can from stones."

After Sheila left the drugstore I went to the lending library to see what the red book was. It was written by the president of some women's college. The title of it was *Woman, the Wasted Sex, or, The Swindle of Housewifery.*

I looked inside the book and found it was divided in these five parts:

I. 5,000,000 B.C.–A.D. 1865, The Involuntary Slave Sex

II. 1866–1919, The Slave Sex Given Pedestals

III. 1920–1945, Sham Equality—Flapper to Rosie the Riveter

IV. 1946–1963, Volunteer Slave Sex—Diaper Bucket to Sputnik

V. Explosion and Utopia

Reva Owley, the woman who sells cosmetics and runs the library, came up and asked if she could help me.

"You certainly can," I said. "You can throw this piece of filth down the nearest sewer."

"It's a very popular book," she said.

"That may be," I said. "Whiskey and repeating firearms

were very popular with the redskins. And if this drugstore really wants to make money, you might put in a hashish-and-heroin counter for the teenage crowd."

"Have you read it?" she asked.

"I've read the table of contents," I said.

"At least you've *opened* a book," she said. "That's more than any other member of Lovers Anonymous has done in the past ten years."

"I'll have you know I read a great deal," I said.

"I didn't know that much had been written about storm windows." Reva is a very smart widow.

"You can sure be a snippy woman, on occasion," I said.

"That comes from reading books about what a mess men have made of the world," she said.

The upshot was, I read that book.

What a book it was! It took me a week and a half to get through it, and the more I read, the more I felt as if I were wearing long burlap underwear.

Herb White came into my showroom and caught me reading it. "Improving your mind, I see," he said.

"If something's improved," I said, "I don't know what it is. You've read this, have you?"

"That pleasure and satisfaction was mine," he said. "Where are you now?"

"I've just been through the worst five million years I ever expect to spend," I said. "And some man has finally noticed that maybe things aren't quite as good as they could be for women."

"Theodore Parker?" said Herb.

"Right," I said. Parker was a preacher in Boston about the time of the Civil War.

"Read what he says," said Herb.

So I read out loud: "'The domestic function of woman does not exhaust her powers. To make one half the human race consume its energies in the functions of housekeeper, wife and mother is a monstrous waste of the most precious material God ever made.'"

Herb had closed his eyes while I read. He kept them closed. "Do you realize how hard those words hit me, with the—with the wife I've got?"

"Well," I said, "we all knew you'd been hit by something. Nobody could figure out what it was."

"That book was around the house for weeks," he said. "Sheila was reading it. I didn't pay any attention to it at first. And then one night we were watching Channel Two." Channel Two is the educational television station in Boston. "There was this discussion going on between some college professors about the different theories of how the solar system had been born. Sheila all of a sudden burst into tears, said her brains had turned to mush, said she didn't know anything about anything anymore."

Herb opened his eyes. "There wasn't anything I could say to comfort her. She went off to bed. That book was on the table next to where she'd been sitting. I picked it up and it fell open to the page you just read from."

"Herb," I said, "this isn't any of my business, but—"

"It's your business," he said. "Aren't you president of LA?"

"You don't think there really *is* such a thing!" I said.

"As far as I'm concerned," he said, "Lovers Anonymous is as real as the Veterans of Foreign Wars. How would *you* like it if there was a club whose sole purpose was to make sure you treated your wife right?"

"Herb," I said, "I give you my word of honor—"

He didn't let me finish. "I realize now, ten years too late," he said, "that I've ruined that wonderful woman's life, had her waste all her intelligence and talent—on what?" He shrugged and spread his hands. "On keeping house for a small-town bookkeeper who hardly even finished high school, who's never going to be anything he wasn't on his wedding day."

He hit the side of his head with the heel of his hand. I guess he was punishing himself, or maybe trying to make his brains work better. "Well," he said, "I'm calling in all you anonymous lovers I can to help me put things right—not that I can ever give her back her ten wasted years. When we get the ell fixed up, at least I won't be underfoot all the time, expecting her to cook for me and sew for me and do all the other stupid things a husband expects a housewife to do.

"I'll have a little house all my own," he said, "and I'll be my own little housewife. And anytime Sheila wants to, she can come knock on my door and find out I still love her. She can start studying books again, and become an oceanographer or whatever she wants. And any handyman jobs she needs done on that big old house of hers, her handy neighbor—which is me— will be more than glad to do."

With a very heavy heart I went out to Herb's house early that afternoon to measure the windows of the ell. Herb was at his office. The twin girls were off at school. Sheila didn't seem to be at home, either. I knocked on the kitchen door, and the only answer I got was from the automatic washing machine.

"Whirr, gloop, rattle, slup," it said.

As long as I was there, I decided to make sure the Fleetwoods I'd already installed were working freely. That was how I happened to look in through the living room window and see

Sheila lying on the couch. There were books on the floor around her. She was crying.

When I got around to the ell I could see that Herb had certainly been playing house in there. He had a little kerosene range on top of the woodpile, along with pots and pans and canned goods.

There was a Morris chair with a gasoline lantern hanging over it, and a big chopping block next to the chair, and Herb had his pipes and his magazines and his tobacco laid out there. His bed was on the floor, but it was nicely made, with sheets and all. On the walls were photographs of Herb in the Army, Herb on the high school baseball team, and a tremendous print in color of Custer's Last Stand.

The door between the ell and the main house was closed, so I felt free to climb in through a window without feeling I was intruding on Sheila. What I wanted to see was the condition of the sash on the inside. I sat down in the Morris chair and made some notes.

And then I leaned back and lit a cigarette. A Morris chair is a comfortable thing. Sheila came in without my even hearing her.

"Cozy, isn't it?" she said. "I think every man your age should have a hideaway. Herb's ordered storm windows for his Shangri-la, has he?"

"Fleetwoods," I said.

"Good," she said. "Heaven knows Fleetwoods are the best." She looked at the underside of the rotten roof. Pinpricks of sky showed through. "I don't suppose what's happening to Herb and me is any secret," she said.

I didn't know how to answer that.

"You might tell Lovers Anonymous and their Ladies' Auxiliary that Herb and I have never been this happy before," she said.

I couldn't think of any answer for that, either. It was my understanding that Herb's moving into the ell was a great tragedy of recent times.

"And you might tell them," she said, "that it was Herb who got happy first. We had a ridiculous argument about how my brains had turned to mush. And then I went upstairs and waited for him to come to bed—and he didn't. The next morning I found he'd dragged a mattress out here and was sleeping like an angel.

"I looked down on him, so happy out here, and I wept. I realized that he'd been a slave all his life, doing things he hated in order to support his mother, and then me, and then me and the girls. His first night out here was probably the first night in his life that he went to sleep wondering who he might be, what he might have become, what he still might be."

"I guess the reason the world seems so upside down so often," I said, "is that everybody figures he's doing things on account of somebody else. Herb figures this whole ell business is a favor to you."

"Anything that makes him happier is a favor to me," she said.

"I read that crazy red book—or I'm reading it," I said.

"Housewifery *is* a swindle, if a woman can do more," she said.

"You going to do more, Sheila?"

"Yes," she said. She had laid out a plan whereby she would get her degree in two years, with a combination of correspondence courses, extension courses, and a couple of summer sessions at Durham, where the state university is. After that she was going to teach.

"I never would have made a plan like that," she told me, "if Herb hadn't called my bluff to the extent he did. Women are awful bluffers sometimes.

"I've started studying," she went on. "I know you looked through the window and saw me with all my books, crying on the couch."

"I didn't think you'd seen me," I said. "I wasn't trying to mind somebody else's business. Kennard Pelk and I both have to look through windows from time to time in the line of duty."

"I was crying because I was understanding what a bluffer I'd been in school," she said. "I was only pretending to care about the things I was learning, back in those silly old days. Now I *do* care. That's why I was crying. I've been crying a lot lately, but it's good crying. It's about discovery, it's about grown-up joy."

I had to admit it was an interesting adjustment Sheila and Herb were making. One thing bothered me, though, and there wasn't any polite way I could ask about it. I wondered if they were going to quit sleeping with each other forever.

Sheila answered the question without my having to ask it.

"Love laughs at locksmiths," she said.

About a week later I took the copy of *Woman, the Wasted Sex, or, The Swindle of Housewifery* to a luncheon meeting of LA at the drugstore. I was through with the thing, and I passed it around.

"You didn't let your wife read this, did you?" Hay Boyden asked.

"Certainly," I said.

"She'll walk out on you and the kids," said Hay, "and become a rear admiral."

"Nope," I said.

"You give a woman a book like this," said Al Tedler, "and you're gonna have a restless woman on your hands."

"Not necessarily," I said. "When I gave my wife this book I gave her a magic bookmark to go with it." I nodded. "That magic bookmark kept her under control all the way through."

Everybody wanted to know what the bookmark was.

"One of her old report cards," I said.

Hal Irwin's Magic Lamp

Hal Irwin built his magic lamp in his basement in Indianapolis, in the summer of 1929. It was supposed to look like Aladdin's lamp. It was an old tin teapot with a piece of cotton stuck in the spout for a wick. Hal bored a hole in it for a doorbell button, which he hooked up to two flashlight batteries and a buzzer inside. Like many husbands back then, he had a workshop in the basement.

The idea was, it was a cute way to call servants. You'd rub the teapot as if it were a magic lamp, and you'd push the button on the side. The buzzer'd go off, and a servant, if you had one, would come and ask you what you wished.

Hal didn't have a servant, but he was going to borrow one from a friend. Hal was a customers' man in a brokerage house, and he knew his business inside out. He'd made half a million dollars on the stock market, and nobody knew it. Not even his wife.

He made the magic lamp as a surprise for his wife. He was going to tell her it was a magic lamp. And then he was going to rub it and wish for a big new house. And then he was going to prove to her that it really was a magic lamp, because every wish was going to come true.

When he made the lamp, the interior decorator was finishing up the insides of a big new French château Hal had ordered built out on North Meridian Street.

When Hal made that lamp, he and Mary were living in a shotgun house down in all the soot at Seventeenth and Illinois Street. They'd been married two years, and Hal hadn't had her out more than five or six times. He wasn't being stingy. He was saving up to buy her all the happiness a girl could ever ask for, and he was going to hand it to her in one fell swoop.

Hal was ten years older than Mary, so it was easy for him to buffalo her about a lot of things, and one of the things was money. He wouldn't talk money with her, never let her see a bill or a bank statement, never told her how much he made or what he was doing with it. All Mary had to go by was the piddling allowance he gave her to run the house, so she guessed they were poor as Job's turkey.

Mary didn't mind that. That girl was as wholesome as a peach and a glass of milk. Being poor gave her room to swing her religion around. When the end of the month came, and they'd eaten pretty well, and she hadn't asked Hal for an extra dime, she felt like a little white lamb. And she thought Hal was happy, even though he was broke, because she was giving him a hundred million dollars' worth of love.

There was only one thing about being poor that really bothered Mary, and that was the way Hal always seemed to think she wanted to be rich. She did her best to convince him that wasn't true.

When Hal would carry on about how well other folks were doing—about the high life at the country clubs and the lakes—Mary'd talk about the millions of folks in China who didn't have a roof over their heads or anything to eat.

"Me doing velly well for Chinaman," Hal said one night.

"You're doing very well for an American or for an anything!" Mary said. She hugged him, so he'd be proud and strong and happy.

"Well, your successful Chinaman's got a piece of news for you," Hal said. "Tomorrow you're gonna get a cook. I told an employment agency to send one out."

Actually, the person arriving the next day, whose name was Ella Rice, wouldn't be coming to cook, and wasn't from an employment agency. She already had a job with a friend of Hal's whom Mary didn't know. The friend would give her the day off so she could play the part of a jinni.

Hal had rehearsed her at the friend's house, and he would pay her well. She needed the extra money. She was going to have a baby in about six weeks, she thought. All she had to do was put on a turban when the time came, when Hal showed Mary his magic lamp, and rubbed it and rang its buzzer. Then she would say, "I am the jinni. What do you want?"

After that, Hal would start wishing for expensive things he already owned, which Mary hadn't seen yet. His first wish would be for a Marmon town car. It would already be parked out front. Every time he made a wish, starting with that one, Ella Rice would say, "You got it."

But that was tomorrow, and today was today, and Mary thought Hal didn't like her cooking. She was a wonderful cook. "Honey," she said, "are my meals that bad?"

"They're great. I have no complaints whatsoever."

"Then why should we get a cook?"

He looked at her as though she were deaf, dumb, and blind. "Don't you ever think of my pride?" he asked her. He put his hand over her mouth. "Honeybunch, don't tell me again about people dying like flies in China. I am who I am where I am, and I've got pride."

Mary wanted to cry. Here she thought she'd been making Hal feel better, and she'd been making him feel worse instead.

"What do you think I think when I see Bea Muller or Nancy Gossett downtown in their fur coats, buying out the department stores?" Hal said. "I think about you, stuck in this house. I think, Well, for crying out loud, I used to be president of their husbands' fraternity house! For crying out loud, me and Harve Muller and George Gossett used to be the Grand Triumvirate. That's what they used to call the three of us in college—the Grand Triumvirate! We used to run the college, and I'm not kidding. We founded the Owl's Club, and I was president.

"Look where they live, and look where we live," Hal went on. "We oughta be right out there with 'em at Fifty-seventh and North Meridian! We oughta have a cottage right next to 'em at Lake Maxinkuckee! Least I can do is get my wife a cook."

Ella Rice arrived at the house the next day at three o'clock as planned. In a paper bag she had the turban Hal had given her. Hal wasn't home yet. Ella was supposed to pretend to be the new cook instead of a jinni until Hal arrived at three-thirty. Which she did.

What Hal hadn't counted on, though, was that Mary would find Ella so likable, but so pitiful, not a cook, but a fellow human being in awful trouble. He had expected them to go to the kitchen to talk about this and that, what Hal liked to eat, and so on. But Mary asked Ella about her pregnancy, which was obvious. Ella, who was no actress, and at the end of her rope in any case, burst into tears. The two women, one white, one black, stayed in the living room and talked about their lives instead.

Ella wasn't married. The father of her child had beaten her up when he found out she was pregnant, and then taken off for parts unknown. She had aches and pains in many places, and no relatives, and didn't know how much longer she could do housework. She repeated what she had told Hal, that her pregnancy still had six weeks to go, she thought. Mary said she wished she could have a baby, but couldn't. That didn't help.

When Hal parked the new Marmon out front and entered the house, neither woman was in any condition to enjoy the show he had planned. They were a mess! But he imagined his magic lamp would cheer them up. He went to get it from the closet where he had hidden it upstairs, then brought it into the living room and said, "My goodness! Look what I just found. I do believe it's a magic lamp. Maybe if I rub it a jinni will appear, and she will make a wish come true." He hadn't considered hiring a black man to play the jinni. He was scared of black men.

Ella Rice recognized her cue, and got off the couch to do the crazy thing the white man was going to pay for. Anything for money. It hurt her a lot to stand, after sitting still for a half-hour. Even Hal could see that.

Hal wished for a Marmon, and the jinni said, "You got it." The three went out to the car, and Hal told them to get in, that it was his, paid for in full. The women sat in the backseat, and Mary said to Ella, not to Hal, "Thanks a lot. This is wonderful. I think I'm going nuts."

Hal drove up North Meridian Street, pointing out grand houses left and right. Every time he did that, Mary said that she wouldn't want it, that Hal could throw his magic lamp out the window, as far as she was concerned. What she was really upset about was the humiliating use he was making of her new friend Ella.

Hal stopped in front of a French château on which workmen were putting finishing touches. He turned off the motor, rubbed the lamp, buzzed the buzzer, and said, "Jinni, give me a new house at 5644 North Meridian Street."

Mary said to Ella, "You don't have to do this. Don't answer him."

Ella got mad at Mary now. "I'm getting *paid*!" Everything Ella said was in a dialect typical of a person of her race and class and degree of education back then. Now she groaned. She was going into labor.

They took Ella Rice to the city hospital, the only one that admitted black people. She had a healthy boy baby, and Hal paid for it.

Hal and Mary brought her and the baby back to their new house. The old house was on the market. And Mary, who couldn't have a baby herself, fixed up one of the seven bedrooms for mother and child, with cute furniture and wallpaper and toys the baby wasn't old enough to play with. Mother and child had their own bathroom.

The baby was christened in a black church, and Mary was there. Hal wasn't. He and Mary were hardly speaking. Ella named the baby Irwin, in honor of the people who were so good to her. His last name was the same as hers. He was Irwin Rice.

Mary had never loved Hal, but had managed to like him. It was a job. There weren't many ways for women to earn their own money back then, and she hadn't inherited anything, and wouldn't unless Hal died. Hal was no dumber than most men she'd known. She certainly didn't want to be alone. They had a black yard man and a black laundress, and a white housemaid from Ireland, who lived in the mansion. Mary insisted on doing the cooking. Ella Rice offered to do it, at least for herself. But nobody except Mary was allowed to cook.

She hated the new house so much, and the gigantic car, which embarrassed her, that she couldn't even like Hal anymore. This was very tough on Hal, extremely tough, as you can well imagine. Not only was he not getting love, or what looked like love, from the woman he'd married, but she was giving ten times more love than he'd ever gotten, and nonstop, to a baby as black as the ace of spades!

Hal didn't tell anybody at the office about the situation at home, because it would have made him look like a weakling. The housemaid from Ireland treated him like a weakling, as though Mary were the real power, and crazy as a bedbug.

Ella Rice of course made her own bed, and kept her bedroom and bathroom very neat. Things didn't seem right to her, either, but what could she do? Ella nursed the baby, so its food was all taken care of. Ella didn't eat downstairs with the Irwins.

Not even Mary considered that a possibility. Ella didn't eat with the servants in the kitchen, either. She brought upstairs whatever Mary had prepared especially for her, and ate it in her bedroom.

At the office, anyway, Hal was making more money than ever, trading stocks and bonds for others, but also investing heavily for himself in stocks, never mind bonds, on margin. "On margin" meant he paid only a part of the full price of a stock, and owed the rest to the brokerage where he worked. And then the stock's value would go up, because other people wanted it, and Hal would sell it. He could then pay off his debt to the brokerage, and the rest of the profit was his to keep.

So he could buy more stock on margin.

Three months after the magic-lamp episode, the stock market crashed. The stocks Hal had bought on margin became worthless. All of a sudden, everybody thought they were too expensive at any price. So what Hal Irwin owed to his brokerage, and what his brokerage owed to a bank in turn, was more than everything he owned—the new house, the unsold old house, the furniture, the car, and on and on. You name it!

He wasn't loved at home even in good times, so Hal went out a seventh-story window without a parachute. All over the country, unloved men in his line of work were going out windows without parachutes. The bank foreclosed on both houses, and took the Marmon, too. Then the bank went bust, and anybody with savings in it lost those savings.

Mary had another house to go to, which was her widowed father's farm outside the town of Crawfordsville. The only place Ella Rice could think of to go with her baby was the black church where the baby had been baptized. Mary went there with them. A lot of mothers with babies or children, and old people, and cripples, and even perfectly healthy young people were sleeping there. There was food. Mary didn't ask where it came from. That was the last Mary would see of Ella and Irwin Rice. Ella was eating, and then she would nurse the baby.

When Mary got to her father's farmhouse, the roof was leaking and the electricity had been shut off. But her father took her in. How could he not? She told him about the homeless people in the black church. She asked him what he thought would become of them in such awful times.

"The poor take care of the poor," he said.

Coda to My Career
as a Writer
for Periodicals

Some of these stories have been edited for this book, with minor and major glitches repaired, which editors and I should have repaired before they were printed the first time. Rereading three of them so upset me, because the premise and the characters of each were so promising, and the denouement so asinine, that I virtually rewrote the denouement before I could stop myself. Some "editing"! They are "The Powder-Blue Dragon," "The Boy Who Hated Girls," and "Hal Irwin's Magic Lamp." As fossils, they are fakes on the order of Piltdown Man, half human being, half the orangutan I used to be.

No matter how clumsily I wrote when I was starting out, there were magazines that would publish such orangutans. And there were others that, to their credit, would not touch my stuff with rubber gloves. I wasn't offended or ashamed. I understood. I was nothing if not modest. I remember a cartoon I saw long ago, in which a psychiatrist was saying to a patient, "You don't have an inferiority complex. You *are* inferior." If the patient could afford a psychiatrist, he was earning a living somehow, despite his genuine inferiority. That was my case, too, and the evidence seems to be that I got better.

Thanks to popular magazines, I learned on the job to be a fiction writer. Such paid literary apprenticeships, with standards of performance so low, don't exist anymore. Mine was an opportunity to get to know myself. Those who wrote for self-consciously literary publications had this advantage, their talent and sophistication aside: They already knew what they could do and who they were.

There may be more Americans than ever now embarking on voyages of self-discovery like mine, by writing stories, come hell or high water, as well as they can. I lecture at eight colleges and universities each year, and have been doing so for two decades. Half of those one hundred sixty institutions have a writer-in-residence and a course in creative writing. When I quit General Electric to become a writer, there were only two such courses, one at the University of Iowa, the other at Stanford, which my President's daughter now attends.

Given that it is no longer possible to make a living writing short stories, and that the odds against a novel's being successful are a thousand to one, creative-writing courses could be perceived as frauds, as would pharmacy courses if there were no drugstores. Be that as it may, students themselves demanded creative writing courses while they were demanding so many other things, passionately and chaotically, during the Vietnam War.

What students wanted and got, and what so many of their

children are getting, was a *cheap* way to externalize what was inside them, to see in black-and-white who they were and what they might become. I italicize *cheap* because it takes a ton of money to make a movie or a TV show. Never mind that you have to deal with the scum of the earth if you try to make one.

There are on many campuses, moreover, local papers, weeklies or monthlies, that publish short stories but cannot pay for them. What the heck, practicing an art isn't a way to earn money. It's a way to make one's soul grow.

Bon voyage.

I still write for periodicals from time to time, but never fiction, and only when somebody asks me to. I am not the dynamic self-starter I used to be. An excellent alternative weekly in Indianapolis, *NUVO,* asked me only a month ago to write an essay for no pay on the subject of what it is like to be a native Middle Westerner. I have replied as follows:

"Breathes there the man, with soul so dead, who never to himself has said, this is my own, my native land!"

This famous celebration of no-brainer patriotism by the Scotsman Sir Walter Scott (1771–1832), when stripped of jingoistic romance, amounts only to this: Human beings come into this world, for their own good, as instinctively territorial as timber wolves or honeybees. Not long ago, human beings who strayed too far from their birthplace and relatives, like all other animals, would be committing suicide.

This dread of not crossing well-understood geographical boundaries still makes sense in many parts of the world, in what used to be Yugoslavia in Europe, for example, or Rwanda in Africa. It is, however, now excess instinctual baggage in most of North America, thank God, thank God. It lives on in this country, as obsolescent survival instincts often do, as feelings and manners that are by and large harmless, that can even be comical.

Thus do I and millions like me tell strangers that we are Middle Westerners, as though we deserved some kind of a medal for being that. All I can say in our defense is that natives of Texas and Brooklyn are even more preposterous in their territorial vanity.

Nearly countless movies about Texans and Brooklynites are lessons for such people in how to behave ever more stereotypically. Why have there been no movies about supposedly typical Middle Western heroes, models to which we, too, might then conform?

All I've got now is an aggressively nasal accent.

About that accent: When I was in the Army during the Second World War, a white Southerner said to me, "Do you *have to talk* that way?"

I might have replied, "Oh, yeah? At least my ancestors never owned slaves," but the training session at the rifle range at Fort Bragg in North Carolina seemed neither the time nor the place to settle his hash.

I might have added that some of the greatest words ever spoken in American history were uttered with just such a Jew's-harp twang, including the Gettysburg Address of Abraham Lincoln of Illinois and these by Eugene V. Debs of Terre Haute, Indiana: "While there is a lower class I am in it, while there is a criminal element I am of it; while there is a soul in prison, I am not free."

I would have kept to myself that the borders of Indiana, when I was a boy, cradled not only the birthplace of Eugene V. Debs, but the national headquarters of the Ku Klux Klan.

Illinois had Carl Sandburg and Al Capone.

Yes, and the thing on top of the house to keep the weather out is the *ruff*, and the stream in back of the house is the *crick*.

Every race and subrace and blend thereof is native to the Middle West. I myself am a purebred Kraut. Our accents are by no means uniform. My twang is only fairly typical of European-Americans raised some distance north of the former Confederate States of America. It appeared to me when I began this essay that I was on a fool's errand, that we could be described en masse only as what we weren't. We weren't Texans or Brooklynites or Californians or Southerners, and so on.

To demonstrate to myself the folly of distinguishing us, one by one, from Americans born anywhere else, I imagined a crowd on Fifth Avenue in New York City, where I am living now, and another crowd on State Street in Chicago, where I went to a university and worked as a reporter half a century ago. I was not mistaken about the sameness of the faces and clothing and apparent moods.

But the more I pondered the people of Chicago, the more aware I became of an enormous presence there. It was almost like music, music unheard in New York or Boston or San Francisco or New Orleans.

It was Lake Michigan, an ocean of pure water, the most precious substance in all this world.

. . . .

Nowhere else in the Northern Hemisphere are there tremendous bodies of pure water like our Great Lakes, save for Asia, where there is only Lake Baikal. So there is something distinctive about native Middle Westerners, after all. Get this: When we were born, there had to have been incredible quantities of fresh water all around us, in lakes and streams and rivers and raindrops and snowdrifts, and no undrinkable salt water anywhere!

Even my taste buds are Middle Western on that account. When I swim in the Atlantic or the Pacific, the water tastes all wrong to me, even though it is in fact no more nauseating, as long as you don't swallow it, than chicken soup.

There were also millions and millions of acres of topsoil around us and our mothers when we were born, as flat as pool tables and as rich as chocolate cake. The Middle West is not a desert.

When I was born, in 1922, barely a hundred years after Indiana became the nineteenth state in the Union, the Middle West already boasted a constellation of cities with symphony orchestras and museums and libraries, and institutions of higher learning, and schools of music and art, reminiscent of the Austro-Hungarian Empire before the First World War. One could almost say that Chicago was our Vienna, Indianapolis our Prague, Cincinnati our Budapest, and Cleveland our Bucharest.

To grow up in such a city, as I did, was to find such cultural institutions as ordinary as police stations or firehouses. So it was reasonable for a young person to daydream of becoming some sort of artist or intellectual, if not a policeman or fireman. So I did. So did many like me.

Such provincial capitals, which is what they would have been called in Europe, were charmingly self-sufficient with respect to the fine arts. We sometimes had the director of the Indianapolis Symphony Orchestra to supper, or writers and painters, or architects like my father, of local renown.

I studied clarinet under the first-chair clarinetist of our symphony orchestra. I remember the orchestra's performance of Tchaikovsky's *1812 Overture*, in which the cannons' roars were supplied by a policeman firing blank cartridges into an empty garbage can. I knew the policeman. He sometimes guarded street crossings used by students on their way to or from School 43, my school, the *James Whitcomb Riley School*.

It is unsurprising, then, that the Middle West has produced so many artists of such different sorts, from world-class to merely competent, as provincial cities and towns in Europe used to do.

I see no reason this satisfactory state of affairs should not go on and on, unless funding for instruction in and celebration of the arts, and especially in public school systems, is withdrawn.

Participation in an art is not simply one of many possible ways to make a living, an obsolescent trade as we approach the year 2000. Participation in an art, at bottom, has nothing to do with earning money. Participation in an art, although unrewarded by wealth or fame, and as the Middle West has encouraged so many of its young to discover for themselves so far, is a way to make one's soul grow.

·　·　·

No artist from anywhere, however, not even Shakespeare, not even Beethoven, not even James Whitcomb Riley, has changed the course of so many lives all over the planet as have four hayseeds in Ohio, two in Dayton and two in Akron. How I wish Dayton and Akron were in Indiana! Ohio could have Kokomo and Gary.

Orville and Wilbur Wright were in Dayton in 1903 when they invented the airplane.

Dr. Robert Holbrook Smith and William Griffith Wilson were in Akron in 1935 when they devised the Twelve Steps to sobriety of Alcoholics Anonymous. By comparison with Smith and Wilson, Sigmund Freud was a piker when it came to healing dysfunctional minds and lives.

Beat that! Let the rest of the world put that in their pipes and smoke it, not to mention Cole Porter, Hoagy Carmichael, Frank Lloyd Wright, and Louis Sullivan, Twyla Tharp and Bob Fosse, Ernest Hemingway and Saul Bellow, Mike Nichols and Elaine May. Toni Morrison!

Larry Bird!

New York and Boston and other ports on the Atlantic have Europe for an influential, often importunate neighbor. Middle Westerners do not. Many of us of European ancestry are on that account ignorant of our families' past in the Old World and the culture there. Our only heritage is American. When Germans captured me during the Second World War, one asked me, "Why are you making war against your brothers?" I didn't have a clue what he was talking about. . . .

Anglo-Americans and African-Americans whose ancestors came to the Middle West from the South commonly have a much more compelling awareness of a homeland elsewhere in the past than do I—in Dixie, of course, not the British Isles or Africa.

What geography can give all Middle Westerners, along with the fresh water and topsoil, if they let it, is awe for a fertile continent stretching forever in all directions.

Makes you religious. Takes your breath away.

Grateful acknowledgment is made to the following publications, where the stories collected here first appeared:

Argosy, for "A Present for Big Saint Nick" (published as "A Present for Big Nick") and "Souvenir."

The Atlantic Monthly, for "*Der Arme Dolmetscher.*"

Cape Cod Compass, for "The Cruise of *The Jolly Roger.*"

Collier's, for "Any Reasonable Offer," "Mnemonics," "The Package," "Poor Little Rich Town," and "Thanasphere."

Cosmopolitan, for "Bagombo Snuff Box," © 1954 Hearst Communications, Inc.; "Find Me a Dream," © 1961 Hearst Communications, Inc.; "The Powder-Blue Dragon," © 1954 Hearst Communications, Inc.; and "Unpaid Consultant," ©